Of Ash and Ivy

THE ITHENMYR CHRONICLES
BOOK THREE

ELAYNA R. GALLEA

Cover by Getcovers

Map designed on Inkarnate

Ebook ISBN: 978-1-7388342-1-1

Paperback ISBN: 978-1-7388342-0-4

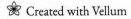 Created with Vellum

For those who are tired of being pushed down.
Fight back.
I believe in you.

Map of Ithenmyr

FOR A LARGER VERSION, PLEASE GO TO:
HTTPS://WWW.ELAYNARGALLEA.COM/MAPS

Pronunciation Guide

Hello dear readers,

I am so glad you are here for the third instalment of the Ithenmyr Chronicles. This is a fantasy world, and some of the pronunciations might be a little unfamiliar.

I have included this pronunciation guide in case you find it useful. (But please feel free to ignore me and pronounce the words as you see fit.) After all, that is the beauty of reading.

I have expanded the pronunciation guide to include new characters we will meet in Of Ash and Ivy.

Characters:
Aileana: Ay-lee-ah-na
Xander: Zan-der
Daegal: Day-gal
Myhhena: my-hen-na
Uhna: ohh-nah
Niona: Nigh-oh-na

Saena: Say-nah
Elyx: Eee-licks
Elyxander: Eee-licks-zan-der
Maiela: May-el-la
Kysha: Key-sha
Ryllae: Ry-lee
Tiaesti: Tie-ay-stee
Castien: Cas-tee-in
Erwen: Ehr-win
Kethryllian: Keth-reh-lee-yan
Firana: Fir-ah-na
Dirhinth: Dir-in-th
Erthian: Er-thee-in
Linthi: Lin-thee
Galahad: Gah-lah-had
Braern: Bray-urn
Mareena: Mah-ree-nah
Calix: Cah-licks

Gods:
Aemiis: ay-mees
Kydona: Key-doh-na
Thelrena: Thel-ray-na
Ithiar: Ih-thigh-ar

Places:
Thyr: Th-ur (Like sir, but with th)
Ithenmyr: Ih-thin-meer
Ipotha: Ih-poh-tha
Niphil: Nigh-fill

Breley: Breh-lee

Houses:
Irriel: Ih-ree-el
Ignis: Ig-nis
Corellon: Coh-reh-llon

Contents

Author's note — xiii

1. Something was Extraordinarily, Terribly Wrong — 1
2. Kill the Dragon — 11
3. Death's Embrace — 17
4. Hold On, Sunshine — 20
5. The Keeper of the Earth — 25
6. Welcome to the Sanctuary — 38
7. A Bundle of Leaves and Twigs — 52
8. I Hated Them All — 71
9. Nothing Wrong with a Touch of Paranoia — 85
10. A Very Important Question — 100
11. Safe was a Relative Term — 114
12. The Guardians of the Sanctuary — 125
13. What is Blood? — 138
14. No One Will Survive — 158
15. Practicing Magic and an Unexpected Arrival — 175
16. Kydona has No Place Here — 195
17. The High Lady — 216
18. Death Knocked on my Door — 226
19. A Multitude of Distractions — 237
20. Gone — 249
21. The Forgotten One — 258
22. Happiness Had No Place Here — 272
23. Racing Against Time — 283
24. Life and Death Would be Torn Asunder — 287
25. Absolute Darkness — 296
26. Curses and Nightmares — 299
27. Absence Makes the Heart Ache — 310
28. A Summons and a Healing — 318

29. Alone Once More   330

30. A Myriad of Problems   342

31. The High Tide Waits for No Fish   350

32. They're Going to Kill Me   362

33. Coral City   379

34. Running Out of Time   392

35. Two Paths Ahead   400

36. How Had Everything Come to This?   409

37. I Believe You   414

38. Come Get Him   422

39. A Masterful Curse   432

40. The Worst Listener   438

41. Time for a New Game   448

42. A Broken Curse   458

43. A Lovers' Reunion   465

44. Running Out of Time   472

45. Epilogue - Darkness is Coming   482

Of Thistles and Talons   485

Tethered: An Arranged Marriage Fantasy Romance   487

Acknowledgments   499

About the Author   501

Also by Elayna R. Gallea   503

Author's note

Welcome back to Ithenmyr.

Of Ash and Ivy takes place in a medieval setting that contains violence in several different forms.

This book contains references to violence, including violence against women and children. It also contains language, death, assault, sexism, child abuse, severe misogyny, and references to off-page sexual assault.

Something was Extraordinarily, Terribly Wrong

DAEGAL

Jolting upright in my bed, cold sweat beaded on my forehead. My pulse beat rapidly in my ears, and my lungs were tight. A thick sense of wrongness slid over my skin like an ill-fitting shirt. Something was wrong. I felt it like a pounding drum in the core of my being.

My first thoughts went to Aileana and Xander, but that couldn't be right. They weren't supposed to return until the morning. A peek out of the window confirmed the late hour. The moon was high, the stars barely making it through the leafy cover around Nonna's cottage.

It was far too early for them to be back.

Still, that feeling of wrongness did not go away. A warning beat in my veins, washing over my skin like the prick of a thousand tiny needles. I couldn't hear anything out of the ordinary, and nothing seemed out of sorts, but I couldn't shake the feeling that something was extraordinarily, terribly wrong.

My magic thrummed in my veins, begging to be used. It pulsed with

1

an urgency I wasn't used to feeling. Very few times in my long life had my magic called to me like it was right now.

Its voice was deep, ancient, and eternal, begging me to See the future. *Come. Use me. See what happens next.*

Perhaps at another time, I would have questioned how the magic spoke. I would have paused to consider why its call was far more urgent than normal. But this was not the time for introspection.

Not willing to waste another moment, I sucked in a deep breath and reached within myself. Pulling on my core of power was as natural as breathing. It should, after all this time. I'd been on this planet for over two hundred years, and my magic was like another limb.

I couldn't imagine living without it. I didn't know how Ryllae, the Death Elf princess we rescued from Nightstone Prison, woke up every morning without being able to access the well of magic within her.

For Mature Elves who weren't born Without, magic was a part of our very beings.

Letting my power flood through me, I sucked in a deep breath. A heartbeat later, silver light filled my vision. Thick, heavy ribbons that carried the weight of the future were all that I could see. The silver planes were sacred, and the paths they housed were only visible to me. They held everything I needed to know.

As soon as the silver paths appeared, dozens of voices filled my ears at once. I sifted through the ribbons of the future, running my hands over them as flashes of things that were to come appeared before my eyes. Many were faint, mere probabilities that might occur at some point, but others were brighter and more solid. Of all of the paths before me, these were the most likely to occur.

Hundreds of silver ribbons made up the planes, sifting past me like water rushing in a stream past a stone. I couldn't stop to focus on all of them. There were too many, and I could get lost here for hours.

In the past, I had done just that.

Hurry, a dark voice urged me from within. *Time is running out.*

I heeded its call. Urgency pricked at me, and the looming darkness was like a heavy cloud as I sifted through the future.

I was inundated with the things that had yet to occur. Many paths were of little consequence, but others...

They were important, bearing the weight of decisions that would irrevocably change our world. There were many of those looming nearby. The future was the darkest I'd ever seen. Not just in Ithenmyr, but throughout all the Four Kingdoms.

The Vampire Queen was doing something with the ruling council in Ipotha. My brows furrowed, and I ran my hand down the path. I Saw a union being forged between the Western and Northern countries. A marriage and a Binding. A treaty. Darkness.

There was unrest in the Southern Kingdom. A cloud of thick gray mist shrouded their black-haired queen, but I Saw many potential paths streaming out from beneath her feet.

Next to her, the cries of Ithenmyrian females struggling beneath the burden of High King Edgar's rule filled my ears. Slaves screamed as new laws were created to keep them in check. I took note of these to study later.

A prickling sensation tickled the back of my neck, and I turned in a slow circle.

"Good gods," I murmured, my heart pounding as cold fear washed through me. This couldn't be real. Dread twisted in my stomach, and everything felt cold. Crouching, I ran my fingers over the fiery path before me. Green vines intertwined with bright red flames.

Xander and Aileana's path was all wrong.

Before they left, I Looked into the future. I hadn't Seen any of this.

The duo was supposed to go to the Midnight Ball, steal the map, and come back.

This was never supposed to happen.

I ran my fingers over the silver ribbon as if doing so would change what I Saw.

It didn't work.

Shaking my head, I swallowed the lump growing in my throat. Xander was the closest thing I had to a brother, and my only family left besides Maiela. This couldn't happen. I couldn't let it.

We had to do something to save them.

And yet, at that moment, I did not know what to do. The bonded pair was hundreds of miles away and in perilous danger. My magic allowed me to See what was to come, but what good was Seeing the future if I couldn't save them?

My breath caught in my throat, and my head grew light as I stared at their path. It was unmoving, lacking the ripples that signified potential change.

And a few feet away from where I stood, the path just...

Disappeared.

Beyond it was an inky fog so dark, I couldn't See anything past it.

Death.

"No," I whispered, my voice shaking as horror washed through me. It coursed through my veins, and a cold sweat broke out on my skin. "It can't be."

There was nothing left for me to See here. If I was going to help the bonded pair, it would have to be right now.

I needed to leave.

We had to save them.

Shutting my eyes, I pushed myself away from my magic. Leaving the silver planes behind, I slipped back into my body. When the wooden floorboards came into view, I shoved myself off the bed. My toes curled as the cold seeped into my bare skin, but I didn't care. Yanking on the first tunic and trousers I found, I wrenched my door open. I rushed into the hallway, only to come to an abrupt stop.

The elderly witch stood before me, her eyes wide as she looked up. She insisted we call her Nonna and treated us as her grandchildren. It wasn't difficult to understand why Xander loved her. Nonna's white hair hung over her shoulders in a thick white braid, and a blue shawl was warped tightly around her arms. An aura the same color as her shawl surrounded the witch, pulsing with urgency, and her magic rippled in the air.

"Do you feel it, too?" Nonna asked. Her voice had an odd quality that I had never heard before, and it took me a moment to pinpoint it.

Fear.

The elderly witch had seen four centuries come and go. She bore witness to countless horrors, and yet here she was, afraid.

A shudder ran down my spine before I could tamp it down.

Rubbing my hand over my face, I sucked in a deep breath. Despite myself, my voice was shaky as I met the witch's gaze. "I can't See their future. Aileana and Xander...... It just ends. We have minutes to act. If we don't, their path just...... stops."

Nonna's eyes widened as the implication of my words sunk in. A beat passed before she nodded. Her jaw hardened, and she straightened her back. She tightened the shawl and spoke with authority, saying, "Wake your sister-in-law. We'll need her."

"Of course." I nodded.

"Hurry, Daegal," Nonna added. "We have no time to waste. Meet me in the living room."

She turned on her heel, marching down the hallway toward the main living area of the cottage.

Hurrying over to the room my sister shared with her wife, I knocked. My fist barely made contact with the wood before the door swung open, revealing my disheveled sister-in-law. Kysha wore a black shawl over her nightgown but nothing else.

I looked over the Light Elf's shoulder, noting my sister's black curly hair spread over her pillow. Maiela's chest rose and fell steadily as the soft sounds of snoring filled the air.

"What do you need, Daegal?" Kysha asked, her purple aura around her like a veil. "Maiela just fell asleep an hour ago, and she needs to rest."

A pang went through me at the reminder that the Winged Soldiers had brutally attacked my sister a few short weeks ago. After stabbing Maiela, the Crimson King's black-blooded soldiers set fire to their home, causing my sister and her wife to flee before coming here. When they arrived, Maiela had been on the edge of Fading. It had taken everything Nonna had to heal her.

Thank the gods, Nonna had been successful. Maiela was healing. She would be okay.

I couldn't say the same thing for Xander and Aileana.

"We need your help, Kysha." My words came in a rush, and I tilted my head toward the living room. "There's trouble."

"Xander and Aileana?"

I nodded.

Kysha's face paled. "Did you See something?"

"Yes." The tone of my voice said everything I couldn't put into words.

I didn't even know what we could do to help, but we needed to try. Kysha was a halfling—her mother was a witch, and her father was a Light Elf. Hopefully, she'd be able to help us do... something.

Anything.

We needed to act before the future came to pass.

Kysha reached behind the door, grabbing a dark robe. Dropping the shawl on the ground, she pulled the robe over her shoulders and slid the door shut behind her.

It clicked into place, and the Light Elf nodded. "Lead the way."

I prayed to all the gods for help.

We needed all the assistance we could get.

By the time Kysha and I got to the living room, Nonna was pulling out various candles and laying them over every available surface. A large book was open on the table, the yellowed pages rustling beneath the touch of an unseen wind.

Xander's grandmother glanced at the book, murmuring under her breath as she rearranged a few things before her. Her movements were quick and filled with purpose. Nonna didn't even look up as we entered the room. "Hurry, young ones. Come here."

We obeyed. As soon as we stood in the middle of the room, the witch waved a hand. Instantly, all the candles burst into flame. The firelight flickered ominously, casting deep shadows on the walls.

Nonna said, "If we are to help them, we must act now. Sit."

Kysha and I sat on the floor, crossing our legs beneath us as we formed a triangle with the elderly witch. The three of us joined hands, and Nonna murmured under her breath. The candles flickered, and a heavy cloud settled over us. A thick sense of foreboding filled me, and my entire body screamed at me to be alert.

Footsteps came from the loft upstairs, and moments later, Ryllae's blond head popped around the corner.

"What's going on?" she asked sleepily, her long blond hair hanging in a braid down her back. Her horns seemed starker in the candlelight. Sharper, somehow.

She stepped into the living room. Tonight, the crimson, almost black aura I associated with the Death Elf princess was darker than usual. When I first met Aileana, her aura was similar, tainted with wrongness. It was a side-effect, I thought, of the prohiberis both females had been forced to wear.

The darkness in Aileana's aura had worn off over time. Perhaps the Death Elf's aura would as well. I hoped so. There was something about Ryllae that drew me to her. A magnetic pull that made me constantly aware of her presence. Ever since we rescued her, I have always wanted to remain by her side.

I met Ryllae's blue gaze, still holding hands with Nonna and Kysha. "We aren't sure, but Aileana and Xander are in trouble."

The princess cursed. "Can I do anything to help?"

"Not really—" I began, but Nonna cut me off. "You can run into the garden, Princess. There is a plant growing near the cottage. It has bright purple petals and a blue stem. Grab as much of it as you can."

"Of course."

"Make haste, young one," Nonna ordered. "Time is running out."

Ryllae nodded, rushing to do the witch's bidding. I met Nonna's gaze, raising a brow.

She answered my unspoken question. "The plant will act as an amplifier for our magic."

"I see."

Kysha tightened her grip on my hand. Her palm was sweaty, and I was certain mine was as well. "I hope it's enough."

It had to be enough.

"There is no room for doubt here. We must put all our positive energy into this." Nonna shut her eyes, and a brilliant blue light surrounded her. The witch's aura grew brighter and brighter until it rivaled the candlelight filling the room. "There are very few poisons that could injure my grandson to the point of death. We must do everything we can to help him."

A cold gust of wind came from the entryway, and I shivered as Ryllae ran into the living room. She held several flowers and chunks of black dirt sprinkled on the carpet as the princess extended them toward Nonna, roots and all.

Ryllae panted, trying to catch her breath. "Here you go. I grabbed as much as I could."

"Thank you, child." Nonna released my hand, taking the flowers from Ryllae and ripping off the blue stems. The witch dropped them on her lap before crushing the petals between her fingers. Murmuring under her breath, Nonna scattered the petals around the three of us before taking my hand in hers once more.

A cloying, floral scent tickled my nostrils as Nonna shut her eyes and chanted. Ryllae stood back, wringing her hands in front of her as Nonna's magic worked. A tugging came from within me, and moments later, colored ribbons filled the air. My chest ached as the witch forced my magic out of me, but I didn't resist.

Silver, blue, and purple ribbons swirled between the three of us, carried by an unseen wind. Light and Fortune Elf magic intermingled, joining Nonna's blue healing power. Together, the three magics wove themselves tighter and tighter until their colors were indistinguishable from the others.

Nonna's voice, which had been unintelligible until this point, became much louder. A musical, lilting language I'd never heard came out of the witch's mouth. The magic swirled, increasing in speed until it resembled a cyclone spinning in the center of the room.

Sweat broke out on the back of my neck, and my tunic's collar felt too tight as the air thickened. My lungs struggled to draw in a breath, and my heart raced.

Beads of sweat dripped down Nonna's face, and Kysha's hand was clammy in mine.

When it seemed like we wouldn't be able to take another moment of this, the witch stopped speaking.

The silence was so abrupt; it was like a heavy weight as it fell upon us.

For a long moment, nothing happened.

Then, the multi-colored magic shrank into a tight ball before disappearing with a *pop*.

A solemn silence filled the room. It was palpable and nearly suffocating, hanging in the air like a thick fog. The candles flickered again, and then the flames disappeared into a puff of smoke. The lingering scent of ash and flowers filled the room as exhaustion pulled at me.

"What now?" I asked wearily. My eyes threatened to close, and my head felt like it was too heavy for my body. Losing magic at such a rapid rate was draining, even for Mature beings.

Nonna sighed, closing her eyes as she leaned against the armchair behind her.

"Now we wait."

Kill the Dragon

XANDER

A few minutes ago

"Aileana!" I screamed at the top of my lungs. The cloudy night sky seemed to laugh at me as I stared at the space where my bonded mate had stood a mere moment before.

Now, it was empty.

She was gone.

This tower was high but at the bottom...

Aileana was going to die.

I *roared*, thrashing beneath the iron net, pinning me to the ground. Dragonsbane burned through my tunic, pressing into my skin as I stared at the empty space where Aileana had been moments before.

"No!" High King Edgar yelled. His hands clenched into fists, and red sparked all around him. He turned to me, seething, "This is all your fault, dragon."

One of the Winged Soldiers kicked me in the stomach, and another slammed their foot into my ribs. They pushed the dragonsbane further into my body, and I screamed.

It felt like I was being torn apart from the inside out. Agony, unlike anything I'd ever known, ran through me. My entire body trembled, and my nerves felt like they were on fire.

Everything that could have gone wrong did.

Tonight was supposed to be a good, easy night. A night of celebration. We were supposed to steal the map and then fly back to Nonna's under the cover of darkness.

How had everything gone so wrong?

I couldn't shift, not with the dragonsbane coursing through my body. My blood painted the stone floor of the tower, but I paid it no attention.

Aileana.

Her name echoed in my mind like a pounding drum.

Ash filled the air, and my lungs tightened as I tried to breathe. My eyes darted around the destroyed tower, seeking a weapon. I would settle for anything.

Mere seconds had passed since Aileana fell, but it felt like hours.

Red ribbons swarmed around the Crimson King as he took a threatening step toward me. He gathered magic in his palms, and my heart thundered within me.

I needed to get up. To fight.

My mating mark burned with the fire of a thousand suns. Poison leaked into my blood, and I knew I was looking death in its face.

Aileana.

Every breath that I took brought Aileana closer to her demise.

Time was running out.

Mere moments had passed since she fell out the window, yet it felt like an eternity. How far were we from the ground?

Not far enough.

Time was running out.

This couldn't be the end. Not now. Aileana couldn't die because of me.

If she did...

Nothing else would matter.

To live without one's bonded mate was to exist in perpetual torture. My heart would beat, but what was life when one's other half was dead?

Aileana tugged on the bond, and I *felt* her anguish run through me.

"No!" I yelled.

The Crimson King took another step closer, and the red ribbons wrapped around his arms sparked as death called my name.

I roared, forcing myself to move despite the poison burning through my skin.

Death called my name, but I refused to heed its summons.

"Hold on, Aileana!" I screamed.

High King Edgar laughed, the sound tinged with madness.

As he approached, his deathly magic swirling around him, I knew one thing.

This couldn't be the end.

Not for us.

Our story could not end like this.

Somehow, Aileana was still alive. The bond we shared pulsed with life, and I knew the fall hadn't killed her yet.

Had she found something to hold? A way to slow her fall? Whatever the reason for this brief reprieve, I knew it couldn't last.

I needed to save her.

I struggled against the Winged Soldiers. My blood boiled within me, and agony filled my veins, but I didn't care.

The Crimson King screamed profanities at me, but I didn't pay him any heed.

I couldn't.

Aileana occupied every part of my mind. Her sorrow tasted like the ocean as it flooded me through our bond.

She was saying goodbye.

"No!" I roared.

I refused to let this be the end.

High King Edgar readied his magic, and I swallowed.

Shoving past the agony created by the poison, I tried to summon my dragon.

Thick, black mist hid the creature from view. I knew it was there—it was always there—but I couldn't touch or speak to it. I couldn't even feel it.

The dragonsbane was holding the dragon hostage, out of my reach.

But giving up was not an option. Aileana never gave up on me. I would do her the same courtesy.

I had to move quickly.

Ignoring the searing pain in my arms, I shifted beneath the iron net. Reaching toward my thigh, I felt the cool hilt of one of my daggers. Slipping the weapon out of its sheath, I adjusted my body as well as I could beneath the net.

My skin sizzled, and I clenched my jaw against the searing pain as I eyed the nearest soldier. His wings cast a long shadow over me, but he wasn't looking at me. None of them were.

All three soldiers eyed the Crimson King. As he gathered his magic, a thick haze of red magic surrounded the Death Elf.

High King Edgar was readying to kill me.

This was my chance.

Gripping the hilt of my dagger, I eyed the nearest Winged Soldier's chest. I had to hit his heart. Somehow.

I shoved myself to my knees, and the net tightened on my back. Fiery pain erupted as the horrifying scent of burnt flesh and cloth filled my nostrils. Ignoring the agony, I reached for the Winged Soldier's leg.

One chance.

For Aileana.

My fingers ran over the coarse material of his trousers. The unsuspecting soldier sucked in a deep breath just as I yanked. Brandishing my dagger, I rolled and pulled the soldier down.

The gods-damned poisoned net remained over my head, but with the Winged Soldier falling to his knees, I had slightly more room to move. Even as my flesh sizzled from the dragonsbane, I drove my dagger straight into the Winged Soldier's heart.

I knew before the blade pierced his flesh that my aim was true.

The guard screamed, his black wings snapping behind him, but it was too late. Black blood spurted from the soldier's chest, and his cries ended in a horrifying gurgle.

"Kill the dragon!" High King Edgar screamed as I tightened my grip on my dagger, readying myself to fight until the very end. "Whatever you do, don't let him shift!"

The strangest sensation began in the middle of my chest. It started as a soft thrum, but soon, it increased in intensity. Time slowed to a crawl as the thrumming became a steady drumbeat within my torso.

Glancing down at my blood-covered hand, my eyes widened as ribbons of silver, blue, and purple magic swirled around me.

I knew this magic.

The blue ribbons spoke to my soul, twisting with the silver and purple magic before they sank into my battered body. The moment they touched my skin, the pain lessened.

The dragon twinged, stirring once more.

My skin sizzled, but I felt stronger.

Better.

Faster.

My heartbeat steadied, and I blew out a long breath.

Thank you, Nonna.

Hopefully, one day, I'd get to thank her in person.

Where is she? the dragon cried out within me, breaking through the hold of the dragonsbane. *Where is Aileana?*

Falling. I didn't have time to say anything else.

The creature that lived beneath my skin *roared*; its fury was the fuel I needed. The two remaining soldiers turned towards me, their faces painted in anger. Their wings snapped behind them as they snarled, stepping over the black blood of their companion.

Metal twanged. One of them drew a sword. The other's fingers sharpened into talons. But it was too late for them.

White-hot anger pulsed through my body.

Every single second counted. If I waited even a moment too long, it could be too late for Aileana. Her intense terror was a bitter coating on my tongue as it flooded through the bond.

The final two Winged Soldiers approached. The High King yelled, ordering his soldiers to kill me, but it didn't matter.

I focused everything I had on the dragon.

This was our only hope.

I wrenched the beast forth, praying to Kydona that I wouldn't be too late.

Death's Embrace

AILEANA

Death's embrace was not gentle. It was not kind. Nor was it calm, loving, or warm. It was not welcoming at all.

Death's embrace was worse than being touched by Remington. Worse than High King Edgar and his punishments. Death's embrace was slow, painful, and drawn out.

Every second felt like an eternity as I tumbled head over heels to my death.

Death's embrace was rough. It was cold and bitter and cruel. It was a roaring, rushing wind yanking me away from life.

From Xander.

Even now, as I fell from the tower, I refused death's touch.

I would not go to it willingly.

This was not what I wanted. I had so much life left to live.

My life couldn't be over now. Not when mere months had passed since I learned the power of freedom. The beauty of family.

Not when I had just fallen in love and found my mate.

I had so much left to do. So many battles were left unfought.

And yet, here I was.

I should have been fighting to free the females of Ithenmyr, but instead, I was careening through the skies. I should have been flying through the skies with Xander, but I was tumbling head-first toward death's cold hands.

With every beat of my heart, every second that passed, I drew nearer to my end.

I heard death's cold, cruel voice as I fell from the Queen's Tower. Blackness pushed at the edges of my vision, and the ruined, tattered remains of my skirts billowed in the air.

They were the last remnants of my battle with Edgar. My life flashed before my eyes as I tumbled towards the ground.

Death opened its arms.

One last scream crawled out of my throat as death's claws dug into me. A single, salty tear slipped down my cheek. I glimpsed the tower where my bonded mate lay under a net of chains one last time.

"I'm so sorry, Elyx," I whispered.

My heart thudded as a feral roar shook the tower above me. The wind carried the sound to my ears as I fell toward the forest that surrounded Kaerndal Castle.

There would be no saving me now.

I was not Mature. I had no wings.

Death was waiting for me, and there was no way out.

I was never going to see Xander again.

Leaves rustled, and shouts came from the walls of the city built into the mountain. A brisk, bitter, arctic wind kissed my cheeks, and strands of my hair fell on my face.

The poetic injustice of my death was a dagger to my heart. I found life by escaping all those months ago, and now, another tower was going to be the death of me.

The leaves grew near enough to touch. My heart stuttered, and my lungs tightened. A roar shook the entire world.

"Goodbye, Elyx."

Then, darkness was all I knew.

Hold On, Sunshine

XANDER

I let the shift take over even as the dragonsbane from the net burned into my flesh. My neck cracked, and my bones broke and reshaped as the dragon emerged from within. High King Edgar shot red ribbons of magic at me, but it was too late for that.

My eyesight sharpened, and my sense of smell strengthened. The lemon and cedar scent of the dragonsbane was so overwhelming that it was all I could smell.

In this form, Aileana's screams were ear-piercingly loud. Each one was a bolt of fire sent directly into my heart.

Hold on, Sunshine.

I drew in a deep breath, and my wings snapped out at my sides. Or at least, they tried to. This tower was not built for a dragon. The gray stones of the Queen's Tower bore down on me, pressing against my body from above as my wings struggled to expand. Even with Nonna's magic and my rapid healing, my body still screamed from the amount of dragonsbane running through my veins.

20

At any other time in my life, the pain would have been too much. But not today. Not with my bonded mate's life on the line.

I *roared*, gathering every single ounce of strength I had, and the tower shook. Stones crumbled to dust above me.

Bright, scorching red flames ripped from my mouth, eating through the remnants of the tower. The last two Winged Soldiers screamed, and High King Edgar threw up a red shield of magic seconds before my fire hit him.

Ash filled my mouth, and finally, I beat my wings.

Once.

Twice.

The stone roof gave way. It crumbled, turning to dust, and the cold autumnal air kissed my scales. Ribbons of red magic lit up the night like deadly bolts of lightning.

I flapped my wings, flying away from the tower. Dust and ash swirled in the night air around me, falling slowly around me as a pair of black wings rose from the tower.

Flying above the rubble of the tower, High King Edgar roared, "I will kill you, dragon!"

Red flashed.

Pain erupted on my back, but I didn't stop.

It would heal, eventually.

Or not.

At this point, I needed to find Aileana. Nothing else mattered.

Ignoring the scorching pain making its way through my body, I soared towards the earth. Behind me, the tower shook and rumbled, but I paid it no attention.

Vibrant red Death Elf magic filled the air, and I continued my descent.

Aileana! I screamed through the mate bond. The fact that we could speak like this was a blessing.

Silence was my only response.

Please, Kydona, let her be alive.

Narrowing my eyes, I flew in a downward spiral much faster than usual. Keeping my wings tight against my side, I spun until a flash of red hair caught my eye.

Aileana! Her name sounded on repeat in my mind as I sent it down the bond.

She approached the trees quickly, and I barreled toward her.

My heart raced in my chest, and I roared. Fire shot from my mouth as I careened toward my mate. Flying faster than I had ever done before, I only had one thing on my mind: I had to save her.

I couldn't let her die.

She was *mine*.

My reason for living. My bonded mate. My *everything*.

She fell, and I flew toward her. My back ached, and my wings weren't flapping properly, but I didn't stop.

I couldn't stop.

Aileana was twenty feet away from me.

Fifteen.

Ten.

Reaching out with my talons, I grabbed for her.

And...

They closed on nothing but air.

I shrieked, the sound of my anguish filling the night air as I continued to dive.

One chance.

That was all I had left. Just one.

The trees were so close that I could make out the ribbing on each individual leaf.

Then she looked up. Her emerald eyes met mine, and she smiled.

I love you, Elyxander, Aileana said through our mating bond. Her voice was so soft, so filled with anguish, that my heart shattered. *I only wish we had more time.*

I snarled, smoke coming from my mouth. *Don't talk like that. You can tell me how much you love me in person.*

Flexing my talons, I flapped my wings once to stabilize in the air. *Hold on.*

This time, when I reached for Aileana, my talons wrapped around her.

Instant relief flooded through me like a rainstorm after a summer drought.

This was all I needed. *She* was all I needed.

I tightened my grip around her and flapped my wings, pulling us away from the trees.

I'm... not dead, Aileana whispered through the bond.

My wings beat against the air as bolts of red magic rained down from the crumbling tower. We rose as crisp relief flooded the bond. It tasted like a fresh spring morning after a long, cold winter.

It tasted like a second chance at life.

Shaking my head, I roared as we rose higher and higher. *No,* I said. *You are definitely not. Now, hold on tight, Sunshine.*

Aileana's hands found their way around my talons, and she gripped me tightly. My wings flapped, and I ignored the searing pain in my back as I continued to climb.

What are you doing? she asked.

I leveled myself with what was left of the stone tower, narrowing my eyes. *Taking care of something.*

ELAYNA R. GALLEA

He was still there. Flying above the remains of the Queen's Tower, High King Edgar's wings blended into the night. His horns curled above his head, and his blond hair blew around him as he summoned ribbon after ribbon of deadly magic.

I locked eyes with the evil king and pulled on the flames that were my dragon's birthright.

The Crimson King was powerful.

But I was angry.

There was little in this world that was more powerful than a dragon shifter whose bonded mate had just been threatened.

Ignoring the agonizing pain running through my body, I drew a deep breath. Flames erupted from my maw, lighting up the night sky.

Instantly, fire engulfed the tower. The flames were so hot that they burned right through the stone.

Red flames licked the Crimson King's wings, and a scream that would haunt my nightmares for years escaped his lips as he tumbled to the ground.

I didn't stay to watch him burn.

The Keeper of the Earth

AILEANA

I was still alive.

Laughter bubbled up within me at the thought. *Alive*! I couldn't believe it.

I had honestly thought I was going to die.

But instead, Xander saved me.

Again.

My hands tightened around the rough skin of Xander's talons, and my heart raced in my chest. His wings beat against the night sky, the powerful membranes blocking the moonlight as he carried me. Xander's enormous wings were little more than black shapes against the dark sky.

I would be delighted to never set foot in the capital of Ithenmyr again. In fact, if I never saw another Winged Soldier for the rest of my life, I would be a happy elf.

Shadows of trees and mountains passed at what would likely have been an alarming rate if not for the life-threatening situation we were fleeing. Eventually, my heart rate slowed enough that I paid more attention to our surroundings.

Xander's wings, which were usually so powerful, were faltering. He remained above the clouds, the dark sky hiding us from prying eyes, but his movements were weakening. The space between his wingbeats stretched, and his body shook as he flew. Through the bond, I felt his complete and utter exhaustion.

Pressing my hand against his talon, I squeezed gently. *Xander, we should stop and find a place to sleep.*

We'd been awake for nearly twenty-four hours, attacked by a murderous king and his soldiers, and we both nearly died. Even if Xander was only half as tired as I was, I could not believe he was still flying.

A beat of his wings blew a gust of cool air toward me before his reply echoed in my mind. *We aren't far enough from that black-hearted bastard yet.*

That bastard was also known as High King Edgar, the Crimson King, Ruler of Ithenmyr, and the male responsible for the majority of my trauma and pain. He was the reason for the dragon massacre. It was his fault I had no family left.

I hated High King Edgar with every fiber of my being.

Do you really think he could have survived the flames? Even in my mind, my incredulity was clear.

Xander's fire had been so hot that it singed the edges of my destroyed dress. How could anyone have survived that?

We can only hope. The dragon who held my heart shook his head, and bright flames lit up the night.

I supposed there was no need for secrecy. Not anymore.

By the time the sun rose, everyone in Ithenmyr would know the Last Dragon still lived.

Xander kept flying, and comfortable silence fell between us. The necklace with the four map pieces bounced between my breasts, the rhythm steady against the beating of my heart. I should have been cold. After all, my dress was destroyed, and the air was freezing. But I wasn't. The heat from my dragon warmed my entire body.

Soon, my eyes grew heavy. Rays of sunlight pushed away the darkness, and the trees blurred beneath me. My limbs were leaden, and my body was weary. The pool of magic within me was far lower than it ever had been before. I'd used so much magic fighting High King Edgar, and he still managed to beat me.

My face and arms stung, reminding me that I'd suffered dozens of cuts when the glass windows of the Queen's Tower had imploded.

And yet, even with all that, I smiled.

My bonded mate and I were alive.

Night gave way to early morning, and Xander flew. My eyes slipped shut, and I drifted into a fitful sleep, held by my mate.

I dreamed of fire.

Soft, dewy leaves brushed up against me, tickling my skin. Birds chirped. Their song was incongruous with the death and destruction we left behind us mere hours ago.

Wake up, Sunshine. Xander's voice caressed my thoughts like a warm kiss, brushing against me and pulling me from sleep.

My lips twitched, and I pried my eyes open. Green filled my vision, and the warm, yellow rays of the early morning dawn cast light over the forested canopy above us. My hands stretched out, and I ran my fingers over the soft bed of moss beneath me as I pushed myself up onto my elbows.

Larger than four horses put together, my dragon was massive and took up most of the clearing. Xander's wings were pressed tight against his body as he stood a few feet from me. His slitted golden eyes watched me carefully as he stomped once, his foot leaving a massive indent in the damp grass beneath him.

His message was clear: *Stand.*

"Even as a dragon, you're bossy." There was no anger in my tone, though, and my lips twitched as I pushed myself to my feet. Or at least, I attempted to do so.

In reality, I got one foot underneath me before both my legs shook, and I collapsed to the ground on all fours. I grasped the dewy grass, my entire body shaking, as a flash of bright white light filled the forest.

Moments later, a very familiar set of legs appeared in my vision, and a pair of warm hands rested on my face.

"Are you okay, Aileana?" Concern filled Xander's voice, and I looked up. He crouched before me, wearing nothing but the skin he was born in, and my eyes widened as I got a good look at him.

Gasping, I pushed his hands off me. Confusion pulsed through me, but it didn't belong to me. It was his.

"Am I okay?" I repeated the question, and my voice was hoarse as I looked Xander over.

Red and black blood covered his usually pale skin, and a large purple bruise was blooming on his left flank. Fresh blood oozed out of dozens of open cuts that spanned Xander's legs, chest, and neck.

His mating mark was barely visible beneath the blood and grime that covered his flesh. How had he even flown us here?

Why isn't he healing?

That question became the only thing that mattered to me. Xander healed fast—far faster than anyone I had ever met in my entire life.

But right now, he wasn't healing at all.

My stomach twisted into a tight knot. With every passing moment, I noticed another cut. Another bruise.

"Aileana, what's wrong?" Xander's brows furrowed, and he bent, uncaring of his lack of clothing, as his hands quickly roamed over me. He felt my shoulders, my arms, and my stomach. "Are you injured? Tell me where it hurts."

"I'm fine," I mumbled. I had some cuts and bruises, but they would heal. Even with my magic levels far lower than normal, I was connected to the earth.

Already, I felt better than before. The ground hummed beneath my fingertips and the wind blew around me in a gentle caress, as if it was inviting me to play. I had other things on my mind. "It's not me you should be worried about."

Xander raised a bloody brow. "What are you talking about?"

My hand trembled as I lifted it off the ground, running it down his exposed arm. He hissed as my finger ran over the mark of our mating. It seemed alive beneath my touch, pulsing as I pressed my finger into it.

"You're hurt," I said accusingly. The breeze blew by, bringing the scent of lemons and cedar to my nose. My heart thudded as realization dawned on me. "The dragonsbane."

Xander glanced down.

"Oh," he whispered. His voice wobbled and was far lower than normal. "Somehow, I forgot about that."

"Forgot?" My eyes widened. "How could you forget about being injured?"

"You're safe," he murmured. Xander's eyes fluttered shut. "That's all that matters."

"Xander!" Worry knotted my stomach as the enormous male's shoulder fell against my chest. Air escaped me in a whoosh, and I could barely breathe as Xander's weight pushed down on me. "What are you doing?"

Those golden eyes turned glassy moments later as they rose to meet mine. Panic whirled within me like a windstorm. I placed my hand on his skin, and I gasped as a flurry of curses escaped me. "You're burning up."

"Am I? That's interesting." He blinked, his eyes unfocused, as he raised a bloody hand and patted my cheek. "Don't worry, Aileana. It's going to be okay."

Okay? No. This was not okay. In fact, this was the opposite of okay. Was he delusional? Good gods. If so, we really had a problem. I did not know how to care for an ill dragon shifter, especially in the middle of a gods-forsaken forest in the middle of Ithenmyr.

Xander's eyes slipped shut, and a shuddering, ragged breath escaped him. My heart raced, and my lungs tightened as I shook his shoulders. Calling his name, I prodded him, but he didn't respond.

"Xander, can you hear me?" Urgency leaked into my words, and I kept calling out as my voice reached a fever pitch.

Still, he didn't move.

My heart sped up, and my hands grew clammy as I looked around. The sun was slowly cresting the tops of the trees, casting bright rays of light on the leaves.

"Wake up, Xander!" Tears lined my eyes. "I don't know where we are!" I drew in a shaky breath. "Please. I don't know what to do."

Fear unfurled in my stomach.

What am I going to do?

"Oh my gods," I moaned.

My pulse quickened, and my chest constricted as a cold sweat broke out on the back of my neck. I took in deep, shuddering breaths, and panic loomed over me like an unwelcome acquaintance, just waiting for me to let it back into my life.

I had to think of something.

Xander needed me to remain calm. Forcing myself to breathe, I ran through my options. Obviously, I couldn't fly. While I wasn't a healer...

Nonna was.

Reaching beneath the neckline of my destroyed dress, I felt around for the ribbon securing Nonna's locket around my neck. She could help. She was a powerful witch. Maybe she could...

Dammit.

My fingers ran down the leather string around my neck. The small tube containing the four pieces of the map was there, but that was all.

Nonna's locket was gone. We were alone. A sob crawled up my throat, but before it could come out, I forced it down.

Stop. Focus. Xander needs you.

One of us needed to remain calm, and whether I liked it or not, that task landed on me.

Finding a healer was not going to happen.

I needed to figure out where we were. At least then, I could plan the next steps.

We were in a forest. That wasn't all that surprising. Forests, mountains, and rivers covered most of the land in Ithenmyr.

This specific forest was beautiful. Leaves ranging from the deepest reds to the brightest oranges hung from trees and covered the ground at our feet.

I inhaled. I couldn't smell any salt, so it was a pretty good assumption we weren't close to the Indigo Ocean.

Even so, there were dozens of forests in Ithenmyr. Hundreds, even.

Why does this keep happening to us?

Xander's face was growing alarmingly pale. His every breath was shallow, and a thin sheet of sweat coated his forehead.

"Please wake up, Elyx," I whispered.

Placing my hand on his cheek, I yelped. His skin, which had been

31

burning hot a few moments ago, was now cold and clammy to the touch. I wasn't a witch or a healer, but I knew this was extremely bad.

Not for the first time, I wished I could take all knowledge of ridiculous etiquette and trade it for something useful. I would gladly forget how to properly serve tea service if it meant I could help my bonded mate.

The poison was still in his body, and now it was killing him.

Figure it out.

Sliding Xander's head off my shoulder, I gingerly laid his body on the ground. Even now, in this terrible state of illness, he was breathtaking. Blood coated his silver-white hair, and our mating bond was visible even through the blood. The gold and green tattoos were a sign of our bond—a visible marking of our connection.

I hoped it would be enough to help us get through this next obstacle.

Crouching, I brushed my lips over his.

"Hold on, Xander," I whispered, pressing my forehead against his. "Don't you dare die on me, alright? I'm going to need you to listen to me for once."

He remained still, but the bond pulsed with a sense of awareness.

"Can you hear me?" I asked.

A flutter came through the bond.

"Thank the gods."

At least he was alive.

Sending as much warmth and love as I could through our connection, I kissed his forehead before shifting back.

"I'm going to figure this out, Xander," I whispered, taking his marked hand in mine. "We'll get the poison out of you, and you'll be fine."

Leaves rustled beneath me as I shifted. Leaning against a nearby tree, the rough bark dug into my skin as I tightened my grip around Xander's hand. Our mating marks lined up, even though his arm was much larger than mine.

Placing my free hand on the ground, I reached within myself to my well of magic. It was far lower than ever before, but slips of green ribbons were waiting for me. There were more now than before, and I made a mental note to find out how my magic was replenished.

Thanking Thelrena, the goddess of the Earth Elves, for my magic, I dug my fingers into the ground. My magic thrummed in my veins, and the dirt was cool. The earth called to me as I crumbled the soil beneath my fingers. The wind swirled around me, blowing strands of my hair in my face as it sang a soothing lullaby.

Protectress of the Woods, the earth cried out. Its ethereal voice rang through me, and my magic pulsed in response.

Once, the cry of the earth frightened me. Now, it brought me comfort.

My eyes slipped shut, and my consciousness spread out from me as I connected to the earth.

I could *feel* everything in Ithenmyr.

As one, all the insects and the animals in Ithenmyr ceased what they were doing. From the tiniest ants born minutes earlier to the oldest giant leopards who lived in the Koln Mountains, all the life in Ithenmyr paused what they were doing and acknowledged me.

We see you, they said as one. Their voices merged, echoing in my mind as I connected to the earth.

The thrumming in my veins became a heady pulse that took over everything else. My breath came harder, and my heart pounded as I acknowledged the life around me. The trees, the insects, the plants, and the animals were all a part of me at that moment.

For the first time in my life, I knew what it meant to be an Earth Elf. My heart swelled at the presence of these lives who depended on me.

The living things in Ithenmyr needed me.

They were mine. Mine to protect. Mine to care for.

They were mine to love.

As I poured my magic into the earth, connecting with the life in Ithenmyr, I tightened my grip on my bonded mate's hand. His skin was clammy, but that faint pulse of life still came through our bond, a constant reassurance.

"I hear them, Xander," I whispered in awe.

Green ribbons poured out of my palm, but I wasn't exhausted.

The earth was feeding me as much as I was feeding it.

This was how my magic replenished, I realized with a jolt. The earth was giving back to me, even as I provided for it.

Feeding my magic into the earth, I felt *alive* in a way I never had before. My lungs expanded, and my skin tingled. The ground sang and rumbled beneath my feet as the wind brushed my cheeks.

The trees shook, the rustling of their leaves echoing the cries of the life in Ithenmyr. *The Keeper of the Earth is here.*

Over and over again, they chanted the title. The chorus of their voices filled me, rejuvenated me, and the pool of magic within me expanded.

Something within me *clicked*.

It felt as though, for the first time in my life, I could really breathe. My lungs expanded, drawing in far more air than ever, and I was... renewed.

Myself, and yet more.

Slipping back into my body, I released my grip on the earth. It was far easier than it ever had been to step away from the call of the earth.

Tightening my grip on Xander's hand, I ran my thumb over his skin. His eyes were shut, and his breaths were shallow, but that faint pulse came through the bond.

Pulling my free hand out of the dirt, I stared at it.

This was new.

My skin glowed a vibrant green, and bright whorls and swirls covered the backs of both my hands, stopping at my wrist.

The tingling continued. A feeling of life spread through me, and I felt better than I had in a long time. Strength ran through my veins.

My cuts were gone, healed as though they had never existed. The leaves rustled, and the wind murmured as green ribbons slipped from my hands once more.

"Oh, my gods."

I knew what this was.

The ground shook, and I tightened my grip around Xander's hand. A hoarse, disbelieving laugh escaped me.

I peeked at the pool of magic within me.

It was brimming with magic.

Fate possessed a strange sense of humor.

I wasn't sure if it was the fall or the fight with High King Edgar, but something over the past day must have triggered this. Once the laughter started, it was harder and harder to keep it in.

I just underwent the first stage of Maturation.

This should have been a moment of joy. Xander and I should have been able to celebrate this together. After all, once I was fully Mature, things would probably be easier. I would be more difficult to kill. Stronger. More powerful.

But instead, we were stranded in the middle of a random forest.

What good was Maturing if I couldn't find out where we were?

I wasn't sure what made me do it, but I placed my hand on the ground again. Sucking in a breath, I directed my question toward the earth. *Where are we?*

No sooner did I think the question than the answer arose within me. The earth showed me where we were, painting a picture in my mind's eye.

We were far from everything.

Xander had flown us in the opposite direction from Nonna's cottage. There were trees for miles, but that was it. I should have been afraid. The night would come, eventually. Animals much larger than the two of us called this forest their home.

But I wasn't. A strange sense of peace filled me.

The earth had shown me something else. Something... good. I hoped. I still remember how the earth tried to claim me as its own when my magic first emerged.

We will never harm you, the earth said in reply to my thoughts. I hadn't realized I was still connected to it. *You are the Protectress and the Keeper of the Earth. You are* ours.

Murmuring my thanks to the earth, I withdrew my fingers from the dirt.

Leaning over, I pressed a kiss to Xander's bloody cheek. His eyes were still closed, and his chest moved up and down in a reassuring manner. "Hold on, my love."

Laying down next to my mate, I curved my body around his.

The earth vibrated beneath me. *Help is coming, Keeper of the Earth.*

Acting on an instinct from deep within me, I ran my hand over Xander's chest. Careful not to touch any of the cuts, I released my grip on my magic. Green ribbons slipped from my fingers, sliding over Xander's skin before disappearing beneath his flesh. Soon, his breathing evened out. Color returned to his face, and his cuts looked better than before.

OF ASH AND IVY

I wasn't sure what my magic was doing, but I didn't stop.

After a short while, Xander no longer looked like he was on the brink of death. But still, his eyes were closed, and his breathing was ragged.

He needed help.

Shifting, I placed my hand on the tree truck behind me. The bark was rough beneath my fingers, and birds chirped above me as I murmured, "Hurry."

The answer came moments later. *We are coming for you, Keeper of the Earth. Hold on.*

The ancient voice echoed in my mind, and I took a long breath. Something warm and comforting kindled within me. It took me a moment to realize what it was.

Hope.

37

Welcome to the Sanctuary

AILEANA

The sound of hoofbeats on the forest floor was the first thing I heard.

Help is coming, Keeper of the Earth.

An eager silence filled the forest. The birds stopped chirping, and even the wind ceased to blow as the air hummed with anticipation.

Settling in to wait, I ran my thumb over Xander's calloused skin. Even now, vibrant green ribbons of magic slipped from my fingers. They sank beneath his skin as my eyes searched the nearby trees.

Leaves of various shades of orange and red glinted in the early morning autumn sunlight. A flicker of white caught my attention through the trees, and I tensed. My left hand tightened around Xander's as my other clenched helplessly at my side. I wished we had our weapons, but they were gone. Xander must have lost his weapons and clothes when he shifted, and my daggers disappeared during my fall.

Our rescuers broke through the trees, and my breath caught in my throat.

Two enormous, majestic elks stood in the clearing. They were as

38

white as freshly fallen snow, a stark contrast to the red and black blood marring Xander's body, and their coats glistened in the sunlight. The larger one's head was as high as my shoulder, and its companion wasn't much smaller. Instinct told me they were a mated pair.

Pressing a kiss to Xander's brow, I covered his naked form with some fallen leaves and pushed myself to my feet. My legs shook, and I wobbled before finding my footing, never taking my eyes off the incredible creatures.

The male's enormous antlers extended two feet from the center of his head. He stepped forward, the powerful muscles in his legs tightening as he slowly approached. The ground quaked with every movement, and my heart beat quickly. It looked as though he could run for days on end without stopping.

The female didn't move at all, but she met my gaze. Her eyes were a brilliant blue, like a cloudless sky on a spring day, and filled with intelligence. If I hadn't already known these weren't normal creatures of the woods, that would have confirmed it for me.

A long moment passed in complete silence.

I was about to speak when a warm breeze rustled my hair. It kissed my temples and caressed my cheeks before hurrying on.

An ancient, powerful voice swirled through the clearing, and goosebumps erupted on my arms and legs as the male elk stepped forward. *Greetings, Aileana of the House of Corellon, Earth Elf, Bonded Mate of Elyxander, Protectress of the Woods, and Keeper of the Earth.*

His eyes were a deep, glowing amber as they met mine. A brilliant golden light that rivaled the sun shone from them. His mouth curved into a strange semblance of a smile before he dropped to one knee. Leaves crinkled beneath the elk as he dipped his head in reverence. *We are here to serve you.*

Bowing.

This magnificent creature of the woods was bowing... to me?

I could scarcely breathe as my mind raced to comprehend what was happening. Something within me stirred, even as my feet moved without volition. They carried me toward the elk, and he remained on one knee. Waiting.

When I was close enough to touch the elks, I extended a trembling hand. The female's gaze was watchful as I placed my shaking hand on the male's snout. He remained as still as a statue as I rubbed my hand slowly over his mouth. Warm air tickled my skin as I explored his soft, warm fur. The elk nuzzled my hand, his snout wet against my skin.

"Hello there," I whispered reverently. Glancing over my shoulder at Xander, I frowned. A faint green tinge came from his skin, and the blood looked worse in the daylight. "Are you... can you help us?"

The elk snorted against my hand. The warm air came as a shock against my arm, and I stepped back.

This is your bonded mate? The same voice echoed in my mind.

"Y-yes," I stammered. "He is mine." My claiming words swirled in the air, and my mating bond tingled. "We need help. There is poison in his blood, and he shifted earlier, but now he isn't healing..." My voice trailed off. "I healed myself, but I can't seem to help him."

He is yours. The elk's voice echoed sagely in my mind. *The bond between mates is sacred.*

"It is."

The male looked at his mate, and they seemed to communicate silently. *Calea and I will take you both to the Sanctuary.*

I had never heard of such a place. The male elk moved around me, trotting to Xander. His eyes glowed gold once more as ribbons of the same color filled the air.

My mouth fell open. "Golden magic?"

I'd never seen that before. To be fair, I'd never seen a woodland creature wield magic, either. Calling my upbringing "sheltered" would be an understatement of epic proportions, but even I knew this was not normal.

I ran through the types of magic in my mind. Red for death, purple for light, silver for the future, blue for healing, and green for the earth.

But gold?

That was definitely new.

This time, another voice spoke as a wet nose touched my arm. My destroyed dress was little more than ribbons of fabric as it swished around me. I turned and met the smaller elk's blue eyes.

Golden magic is a gift from the gods. The soft, feminine voice belonged to the smaller elk—Calea, I assumed—nuzzled my arm. *Watch.*

Golden ribbons slipped from the male elk, swirling in the air and forming a thick, shimmering net. It moved on its own, sliding beneath Xander. My breath caught in my throat as the net lifted him off the ground, creating a sled beneath his large body.

The golden magic shifted into cords that quickly knotted themselves tightly around Xander, securing him to the sled. The cords were thicker around his middle, forming a loincloth of sorts. If not for the blood all over him, he looked like he was sleeping.

Come, Protectress, Calea said softly as she bumped her hip against me. *Climb on.*

I blinked. "You want me to ride you?" Incredulity filled my voice, and I took a step back. Riding an animal who had been touched by divinity seemed blasphemous, even for someone like me who didn't pray anymore.

As if she could read my mind, Calea snorted. *It is an honor for Beor and me to escort the Protectress of the Woods and her bonded mate to the Sanctuary.*

Maybe she could read minds?

I sucked my bottom lip through my teeth. "Will Xander... will he be okay?"

Calea smiled. *He will not wake until we have arrived at the Sanctuary, but he is safe. No harm will come to either of you, Protectress of the Woods. This is my vow to you.*

Her words echoed with certainty in my mind, and a feeling of safety washed over me. The male—Beor—watched us both, the golden magic having created some sort of harness attaching the sled to his back.

"All right." Placing a hand on Calea's flank, I shoved aside the feelings of oddness and did as she asked. Once settled on her back, a thought struck me. "Where is this Sanctuary?"

Calea seemed to hum, her aura pensive before she replied, *It is a place of safety.*

My brows furrowed. "Can you be more spe—"

Beor stiffened, and the words dried up in my throat.

We must go. His voice echoed in my mind as the golden magic ribbons ran from him again. The threads sank into Xander, giving his skin a soft golden sheen before Beor took off in a run.

The elk beneath me turned her head, her eyes meeting mine.

Hold on, Calea warned. *Danger lurks in these woods. Darkness is rising in the Southern Kingdom. We must hurry.*

Leaning forward as my heart raced, I wrapped my arms around her neck as tightly as I could.

Then we were off.

Riding bareback on an elk was not precisely what I'd call a pleasant experience. When Calea took off into the forest, the trees became nothing more than blurs. Their leaves were little more than patches of orange and red, and their trunks were barely visible. The elks leaped over logs, their movements quick and graceful as they easily navigated the thick growth.

Wherever we were, autumn was in full swing in these woods. The leaves had only begun to change at Nonna's cottage, but the air was colder here.

Winter was quickly coming.

As the elks ran through the forest, the earth sang to me. It whispered gentle encouragement, even as my stomach churned from the rapid movements. If I'd eaten anything recently, I was sure it would have come up.

Soon, all I could do was grip Calea's neck and squeeze my eyes shut, praying this would be over soon.

No one answered my prayer. The sun rose high in the sky, and hours passed. My muscles burned, cramping as I held onto the back of the massive creature.

Eventually, the elks slowed and stopped at a small, clear, babbling brook. The moment Calea stopped moving, I slid off her back. My legs wobbled, but I paid them no heed as I rushed to Xander's side. Crouching, I sucked in a breath.

He was completely immobile on the sled, his skin a sickly hue despite the golden sheen.

"Please don't die," I whispered, pressing a hand on his chest. His heart beat steadily beneath my fingers, and I yanked on the bond between us. A reassuring flutter of life came back to me. "I need you, Elyx."

He will be alright, Calea reassured me, nuzzling me from behind. *Once we arrive, he will heal quickly.*

Nodding, I kept my eyes on Xander as I crouched before the brook. Cupping my hands, I dipped them into the cool water. I scooped up the liquid, drinking whatever water did not fall on my shirt. Once my thirst was quenched, I ripped off a piece of my torn ball gown and soaked it in the water.

I washed the blood off myself as best I could and rinsed the cloth before turning towards Xander. The rag was cool in my hand as I gently wiped his face. Black and red blood came away from his skin, revealing the face of the male I loved.

The more I washed, the angrier I became.

This was High King Edgar's fault. His hatred for dragons and all femalekind brought us to this point.

It was his fault that Xander and I couldn't live quiet, peaceful lives.

It was his fault my mate lay here, with blood oozing from cuts that refused to heal.

Forcing my movements to remain gentle despite the anger running through my veins, I cleaned Xander as best I could around the golden cords that secured him to the sled.

Cleaning Xander was intimate in a way that I had never experienced. I only wished he was awake to experience it with me.

He did not move, nor did he respond. Even the fluttering pulse of our bond felt weaker.

"Hold on," I whispered.

It's time to go, Protectress, Beor said.

"All right." Sending warmth and love through the bond, I pressed my lips to Xander's forehead and squeezed his hand. "I love you."

I mounted Calea, and once again, her feet pounded on the forest floor.

∽

SLOWLY, the forest around us changed. The shift was subtle at first, but soon, I realized all the trees were taller. Their trunks were thicker, and the call of the earth was stronger here than before. The leaves were more vibrant, drawing the eye as Calea ran by them. The forest looked like it was on fire, and I loved it.

To say that the autumnal forest was beautiful would have been a disservice to the word itself. It was stunning. Fantastical, even. It boggled my mind to think that these leaves were green a few weeks ago. Now, they paid homage to the beauty of fire and flames.

The beauty of the dragons.

The elks ran until the sun was dipping below the horizon, only slowing once the air chilled.

We have arrived, Protectress. Beor's voice echoed in my mind as he came to a stop.

My brows furrowed, and I frowned. As far as I could tell, we were still in a forest. Trees and bushes covered the hilly woods on all sides. Birds flew above, and a squirrel hopped from one tree to the next.

It looked like every other forest I'd seen. I couldn't see this so-called Sanctuary anywhere.

"Really?" I asked.

Trust us, Caela replied.

It wasn't like I had any other options. Sliding off Calea's back, I hurried over to Xander's side and kneeled before him. His chest rose and fell beneath my hands, and I exhaled, pressing my forehead against his chest.

"Thank Thelrena, you're alive," I murmured. I rubbed his mating mark. "Come back to me, okay?"

For a long time, I believed the gods and goddesses had forgotten about me. Now, I thought that perhaps that wasn't the case. They blessed me with a bonded mate who loved me despite my less-than-desirable violent tendencies, one who would do anything for me.

The dragonsbane running through Xander's veins was proof of that.

Maybe they hadn't turned their back on me. Maybe they knew something we didn't. Something about what was to come.

Maybe there was a purpose to all of this.

Turning, I rose to my feet. Grabbing strips of fabric from the bottom of my dress, I curtsied toward the elks who brought us here. "Thank you for all you've done."

Anything for the Keeper of the Earth, Calea said as they dipped their heads in unison.

Then, the wind began to blow. Leaves swirled in the air, and a chill ran over my skin as a familiar being appeared in the forest before me.

"Hello, Myhhena," I said.

Made entirely of leaves and twigs, her corporeal body not requiring clothing, Myhhena's moss-green eyes stared at me. Her lips tilted up, and her eyes shone. The Spirit of the Woods looked me over with her knowing gaze before she spread her arms out at her side.

"Aileana of the House of Corellon, Earth Elf, Protectress of the Woods, Keeper of the Earth, Bonded Mate of Elyxander, son of Aranuil." Myhhena bowed, and her leaves rustled. "The Spirits of the Woods and Waters welcome you and your mate."

I had so many questions, but all I said was, "Thank you."

"I expect you are seeking sanctuary?" She returned to her full height, a twinkle in her eye as if she knew something I didn't.

"We are." Crouching, I took Xander's hand in my own. "He needs help."

"It shall be taken care of, Protectress."

Lifting her arms at her side, Myhhena spoke in an unfamiliar, lilting tongue. She chanted, and the pool of magic stirred within me. It bubbled, swirling in my veins as my skin tingled. My lungs tightened, and a strange sensation washed over me as the Spirit of the Woods spoke. A sense of peace that I had never felt flooded my veins.

Myhhena raised her hands above her head, and golden ribbons erupted from the Spirit's fingers. They swirled in the air, dancing to a tune only they could hear as they increased in numbers. When there were hundreds of golden ribbons twirling through the forest, Myhhena lowered her hands. As one, they slithered into the ground. My magic thrummed in my veins as if it wanted to come out and play with the golden ribbons.

A tremor ran through the earth, and the woods, which had appeared completely normal mere moments ago, now *moved*.

The trees behind Myhhena shifted as the entire forest rearranged itself. My eyes widened, and my jaw fell open as enormous trees parted.

Myhhena chanted, her leafy hands raised above her head again, as leaves swirled around her. Golden ribbons escaped her in droves, but this time, they slammed into a shimmering wall before disappearing into thin air.

A loud *crack* filled my ears, and the earth rumbled beneath my feet. My eyes widened as four enormous white marble pillars rose out of the ground like flowers in the springtime. They burst through the dirt, reaching high into the heavens. Long vines of ivy crawled up the pillars and beyond them...

"It's a city," I murmured, tightening my grip on Xander's hand.

Dozens of ancient stone buildings covered in dark green crawling vines sat on the edge of cobblestone streets shrouded in moss. Birds flitted through the canopy of trees, deer ran through the streets, and chipmunks balanced on the vines stretching between buildings.

Myhhena took a rustling step forward, and I pulled my eyes back to her.

"Welcome to the Sanctuary," the Spirit of the Woods said. She conjured a cloak out of thin air, handing it to me. I laid it over Xander's chest, and Myhhena continued. "You have reached the home of my people. Under the laws that govern this continent, I can provide you with care."

"And Xander?" I asked, squeezing his hand. "Can you help him?"

Myhhena smiled. "I sense that he has already started to heal, but I can finish that for you, Protectress."

The Spirit of the Woods bent, placing her hands on Xander's chest before speaking in the same lilting tongue. Golden ribbons of magic flowed from her fingertips, sinking into his skin.

Xander moaned, twitching as the magic entered him.

My grip tightened on his fingers.

Please work, I begged silently. *This has to work.*

The Spirit of the Woods continued chanting. Her voice boomed.

I pressed our joined hands against my forehead. "If you wake up, Xander, I promise I'll never call you bossy again."

Nothing.

"I mean it," I murmured. "I won't even try to stab you anymore."

His eyes didn't open, but this time, a groan rumbled through him. Moments later, a thick, black substance oozed from multiple cuts on Xander's skin.

I must have made a sound because Myhhena looked up. Switching back into the Common Tongue, she said, "Do not fear, Protectress. This is simply the poison leaving his body."

That was easy for Myhhena to say. Her bonded mate wasn't the one with poison running through his veins, lying on the ground, completely immobile. She wasn't the one High King Edgar had tried to kill.

But the Spirit of the Woods was trying to help us.

I had to keep that in mind.

Forcing myself to ignore the black seeping out of Xander's body, I ran my thumb over the back of his hand as Myhhena worked. The sun dipped even further, and a cool breeze blew by as the Spirit's words lilted over us.

Time passed in agonizing slowness as the black substance left his body until, finally, Xander's face contorted. He winced, his fingers squeezing mine. I gasped, clutching his hand in return.

Myhhena stopped talking, taking a step back. Her leaves rustled as she waved her hand, and the golden cords binding Xander to the sled disintegrated into thin air.

"Elyxander?" I whispered, raising a hand and cupping his cheek. A pleasant warmth met my hand, and I nearly wept. I had never been so excited to feel the heat that burned through my bonded mate than I was at that moment. "Can you hear me?"

Xander's golden eyes blinked open, and a breath whooshed out of me. "Yes, Sunshine." He chuckled, his lips tilting up as his gaze swept over me. "I can hear you just fine."

"I'm glad," I replied softly. I bent, brushing my lips over his. "You really scared me, Xander. For a second, I thought... I thought you were gone."

A long moment passed, and the air thickened between us.

Xander pushed himself onto his elbows, and the cloak covering him slid to his hips. "Don't you know already, Aileana?" He reached out, running his hand over my mating mark. "I will never leave you."

His words echoed all around us, striking a chord deep within me.

"I am yours," I murmured. "And you are mine."

The claiming words were a reminder of the promises we had made.

Xander raised his hand and threaded it through my hair, pulling me closer. My breath hitched as we hovered above each other, sharing the same air.

His voice was husky, and his eyes darkened as they swept over me. "Always. No matter what. I will always be yours. I will always be here for you."

Then, there were no more words as he closed the distance between us.

Our lips met in a kiss that was not gentle. It was not kind. Nor was it soft. Our lips crashed together like waves against rocks, and our hands grasped at each other like we were the only thing stopping the other from drowning in a storm of want.

This kiss was a testament to our survival. Despite the odds, we survived the king's wrath. We were alive. And we were together.

Our kiss was powerful. It was a claiming and a declaration of things to come. We were nothing but lips, tongues, and teeth for an untold amount of time until a throat cleared behind us.

"Excuse me, Protectress?" Myhhena asked.

The moment she spoke, blood rushed to my cheeks. I forgot the leafy spirit was even there. Breaking the kiss, I rested my forehead against Xander's, both of us breathing in deeply.

Amusement tinged the Spirit's words as she said, "If you'll both come with me, I'll escort you to your residence."

"Thank you, Myhhena." Pushing myself to my feet, I held out a hand to Xander.

He glanced at it, chuckling to himself as he grabbed the cloak. Xander stood, wrapping the cloak around his middle and tied it in a knot.

"Showoff," I muttered.

"It's the magic." Xander drew me towards him, pressing a kiss against my head before dipping his head toward the Spirit of the Woods. "You have my gratitude, Myhhena. I've never felt better."

"The honor was mine, dragon." The Spirit of the Woods smiled. "We have been waiting for the Protectress for many years."

Stepping forward, I clasped the Spirit's leafy hand in mine. The veins of each leaf and twig rubbed against my skin as I vigorously shook her hand. "Thank you for saving Xander."

Myhhena's lips tilted into a small smile. "He is yours, Protectress. You carry his mark on you, and he yours. We will watch over him as best we can."

We?

I automatically looked around but didn't see anyone else in this strange city. Even the elks had disappeared back into the forest. A pang of disappointment went through me—I wanted to thank them for their aid.

Before I could ask what she meant by "we," Myhhena started down the mossy cobblestone streets. The wind blew past, rustling her leaves as she walked towards the large stone buildings. The empty city stretched as far as my eyes could see, disappearing into the thick forest.

A beat passed before a familiar, warm hand pressed against mine. "Shall we, Sunshine?"

I smiled at my bonded mate. Was it only a day ago we were preparing to enter the Crimson King's castle?

So much had changed, and yet, we were both still here.

Alive.

"We shall."

A Bundle of Leaves and Twigs

AILEANA

With every step, we went deeper into the place called the Sanctuary. Stone structures of varying sizes lined the streets of the abandoned city. Some were short, no taller than a story, but others rose high above our heads, tickling the leafy canopy. The setting sun cast deep shadows over the city, and night insects woke.

Despite having napped in the dragon's talons, tiredness was pulling at me. My eyes were heavy, and my feet dragged as we followed Myhhena through the city. Although my body was exhausted, my mind was whirling.

Were we still in Ithenmyr? I thought so. The earth still hummed beneath my feet, and its call was as strong as ever. This hidden place was beautiful. The Sanctuary might once have been a thriving metropolis the size of Vlarone, but now, the forest had reclaimed it.

Somehow, the presence of the buildings wasn't odd or out of place. If anything, the flora looked like it should have always been a part of the city. As though the buildings were constructed to honor the ethereal, otherworldly beauty of the forest.

Beside me, Xander was quiet. His hand gripped mine, his scent of smoke and ash and pine a comfort as we walked across the cobblestone paths. Myhhena led us in silence, and our footsteps were the only unnatural noise in this place of respite.

By the time the first stars appeared in the evening sky, we were deep in what must have once been a residential part of the city. Stone structures covered in greenery, some short and others three stories high, towered above us. Trees replaced roofs, vines crawled out of windows, and strands of dark green ivy covered every inch of the gray stones.

Laying near the entrance of one such home was a tiny wooden toy. I bent, picking it up and rolling it over in my hands.

It was a carved dragon.

A warmth filled me, and I gripped the carving in my hand. A child must have played with it in years past. How long ago had they lived? A century? Two? More?

The grooves in the toy spoke of many hours of play. Of a childhood well lived.

Of peace.

We kept walking, turning left and then right before Myhenna finally halted in front of a stone building. A large garden flourished out front, setting it apart from the other empty buildings.

The Spirit of the Woods turned, her leaves shaking as she bowed. "This building is for you, Protectress."

I nodded, leaning against Xander. My limbs felt heavy, and my head spun. Exhaustion pulled at me as I yawned, covering my mouth with my hand. "Thank you."

Xander cleared his throat, wrapping his arm around my waist. "Do you have a way to contact others in this place?"

Myhhena raised a leafy brow. "You're referring to the witch, correct?"

"Yes. We need them to know we're safe, thanks to their intervention. If it wasn't for them, we would be dead right now."

I had suspected Nonna's magic had saved us, but this served as confirmation.

"Consider it done." Myhhena smiled, bowing at the waist once more. The moonlight shone on her leaves, and her green eyes glowed in the dark. "I will leave right away and deliver the message myself. There is running water in the building. Please, make yourselves at home. When I return, I will have one of my sisters attend to you."

Myhhena's words echoed through me. *Home.*

At that moment, I wasn't sure what I was more excited about. The chance to clean up sounded terrific, but falling into bed was also highly appealing.

Perhaps there would be time for both.

Myhhena disappeared in a brisk wind, leaving Xander and me alone in this strange city of stone and ivy. I let out a shaky breath, sagging against him. His arms wrapped around me, and he pressed me to his bare chest. Despite his lack of clothing, he was warm, and my eyes slipped shut as a sigh escaped me.

"We're alive," I whispered against his chest.

No matter how often I said the words, they still didn't feel real.

"We made it." His lips brushed my forehead. "Try not to get yourself killed for the next few days, Sunshine. I could use a break from having my heart ripped out of my chest."

A morose chuckle escaped me, and I pulled back just a touch, punching Xander in the arm. "*You* could use a break? I thought you were going to die at the hands of the king tonight."

"Maybe we can both agree to put a pause on risking our lives for a few moments," he said, stifling a yawn.

"On that, we are in agreement." I peered at Xander, frowning as I took in the bags under his eyes and the lines bracketing his mouth. "For now, why don't we explore our new home? If we're lucky, perhaps there will even be a bed."

"That might be the best idea you've had yet."

Suspecting Xander was far more tired than he was letting on, I opened the door and pulled him inside. "Welcome home."

Moonlight shone through a large window, casting a soft light on the small kitchen area, complete with a wooden table, two small chairs, and a red rug. A few pictures hung on the walls, and to my right was a fireplace waiting to be lit.

A small spiral staircase stood across from the entrance, leading to what I presumed was the bedroom upstairs. At the base of the stairs, the bathroom door was ajar.

I had never seen such an inviting sight in all my life.

The building was quaint and quiet. Somehow, it already felt like home.

I let go of Xander's hand and ran my fingers over the kitchen table. It was worn beneath my touch, filled with grooves that spoke of previous users.

I loved that.

Someone else had lived here before. This table was proof of that. They were gone, but parts of them lived on.

When I was gone, what would I leave behind?

Xander's hand landed on my arm, and I jumped, lost in thought.

"Come on, Sunshine," he murmured. "Let's get cleaned up and go to bed."

Taking my elbow gently, Xander led me into the bathing room. It was dark, with barely enough light to see.

"I'll wait right outside," he murmured.

The door shut behind him, and I pulled off my ruined clothes. Taking care of my personal needs, I washed my hands before exploring the bathing room. A strange wooden contraption was in the corner, and I furrowed my brows. I had never seen something like this. A spout came from the ceiling, and when I pulled on a nearby lever, water gushed out of it.

I squealed as water poured onto me. A fist pounded on the door.

"Aileana?" The knob rattled. "What's wrong?"

Rolling my eyes, I left the spout running.

I saved Xander, and he was still being overprotective. Normally, I would argue with him about this, but I supposed since we nearly died earlier, I would forgive him.

Just this once.

Pulling open the door, I raised a brow. "Nothing's wrong."

Xander gripped the doorframe. His eyes were wide, and his nostrils flared as he searched the bathing room. Fear pulsed through the bond, and my frustration melted away. He was really worried about me.

"I'm sorry. I didn't mean to worry you. I just... I've never seen something like this." I gestured to the running water behind me.

His gaze softened, his shoulders relaxing.

"I see." Xander's eyes roamed over my bare skin, reminding me I hadn't covered up before opening the door. His voice lowered, and a gleam entered his eyes. "Well, it wouldn't do for my bonded mate to take her first shower alone, would it?"

"Do you mean..." My voice trailed off, but I gestured to the cloak covering his middle as blood rushed to my cheeks. "It's not that I don't enjoy it, because I do, but it's been a long day, and there was the poison, and—"

Xander stepped forward, placing his finger on my lips. "Not tonight, Aileana." He shook his head, letting the cloak fall to the ground and exposing his naked body to me. I couldn't help the downward trajectory of my gaze.

I was still a female, after all, even if I was exhausted.

He chuckled, noticing where my eyes went. "As much as I love your train of thought, this isn't the time. We'll just wash and go to bed. I promise."

The shower was tight with both of us in the wooden enclosure, but I didn't care. The water falling from the ceiling felt amazing. Someone had left a bar of sweet-smelling soap on a ledge, and we took turns lathering each other. It was intimate and quiet, which was exactly what I needed after this never-ending day.

We washed and dried off, wrapping the towels around ourselves before, *finally*, it was time to sleep. I was so tired I could barely lift one foot in front of the other to climb to the second story.

When we reached the top of the stairs, I stopped. This bedroom was a study in green, and it looked like it was made for me. An enormous forest-green comforter was on top of the massive bed, half a dozen large pillows of various shades of green rested against a carved wooden headboard, and a long green couch rested against one wall. Against another was a massive wardrobe, and three windows lined the largest wall. Their shutters were wide open, letting in the soft moonlight.

A folded white slip was sitting on top of a small table at the top of the stairs. I let my towel fall to the floor and pulled the slip over my head. It fit me perfectly, falling to my knees and hugging my skin comfortably.

Walking over to the bed, Xander pulled down the edge of the comforter before slipping a knife under his pillow.

"Where did you get that?" I asked. I hadn't even seen him pick it up.

He raised a brow. "Downstairs. Did you think I would let us go to sleep defenseless? This place might seem safe, but I don't trust anything or anyone right now."

I didn't blame him at all.

That I wasn't even alert enough to consider arming myself was all I needed to know about my current mental state. Slipping beneath the covers, I snuggled into the warm bed.

"Thank you for looking after me," I whispered.

The mattress dipped, and Xander pulled me against his chest. I sighed, pressing myself against him.

"I will always look after you," he whispered. Running his hand over my thigh, Xander kissed my head. "Sleep, Aileana. When we wake, we will talk about everything that happened."

"EXCUSE ME?" a high-pitched voice whispered in my ear. "Protectress of the Woods?"

I hummed, batting away the voice that dared intrude upon my pleasant dreams of warm caves and days spent alone with my dragon shifter. "Go away."

"Can you hear me?" The voice seemed closer now, and something tickled my ear. "You've been asleep for eight days. Our magic has kept you alive, but the Eldest says it's time to wake. You need food and water, or you will begin to Fade."

Eight days?

Startled, I pulled my eyes open. Curtains covered the windows, but thin strips of light made it through cracks at the bottom, illuminating the space.

I blinked. Maybe this was still a dream.

A fuzzy green shape stood in front of me. Rubbing my eyes, I blinked again. The shape became less fuzzy and more... leaf-like. And twiggy.

A short, tiny being made entirely of twigs and leaves was staring at me with large brown eyes.

"Well, this is strange," I muttered. "Am I still sleeping?" Flopping back down, I pressed my head into the pillow. "It's rude to wake people who are having nice dreams, you know."

"Protectress of the Woods? Miss?" Something hard prodded my hand where it hung off the mattress, and I snatched my limb away.

I was *definitely* not dreaming.

Mumbling into the pillow, I asked, "Are you going to leave?"

"I cannot leave you," the tiny being said resolutely. "I am under strict orders to remain here."

Behind me, Xander snored loudly. I wished I was still sleeping. How was it fair that I was awake, and he continued to slumber?

The male's ability to sleep through practically anything irritated me to no end.

"Is it even morning?" I asked, my head still tucked into the pillow.

"The sun just rose, Protectress!" the bundle of leaves said exuberantly.

I groaned, raising my head and glaring at the intruder. No one should be awake before the sun was fully in the sky. "Who *are* you?"

The leafy bundle giggled. Now that I was more awake, I could see that the tip of the strange creature's head came up to the top of the mattress. "I am called Tiaesti, Protectress."

"Tee-stay?" I tried the name on my sleepy tongue. The syllables were strange, more drawn out than I was used to.

Tiaesti shook her head, giggling again. "Tie-ay-stee."

"Tiaesti." I tried again, raising a brow. "Is that right?"

"Yes!" The leaf-child clapped, her leaves rustling as she laughed. This time, it was too loud.

With a roar, Xander leaped out of bed. He was stark naked as he yanked the knife out from beneath his pillow.

When his gaze landed on Tiaesti, he groaned. "Ashes and smoke." Running his hand through his sleep-mussed hair, Xander waved the blade toward the tiny creature. "What is *that*?"

The leafy child shrieked, darting around the bed to poke Xander in the leg.

He swatted her away even as she screeched, "How dare you? I am not a 'what'."

"*Who* are you, then?" Xander snarled.

"Obviously,"—Tiaesti drew out the word as though it were a sentence—"I am a Spirit."

"A Spirit," he said flatly.

"Yes." Tiaesti pointed a twiggy hand across the mattress in Xander's direction, clenching her jaw. "If you didn't belong to the Protectress of the Woods, you wouldn't be here right now. The gates of the Sanctuary don't just open for anyone, you know."

"Are you threatening me?" Xander growled, raising himself to his full height even as he grabbed a pillow and held it over his middle. "You're nothing but a bundle of leaves and twigs."

Tiaesti gasped, her leafy hand fluttering to her heart. "How dare you? You... you... fire-breather."

She said the last words like they were a curse, and I couldn't help but huff a laugh.

"Something funny, Sunshine?" Xander snapped, his golden eyes burning as they turned towards me. If he were in his dragon form, I was certain smoke would be coming from his maw. As it was, scales rippled over his skin.

"No," I shook my head quickly, stifling my laugh. "Nothing at all. I wouldn't want to upset you, my enormous fire-breathing dragon."

The last word came out as a chuckle that I tried and failed to tamp down. My dragon shifter snarled, and I successfully kept a straight face.

The last thing we needed was his dragon emerging in the middle of a forest. Fire and trees didn't seem like they would play well together.

A beat passed before Xander huffed, glaring at Tiaesti. "Do you think we could have some privacy?" He raised a brow, gesturing to the door. "Maybe you could leave us so we could get dressed?"

"I am here to serve the Protectress. Not you, dragon." Tiaesti smirked, clearly enjoying herself. She shook her head, taking on a tone I had overheard teenage females using in the markets when they spoke to others. "*You* can't tell me what to do."

Xander scoffed. "Well, that's rude."

"Rude or not, it's the truth." Tiaesti walked over to me and took my hand in hers. The gesture was so childlike that part of me melted. "Whatever the Protectress of the Woods needs, I will do."

I opened my eyes wide, making a face at Xander. *Isn't she cute?* I mouthed.

He growled, speaking through clenched teeth as he waved in the small Spirit's direction. "Do *something*, Aileana."

Turning to Tiaesti, I raised a brow. "You mentioned you have orders?"

The Spirit nodded vigorously, her leaves rustling. "From the Eldest. I cannot disobey her."

"I see." Xander glowered, turning to me as he held the pillow over his middle. It didn't hide much, but the sight was rather comical. "Sunshine, perhaps you could ask your new friend to give us some privacy?"

The way he emphasized the last word made it clear it wasn't really a question. If I was being honest, I could use a few minutes to myself as well. An urgent pressure weighed down on my bladder, and I raised a hand to my hair, finding far more knots than I'd like.

Turning back to the small creature, I found her staring intently at me. "Ah, Tiaesti?"

She nodded vigorously, her brown eyes unblinking. "Yes?"

"Would you mind stepping out?"

"Stepping out?" The Spirit wrung her hands in front of her. "What does that mean?"

"Oh my gods, save me now," Xander murmured. "Not only is the Spirit annoying, but she's as dense as the wood she's made from."

I glared at him. His attitude was not helping anything. Dropping to my knees, I knelt in front of Tiaesti. "Ignore him. He's just a cranky male who hasn't eaten his breakfast. You said you're here to... serve me?"

Tiaesti nodded vigorously. "I was created to serve you, Protectress. I have been waiting for my entire existence for you to join us. Finally, you have arrived. I am here to do your bidding."

Created to serve me?

My mind whirled. It was too early in the morning to deal with things like this. I was of the opinion that nothing important should be dealt with before noon. "How long have you been waiting for me?"

Tiaesti shook her head, stepping back and clenching her twiggy hands together. "Oh, not long."

"How long is 'not long'?"

Having lived with one cantankerous century-old creature for some time, I knew some of the oldest beings in Ithenmyr considered themselves young. If not in body, then in spirit.

The leafy creature grinned, twirling on the spot. "I sprouted five hundred and thirty-six years ago. I am the first offshoot of the Twelve, and will one day serve Thelrena herself."

Xander whistled, and I choked on my breath. "You think five centuries is young?"

The Spirit giggled, nodding enthusiastically. "Yes. I am still young. The Eldest was made when the gods first created the world. In fact, did you know that the wards that hide the Sanctuary from sight were first made by—"

"Aileana," Xander coughed pointedly, interrupting the Spirit. "You need to ask her to leave before we get an entire history lesson we did not ask for."

I glared at him. "Don't tell me what to do."

Tiaesti stood to her full height, placing her hands on her hips as she raised a wooden brow. "Would you like me to take care of him for you, Protectress? I can, you know." She held out her hand, and small golden ribbons appeared in her palm. "Bonded mate or not, this male is still a you-know-what." She hissed the last word as though it were a curse.

"A dragon?" I filled in the blanks.

The child sucked in a sharp breath. "Yes. A *destroyer* of the woods."

My lips tilted up into a small smile. "Thank you for your willingness to help, Tiaesti, but it just so happens I am rather fond of this dragon." Xander snarled as I reached out and placed my hand on Tiaesti's shoulder. "I'd rather you leave him alone if it is all the same to you."

She huffed, pouting as she glared at Xander one final time. "Fine. I'll let him live. But if you change your mind, you just need to ask. I would be happy to take care of him for you."

"Um... thank you." Chuckling, I stood and stretched. "On that note, if you wouldn't mind leaving the house, my bonded mate and I need to have a little chat."

"As you wish, Protectress." The Spirit of the Woods curtsied. It was only then that I realized she was wearing a dress made entirely of bark. "I shall wait for you outside your residence."

The leaf child scurried out of the room, and moments later, the front door slammed downstairs.

Running down to the main floor, I hopped into the strange contraption Xander called a shower. My second experience was just as good as the first, minus the hulking naked male.

I'll have to remedy that.

Already, my mind was thinking about all the interesting things we could do in the shower.

But we had other problems to deal with. Drying myself off, I pulled my slip back on and walked back upstairs. Running a brush through my hair, I pulled out the knots that had formed during our eight-day sleep.

Xander was still naked, the pillow back in its place as he sat on the edge of the bed. He had opened the curtains and was running his fingers over the hilt of the knife. I couldn't help but notice how the sun shone through the open windows, illuminating his musculature. Even after sleeping for days, the male looked like a sculpted god.

My core twisted at the sight of him.

"Tiaesti is adorable, don't you think?" I said by way of greeting, waving the wooden brush in the air.

"Adorable?" Xander ran his hand through his long, silver-white hair. Of course, there wasn't a single knot anywhere to be seen. "Kydona, help me. First, we get woken up by this creature, and now you think she's adorable? The next thing I know, you will want to adopt her."

I laughed, walking over to the large mahogany wardrobe in the corner of the room. "No, I think we have enough problems without adding a five-century-year-old child to the mix, don't you?"

Xander snorted. "Aileana, we have so many problems it would take days to catalog them all."

That was true.

"Do you think..." My voice trailed off as I stared into the wardrobe, open-mouthed.

There wasn't a single dress in sight. Not one.

Whoever was responsible for outfitting the wardrobe must have known how much I hated the oppressive dresses forced upon females of Ithenmyr. Leggings and tunics of varying shades of green were stacked in neat piles, along with cloaks and clothes for warmer weather. The fabric selection was a veritable showcase of the colors of the forest, and I loved them.

Reaching inside the wardrobe, I ran my hand down a pine-green tunic. It was as soft as a cloud, and instantly, I made my choice. Pulling it off the hanger, I slid out of my slip before pulling the new tunic over my head. It fit perfectly.

The scoop-neck collar gave me lots of room to breathe while still covering my breasts, and the three-quarter sleeves put my mating mark on full display. Today, it was glowing brighter than usual. Grabbing a cloth belt from the wardrobe, I buckled it around my waist before pulling on a pair of thick, dark green, almost black leggings. They, too, fit perfectly. It was like wearing a hug.

I was never going to put on a dress again.

Behind me, Xander coughed.

"Aileana," he said roughly. "I can see... everything in those."

I glanced down, noting the way the leggings hugged the curves of my hips before tapering at my feet. Shrugging, I winked over my shoulder at him. "Then I hope you like the show."

Pushing through the garments, I found a second set of much larger clothes clearly intended for Xander. Tossing the clothes toward him, I tightly braided my now tangle-free hair against my skull as he dressed.

I was almost done with the second braid when a pair of hands landed on my hips. I stilled as Xander came up behind me.

He pressed a kiss to my forehead. "Are you ready to talk about what happened in the tower?"

A shudder ran through me. "Do we have to?"

I never wanted to talk about it again. The Queen's Tower was horrible. I said as much to Xander, and he shook his head.

"You were incredibly courageous in the tower, Aileana. Most people would run in fear when faced with the demon of their past, but you met that bastard head-on." He pressed a kiss to my forehead. "You were amazing."

My eyes watered as I took in a shuddering breath.

"I didn't feel brave," I whispered. Bravery was so far from the word I would have used to describe how I felt; it wasn't even funny. "I was weak. I gave everything I had, and it wasn't enough. Edgar defeated me. If I hadn't fallen from the window, you'd be dead, and I would be in a hole somewhere, mourning you for the rest of my life."

"Aileana," Xander breathed.

My hands trembled at my sides. "I didn't... I should have done more." I shuddered, recalling the way Xander had thrashed beneath the iron net. "You were suffering, and I couldn't stop it."

Xander shook his head, pulling me tightly against his chest. His warmth seeped into me, and I sagged against him. He ran his hand up and down my back, and for a long moment, we remained like that.

"I couldn't save you," I whispered. "I wanted to, but I couldn't."

If Xander had died, nothing else would have mattered. When I gave myself to him, and we solidified our bond, we pulled down all the barriers around our hearts.

"We survived," he said gruffly. "That is the most important part."

A hoarse laugh escaped me, and I shook my head. "For once, I'd like to do more than survive. I'd love to thrive. To live without fearing what will happen to us next."

Xander pressed me tightly against him. "I promise you, Aileana. One day, we will live without fear of anything."

I sucked in a breath, shutting my eyes as I leaned against him. "Don't do that."

"Do what?"

"Don't promise things you can't," I whispered. "Please."

My heart was already so fragile. Surviving was exhausting. Ever since escaping my tower, it felt like we were running from one thing to the next. Peace was nowhere to be found.

"Aileana." Xander drew out my name, pressing quick, butterfly-light kisses to my face. "Look at me. What happened in the tower is over. The High King burned. I watched him fall. If he somehow survived that, I'll kill the bastard myself."

If anyone could survive a fall like that, it was the king. He was like a cockroach, always coming back to haunt us.

We stood together for a long time. My mind refused to stop, constantly whirling as it went over the events that led us to this place.

Would the Sanctuary really be a safe place for us?

Pulling my head from Xander's chest, I looked up. "Did you hear what Tiaesti said?"

"The child made of leaves?"

I raised a brow. "Do you know another being with a name like hers?"

"Yes, Sunshine, I heard her. She called me a fire-breather before making it clear she was here to serve you and only you." He sighed.

"Honestly, what do these Spirits have against me? First Myhhena and now this child."

I chuckled. Xander got along well with nearly everyone, so the fact that the Spirits of the Woods seemed to hate him amused me greatly.

"I meant the part where Tiaesti said we'd been sleeping for eight days. I know it's not exactly unexpected, considering the events that led up to our arrival."

In the past, when I used large amounts of magic, I fell into an exhausted state for days, but it had never happened for this long, though.

Xander raised a hand, cupping my cheek as his eyes searched mine. "How do you feel?"

Furrowing my brows, I peered within myself and searched for the place where my magic resided within me. Vibrant green ribbons were everywhere, waiting eagerly to be used as the familiar presence of power thrummed through my veins. "I feel fine."

"Good." The corner of Xander's mouth twitched upwards as he reached out, clasping my hand in his. He led me towards the bed, pushing me down gently until the two of us were sitting side-by-side on the large mattress.

Holding my hand up to the light, Xander traced the new markings covering my skin from my fingertips to where my wrist met my arm. "Then maybe this is the right time to tell me what happened when I was unconscious."

"Oh," I whispered. "That."

I held my other hand up, staring at the glimmering green marks. Beneath my watchful gaze, they seemed to swirl beneath my skin, pulsing in time with the thrum of the magic in my veins.

"Yes, *oh*." Xander raised a white brow. "What happened? Where did they come from?"

Sucking my bottom lip through my teeth, I let out a long breath. "When you... when the poison pulled you under... I connected with the earth."

Xander rubbed his thumb over my new markings as I told him everything that had happened, from connecting to the earth to the elks who had brought us here.

"I'm fairly certain I went through the first stage of Maturation," I concluded.

For a long moment, Xander didn't say anything. Those golden eyes searched mine, and a knot twisted in my stomach. Then his lips broke into a wide grin, and a deep, masculine laugh filled the air. Joy tasting like a bright summer's day came through the bond, and I couldn't help but laugh alongside Xander.

Picking me up around my waist, he stood, twirling me around the room. My legs flung out behind me as he spun us in a circle. Our mirth filled the early morning air as green ribbons slipped from my hands. They crawled over the walls, and my magic pulsed in my veins.

One moment, the ribbons were shimmering threads of magic, and the next, *life* exploded in our room. Thick green vines covered in yellow and purple flowers filled the room, hiding the stone walls from sight.

"You're Maturing." Xander laughed, hoisting me up around his waist. My legs hooked around his middle, and he grinned, pressing a searing kiss to my lips. Our mouths moved in tandem, promising everything we couldn't say.

He was mine, and I was his.

"This is amazing news, Aileana," Xander said against my lips. "And it deserves celebration."

I hummed. Slipping my hands beneath his tunic, I traced the lines of his chest. "What did you have in mind?"

No sooner had the question left my lips than Xander's tongue swept into my mouth, tasting every part of me. I moaned, my core twisting as he continued to run his hands over me. He placed me on the edge of the bed, his mouth dipping lower and lower until he was kneeling in front of me.

My clothes soon ended up on the floor, but I found I did not care.

Xander was exactly what I needed. I was broken and remade beneath my mate's skilled touch.

He showed me *exactly* how pleased he was by this new development.

I Hated Them All

RYLLAE

I hated three things in life: my father, the gods, and my mother.

The reasons I hated my father were pretty obvious. I could trace all the bad things in my life back to him. It was his fault that I had spent the past two and a half centuries living in a dungeon. It was his fault I'd worn prohiberis for all that time. And it was his fault that even though those damned manacles were off my wrists, I still didn't have my magic.

I hated the gods because they hadn't made me a male. If I'd been born with what my father considered the "right parts," my life might have gone in a very different direction. I would have been the prince he always wanted.

I would have been the perfect Death Elf heir.

But for some unknown reason, the gods cursed me to live in this female body. It was their fault my father hated me. Their fault I could never live up to his expectations. The gods abandoned me the moment I left my mother's womb. If they cared about me at all, they would have saved me from Nightstone Prison. They wouldn't have left me to rot.

But they did not care about me.

No one cared about me.

I stopped praying to the gods long ago.

They weren't the only ones who had abandoned me. I hated my mother for the way she left me alone. She died on the day I was born, leaving me to face this cursed world on my own. They say she Faded so fast that no one knew what was happening. One moment, she was holding me to her breast, and the next, her body disintegrated in a flurry of red magic.

My nursemaid Cristin had told me that when my father heard the news, red lightning bolts shot from his hands for an entire day. She said when Mother was alive, Father was different. Kind.

She never described him as loving. I didn't think Father knew how to love. But she said my father cared about my mother in a way he never cared about anyone else.

All that changed the moment Mother Faded. From that day forward, it was as though my father's soul had been ripped from his body.

He never let me forget I was the reason Mother wasn't with us. Even when he told me I would be queen—an outright lie since he tossed me in the prison the day I Matured—Father made sure I knew that even as a babe, I had been a murderess.

As if I could ever forget.

The day my mother died, she condemned me to a life without parental love.

I hated them all.

That hatred fueled me. It burned within me, giving me the strength to survive the nightmare that was my life. For decades, my hatred kept me alive through the worst my father's Winged Soldiers had to offer.

My hatred fueled my survival in prison, and now, it gave me a reason to live.

Once I figured out why my magic wasn't returning to me, I would kill my father and take my rightful place as Ithenmyr's queen. It was my birthright, and I would no longer be denied it.

Until then, I was stuck in this tiny little cottage in the woods.

Right now, I was the only one awake. Four days had passed since the dragon shifter and his mate left. The elf who had been stabbed was still healing, and the others were drained from sending their magic into the world to help the dragon and his mate. They'd been sleeping on and off since the night of the Midnight Ball.

Pouring myself a cup of tea, the warming liquid seeped into my still-frail hands. The sleeves of my dress were long, but I caught a glimpse of the red tattoos that covered most of my body.

One good thing about being out of prison was that my flesh was filling out. My curves were returning to me, and my blond hair was regaining some of its previous shine.

Even though my body was returning to the way it was before my father threw me away like a piece of discarded trash, it would never erase the marks Nightstone Prison left on my soul.

A shudder ran through me as unwanted memories flashed before my eyes.

There were far too many ways to inflict pain upon someone without breaking their skin. I knew them all. The Winged Soldiers had used me as their plaything for so long that I lost sight of who I was.

Too often, I found myself seeking a retreat from the loudness that was my mind.

This cottage wasn't it. It was far too quiet, and though the females here were kind, they didn't understand what I had gone through.

The loudness of my mind juxtaposed with the quiet cottage left me feeling strange. I couldn't sleep. I could barely sit still. After spending centuries surrounded by never-ending sounds of pain and agony, the cottage was far too tranquil.

The last thing I needed was to feel any stranger. Already, I was walking a fine line between sanity and madness. My mental state could be described as fragile, at best.

Every so often, I could feel myself slipping into the insanity that I had avoided for so many years.

How horribly ironic would it be if I fell into the madness now that I was free?

During those early years in Nightstone Prison, when I thought that perhaps Father might change his mind and free me, I hid the most intrinsic parts of myself deep in the recesses of my mind.

When I realized I was never being freed, I tucked those memories away in a box within my soul. Locking them up for safekeeping, I never gave them away.

Not for lack of trying. My father and, eventually, my brother, Remington, had delighted in torturing me. They tried to break me. To ruin me. They took my freedom and magic, but I never gave them my memories.

The problem was that in burying my memories, I shoved a large part of myself to the side. In order to survive the nightmare that was my life in prison, I became a shell.

It turned out that after two and a half centuries in a hellhole, even shells could break.

Now, I was desperately trying to pull my memories back out of that box and become a whole person once more. No matter how much I pulled, they didn't want to come. There was a hole inside of me, but I didn't know how to mend it.

Maybe it could never be fixed. Perhaps I was doomed to live my entire life as this shell, teetering between sanity and madness.

I was so lost in my thoughts that I forgot about the cup of tea I was holding. The porcelain became so hot it was like touching a piece of burning coal. Cursing, I adjusted my grip on the cup. Bringing it to my nose, I inhaled sharply.

The scent of strong herbs reached me, and almost instantly, I felt more relaxed.

Tea helped. It was one of the only things that helped. This was my second cup of the day. The hot liquid reminded me of simpler times before I understood the depth of my father's hatred. Sharing tea with my nursemaid was one of the only highlights of my childhood.

Sipping the herbal liquid, I padded out into the living room. A crackling fire blazed in the fireplace, casting flickering flames on the mural of the dragon above the mantle.

I rested against the settee, trying not to touch anything.

Being here was strange. I didn't belong in this place. It was too nice. Too small.

I couldn't stay here but didn't know where else to go. My next steps were fuzzy. Home was a foreign concept. I was no longer my father's daughter—I renounced him the moment he threw me in Nightstone Prison.

Could I even still call myself a Death Elf if I never regained my magic?

Sipping the last dregs of my tea, I placed my empty mug on the side table and stretched out my hands. Resting them palm up on my knees, I reached within myself and sought out the pool of magic within me.

Pulling on the red ribbons used to be as easy as breathing. At one point in my life, the dark pool within me brimmed with potential.

Once, I was known as the Bringer of Death.

Now, I couldn't even produce a single red ribbon. A thick, black cloud of smoke hung like a shroud over the place where my magic should have been.

Before, I'd been so powerful that I could destroy an entire army with a single flick of my wrist.

Now, my veins were quiet.

Perhaps even my magic did not want to be near me. Maybe that was the problem. I was too broken for it.

Frustration bubbled up within me, and I groaned. Picking up the empty teacup, I ran my finger over the ridges of the flowers painted on the porcelain, trying to empty my mind.

What is wrong with me?

A dark memory remained hidden in my mind, deep enough that I couldn't see it, but I knew it was there. If I pushed hard enough, trying to pull it out of the box within me, faint traces of the memory flashed before my eyes.

My lungs tightened as though the darkness was trying to choke the very life out of me. Pain ran through me like scorching flames, licking at my skin. A cloaked figure stood before me, their face hidden in the shadows. Laughter, a cruel and mocking sound, slammed into me with the force of a gale wind.

I tried to move. To run. To escape. But I couldn't do anything.

I was all alone, unable to escape my father's cruelty.

That memory...

My father had cursed me before throwing me into prison. It was the only explanation that made sense. The curse must still have been on me, waiting to be broken.

But how did one break a curse they didn't create?

Dropping my head into my hands, I groaned.

Maybe I was wrong. Maybe the memory wasn't real. But it felt real... or at least, I thought it did.

I couldn't trust my own thoughts. Not anymore.

I couldn't trust myself.

A rustling came from behind me, and I stiffened. My grip tightened around the mug, and I turned. The injured Fortune Elf shuffled toward me. My father's Winged Soldiers had stabbed her before they attempted to kill her and her wife.

The two elves had escaped and barely made it here before the witch —the one the others called Nonna—healed Maiela. The injured elf and I hadn't spoken much.

I liked that.

"Maiela."

She sat on the settee across from me, pulling a black blanket with frayed edges over her lap. Maiela's face was pale, and dark shadows hung beneath her eyes. "Princess."

A few minutes passed in silence.

I refilled my teacup, letting the warmth seep through my hands again before I met Maiela's gaze. "What are you doing awake?"

She raised a brow. "I Saw you."

"Oh?"

This wasn't the first time I'd been around Fortune Elves. I knew how to talk to them. Or rather, how not to talk to them. Fortune Elves —the entire group of them—seemed to enjoy making their messages as cryptic as possible. The key was to ask a few questions and allow them to get their entire story out without too many interruptions.

Maiela nodded. Her eyes took on that silver gleam of her kind, and for a long moment, she didn't speak.

After her eyes cleared, she said, "My brother will take you where you need to go."

I blinked. "Daegal?"

"Yes. But beware, Princess of Ithenmyr. The path you will take is one of fate."

"What are you saying?" I tightened my grip around my mug as the Fortune Elf pinned me with a blue glare.

Maiela's voice dropped, and suddenly, it was as though a dozen voices spoke at once. "Ryllae of the House of Irriel, you will find what you seek at the end of this road. But be forewarned. The journey you will embark on is neither kind nor gentle. There will be trials, but they are necessary to achieve balance."

I sucked in a breath.

Balance.

The word echoed inside me, and something deep within me twinged. It was important. I could feel it in the depths of my soul.

"Where do we have to go?" I asked when it was clear Maiela was done.

She drew in a breath, her eyes turning silver once more. I waited, counting my heartbeats until the blue in her eyes was back.

"You must find the bearer of the Coral Scepter. She will know how to undo what was done to you." The Fortune Elf raised a shoulder, her voice sounding normal once more. "That's all I know."

"The Coral Scepter..."

A memory flashed through my mind, and my voice trailed off. At least, I thought it was a memory. Maybe it was a dream. Or perhaps it was just a vivid thought pulled from the recesses of my broken mind.

It was hard to tell what was real these days.

Blue and green waters stretched as far as I could see. Beings with long, dark tails covered in shimmering scales swam in the cove. There had to be at least a hundred of them, and their brightly colored heads bobbed as they observed us. Their golden tridents reflected the sunlight, only adding to their otherworldly beauty.

My father stood next to me. I wasn't sure how old I was. Five? Ten? I came up to his waist, no higher. The bottom of my crimson dress was sodden. I'd begged to wear trousers and boots like him, but he refused.

I swirled small red ribbons between my fingers, watching them dance in the air. No one else came close, and I heard them murmuring about me.

"She's strange..."

"... My wife says she never speaks to anyone."

"Can you blame her?"

"... all alone."

I tuned them out.

People were always talking about me.

Most of the merfolk stayed in the deep water, but one of them swam toward us. His skin was as dark as the night, and he held a coral scepter. A coral crown rested upon white hair that was so long it swirled in the water around him. The male's eyes were bright and shrewd as he looked over us.

"I told you before, this meeting is pointless." The mermale's loud, regal voice rang out over the water. He spoke in the Common Tongue without a trace of an accent, and even at my age, I recognized the authority with which he spoke. "My people will not bow to you."

Beside me, my father stiffened. Red magic shot out of his palms, swirling at the water's edge.

I straightened my back, steeling myself against what I knew would come next.

Blood. Tears. Death.

No one ever went against my father and survived.

Except for this time, death never came. The ribbons didn't make it to the mermale.

The dark-skinned mer laughed. "That magic won't work here."

A brilliant pink light shot out of his scepter, obliterating my father's ribbons as they danced above the shore.

I gasped, and my father swore. Behind us, elves murmured their shock. The two kings faced off.

I thought Father was the strongest male alive, but no matter how many red ribbons slipped from his palms, the mer king destroyed them.

The sun rose and fell as we remained in a strange standoff with the people of the sea. When the moon rose, my clothes were drenched from the ocean spray. The merfolk never came any closer, and my father could not bend them to his will.

A cool, salty breeze blew around us as dark clouds filled the skies.

"Father?" I asked, tugging on his sleeve. "What are you going to do?"

He ground his teeth, seething. "I will make these ungrateful talking fish rue the day they ever laughed at your father. No one makes a fool of Edgar of the House of Irriel."

My chest puffed up. My father would take care of these people who dared defy him.

He was going to take care of us all. He was the strongest Death Elf in Ithenmyr, and no one stood against him.

And one day, when he Faded, I would be queen.

Deep shame knotted in my stomach at the memory. How could I have felt anything close to pride? My father was a tyrant, trying to push himself on the merfolk.

I saw his true colors the day I Matured. He slapped those manacles on me and threw me into the deepest, darkest dungeon he could find.

A shudder ran through me at the thought.

"Ryllae?" A hand landed on my shoulder, and I jolted out of the dark swirl of my mind.

"Don't!" I screamed, dropping my teacup on the floor.

Maiela lifted her hand, darting away from me. The sound of shattering porcelain was the backdrop to the thundering of my heart. My stomach twisted, and I pulled my legs against my chest, shutting my eyes.

I gasped, "Don't touch me."

Memories flashed before my eyes. Darkness. Pain. Hands skittering over my skin. My clothes being removed. Being touched against my will.

I shook, darkness edging on my vision.

"I'm sorry, Ryllae," Maiela murmured. She was close. Far too close.

My entire body trembled as I danced right on the edge of sanity. I squeezed my eyes shut, shaking my head. "Please, don't touch me."

"All right," she whispered. "I'm sorry."

Fabric rustled, and the sound of footsteps reached my ears.

My heart thundered in my ear, and my lungs grew impossibly tight, but I forced myself to draw in a shuddering breath. Then another. A third.

I forced myself to keep breathing as I shoved those horrible, violent memories deep into the recesses of my mind.

The fire crackled, and I inched away from the madness threatening to swallow me whole.

Eventually, my lungs loosened, and my heart rate slowed. I pulled my head out of my hands, and a shuffling sound came from nearby.

Only then did I open my eyes.

Daegal crouched before me, his hands resting mere inches from mine. His brows were furrowed, and his mouth was pinched in a straight line as his blue, concern-filled eyes watched me as if I were an animal about to bolt.

Too bad his concern wouldn't fix me. I wasn't sure anything could fix me.

I was far too broken to be fixed.

Maybe they should have just left me to rot in prison.

Daegal ran a hand through his short, curly hair, his dark skin catching the light of the rising sun through the window. "Ryllae... I... Maiela didn't mean to upset you."

I sucked in a deep breath. "I... I know she didn't."

She didn't know what happened to me. Why I couldn't be touched. No one knew.

That part of me was buried in a box along with my memories.

Daegal watched my every movement. Sympathy radiated from him, and for a long moment, neither of us spoke.

He cleared his throat. "Are you... what do you need from me, Ryllae?"

The Fortune Elf was one of the nicest males I'd ever met. Not that the bar was especially high, but still. There was a kindness about Daegal that I had never known before. When I was around him, I felt... safe.

No one made me feel safe these days.

Daegal was built like a warrior, and from the tales he told, I knew he fought like one, too, but he wasn't gruff with me. He was gentle, his actions were thoughtful, and he always spoke to me in a quiet voice.

He was kind.

"I don't need anything," I whispered. Forcing myself to unfurl from the ball I'd placed myself in, my feet landed on the floor again. I gripped the fabric of my dress, twisting it tightly. "I'll be... it's okay."

Daegal shook his head. "It really isn't okay, Ryllae." He paused. "Do you want to talk about it?"

"No," I replied vehemently. That was the last thing I wanted to do.

"Ryllae..."

I shook my head. Talking would mean giving voice to the things that were done to me against my will. And I wasn't sure I was ready for that. If I would ever be ready for that.

"Daegal, I don't... I just..." Reaching through my mind for something to say, anything that would get us off this topic, I latched onto what Maiela had said earlier. Anything to get his concerned gaze off me. "Your sister told me she Saw us going to the Indigo Coast."

"Did she now?" Daegal raised a brow, glancing at Maiela, who nodded in affirmation.

She cleared her throat. "As far as I can see, brother, you two are leaving within the next few days. Whatever ails the princess can only be solved by visiting the merfolk."

Daegal looked back at me. "How do you feel about that?"

He spoke softly, keeping his hands to himself as he eyed me carefully.

"I trust you," I whispered. "I don't trust anyone. That doesn't really answer your question—"

"It's okay, Ryllae." A small smile stretched on his face. "I trust you, too. Does this mean you'll come?"

"I will go with you," I said. "I know I'm not great company, but I want to go."

Daegal pushed himself to his feet. "Alright, Ryllae." Offering me his arm, I placed my hand on it warily. A jolt of electricity sparked between us as he helped me to my feet. His hand slid to mine, gripping it lightly. "Then I suggest we get ready."

He held onto my hand for a moment longer than necessary before letting go and heading toward the bedroom he claimed as his own.

When Daegal was out of sight, Maiela leaned over. "Don't hurt my brother, Princess."

My mouth fell open, but before I could do more than stutter, "W-what?" she turned and followed Daegal.

I stood there for a moment, staring at the empty room, before grabbing a broom and sweeping up the remnants of my teacup.

Maiela was right. I would have to be careful. Already, I could feel that this was a turning point in my life.

On one hand, I might find healing.

On the other hand, I might end up in as many pieces as the mug.

Right now, I wasn't sure which one was more likely to occur.

Nothing Wrong with a Touch of Paranoia

XANDER

I followed Aileana down the stairs, which was a strategic move on my part. My bonded mate looked amazing in those leggings, and I could see every part of her. The leggings were absolutely indecent in the best ways.

My eyes trailed the curve of Aileana's arse to where the material accentuated the tightness of her thigh muscles and her long, lean legs. Twin daggers, gifts from the Spirits that I found inside the night table, were strapped to her thighs.

Clearly, they knew of her violent streak.

Jumping over the last step, Aileana waited for me by the door.

"Come on, dragon boy," she said, waggling her brows. "Let's find Myhhena and see if this place has some food. I don't know about you, but I'm starving."

At the mention of food, my stomach gurgled. Whatever magic the Spirits had used to keep us alive certainly hadn't done much for us nutritionally. My mouth watered at the thought of food, and I eagerly laced my hand through Aileana's. Drawing her close, I pressed my lips against hers in a fleeting kiss.

I couldn't get enough of her. After almost losing her in the Queen's Tower, I vowed to appreciate every moment as though it might be our last. "I would love that."

Her mouth tilted up, and she pushed the door with her shoulder.

It swung open, but Aileana stopped just a few feet from the door.

The same bundle of twigs and leaves was hunched over, facing in the other direction. The creature called Tiaesti hummed beneath her breath as she traced squiggles in the dirt.

I groaned.

"Be nice," Aileana hissed under her breath, squeezing my hand.

I stared at her. She thought *I* was the problem here? The twiggy Spirit was the one who had a problem with me.

However, deciding I would rather not meet the sharp end of one of Aileana's daggers, I chose not to speak.

Instead, I gestured toward the creature as if to say, *Go ahead. You deal with this.*

Aileana cleared her throat. "Um... Tiaesti?"

At the sound of her name, the leaf-child bolted upright. She straightened her dress made of bark, turning back around to face us.

"Greetings, Protectress." The small Spirit curtsied in my mate's direction. To me, she sent a withering glare. After making sure Aileana's back was turned, I gladly returned it.

The Spirit of the Woods stuck her tongue out at me before turning back to Aileana. "How can I help you?"

Aileana raised a brow. "I... uh... we didn't expect you to be waiting here for us."

"This is what you told me to do," Tiaesti said. "I followed your orders."

"Not really…"

"Yes, it is." The child-like Spirit raised a brow. "You told me to leave your home. I left."

Apparently, she took orders quite literally. We would certainly have to keep that in mind.

A choked chuckle escaped Aileana. "Yes, I see that." She tilted her head, her red braids tight against her skull. "We were hoping to get some food…"

Aileana's voice trailed off as Tiaesti jumped a foot above the ground. "Oh, my heavens. Thelrena, help me. I should have known you would be hungry."

The Spirit rushed toward us, taking Aileana's hand in her twiggy one. "Please, Protectress, forgive me for this." Tiaesti sucked in a sobbing breath. "I did not mean to forget about your needs."

The last word sounded like a wail, and a pink tear shaped like a flower petal escaped Tiaesti's brown eyes.

"It's fine," Aileana said sincerely, reaching up and wiping the tear from the Spirit's cheek. "There's no need to cry."

"Really?" Tiaesti hiccuped as three more petals drifted from her eyes. "You don't think I am the worst Spirit ever?"

Aileana smiled softly, pulling the small Spirit in for a hug. "I could never think that."

Something within me sparked at Aileana taking such good care of the child-like Spirit.

She will be a good mother, the dragon remarked, stirring within me for the first time since I woke.

I bristled. *What are you talking about?*

I was fairly certain Aileana's comment about adopting Tiaesti had been a joke. Notwithstanding the fact that our lives were in near-constant turmoil thanks to the High King and his winged minions, we had never spoken about children.

The dragon twisted within me. *No need to get snippy with me. I'm just pointing out the truth.*

Be quiet, I grumbled.

Aileana smiled softly, running her hand down Tiaesti's arm. "Can you show us where the food is?"

The Spirit nodded, taking Aileana's hand before tugging her along. I followed, keeping my eyes and ears open as Tiaesti led us down the moss-covered stones.

The entire time, she muttered to herself, "Stupid Tiaesti. How could you forget the Protectress needs to eat? The Eldest will have your bark for this. You'll never become a full Spirit now."

My brows raised. This was... interesting. I was not a fan of the tiny Spirit, but she seemed truly upset that she hadn't foreseen that we needed to eat.

I made a mental note to try to be kinder to the Spirit in the future. After all, she just wanted to look after my mate. I couldn't fault her for that. We wanted the same thing.

We walked down the stone streets, the sounds of our footfalls echoing through this strange place. I'd been to many cities in the Four Kingdoms, but none were quite like this one. For one thing, it was massive. For another, it appeared to be empty.

Extending my senses, I listened to the sounds of the forest around us. Birds chirped, foxes yipped, and leaves the color of fire rustled as the wind blew past.

That was it. There wasn't anything else. No conversations. No voices.

The stillness was almost eerie, and uneasiness crept up my spine.

Myhhena called this place the Sanctuary, but I couldn't help but feel like something was wrong.

Maybe you're just being paranoid, the dragon remarked. *Spending a century on the run would cause anyone to feel on edge.*

First, you talk of babies, and now paranoia?

The creature huffed. *I'm just saying that it doesn't seem all that bad.*

Talking of children was one thing. The thought of having small red-headed halflings made me feel strangely warm inside.

But there was nothing wrong with a touch of paranoia. Besides, was I truly being paranoid when we both almost died mere days ago?

Aileana seemed at ease as she followed the child made of leaves, but I would not let my guard down.

My desire to reunite the pieces of the map had led us here in the first place. If it weren't for me, we wouldn't have walked into the Crimson King's trap.

Unease bloomed, flickering like a small flame in my gut.

Happiness filtered through the bond from Aileana, and I did everything to keep my distrust within me.

I didn't want to worry her, but I did not trust Myhhena. We needed more information. Where was this so-called Sanctuary located? Why was it considered so safe? And perhaps most importantly, why was Myhhena helping us now?

As we walked down the green cobblestones, Tiaesti mumbled to herself. Every so often, she shot me a glare over her shoulder, but for the most part, she acted as though I was not there.

Eventually, the abandoned city widened, and the small Spirit of the Woods led us up a steep set of stairs carved into a hill. Large looming trees with red and orange leaves walled in the stairs on both sides. Aileana's breath came in short bursts, and I placed my hand on the small of her back.

"I've got you, Sunshine," I murmured, relishing how her body curved around my hand.

She sent me an appreciative glance over her shoulder.

We climbed roughly a hundred steps before reaching a small landing. Tiaesti scurried onto another path, and red and orange leaves trailed behind her as she led us toward an enormous stone archway.

"This is it!" Tiaesti proclaimed.

My brows furrowed as I peered beyond the archway. A sea of endless trees stretched as far as the eye could see, but there was no food in sight.

The Spirit of the Woods curtsied, clearly proud of herself. "Welcome, Protectress."

"Thank you?" Aileana sounded confused as she peeked around the young Spirit. "But all I see is a forest."

Tiaesti gasped, the sound incredibly human, before giggling. "Whoops!" A joyous laugh that sounded like a playful wind blowing through trees came from the Spirit. "I forgot."

Holding out her hands, Tiaesti murmured under her breath. Her voice was barely audible as golden ribbons slipped from her twiggy fingers. They swirled in the air, weaving themselves around the stone archway.

A bird landed on a nearby tree just as Tiaesti clenched her fists. The golden ribbons disintegrated into thin air.

The silence gave way to sounds of life. Dozens of voices came out of nowhere, and my nose tingled as the scent of many beings slammed into me all at once.

None of this had been here a moment ago. Where had they come from?

A heartbeat later, the scenery behind the archway changed.

The trees were gone, and in their place was a massive cobblestone square. Ivy-covered walls that stretched towards the heavens formed a boundary around the eating area. There was no roof, but trees provided much-needed shade to the dozen or so tables filling the square. Nearly a hundred Spirits sat at these tables, their laughter and conversations incongruous with the quiet of the abandoned city.

And their bodies...

Every single one looked a little different from the next. Male and female Spirits made of leaves, grass, moss, and twigs sat around the benches, but that wasn't all. Other Spirits were made of water, and their bodies were fluid as the liquid ran through them.

Myhhena sat at a large stone table at the far end of the courtyard. The Spirit's head was bent, and she spoke with a watery female standing on the other side of the table.

Beside me, Aileana laced her fingers through mine. Happiness and awe came through the bond.

"Isn't this amazing?" she whispered.

I grunted. I still wasn't convinced this place was safe. What were they hiding here? My eyes swept the courtyard, looking for threats, but I didn't see any.

Nonetheless, I would not let my guard down.

Tiaesti turned with a smile carved on her wooden face. She curtsied, and her leaves rustled. "Protectress, the Spirits of the Woods, and the Waters welcome you and your bonded mate to the Sanctuary."

Aileana dipped her head. "Thank you for your hospitality."

The small child grinned. Without missing a beat, she wrapped her hand around Aileana's free one and pulled us through the archway.

The moment we stepped into the courtyard, the chatter stopped. Thick tension filled the air, making it harder to breathe. My heart pounded, and my dragon stirred. It was watching. Waiting.

I tightened my grip, not wanting to lose control.

The Spirit of the Waters speaking with Myhhena glided away, and everyone watched us.

Well.

They watched Aileana. Most of them glared at me. Like Tiaesti, they seemed to be predisposed against me.

Aileana shifted on her feet. She squeezed my hand tightly, pressing herself against my side. That she came to me for safety filled me with a strong sense of male pride. She was mine, and I would protect her until my very last breath.

Releasing my grip on her hand, I wrapped my arm around my bonded mate and drew her against my chest. Her scent of honey and earth floated up to me, and I held her tighter against my side.

Raising a brow, I glanced at our leafy escort. She was currently standing next to Aileana, picking at her dress with her free hand as she hummed a tune under her breath.

"Tiaesti," I grumbled.

She looked up, glaring at me. "Yes, dragon?"

Clearly, her kindness only went so far.

"Did you say there was some food?" I asked, raising a brow.

Tiaesti gasped, releasing Aileana's hand as she performed what I could only describe as a nervous dance. "Oh, my goodness, Thelrena save me. Right this way, please."

The small Spirit hurriedly led us through the maze of tables towards Myhhena.

Aileana pressed herself against my side. "They're all watching us," she whispered. Nervousness filtered through the bond, and I tightened my grip around her waist.

"Don't worry, Sunshine," I murmured, brushing back a stray hair that had escaped her braid as we walked past a male made entirely of water. His sharp blue eyes followed our every move, and I glared at him. "I've got you."

The atmosphere was filled with apprehension, the air growing thicker with every passing moment. They all seemed to be waiting for... something.

When we reached Myhhena's table, Tiaesti dipped into a deep curtsy. Her head nearly touched the ground as she bent in half.

"Speak," Myhhena commanded.

Tiaesti rose, clearing her throat. "I have brought the Protectress of the Woods, Eldest Sister."

Myhhena raised a leafy brow. "I see that. Thank you, Tiaesti. You did well."

Tiaesti giggled, clearly pleased by the compliment.

"You may go," Myhhena commanded. "I will look after them from here."

Curtsying once more, Tiaesti murmured, "Of course, Eldest Sister," before disappearing in a flurry of leaves.

Once Tiaesti was gone, Myhhena's moss-green eyes swung over to us. She studied us with the care of an ancient being. There was an eeriness about her gaze, and I wasn't shy about staring right back at the Spirit of the Woods. The last time I saw Myhhena was when we finally got the prohiberis off Aileana. At that time, she had been extremely clear that she couldn't help us.

What changed?

"Have a seat, please," Myhhena said in her eternal voice, her words brokering no room for discussion.

Aileana dropped into an open spot on the bench across from the Spirit. After a moment, I slid in beside her.

Keeping a hand on the knife I'd pilfered from the kitchen of our small abode, I kept my eyes on Myhhena as the Spirit clapped her hands.

Blue clay plates filled with bread, cheese, and fruit emerged out of thin air.

"Eat," Myhhena commanded, her voice ringing through the courtyard.

Aileana went to dig in right away, but I narrowed my eyes, holding out a hand to stop her.

"Wait." I shook my head. "You don't know if it's safe."

"Are you serious, Xander? We are in a strange place where golden magic exists, and you think the food is poisoned?" She scoffed, crossing her arms in a move that served to accentuate her breasts.

Being the strong male I was, I refused to be distracted. I shrugged, not removing my hand. "Stranger things have happened."

Aileana shook her head, muttering something about incorrigible males under her breath before uncrossing her arms. Deliberately reaching under my outstretched arm, she grabbed a flatbread sprinkled with sesame seeds.

I snarled, "Aileana."

She turned to me, her green eyes wide as she took an over-exaggerated bite of bread. "Mhmm," she said, dramatically moaning. "This is delicious. You should try some."

"Can't you listen to anything I say?" I snapped, pulling back my arm and glaring at her. "It might not be safe."

"Can't you try to be less bossy?" Aileana looked at me pointedly before raising a hand and showcasing her body. "Look, I'm still alive. I'm sure the food is fine."

She took another bite, and I knew it was a lost cause. Despite the enjoyment I got from arguing with Aileana, I had other things on my mind.

Turning my gaze to Myhhena, I narrowed my eyes. Something

about this place felt strange. I couldn't quite put my finger on it, but I wouldn't rest until I figured out what it was.

"Why are you helping us?" I asked the Spirit of the Woods.

"What do you mean?" she asked innocently.

"I mean, *this*." Gesturing to the surrounding forest, I raised a brow. "Last time we talked, you told me you could not interfere with our affairs."

"Xander," Aileana hissed. "Do you need to do this now? Myhhena opened this place to us in our time of need. She has done nothing but show us kindness."

I squeezed Aileana's hand, whispering. "Just because someone is kind to you doesn't mean they don't have ulterior motives. We can't trust anyone." Returning my gaze to Myhhena, I raised a brow. "Why couldn't you help us before now?"

"In Ithenmyr, the Spirits of the Woods and the Waters cannot lend assistance to those who live within its borders." Myhhena's voice was matter-of-fact as she spoke. "We are guides and nothing more. There are laws that even we must follow, rules that govern our very existence. They are created by the gods and goddesses themselves."

"So, how do you explain this?" I asked as Aileana bit into a rain berry.

She made a sound of appreciation as it exploded on her tongue, and I shifted uncomfortably in my seat.

"I didn't bring you here." Myhhena gestured to Aileana. "Your bonded mate summoned the gatekeepers of the Sanctuary herself. They brought you here, placing the two of you under my protection. By the ancient laws that govern the Sanctuary, my sisters and I can provide you with food and shelter." She raised a brow. "You should know you are the first dragon shifter ever to make their way through the gates."

Her words made sense, in a way. Despite the obvious aversion the

Spirits had towards me, I seemed as though Myhhena had Aileana's best interests in mind.

I still didn't trust the Spirit of the Woods, but it seemed safe enough for us to remain here. At least until we figured out what to do next. We couldn't stay here forever, but maybe this Sanctuary would provide us with a well-earned reprieve from the chaos that was our lives.

Aileana pushed a piece of bread in my direction. "You should eat, Xander," she whispered.

I eyed the bread. It *did* look delicious.

Gods, please just eat, the dragon said. *I'm starving.*

Fine, I snapped. *But if we die from being poisoned, it's your fault.*

We won't, he said smugly.

Sighing, I reached over and took a thin slice of white cheese. Placing the cheese on top of the bread, I folded the entire thing in half before slipping it into my mouth. It practically melted against my tongue, leaving me with the lingering flavor of pepper.

"Oh my gods, this is delicious," I groaned as I tossed another two slices of cheese in my mouth.

Aileana giggled, elbowing me in the side. "I told you so."

Wrapping an arm around her, I kept one hand around her waist and piled a plate full of food with the other.

The flow of conversation resumed around us, and I listened to snippets as we ate.

"They came from Vlarone...."

"... Can't you scent the ash on him? He's a dragon shifter..."

"Dangerous..."

"Can't hurt him..."

"My mother was in Breley when the dragons..."

"... Bonded mate."

Apparently, the love of gossip transcended species. These Spirits talked about us as though we weren't even here.

I bit my tongue, holding in my outrage. Kysha's words from before we left for the ball echoed in my mind. They were a reminder of why we needed to remain hidden.

The king has ordered the Winged Soldiers to search the entire country for you both.

If High King Edgar survived the flames, I was certain he would not put an end to his search until he found us. That meant I needed to keep Aileana safe above everything else. If staying here with these gossiping, dragon-hating Spirits was our best bet, then I would put any personal discomfort aside for her sake.

She was the most important thing. Nothing else mattered.

It struck me that my life always seemed to revolve around females.

First, my mother. Then my sister. After I lost Saena on that bloody day in the Southern Kingdom, I found Nonna.

Now, I had Aileana by my side.

This time, though, our story wouldn't end in blood and tears. I wouldn't let it. I couldn't fail.

Not again.

My fist tightened around the clay mug in front of me. Visions of my beautiful black-haired sister lying broken on the palace floor in Drahan, blood leaking from her broken body, flashed through my mind.

That day when I found Saena nearly broke me. I would not let that happen again.

I would do anything to keep Aileana safe. Kill anyone who crossed her.

So I let the Spirits gossip about us, and I ate in silence.

Eventually, Aileana pushed back her plate. "Thank you, Myhhena, for opening the doors to the Sanctuary."

The Spirit of the Woods dipped her head. "It is our pleasure to house the Protectress of the Woods and her bonded mate."

Aileana smiled, but before she could speak, a *screech* came from above us. A hush filled the courtyard as all conversations dried up at once.

I looked up at the brilliant blue sky, my eyes widening. Thrusting out an arm, I shoved Aileana to the ground as a massive black raven flew directly toward us. Withdrawing my knife, I gripped the hilt as the bird approached.

It was four times the size of a normal raven, and the look in its eyes...

This was not a normal creature. If its size wasn't enough of a clue, blood dripped from its claws.

Aileana sucked in a deep breath, and a wave of frigid fear splashed through the bond. The raven landed on the table, its black, beady eyes wide as it turned in a slow circle, leaving bloody claw prints behind.

The twang of metal came from behind me, and Aileana pressed herself against my side. She clutched her dagger, eyeing the creature warily.

It pleased me to no end that my mate could defend herself.

"It's a shifter," I whispered.

I knew as soon as it landed. Its scent was different from its animal counterparts. Even without the scent, the raven's size was a dead give-away. Only shifters could change their size so dramatically.

Myhhena rose, her leafy hands gripping the table as she stared at the raven. "The dragon speaks the truth." Her voice was cold, and fear laced her words. "Do not touch it. This creature does not belong here."

I shook my head, holding out an arm and pulling Aileana back. "Don't worry, we won't."

As far as I was concerned, this just proved my point.

The Sanctuary was not a safe place.

Raising her voice, Myhhena called out. "Spirits of the Woods and the Waters. Return to your homes and await further instruction. Do not speak of this to anyone."

A rustling filled the air. When I glanced over my shoulder, we were alone.

Then, the raven opened its beak.

A Very Important Question

Xander drew me tight against him, and even Myhhena seemed affected as the raven spoke. Its voice was deep and tinged with echoes of darkness. "Spirit of the Woods and Eldest of the Twelve. You have committed a grave sin against Ithenmyr."

"Do not speak untruths such as these in my presence," Myhhena hissed.

"In housing these traitors, you have broken the Treaty of the Seven Roses," the raven said smugly.

I shuddered. *Traitors*. Was that what we were? I'd seen what High King Edgar did to traitors. The way his Death Elf magic ran through their bodies, pulling them apart from the inside out.

How was fighting against the male who had made my life a living hell considered treachery? Not just my life but that of all females in Ithenmyr.

If fighting for freedom was treasonous, I would gladly accept the mantle thrust upon me.

Myhhena scoffed, shaking her head. "I have done no such thing."

She grew larger, looming over the table as her voice echoed with authority. "The guardians brought them here. No laws were broken in the process. We followed everything to the letter. The Treaty of the Seven Roses still stands."

"Lies," the raven hissed, flapping its black feathers.

My heart pounded, and my palms grew sweaty around the hilt of my dagger.

A snarl sounding like the snapping of twigs came from Myhhena as golden ribbons slipped from her leafy palms. They swirled around her, awaiting her command. "You know as well as I that they are welcome here."

The raven *cackled*. It walked on the stone table, leaving red marks in its tracks. A shiver ran through me at the sight of them. Even here, in the safety of the Sanctuary, it always came back to blood.

Would I ever escape the crimson curse? Or was it my birthright to be haunted by blood until the day I Faded?

"Nowhere is safe," the raven hissed, pulling my attention back to it. "No one is safe."

Myhhena waved a hand. "Begone with you," she snapped. "Leave. Your kind is not welcome here."

The raven shook its head. "I cannot." Black, beady eyes turned toward me, and I shivered at the deadness in the shifter's gaze. "I have a message for the Earth Elf."

"A message?" I blinked.

Xander tightened his grip on my arm and tried to pull me back.

"Don't talk to it, Aileana," he snarled, trying to block the raven from my sight. "Whatever it wants to say isn't important."

Despite Xander's insistence, I paused.

It would be foolish to ignore the creature... right? It had come all this way with a message.

The last time I ran into a shifter, it turned out to be incredibly violent. I would never forget Kolvar. The cat shifter worked for Remington, and he had stalked me in my tower for years, watching my every move. Until a few days before his death, I hadn't even known shifters existed.

Then I learned that he had been watching me for the majority of my life, invading my privacy in the worst ways. Now, Kolvar was dead. I couldn't do anything about him anymore. The moments he stole were gone. Everything he did to me was out of my control.

But this... I could control this.

I shook my head, standing my ground. "I want to hear what the bird has to say."

Xander cursed. "Seriously?"

"Yes," I insisted.

The raven cackled, and the hairs on the back of my neck rose. My magic pounded steadily in my veins, begging to be released as the earth hummed beneath my feet.

They wanted to protect me, but I had made my choice.

I wanted to hear what the raven had to say.

The shifter's black feathers fluffed, and he spread his wings wide as he eyed me. His voice deepened impossibly further until it boomed around the now-empty courtyard. "The message is this: High King Edgar knows where you are. He *will* find you. And when he does, you will pay for your sins in blood. You should have died, but he will find pleasure in draining—"

Xander snapped out a hand, grabbing the massive raven around the neck. It squawked, pecking at my mate. Blood welled on Xander's hand, and he cursed, dropping his knife and wrapping his hand around the bird's back. With two fingers, he pinched the raven's beak shut.

"That's enough out of you." Lifting his gaze to Myhhena, Xander snapped, "Do you have a cage in this so-called Sanctuary of yours?"

"We do." Myhhena nodded, her mossy eyes wide even as her leafy hands remained at her sides. "One moment."

The Spirit of the Woods disappeared in a flurry of leaves and wind. Xander tightened his grip around the shifter, who flailed in his hands, and he turned to me.

"Now, do you see why I asked you to be careful?" His golden eyes flashed, and he growled. "Nowhere is safe, Aileana. *Nothing* is safe. We always have to be on our guard."

"That's no way to live," I snapped, waving a hand. "What kind of life is that, Xander?"

"The kind where we *survive!*" he yelled. "The kind where we don't die because we got too comfortable and forgot to pay attention."

"I pay attention, Xander. How dare you say anything to the contrary?"

"How dare I?" He raised a brow, holding the shifter in front of him. "Do you see this bird?"

I glared at him. "Obviously, I see it."

"This raven works for Edgar," Xander snarled.

The bird tried to peck him again, and he adjusted his grip on the bird.

"I am aware," I said through clenched teeth.

"Then why are you fighting me on this?" Xander seemed exasperated.

Recognizing that this probably wasn't the best time for this argument, I sighed and stepped back.

Running my hand over my braid, I groaned. "I just... I don't want to spend our lives on the run."

A long moment passed, and Xander stared at me.

"Neither do I, Aileana."

Moments later, the wind swirled. Our argument was forgotten as Myhhena reappeared in a flurry of leaves, clutching a massive golden birdcage. It was at least four feet tall and two feet wide. It seemed miraculous that the Spirit of the Woods could carry the cage since it was more than half her height, although I thought her magic was probably helping her with the weight.

Without a word, the Spirit unlocked the gilded door. Xander opened his hand, loosening his grip on the bird's beak.

When its beak was free, the raven squawked, "Traitors! Traitors! You will pay in blood for your sins!"

With a spurt of anger that I felt through the bond, Xander smacked the raven on the back of the head. Its screaming stopped with a gurgle as the bird's head lolled strangely to the side.

"Get rid of it," Xander ordered, thrusting the unconscious bird into the cage. "Take that thing away from here and kill it."

Myhhena's eyes widened. "We aren't beasts," she snarled, pulling the cage away from Xander. "We don't *kill* things here, dragon."

"Of course you don't," he snapped, reaching for the cage once more. His violent intentions were clear.

Myhhena gasped, holding the cage on her other side. The wind swirled, and gold sparked off her as she shook her head. "I won't let you hurt it."

"It's a shifter," Xander hissed. "Not a bird."

"We cannot shed blood within the walls of the Sanctuary. This is a safe place."

"Not that safe," he snapped angrily, gesturing to the bird. "*Clearly!*"

Anger bubbled between them, and despite Myhhena's words, violence was in the air.

Holding up my hands, I stepped between the two of them.

Placing a palm on my bonded mate's heaving chest, I looked up at him. "Stand down, Xander."

He snarled, and scales rippled on his skin.

That was *not* a good sign.

Deciding it would be safer to deal with Myhhena, I turned. "If you don't want to kill it, can you... take it away? Put it somewhere safe?"

The Spirit of the Woods nodded. "I can." She waved her hand, and golden ribbons slipped from her palm. They wove around the raven, sinking into its skin. "While I cannot kill it, the shifter will sleep for a few days. This will give us time to... deal with this."

Xander snarled. "You should throw the damned thing in the deepest, darkest hole you have." His eyes flashed. "The shifter is far more dangerous than you know."

Myhhena's mouth pinched in a firm line, and she tightened her hold on the top of the cage. "I know just the place."

My mate cleared his throat. "One more thing before you go."

"Yes?"

"I need a weapon," Xander said gruffly. "I appreciate that your people left these blades for Aileana, but I require weapons to protect my mate."

"Weapons?" Myhhena's tone was dry. "I told you already, we don't allow killing here."

Xander's shoulders tensed. "You may not, but I will do whatever is required to protect my mate. If you want us to stay, you will find me a sword."

A long moment passed as the Spirit of the Woods studied Xander before she dipped her head. "I will have one sent to your residence after I deal with this." She gestured to the birdcage. "The two of you should return home. I'll let Tiaesti know to look out for you."

The wind swirled around her once more, and then she and the raven were gone.

A long breath escaped me, and I groaned. My blood pounded in my veins, and my heart raced as I stared at the red prints the raven had left on the table.

Xander wrapped his arm around me, plucking the dagger from my hands before sliding it into the sheath. He hugged me tightly against his chest, his hands running over my arms. "Are you all right, Aileana?"

That was a strange question.

No, I was not all right. I was never "all right." Why could nothing ever be simple for us? Why did life have to throw one thing after another in our direction? For Thelrena's sake, we couldn't even eat breakfast without it being interrupted by a messenger from the king hunting us.

But that seemed like a lot to say, so I just sighed. "I'll be fine. I was just hoping for a safe, uneventful day. Obviously, that was too much to ask for."

My hand crept up to the necklace beneath my shirt, and I ran my fingers over the long, thin cylinder holding the map.

Xander's hand followed mine, cupping my fingers. "When has our life ever been safe or uneventful?"

"Never. But I had hoped that we might turn over a new leaf, so to speak. Unfortunately, that doesn't seem to be the case. The bloody raven..." My voice trailed off, and I shuddered, tucking my face into Xander's tunic. "It always comes down to blood."

"I will keep you safe, Aileana." Xander tightened his grip around me. "Always."

Silence filled the space between us as I lost myself in my thoughts. The raven had said something, and now, I couldn't get my mind off it.

"High King Edgar is alive," I said, voicing my thoughts. "He didn't die." I needed to say the words aloud and hear them in my own voice.

"It appears that way."

"He's alive, and he's still hunting us." Until High King Edgar was dead, we would not know a moment's peace. The raven's presence served as confirmation. Shaking my head, I met Xander's gaze. "What are we going to do?"

Rubbing his rough, calloused thumb over my cheek, Xander pressed his forehead against mine. His silver hair fell in a curtain around us, closing us off from the rest of the world. "We're going to do what we do best, Sunshine. We're going to figure this out."

He lowered his lips, brushing his mouth against mine.

This kiss was kind. It was gentle. Reassuring.

It wasn't nearly enough.

"Xander," I groaned against him, my tongue sweeping into his mouth as urgent need swept through me. "I need more."

I needed everything he could give me.

In response, he lifted me. My thighs wrapped around his hips, and his hands landed underneath my buttocks.

"What do you need?" he growled, holding me against him. I could feel every part of him, and I knew he wanted me as much as I wanted him.

"To forget."

There was so much I wanted to forget. The raven and its message. The High King and his Winged Soldiers. I even wanted to forget about this Sanctuary that wasn't, despite the implications of its name, all that safe.

I needed to forget about it all.

Xander raised a brow. "I can help with that."

Tightening his grip around my thighs, Xander moved swiftly down the path we had followed earlier. He took the stairs three at a time, and I busied myself with pressing kisses to his face, neck, and shoulders. I did not know where the Spirits had gone, and at that moment, I didn't even care.

I needed my bonded mate, and he needed me, too.

For comfort. For love. For everything.

When Xander used his hip to open the door to our small home, I sighed in relief. Still, he didn't put me down. He climbed the stairs, kicking off his boots before standing before the bed. Slipping my hands beneath his tunic, I ran my hands over the bare muscles of his sculpted chest.

He groaned, finally releasing his grip on my thighs. I tumbled onto the bed, my heart beating quickly as pure need filled me. A glance at Xander's eyes told me he felt the same.

He looked like he wanted to eat me.

And at that moment, I had no problem with that whatsoever.

"Xander," I breathed. His name was a prayer as it passed through my lips. A request. A demand.

The bond between us pulsed, and a multitude of emotions poured through it. Love. Desire. Happiness.

He bent, covering me with his body as he pressed his lips against my throat. His voice was rugged as he kissed my neck. "I've wanted to do this since the moment you put that damned tunic on this morning."

I raised a brow. "Do what?"

"Don't be coy, Sunshine." He ran a finger up my thigh towards my pulsing core. "You know what I'm talking about."

The thrum of magic in my veins increased, pounding in time with my heart. I did, in fact, know exactly what he was talking about.

My voice was little more than a whisper as I said, "Then do it, dragon of mine. What are you waiting for?"

Xander raised his head, his golden eyes gleaming. "And you think I'm bossy?"

"I know you are," I smirked. "I just happen to be a little bossy, too."

He chuckled as his deft fingers quickly undressed me. Soon, I lay bare before him. There was something intensely intimate about being completely naked in front of Xander while he was still fully dressed. My insides twisted, and my core churned as he ran a hand down my chest, leaving a trail of tingling flesh in his wake.

He put his hands on my hips, moving me onto the bed until I was lying in the middle of the mattress. Resting between my legs, Xander supported his weight on his arms as his gaze swept over me appreciatively.

"Elyxander," I breathed, tugging up the hem of his tunic. "Please. Make me forget."

My silver-haired mate raised a brow, tugging his tunic over his head, and displayed himself to me. My breath caught at the sight of him, and I raised a hand, running it over the scars that covered his flesh. These markings of his life as a warrior told the stories of his past. Of the people who tried to hurt this dragon of mine.

I wanted to kill them all for hurting him.

Xander's eyes darkened, but he held still as I traced the scars that covered his body.

Eventually, he rested his weight on one elbow and lifted a hand.

"Aileana," he breathed, "I love you so much." With care, he picked up the necklace holding the pieces of the map, turning it over.

"I love you too," I murmured. "So much. You are my life, Xander."

"When we were in that tower, the only thing I could think of was that we didn't have enough time." He rolled the necklace through his fingers, his voice barely more than a whisper. "There are so many things we haven't had the chance to do."

He placed the necklace back on my chest, trailing a path with his fingers and then his tongue. I shivered, his touch sending sparks through me.

"I know," I whispered hoarsely as Xander's fingers ran toward my twisting core. "I feel the same way."

He made a sound of agreement, his hands running over me. I plucked at the buttons on his trousers. "Take these off," I murmured. "Please."

He did. And then, there were no more words between us.

For that brief moment, I forgot about all our problems. The tower, the king, even the raven. None of it mattered.

The only thing that mattered was Xander and the way he made me feel.

I was his, and he was mine.

WE SPENT the remainder of the day in our small home, resting and spending time together. Tiaesti delivered food for us at night, and we ate before falling back into bed.

During our recreational... activities, I added to the decor, creating a distinct forest-like atmosphere in the small stone house. Dark red roses adorned the vines crawling up the walls, their intensely floral scent adding an interesting note to the autumnal breeze.

For once, sleep came easily.

THREE DAYS WENT by in the same manner. We talked about everything and nothing, wondering about our friends outside the Sanctuary.

For a few days, we were at peace. Somehow, we did it. We had three days of safety and solitude. We didn't hear about the raven or anything else.

It was wonderful.

On the morning of the fourth day, Xander woke me up in the best way possible. After we thoroughly enjoyed each other, I rested in the crook of his arm, drawing circles on his bare chest.

He watched me through hooded eyes, a purely masculine and satisfied look on his face.

"Are you happy, Aileana?" he asked.

I raised a brow. Pushing myself up, I met his eyes. "Of course, I'm happy. We're together. That makes me happy."

"Good," he murmured. "I'm happy, too."

He patted the bed beside him, and I raised a brow, shuffling over.

"What's going on?" I asked.

Xander pushed himself up against the headboard, pulling his hair back into a low bun at the base of his neck before tying it off with a leather ribbon. He shifted, looking suddenly uncomfortable. "Aileana, I... we should talk."

My eyes widened, and I swallowed.

That sounded ominous.

I drew the bedsheets around me as a chill ran down my naked front. "Oh?"

Nodding, he lifted an arm and gestured for me to press myself against him. I took the spot without hesitation, letting his warmth fill me.

Happiness filtered through the bond, but there was something else there, too.

He was... nervous? What did he have to be nervous about?

"We may not have a plan of what exactly we're going to do next, Aileana, but I am certain of one thing. Nothing we do will change that."

"Oh?"

He shifted, his golden eyes meeting mine as he huskily said, "I love you."

Snuggling close, I ran a finger down his bare chest. "I love you, too."

Xander's lips tilted up, but the smile didn't quite reach his eyes.

"Is that what you wanted to say?" I asked.

Nerves were still coming through the bond, and he was shifting beside me.

"No, not really." Xander drew in a deep breath, running his hand over my arm as his eyes darkened to burnished gold. "Aileana, I... I have a question for you."

"A question?"

He nodded. "Yes. As you know, when we first met, we entered into a mutually beneficial arrangement."

"Yes. I *was* present for that occasion." I smirked. "It was mere moments after you surprised me, and I stabbed you."

"I know." His lips twitched, and a small burst of amusement came through the bond. "I won't ever forget. I might even venture to say you're happy you didn't kill me."

"You could say I'm mildly pleased by the outcome," I said.

Chuckling, Xander traced the gold and green lines making up the tattoo marking me as his.

"And we are mated," he reminded me.

"Again," I repeated, my voice edged with dryness, "I am aware of this. I was, in fact, a willing participant in our mating ceremony."

And what a ceremony it was. The cave, the waterfall, the beauty of spending days away from everyone else. I would remember it for the rest of my life.

"You're not making this very easy," he muttered, rolling his eyes.

My brows furrowed, and I pushed myself off his chest, turning until we were face to face. "Making what easy?"

Xander sighed. "Aileana, we are mated."

"Again, that is correct." Reaching up, I lay my hand across his forehead, checking for a fever. "Maybe you were right, and the food was poisoned. I haven't heard of food poisoning kicking in four days after the fact, but perhaps this is it. Are you hallucinating?"

He was warm, but not any warmer than usual.

Frowning, I pulled my hand back as Xander laughed hoarsely. "I'm not ill, Aileana. I just..." He huffed, running his hand over his hair. "The words aren't coming easily to me, that's all."

"What words?"

A moment passed before Xander said, "Aileana, will you marry me?"

All the air was sucked out of the room. I couldn't breathe. I couldn't think. My mind stopped, and I froze. My mouth opened and closed as I stared at Xander.

He thought he had no words? I had no words. This was...

How could he ask me to marry him? Xander knew how I felt about marriage. He knew what Remington was going to do to me. He knew what my marriage would have meant.

I would have been locked up and thrown away, bred like a gods-damned animal.

He knew this, and yet he still asked?

I loved Xander. He was my bonded mate, for the gods' sake.

He was mine. I *chose* him.

Why wasn't that enough? Why did he have to do this? To ask me this? The one thing I couldn't do. I would never do it.

Marriage was a gods-damned gilded cave. And he wanted to put me in one, just like the raven from earlier.

My eyes widened, and I pulled the sheet up further, wrapping it around myself as though it could stop the sting of the words exiting my mouth. "Xander, I... I can't marry you."

Safe was a Relative Term

DAEGAL

The future was far darker than I had ever Seen it before. Dozens of paths lay before me, rippling like water. When Myhhena visited us the day after the Midnight Ball and delivered news of Xander and Aileana, she warned me that the paths I Saw might have been compromised.

I needed to be careful. Thoughtful. It was more important than ever to weigh everything I Saw against what I knew to be true.

But even knowing that my visions could be altered didn't change anything. I couldn't stop Looking ahead. Not now.

The future was too important.

Silver ribbons filled my vision as I sifted through them, searching for one in particular. I held my breath, my heart thudding as I Saw what was to come.

There.

Tinged with hints of dark crimson, the path I sought lay before me. Bending, I picked up the ribbon and ran it through my fingers as I pulled it towards me. Dozens of visions flashed before my eyes. A blond elf walking next to me for days. Curling black horns. Hair blowing in the wind. A growing sense of trust.

I ran my hand down the path, trying to See far ahead. The further I went, the foggier the future became. I Saw us arriving at an endless ocean. It was beautiful, but there were hints of darkness, even there. An unbalanced scale. Brightly colored fins alongside tridents and swords. Something hazy caught my eye.

Gold, perhaps?

I tried to focus on it, but no matter how I shifted my vision, it remained foggy. Sighing, I set down the ribbon. This wasn't the first time this had happened. Often, when paths were fluid like this, the future shifted. It changed.

What I Saw didn't always come to pass.

Over the past ten years, it seemed that the darkest, most dangerous paths were always the most likely to occur. If I were still a betting male, I would put all my money on the dark paths.

But I wasn't a betting male. Not anymore. The last time I made a bet, it ended in the worst way possible.

Pushing thoughts of gambling aside, I dropped the path. It faded back into the rippling silver ribbons surrounding me, and I sought another. This one had been worrying me for days. Since the initial visit from Myhhena, we hadn't heard from Aileana and Xander at all.

I sifted through dozens of paths until I found theirs. It stood out from the rest, the fire and vines marking it as unique before I even picked it up.

Tracing the silver ribbon as far as I could See, I confirmed what the Spirit of the Woods had told us. They were safe, at least for the time being. Their future was fluid, and many paths lay ahead of them.

Dropping their path, I continued on my search. Sorting through the future, I Looked ahead through as many paths as I could until I was satisfied that the time to come was safe.

For now.

Shutting my eyes, I withdrew from the future. I slammed into my body, and a ragged breath escaped me as I blinked.

Bright blue eyes greeted me, shrouded by a dark crimson veil and blond hair. Ryllae wore a dress the same color as her eyes, which only made her black horns stand out more than usual. The corner of her lips turned up as she caught my eye.

My heart sped up at the sight of the Death Elf princess. I couldn't help it. There was something about Ryllae that made me want to protect her at all costs. I felt something for her that I hadn't felt for anyone else in my entire life.

"Well?" Ryllae asked. She sat across from me at the kitchen table at Nonna's, her fingers wrapped around yet another mug of tea. This was her third or fourth of the day, and a strong herbal aroma wafted over to me. "Is it safe?"

Safe was a relative term. Life in Ithenmyr had never been safe. Not really. At least, not in my lifetime.

"It's... interesting," I replied, choosing my words carefully.

She hummed, sipping her tea. I took a moment to study the Death Elf.

Since rescuing Ryllae from Nightstone prison, her physical appearance had dramatically improved. She no longer looked like she was on the brink of Fading. Her cheeks had a tinge of pink to them, and her skin wasn't as gaunt. I would have been lying if I said I didn't notice she was filling out her clothes better, her body's natural feminine curves becoming more pronounced after weeks of eating good food.

I noticed many things about this princess of Ithenmyr who courted darkness.

Perhaps I shouldn't have. Perhaps I should have been more careful around the Death Elf. But I wasn't. Not anymore. I was tired of being careful. Something drew me to Ryllae like a moth to a flame. Maybe it was her pain, or maybe it was the way she persevered despite the challenges thrown her way.

Glimpses of what was done to her had been shown to me on the silver planes. I knew just enough to realize that Ryllae was far stronger than anyone gave her credit for. She had survived the things of nightmares, and she still found the strength to wake up every morning.

Ryllae was angry, but as far as I was concerned, she had every right to be. Honestly, I couldn't believe she smiled at all. I wasn't sure that I would if I were in her shoes. But beneath all her anger, I glimpsed something else. Underneath the vengeance, darkness, and desire for retribution, I saw the person she could be.

"What do you think we should do?" she asked.

"There is no imminent danger in our path." I couldn't guarantee that danger wouldn't find us. I knew better than most how quickly things could change, even before Myhhena had cast doubt on my visions. I drew my bottom lip through my teeth, thinking through all the options.

Ryllae needed her magic, and it was clear that remaining in Nonna's cottage wasn't the answer. She watched me, her blue eyes wide as she waited for an answer.

I exhaled slowly. "I think we should go."

Ryllae exhaled, nodding slowly. "Then it's settled."

She stared at the bottom of her teacup, her brows furrowed. After a long moment, Ryllae whispered, "We will go and leave the witch in your sister's capable hands."

I wished I was a mind reader as well as a Seer. What I wouldn't give to know what the princess was thinking right now.

Clearing my throat, I ran my hand through my coarse hair. "We should go soon, before the future shifts. I'm not certain how long the path I Saw will remain the same."

"A shift." Ryllae's voice took on a strange lilt, and her head tilted, her long blond braid swinging over her shoulder. Her gaze was so heavy that it felt like she was looking into my soul. "Ithenmyr has been shifting for years."

"What do you mean?"

The princess peered into the bottom of her teacup. "I don't think there will be peace until the darkness is gone." She sucked in a breath, her eyes growing wide as they met mine once again. "Or when we die. Then it doesn't matter. Death will bring peace. Death always brings peace."

Her words hung over us like a shroud, and the air grew impossibly thick between us.

I was still thinking of something to say when Ryllae laughed. Just as quickly as it had appeared, her dark mood was gone.

She stood, pushing back her chair. "I feel like taking a walk. Will you join me?"

I blinked, trying to keep up with the rapid shift. "Um, yes. I'd love to walk with you."

Pushing back my own chair, I stood and walked around the table, offering her my arm. Ryllae stared at my proffered limb for a moment, and regret twinged within me. I shouldn't have offered. I knew she had trouble being touched. Not the specifics, but the snippets I had Seen were horrific.

I went to pull my arm back, but she darted out her hand, grabbing my proffered limb.

I froze at the feeling of her hand on my skin. Even through the fabric of my tunic, I could feel the press of her fingers on my arm. It felt like sparks were flying between us.

Ryllae sucked in a breath, staring at the place where her hand touched my arm. "Daegal, I'm sorry."

"Sorry?"

She nodded. "Yesterday... when your sister touched me, and I screamed—"

"Don't," I interrupted, shaking my head. "Please, Princess, there's no need to apologize. You did nothing wrong."

Ryllae chewed on the inside of her cheek. I watched the movement carefully. The last thing I wanted to do was scare her again. The look of fear in Ryllae's eyes when she had dropped the teacup would be seared into my memory for the rest of my life.

"I don't... I just... Maiela startled me," Ryllae said, her shoulders drooping as she sighed.

"I know," I whispered. "It's okay, Ryllae. You don't need to explain."

"She just... I was scared." Her blue eyes widened. "But... Daegal, I need you to know *you* don't scare me,'

Ryllae's words echoed in my mind as I stared at this dark princess. Her crimson aura pulsed around her, and the air in the kitchen thickened.

I stepped toward Ryllae, and her grip on my arm shifted. She didn't push me or run away or shut down.

"You don't scare me," she whispered. Her fingers tightened around my arm, and I raised my left hand, putting it on hers.

"I'm glad," I murmured.

Ryllae sucked in a breath, and her eyes widened. "I... I don't know what this means."

"Neither do I," I murmured.

I had my suspicions, but I couldn't be the one to bring them up. I wouldn't. There had been so many males in Ryllae's past that hurt her. I refused to let myself be added to that list.

Instead, I ran my thumb over the back of her hand as we locked eyes. My heart raced in my chest, and time slipped by as we stood there, looking into each other's souls.

Ryllae's words struck a chord within me that I never knew existed. Part of me wanted to move closer, to move my hand off hers. The other part wanted to leave.

I didn't gamble anymore. I knew better than most how dangerous it was.

So what was I doing, gambling with my emotions like this? I should have shoved them away deep within me, never to be seen again.

I didn't want to hurt Ryllae, but I didn't want to get hurt either.

I should have moved away, but I didn't.

Seconds that felt like hours ticked by before I blew out a low breath. "We should..."

Ryllae jolted, pulling her hand back and running it down her skirt. "Yes, the walk... Let's go."

I felt the ghost of her touch for hours.

"YOU'RE LEAVING." My twin sister didn't even turn around as she spoke, her back bent as she looked over the garden. Her hand hovered in the air as she scanned the garden. A sturdy brown woven basket sat beside her, filled with a bountiful late fall harvest. Multiple varieties of squash grew alongside hearty greens, flourishing despite the late season.

This was Aileana's touch on the earth. Wherever she went, it flourished.

Thanks to her, Maiela, Kysha, and Nonna would eat well when Ryllae and I were gone.

I nodded, shoving my hands in the pockets of my trousers. "We are."

Maiela put down her trowel and turned to look at me. The silver halo around her was bright as she met my eyes. Her black, curly hair was pulled up in a scarf, and a thick violet shawl was draped over her shoulders to ward off the chill in the air. "Tomorrow night."

It wasn't a question. Still, I dipped my head in reply.

My twin pushed herself to her feet, grabbing the cane I'd fashioned for her out of a gnarled stick I found in the forest. Her stomach was healed, but Nonna didn't want Maiela pushing herself too far.

Maiela gave me a knowing look. It was the kind of look that only older sisters knew how to give to their younger brothers. "I knew you would."

I opened my mouth, a reply on the tip of my tongue, but my twin sister sighed before I could give it voice. She crossed her arms, the fabric of her gray day dress crinkling. "I know."

"You know?" My brows furrowed. People thought *I* was cryptic. If that was true, then Maiela was truly mystifying. She spoke in riddles more often than not, her visions of the future far different from mine.

Maiela nodded wisely. "Allow me to save you the time, little brother. I love you too; Kysha and I will be safe, and, of course, we will watch over the witch." She leaned in, whispering, "Although you and I both know Elsbeth can look after herself."

"That we do." I chuckled. Xander's grandmother was nothing if not incredibly strong. Nonna was over four hundred years old, but she barely looked like she had lived sixty human years. "Mai, are you sure—"

"Stop." Maiela whacked me in the side with her cane, I winced. "Don't even say it."

I shouldn't have been surprised that my sister had already Seen our entire conversation. This was her gift from the gods.

I tilted my head. "What if—"

My twin huffed, leaning against her cane. "No 'what ifs.' Yes, I'm sure. No, you can't stay. Kysha and I will be fine. We don't need you to worry about us. We're both Mature, and we can take care of ourselves."

"Okay. I believe you." I raised a brow. "I will still Look for you on the silver planes. I'll never stop trying to keep you safe, Maiela."

"Good." Smiling, Maiela wrapped her arms around me and pulled me in for a hug. "I need you to promise me one thing, Daegal."

"Anything," I replied instantly.

"Promise me you will focus on yourself. Don't spread yourself too thin, and keep your magic stores high. Look into the future often. Do everything you can to stay safe." Maiela drew in a shuddering breath, her voice little more than a whisper. "You're all the family I have left."

"I think that's more than one thing," I murmured.

My twin sister huffed a laugh, punching me in the arm. "Just promise me."

Taking care to avoid touching her stomach, I squeezed Maiela tightly. "I promise." Pulling back, I pressed a kiss to her forehead. "Even though you already Saw this, I will remind you of my love."

We had shared a womb, and even though I lived on the run now— the law and I weren't exactly best friends—I loved Maiela. "I feel it is also my duty as your little brother and only remaining family member to remind you to stay off your feet and let others take care of you."

"I'll be fine," she huffed, waving her cane. "Don't worry about us here. You need to keep your head on your shoulders, little brother. The Death Elf princess... There is something about her. She's... odd."

"She's been through a lot, Mai," I said defensively. "You don't know half of it."

"And you do?" Maiela moved back, putting her hand on her hip. "I'm just asking you to be careful, Daegal."

I blinked. "Like you and your wife were careful, flaunting the Accompaniment Law for decades?"

"That's not the same thing." She huffed. "I'm just saying you should take your time. You haven't even known Ryllae for a full season."

"I know enough," I snapped. "Yes, she's odd, but she's so much more than that. Ryllae is brave. She's strong. You have *no* idea what happened to her in prison. None at all. Anyone would be a little strange after surviving an ordeal like that."

My chest heaved, and my fists curled at my side. Where did this protectiveness come from? I never considered myself an overly emotional male, and yet right now, I knew I would do anything to protect the Death Elf.

I didn't want anyone talking poorly about Ryllae. She didn't deserve that.

Maiela must have seen something in my face because her gaze softened, and she held up a hand. "I'm sorry. I didn't mean to upset you. Please, just... be careful, Daegal."

Blowing out a long breath, I nodded. "I will."

We moved on to safer topics of conversation, and a few minutes later, Maiela returned to the garden.

I wasn't ready to go inside just yet. My feet moved of their own accord, and I walked the perimeter of the cottage as I thought everything over.

A blond, horned female was at the forefront of my mind.

There were moments when Ryllae spoke words so wise that I questioned how such an incredible being ever ended up in front of me. Sometimes, when those sharp blue eyes looked at me, I felt... *seen*.

I'd never felt like that before in my life.

Ryllae was a puzzle, and I would be lying if I said she didn't intrigue me.

Very few things in the life of a Fortune Elf were ever surprises. Such was the burden of a Seer. I had long since given up hope of being surprised in my lifetime.

Until I met Ryllae.

From the moment we came upon this hidden daughter of Kydona, she surprised me. And that, more than anything else, piqued my interest.

Ryllae was broken, but that wasn't a surprise.

We were all broken.

Some were just more broken than others.

Broken people were common in High King Edgar's Ithenmyr.

If the future followed the paths I had Seen, no one in this world would be safe. From the plains of Ipotha to the fae rumored to live on the other side of the Indigo Ocean, we would all feel the effects of the coming darkness.

Eventually, when exhaustion plagued me, and my stomach rumbled, I returned to the cottage. As I packed and readied to leave, my mind wandered to Xander and Aileana.

I hoped they were okay.

The Guardians of the Sanctuary

XANDER

"Y ou won't marry me?" I stared at Aileana, my eyes wide as my stomach twisted into a tight knot. My head swam, and disbelief rooted itself within me.

Maybe this wasn't real? If it were a bad dream, we would probably wake up at Nonna's, and none of this had really happened. The Queen's Tower, the Sanctuary, Aileana's refusal... maybe it was all a nightmare.

Aileana shifted further away, dragging the sheet with her. I sucked in a breath at the assault of cold air on my bare chest.

No, this was real.

Which meant...

She said no. She turned down my proposal.

"Aileana," I breathed. "Why?"

The word held all of my pain and disbelief. It hung between us, and I stared at her, waiting for an answer.

She shook her head sorrowfully. Those emerald eyes widened, and a single tear slipped down her cheek. "I can't. I won't."

Can't. Won't.

The words echoed around in my mind.

Deep within me, the dragon *roared* in anguish.

I could barely form words.

I knew about Aileana's aversion to marriage. Gods, I even under-stood where it came from. I saw what Remington and Edgar did to her. I knew of the marks Aileana carried on her back.

The Red Shadow had terrorized Aileana for years. Remington had been a sick bastard, and he would have been a horrible husband. Aileana was supposed to marry him on that fateful day when she had escaped her tower.

Anyone would be averse to marriage after that.

But time had passed since then, and Remington was dead. Not only that, but I was *nothing* like him. The prince had been a horrible sadist who found pleasure in torturing others.

Marriage to him would have been a death sentence for Aileana.

I was not that male.

I loved Aileana with every single part of my soul. Causing her pain was the last thing I ever wanted.

Marriage seemed like the natural next step. The one that would solidify what we already had between us.

My mouth fell open, and I stared at her. "Why not?"

I couldn't find any other words to say. My entire body felt light, and my head spun as bile rose in my throat. I hadn't planned on asking Aileana to marry me. It had just... felt right.

If I had thought, even for a single second, that she would turn me down, I wouldn't have asked her.

But I had been sure she would say yes. That she, too, would see this as the next step for us.

I had made a mistake.

"Xander," Aileana said softly, her eyes filling with tears as she reached for my hand. I let her take it, my hand much larger than hers as she held it against her chest. Her gentle touch didn't soften the blow of her next words. "I won't marry you. Not now, not tomorrow, not in a century. Not ever."

"Sunshine, I—"

"I *can't*." Her voice was as hard as shards of ice. "Marriage is a cage, and I won't ever let anyone own me like that."

Did she really think I would put her in a cage?

I loved her.

My dragon, who had been silent until now, chose this moment to speak. *You've bonded with her. Isn't that enough?*

I thought it would be... but it's not, I replied.

Somehow, after Aileana and I accepted the mating bond, I had gotten it into my head that our fake marriage would one day be real. I dreamed about our wedding. Even now, I could see it in my mind's eye.

I imagined Aileana walking towards me in a white dress. She wore a ring of flowers around her loose, flowing red hair. In the dragon way, we would walk barefoot down a path of ash, and together, the two of us would show the world how committed we were to each other.

Marriage was a dream I had never dared acknowledge. Now that I had said it out loud, I knew how much it meant to me.

"For the gods' sake, Aileana," I said roughly, still trying to wrap my mind around her refusal, "so we don't get married today. In a year or two..."

"No." Aileana pulled her hand away from me. She shook her head and avoided my gaze. "No, Xander. You're not listening to me."

"I'm listening!" My hands clenched in the sheets, and I wrapped them around my fists. Our chests heaved, and the air hung like a heavy cloud around us.

"I'm listening," I repeated, my voice softer this time.

Her green eyes were as hard as steel when they met mine. "I can't do it. Not now. Not ever."

Not. Ever.

Her words echoed within me, and my heart fractured.

She wanted me to listen but refused to even find out how I felt about this.

"Just like that?" I asked quietly. "It's a no?"

"I can't get married," she confirmed. "I won't."

My head swam. Everything felt too hot. Like the walls were caving in on me. Even thinking was hard.

I closed my eyes, letting the darkness envelop me, and I drew in deep breath after deep breath. I kept doing it until I felt like I could speak without saying something I would regret.

Pulling my eyes open, I met Aileana's gaze.

"You won't marry me," I said, my voice flat.

Her eyes were pained, but she shook her head. "No."

Regret tinged her voice, but it didn't change her answer.

I nodded slowly. "Okay."

"Okay?" She raised a brow as if she couldn't believe it.

Honestly, I was having trouble believing it, too. I repeated the word, and it came out stronger this time. "If you don't want to marry me, I can't force you. I won't. I would *never* do that."

Aileana studied me. She raised a hand as though to touch mine before shaking her head softly and dropping her hand onto the mattress between us. "I know. That's why I love you."

She loved me. In the depths of my soul, I knew that to be the truth. The green and gold markings on our arms were visual proof of our love and commitment to one another.

Even now, as pain pulsed through the bond, love quickly followed behind it.

She loved me, but apparently, her love had limits.

Mine had none.

Aileana would bond with me, but she didn't love me enough to marry me. We'd made a lifelong commitment until we Faded, but it turned out that marriage was one step too far.

My heart raced, and I could barely hear over the roaring in my ears. My dragon twisted within me, and my control of the beast living beneath my skin thinned.

My feelings must have been showing on my face because Aileana scooted away from me. The air in the room thickened impossibly further, and all of a sudden, I was extremely aware that both of us were naked.

Aileana swallowed, and I averted my eyes. I couldn't look at her right now. Not like this.

Slipping out from under the covers, I found my tunic and trousers in a pile on the ground. Had it only been mere minutes ago that we'd been intimate?

Now, it felt like everything had changed.

She loved me, but she didn't want to marry me.

Inside, my dragon was alert. Watchful.

Why is this so important to you? the dragon asked. *She's yours.*

I don't know; I spat at him. *But it is.*

It was becoming more and more important by the second.

When I was young, before my father died and then my village was destroyed, I used to imagine what it would be like to have my own family. Before I was forced to grow up far too fast, I thought about having my own dragon younglings. Teaching them how to master the shift, just like how my father had taught me.

Then, my future had been stolen from me. First, my father had died. Then, High King Edgar murdered my kind.

My dreams died with my family and friends.

As the White Death, marriage had been the last thing on my mind.

But now, I had Aileana. With her, I had another chance at life. Another chance at dreams that I had long since given up on.

Another chance at marriage.

Though not nearly as strong as a mating bond, marriage was important to me.

I wanted Aileana to be mine in *every* single way.

The real problem, the one that was like a sword running through my chest, was that she didn't seem to care that it was important to me. She said no, and as far as she was concerned, that was the end of our discussion.

Running my hand through my hair, I gripped the wooden doorframe. Everything felt too tight. My tunic was too hot. The collar was too tight. The air wasn't right. I could barely breathe.

I needed to get out of here.

"Xander?" Aileana's voice was soft as she spoke from the bed. "Can we talk about this?"

Talk. She wanted to talk.

"I... I need some time, Aileana." My fingers tightened around the doorway, and the wood splintered beneath my touch.

She inhaled sharply. "Oh."

Her voice cracked, and my heart ached. I could feel her pain coming through the bond. It matched the one ripping my heart apart.

But talking wasn't an option right now. If we spoke about it now, the words that came from my mouth would not be kind. They wouldn't be helpful or gentle. They would be laced with anger, hurt, and pain. A reminder of the male I used to be.

A few months ago, I wouldn't have stopped before lashing out.

But now, I didn't want to cause Aileana any pain. Even though her words were like daggers into my heart, I wouldn't do anything to hurt her.

"I can't do this right now." Shaking my head, I walked down the stairs as fast as possible. My gaze caught on a black bundle on the table. "I'm going to go for a run. I need to clear my head."

"Okay," she whispered.

"Lock the door behind me, Aileana."

She appeared at the top of the stairs. The sheet trailed behind her as she rested a hand on the wall.

"I will." She drew her lip through her bottom teeth. "Xander, I... I love you."

"I love you too," I said gruffly.

Grabbing the corner of the black cloth, I pulled it aside. Inside was a short sword with a carved handle, along with a baldric, two sheaths, and a pair of daggers that matched the ones the Spirits had given Aileana. I picked the weapons up in turn, testing their weights. They moved well, the carved handles not impeding their movements at all.

Myhhena had come through.

Sliding the sheaths onto my body, I hid the daggers on my person. I missed the familiarity of my own weapons, but these were better than nothing.

With one last glance upstairs, I pushed open the door. Stretching my senses, I listened to the land around me.

The wind blew, and a few animals rustled through leaves, but that was it.

It was the middle of the day, and I was completely alone.

Satisfied that Aileana would be safe, I stepped out of the building and shut the door behind me. Moments later, the lock clicked into place. With a leap, I burst into a run. My feet pounded on the mossy cobblestones as Aileana's words echoed in my mind.

No.

I turned a corner, barely noticing the looming stone buildings, as my breath came in short bursts.

I won't.

My dragon stirred within me. He was watching. Waiting.

I tightened my control around him as I ran up a steep hill. Letting the dragon out right now was the worst thing I could do.

I can't.

Who knew such small sentences could be so painful? I thought I knew what pain was. How it felt. Dragonsbane was painful. Torture was worse. But it turned out that nothing was worse than the pain inflicted by one's bonded mate.

No.

That one tiny word was like a fire burning in my chest. Aileana's rejection seared through my veins, lodging itself in my heart until it was the only thing I felt.

No.

My feet pounded on the cobblestones, the rhythm filling the otherwise empty air as I ran and ran. I kept going until my muscles burned and my lungs tightened. Sweat beaded on my forehead, dripping down my back, and I ran.

I can't.

I ran until I could think of her words without pain.

I won't.

And then I ran some more.

No.

Eventually, I came to the large vine-covered pillars marking the entrance of the Sanctuary. The pillars loomed tall, stretching high into the trees. The air shimmered between them, and flecks of gold hovered.

My brows raised, and I looked to the left. The same shimmer

stretched as far as I could see, weaving around trees and bushes. A few more moments of investigation revealed the glimmering air also went in the other direction.

Stepping over a small stream near the pillars, I extended a hand and touched the glistening surface. The translucent surface was hard, like leather, but I could see the forest on the other side.

"Interesting," I murmured. Running a sweaty finger over the surface, I tried to push my hand through.

Nothing happened.

Frowning, I pulled back my hand. The air shimmered. I pushed again. Nothing. It didn't give.

Gathering my strength from deep within, I slammed my shoulder against the surface.

All I got in return was a searing pain that ran through my body. A flurry of curses escaped me.

"It won't work."

A male voice came from behind me, and I snarled as I yanked out the dagger strapped to my thigh. Thank the gods, I had the weapons on me. Tightening my grip on the hilt of the dagger, I turned around, keeping my back to the shimmering, hard surface.

Except...

I didn't see anyone. My eyes widened in surprise. There wasn't a single sign of life. The cobblestone streets were empty, the only movement coming from a single red leaf tumbling down the mossy cobblestones.

My shoulders tensed as I extended my senses.

Someone was there. I could feel them. I heard them. But where were they?

Memories of the Northern Kingdom flooded through me. Winged vampires with the ability to cloak themselves in shadows. Others could disappear into the air altogether. Fangs dripping with blood. The Prince of Darkness, whose reputation for draining humans, was whispered about in the darkest corners of taverns.

But the sun.

A quick glance at the sky told me I was being foolish. Vampires could not walk during the day.

Fire and sunlight were their two greatest enemies.

So, where did the voice come from?

"Down here," the voice said, answering my unspoken question.

Narrowing my eyes, I dropped my gaze. There wasn't anyone there. A strange glimmer caught my eye. The small, clear stream rippled before it *expanded*.

Water seeped onto the cobblestones, forming a large puddle beneath my feet. I tightened my grip on the dagger as the tang of magic in the air grew stronger. The water bubbled and churned until something rose from the water.

No.

Not something.

Someone.

A head emerged from the churning waters, followed swiftly by a torso and muscular arms. Pure liquid comprised the male's body, from the flowing hair on his head down to the armor that covered his chest and legs.

"Who are you?" I asked through clenched teeth.

The male bowed at the waist, the water rippling around him like a current. "I am Castien. He straightened, his blue eyes meeting mine. "Spirit of the Waters and a Guardian of the Sanctuary. At your service, sir."

I almost laughed. No one called me "sir".

My gaze swept over the warrior. He was calm, his stance wide as I studied him. His aura was not threatening, and I swiftly concluded that I could trust this warrior—at least as much as I trusted anyone who wasn't Aileana.

"My name is Xander."

A laugh burst out of Castien. It sounded like water rushing through a river. "Oh, I know. Everyone knows who you are. The dragon shifter mated to the Keeper of the Earth. It's quite the story."

She mated me, but she wouldn't marry me.

I was probably going to keep that to myself.

The Spirit of the Waters crossed his arms. His muscles rippled with movement as he stepped out of the puddle. When his feet were free from the water, the remaining liquid returned to the stream.

Tiny water droplets dripped from his body, landing on the cobblestones with small splashes as Castien studied me. "Is there something I can help you with, Xander?"

"Tell me about this." I gestured to the shimmering wall behind me with the dagger.

Just because I felt a modicum of trust toward this male didn't mean I would let my guard down.

I wasn't a fool, after all.

"It's a ward." Castien opened his palm. Golden ribbons slipped out of his hand, sliding through the air and slithering over the wall before disappearing into the shimmering mass. The surface shone brighter, and the wall thickened.

"Interesting." Reaching out, I ran a hand over the surface once more. "And it's secure?"

"Yes. It stretches around the entire border of the Sanctuary. My brothers and I are charged with the safety of this sacred place."

Raising a brow, I studied the wall again. "I see. Then I'm glad I ran into you."

"Oh?"

Mimicking the Spirit's position, I crossed my arms over my chest. I asked Castien about the various safety measures used to keep this place a secret, gathering as much information about this so-called Sanctuary as I could.

The raven got through the wards, so it wasn't as secure as it should have been. That was a problem. If Aileana and I were to stay here for any length of time, I needed to know what we were dealing with. That was the only way I could protect her.

And I would do anything to keep her safe.

She was mine.

Mine to care for. Mine to love. Mine to watch over. Married or not, I would not let her down.

Castien and I walked the perimeter of the large, abandoned city, and he showed me the wards. Built by godly magic, the wards hid the Sanctuary from prying eyes. Or at least, it was supposed to.

The Spirit of the Waters seemed genuinely surprised when I told him about the raven shifter that had broken the wards a few days ago. It seemed as though Myhhena had neglected to tell the Guardians of the Sanctuary about the breach.

I tucked that little piece of information in the back of my mind.

There was something about Myhhena that was making me nervous. She was hiding something. What was it?

When we returned to the vine-covered pillars, Castien assured me he would speak to his commanding officer about the raven. He promised to report his findings as soon as he found anything out.

The conversation with the Guardian of the Sanctuary was good for me. It helped clear my head, allowing me to think about what Aileana said.

She couldn't marry me. She wouldn't.

Something was stopping her.

Around halfway through walking the perimeter of the Sanctuary, during a lull in conversation with Castien, I realized something.

Aileana didn't want to marry me because some part of her was scared I would treat her in the same way that other Ithenmyrian wives were treated. Married females in Ithenmyr were seen as property. Males often treated their wives like their livestock, making it clear that they were good for nothing but breeding.

I knew they were wrong.

For all her vexing, irritating qualities, Aileana was incredible. She was my equal in every single way.

If she thought I would treat her like the other wives in Ithenmyr, I would prove her wrong.

When Aileana agreed to marry me, she would do so because she knew she was my equal in every way.

I strengthened my resolve as I walked back to our home. We were mates, and she had chosen me. She already saved me in more ways than one.

The least I could do was prove to her that I would be everything she needed as a husband.

Even if it took me months. Years. Decades.

No matter how long it took, I would prove to Aileana that I was worthy of being hers in every single way.

What is Blood?

RYLLAE

Drawing my cloak around me, I shivered despite the number of petticoats beneath my simple black dress. Before we left, the witch outfitted us with cloaks, gloves, and scarves. Even with all the garments, the bitter wind still found a way to nip at my skin. It was harsh, feeling like shards of ice against my skin, and no matter what I did, it felt like it was settling into my bones.

Autumn would be over before we knew it. Soon, winter would be here.

Daegal and I had already been walking for hours, having left Nonna's cottage right after dinner. We were going into the city, and he felt it would be safer at night. Matching heavy packs hung on our backs, filled with everything we could possibly need for our long trek. I'd slept earlier to prepare, but my muscles still ached and burned.

I imagined that would be the case for quite a while. After all, exercise wasn't exactly something I spent much time doing in Nightstone Prison.

Based on the pain in my thighs, I knew I was in for a long night. Some people might have taken this as a hint to exercise more.

I would not.

Life was too short and too full of pain for me to willingly go through the torture that some people called exercise.

I would simply accept the pain in my muscles as penance. Besides, it meant I was alive and free. I had survived everything Nightstone Prison had thrown at me. The soreness was a sign of my strength.

One day, I would use that strength to take down my father.

Blood-soaked thoughts of revenge were my companion as we hiked. Moonlight lit our path, guiding us toward the city of Thyr.

Daegal walked silently beside me, clutching a worn, gnarled stick as he led us through the thick forest. Earlier, he told me there was someone he needed to see in Thyr.

The silence between us wasn't awkward. Being alone with Daegal was nice, and the quiet gave me time to think. Time to look around and see the differences in the world around me.

Everything looked new. Different. I'd been in Nightstone Prison for so long that I'd forgotten what the forests were like. The damp, earthy smell of the earth. The crunch of leaves beneath our feet. Even the way the moonlight filtered through the canopy of leaves, illuminating our path.

Before my imprisonment, I didn't notice things like that. I spent most of my childhood training my magic and preparing for the day I would take over as queen.

Look where that got me.

Now, I noticed everything.

My life was split into two parts. Before Nightstone Prison, and after.

Before I went away, Earth Elves roamed the land. They worshiped Thelrena openly, and the land in Ithenmyr flourished. When I was young, Ithenmyr was filled with life. It stretched from the border of Eleyta down to the Southern Kingdom. Before I was in prison, flowers of all different colors filled the land. One couldn't take more than a few steps outside without encountering something beautiful.

When I was young, Ithenmyr was healthy. The land provided for everyone in abundance.

Memories of picnics taken with my nursemaid, of laughter and frolicking through fields of wildflowers, flashed before my eyes.

In that time before prison, there were a few moments when I knew what happiness was.

Now, happiness was a distant memory.

That, too, was part of my "before."

"Watch your step, Ryllae." Daegal's voice broke through my thoughts, and I lifted my skirts, stepping over a large fallen log just in time.

"Thank you," I murmured.

"Always." Daegal turned, continuing to lead us through the woods.

Thick, dense growth stretched as far as I could see. Briars, thorns, and vines were everywhere.

Before, the forests in Ithenmyr felt safe. They were a place where one could go to escape and relax.

Now, a thick sense of unease permeated the land. Leaves rustled ominously as we walked, and wolves howled in the distance. Shivers ran up my spine that had nothing to do with the bitter wind. Everything was darker.

Before I went to prison, the earth used to be happy. Now, it was in mourning.

The forest around the witch's cottage had been different. Touched by the Earth Elf, those forests were flourishing once more.

But out here? Near Thyr? The land was dying.

My father did this. He was the cause of all evil in this country. Stripping Ithenmyr of the Earth Elves and disturbing the balance in such a manner was the act of a male who had gone insane.

I was all too familiar with the dark shadows of madness. On bad days, it beckoned me like an old friend. On good ones, it cackled as I tried to ignore it.

The madness was always there. Always waiting. Always watching.

Before, I was not hovering on the brink of insanity. I might have even been happy. Before, I'd been ready to take my place and rule Ithenmyr as its queen.

Now? I wasn't sure I was fit to be anything. I was no longer a whole person.

Darkness existed inside me. Blood-soaked dreams of vengeance kept me going. Anger was my fuel. Happiness was a distant dream.

The only source of anything other than the bitterness that was my life came from the Fortune Elf walking in front of me.

Trust was growing between us.

Before, I would have been happy about that.

Now, it just confused me.

"We're almost there." Daegal stopped at the top of a small hill, adjusting his pack as he waited for me to catch up. He pointed to a looming wall in the distance. "Have you been to Thyr?"

"Once," I replied. "The year before I Matured, I came to Thyr to celebrate the Festival of the Seven."

Daegal hummed under his breath. "What do you think?"

From our position, we could see over the walls of the city. The moon shone brightly tonight, and I could make out the shadowy forms of the buildings that made up the city.

"I think that it's the same," I whispered.

The Fortune Elf shifted, his dark skin blending into the night as he studied me. "The city?"

"It hasn't changed at all." Shadowy figures with large, dark wings patrolled the walls. Their torches were beacons against the night sky. "How can it be the same? Why hasn't it changed?"

My voice cracked on the last word, and I turned away from the city, wiping a finger beneath my eyes. Treacherous tears threatened to make their way down my cheeks. I pushed my palms against my eyes and forced myself to take deep breaths.

I would *not* cry.

Instead, I allowed anger to bubble up within me.

Thyr was the same. The city hadn't changed. But I had.

The soldiers threw me into prison, and no one cared. People continued to live their lives while I was left to rot. Maiela told me that most people didn't even know I had ever existed.

My father wiped the memory of my life from the planet.

I breathed in and out as Daegal stood by silently. He was just... there.

His presence was a calming balm against the storm raging inside of me. When the tears were gone, and I was sure I wasn't going to fall into the beckoning pit of madness, I withdrew my hands from my eyes.

I found the Fortune Elf watching me carefully.

Daegal held out a hand as though to touch me before pulling it back and rubbing his neck. "I, uh... I'm going to look ahead and See what is coming. Keep watch?"

Nodding, I reached into the pocket of my dress and pulled out the dagger sheathed against my thigh. Saying that weapons were far from my favorite things would be an understatement.

I hated them.

Father had always insisted that I had no need for weapons, so my education never included anything to do with self-defense. And then my time in prison...

Suffice it to say that I knew what weapons could do and was not a fan.

Before we left the witch's cottage, I informed Daegal of this, but he still insisted on arming me.

The weight of the hilt felt unfamiliar in my hand as I turned it over slowly, watching the moonlight glint off the metal.

In front of me, Daegal's eyes turned silver. An intense longing filled me as the Fortune Elf's magic washed over him. I reached into that well of power within me, trying to draw up the red Death Elf magic that was my birthright, but nothing was there. A thick, black veil shrouded my empty pool of magic, covering everything save for a few whips of red ribbons floating in the air. When I tried to grab them, they seemed to laugh at me as though it was my fault I couldn't grab them. An absolute sense of wrongness filled me.

Pulling myself out of that place, I sighed. It was useless. Whatever my father had done to me was too complex. I could not undo it. Hopefully, the merfolk could help me because, at this point, it seemed as though they were my only chance at finding my magic again. I clung to that thin thread of hope because I was afraid I might fall into the darkness that lined my soul without it.

That was my greatest fear.

If I weren't careful, one day, the vengeance that fueled me would destroy me. I could feel it waiting inside of me, ready to pull me apart at the seams. But I couldn't give up.

Darkness or not, I would defeat my father and reclaim my throne.

He locked me in a cage, but I would not return the favor. A cage was far too good for him. He deserved to die a slow and painful death.

One day, I would return things to the way they were before. And hopefully, that would include killing my father and watching his precious red magic seep out of him before rejoining the earth.

I would rejoice at my father's death in the same way that he celebrated when he threw me into prison for two and a half centuries.

I was so lost in my vengeful thoughts that I didn't notice when Daegal's eyes returned to their regular shade of blue.

A branch snapped in two, and somewhere in the distance, a wolf howled. A screech rose from the city, cutting through the darkness, and a shiver ran down my spine.

There were so many noises.

Too many noises.

Daegal stepped toward me, his mouth pinched, and his brows furrowed. "Ryllae?"

Too much.

All of this was too much. My head pounded, a headache coming on out of nowhere, and I gasped, releasing my grip on the dagger. It slipped from my hand, tumbling towards the ground. Without thinking, I reached out and grabbed the blade.

A searing pain flashed through my palm as the metal cut my skin, and I cried out. My hand opened, and I released the blade as quickly as I'd grabbed it. It fell to the forest floor, forgotten, as I stared at my broken skin.

Blood dripped from my palm, a three-inch cut spanning the length of my hand.

"Gods-dammit," Daegal swore. Panic leaked into his voice as he stepped toward me. "Ryllae, close your fist."

I didn't move. Everything was frozen, and my eyes were glued to the wound on my hand. Blood poured out of it, and I trembled.

All those years in Nightstone Prison, I never once cut myself. The guards did unimaginable things to me, but I never bled. My courses had stopped the day I entered the prison, and I never had access to anything sharp.

Two hundred and fifty years, and I never once bled.

Even so, invisible scars lined my soul. At moments like this, when my blood dripped onto the grass beneath my feet, I realized just how heavy their weight was.

"Shit." Daegal darted forward, grabbing my hand before pulling a handkerchief out of his pocket.

I blinked, staring at him as he wrapped the white cloth tightly around my hand. Red coated my fingers and the scent of iron was strong.

The Fortune Elf knotted the cloth, squeezing my hand tightly. "Ryllae, you can't grab knives like that. You could bleed out in minutes if you aren't careful."

Bleakness filled me, and I danced even closer to the edge of madness. Everything felt heavy and dark and altogether too much.

Raising dead eyes, I met Daegal's gaze.

"What is blood?" My voice was quiet and monotone as I ran the fingers of my uninjured hand over the handkerchief.

"What are you saying, Ryllae?" Daegal reached out, taking my intact hand in his.

The motion, which would have frightened me from anyone else, infused warmth and... comfort into me.

That was new.

I inhaled, staring at the place where our flesh met. "Life is nothing if not fleeting. We're all going to die one day. None of us will have the pleasure of Fading in peace." I lifted a shoulder. "We're all going to bleed."

"What?" Daegal's brows furrowed, and he ran a thumb over my hand. "Ryllae—"

"There's no point in denying it." I sighed. "All of us will bleed. Death is our future."

The Fortune Elf shook his head. "No. I refuse to accept that, Ryllae. I've Seen what is to come. Death isn't in the cards. Not right now. Not for us."

Was he being truthful? Or perhaps he had just blinded himself to the fact that the line we walked was a dangerous one. Either way, I knew that death was always waiting in the wings for me. Calling me.

I was a Death Elf, and it was my inheritance.

The Earth Elf gave life, but I took it away.

Death had been with me from the very moment that I entered this world.

"It will be," I said bleakly. "Death is our future. It's kill or be killed, Daegal." My injured hand throbbed, and I sighed. "If my father ends up marrying the Southern Queen as you Saw, if they complete the blood pact, he'll be stronger than ever." I stared into Daegal's blue eyes. "You're signing your death warrant by being here with me."

A long moment passed as the Fortune Elf ran his thumb over the back of my hand. He appeared to mull over my words, his brows furrowed. "I've always known I would die," he began, his voice soft. "Everyone dies."

"I know," I whispered.

He nodded. "Did you know that Fortune Elves cannot see their death?"

That was news to me. "I didn't."

Still holding my hand, he stepped toward me. "It's a cruel twist of fate. One that I rebelled against for many years." Daegal raised a black brow, reaching up slowly toward me. "I'm going to touch your face, Ryllae. Is that okay?"

I nodded mutely. His hand cupped my cheek, and he moved closer as I exhaled softly. There was barely a foot separating us, and the air was thick. All I could do was stare at him.

Daegal whispered, "If I'm going to die, I think doing it alongside a beautiful princess sounds like a noble way to go."

I had no response to that. Everything slipped away as I focused on the Fortune Elf cupping my cheek. My heart beat rapidly in my chest, and deep within me, something flickered to life.

I pressed my cheek into Daegal's hand, and his calloused thumb brushed over the corner of my mouth. My lips opened, and my heart raced as I leaned closer. Mere inches separated us. Daegal's eyes were darker than before, watching me as though I was the most captivating thing in the world.

My tongue darted out, wetting my lips. "Daegal—"

Above us, an owl hooted.

The comfortable silence shattered, and I jolted.

Daegal sucked in a breath. He stepped back, taking his hand with him.

"The blood should be clotted," he murmured. "You should check it."

Peeling back the handkerchief, I glanced at my hand. He was right. The cut was no longer bleeding, but I retied the handkerchief, just in case. Mature elves healed faster than humans, but I didn't want to risk anything.

Bending, Daegal picked up my forgotten dagger and handed it to me. I took it—making sure I was holding the hilt this time—and slid it back into the sheath. "Thank you."

Pulling the hood of my cloak firmly over my horns, I started walking. At least then, we wouldn't have to confront what almost happened. Was he about to kiss me? Why didn't that scare me? Instead of unpacking those questions, I spoke over my shoulder. "We should go."

Within moments, Daegal caught up with me. Together, we walked in silence until we reached a section of the city wall shrouded in shadows.

"Hold on," he whispered. "I know a way to get into the city unnoticed. I'd rather not have to deal with any Winged Soldiers if we can help it."

On that, we were in agreement.

Daegal bent, running his hand over the stones until he appeared to find the one he was looking for. He pushed, and a faint grinding sound filled the air. The rocks shifted, revealing a tunnel running beneath the city wall. A short while later, the two of us emerged inside the city proper. Here, the moon was barely visible, the dim light it usually provided hidden by trees.

But we were inside the walls, and we were safe.

Daegal raised a brow, sweeping into a mock bow. "Welcome back to Thyr, Princess."

I didn't respond. I couldn't. It wasn't safe for me to talk in the city.

The Accompaniment Law was a slap in the face from my father. I couldn't speak in the city proper, let alone walk on my own.

"Ready?" he asked.

I nodded.

In reply, Daegal held out his hand. I stared at it for a moment before sliding my uninjured hand into his.

Remaining in the shadows, Daegal and I walked through Thyr. Whitewashed houses were stacked on top of each other, and the buildings were so close that they appeared to be moments away from falling on each other. The small cobblestone streets were filled with dubious-smelling liquid, and I side-stepped more than a few odorous puddles.

Daegal led me through the streets with the confidence of a male who had been here many times before. I walked silently beside him, squeezing his fingers tightly as I took in the sights. The streets were practically deserted at this late hour, but sounds of life came from the buildings.

Twice, we passed patrols of Winged Soldiers. Both times, they didn't give us more than a passing glance. I knew what they saw when they looked at us. Daegal was just another husband leading his silent, docile wife back home. We had false papers that said as much, but hopefully, no one would ask us to produce them.

Imagine what the soldiers would have done if they'd realized the princess of Ithenmyr was walking past them. They probably would have painted the streets of Thyr with my blood unless they chose to turn me over to my father.

Neither one of those options was particularly pleasing, in my opinion.

Keeping that in mind, I kept my head down and counted the cobblestones. We walked over a large stone bridge, the moonlight reflecting off the water before we turned down yet another tight road. Laughter, the chinking of glasses, and sounds of what was hopefully pleasure and not pain grew louder as we walked towards what appeared to be a tavern.

"We're here," Daegal murmured, his hand tightening around mine as we came to a stop in front of a worn wooden door. "The Opal Spoon."

Shabby wooden planks made up the outside of the structure, and the large grimy window that looked out onto the street reflected candlelight against the otherwise dark night.

The air stank of alcohol and urine, the bitter bite of the wind doing nothing to taper the unpleasant scent. It was very loud, and I fought the urge to press my hands against my ears.

Sighing, Daegal ran a hand through his curly black hair. "I should warn you, Princess, this visit might not go well. I've Seen two paths, and neither of them is particularly pleasant."

I wondered what Daegal would consider "not particularly pleasant."

Thanks to the Accompaniment Law, I couldn't speak. Instead, I raised a brow in a fashion that I hoped conveyed my question. *Is it safe?*

It must have worked because he squeezed my hand. "I would never have brought you into a situation if I thought it would be really dangerous."

I trusted him. If Daegal said it would be okay, I believed him. Swallowing, I nodded.

"All right," he murmured. "Here we go."

Daegal pushed open the door, and the sounds of merriment grew ten times louder. Flickering candles illuminated a dozen wooden tables filled with males and females alike. Their attention seemed to be equally split between alcohol and seeking pleasure. More than one person glanced up as we entered, their glazed eyes sliding over us slowly before they returned to their previous activities.

Females wearing what I could only describe as scraps of fabric bustled about, serving copious amounts of alcohol. The occasional moan came from the rooms upstairs, underlying the sounds of revelry. They didn't bother me at all. People lived their lives to the fullest, finding pleasure wherever possible.

The only females in Ithenmyr who weren't bound by the Accompaniment Law were those who worked in taverns and brothels. This wasn't because they were valued. On the contrary, the only thing my father hated more than a female was one whose body was used by others.

It was painfully ironic, considering his addiction to using the opposite sex for pleasure.

I shuddered, forcing thoughts of my father out of my mind. That was the last thing I needed to deal with tonight.

Daegal tucked my hand into his elbow, leading me toward the large bar that ran across the back of the establishment. A clean-shaven human male with shaggy brown hair was tending the bar. His tunic sleeves were rolled up to show off his chiseled, tattooed forearms, and he wiped down the counter. Six empty stools rested on this side of the bar, and a female elf with opaque navy blue wings sat in the seventh, nursing what appeared to be a mug of ale.

When we were halfway across the room, the bartender looked up. A flash of recognition passed through the human's brown eyes, and he frowned. His voice was sharp, and suspicion leaked into it as he said, "Daegal."

The air thickened, and I looked between the two males. The lines of their faces were drawn as they glared at each other.

A warning bell rang inside me, but it was too late. We were here.

By now, Daegal and I had reached the wooden bar.

The Fortune Elf cleared his throat. "Finn."

The human scowled at us both. An awkward moment passed, and I shifted, rubbing the handkerchief wrapped around my injured hand.

"What do you want?" the bartender asked coolly.

Daegal's hand remained tight around mine, but his voice was the epitome of calmness when he asked, "Can we have two ales?"

The bartender eyed us warily before sliding two full cups our way. Daegal paid for the beverages. I held the cup up, eyeing the frothy liquid warily. I would have preferred a cup of tea, but this tavern did not seem to be the type of place that would serve those types of drinks.

"Here goes nothing." Raising the cup to my lips, I sipped the foamy liquid. A bitter taste filled my mouth before leaving a warming trail down to my stomach.

Beside me, Daegal lifted his stein to his lips. His arm rested behind me, the weight a gentle reminder of his presence. A rumble of male appreciation escaped him, and his throat bobbed as he drank. And drank.

He finished his drink in one gulp.

On the other hand, I took my time. Who knew the next time we would be in a tavern? After this, we were heading to the Indigo Ocean.

Once our cups were empty, Daegal reached into his pocket. The arm behind me tensed, and I stiffened.

When the bartender stood in front of us once more, Daegal cleared his throat. "Finn, I have something to tell you—"

"Don't." The bartender held up a hand, interrupting Daegal. He shook his head, a vein ticking in his jaw. "Not. Here."

Finn's brows furrowed, and he clenched a cup so tightly I thought it might break.

"So be it." Daegal sighed as an air of resignation radiated off him. "Where would you like to talk?"

"In the back," Finn replied gruffly. He looked me over with shrewd eyes. "Who is she?"

Daegal swung a protective arm around me, drawing me against his side. His touch, which would not be welcome if it came from anyone else, was exactly what I needed at that moment. "This is Ryllae."

Before coming into the city, we had decided that using my name would be unlikely to cause us problems. After all, most people in Ithenmyr didn't even know I was still alive, let alone that I had ever existed. As far as history was concerned, Remington was the king's only child.

My father's disdain for me was definitely mutual.

"Ryllae." Finn's tone was flat. "Is she coming too?"

"Yes," Daegal said firmly. "Where I go, she goes."

His words went deep into my soul, twisting together and warming my core from the inside out.

That *thing* between us grew even stronger, and I pressed myself against Daegal's side. He slipped his arm from around my waist, shifting it to rest above my shoulders.

"All right," Finn said gruffly. "Follow me."

The bartender turned, walking into the back. A tight hallway led into a small storeroom filled with bottles and jars. Half a dozen barrels were stacked on the floor, and the scent of alcohol was stronger than before.

Crossing his arms, Finn glared at Daegal. "I know what you came to say."

The Fortune Elf's brows rose. "Oh?"

"It's about Josephine, isn't it?" the bartender asked through clenched teeth.

Daegal stiffened, and the air thickened in the small room. I didn't know who Josephine was, but evidently, both the males did.

An eternity seemed to pass before Daegal let out a ragged sigh. "I... did you... we sent a letter... did you get it?"

A rough, angry laugh came from the bartender. "A letter." Finn shook his head, clenching his fists. "Yes, gods-dammit. I got your letter. The one where you said my sister *died* while on a cursed excursion. It was sparse on details and barely a page long." The human seethed and vitriol laced his words.

I took a step back. Jars rattled as I bumped into the shelves, but I didn't take my eyes off the bartender. I might not have been able to handle weapons well, but experience taught me never to turn my back on people when they were angry.

"That's why I'm here," Daegal said softly as he reached into his pocket. The bartender inhaled sharply but didn't say anything as Daegal pulled out his fist and extended his hand. A silver locket lay in the middle of his palm, a delicate chain dangling off the side of his hand. "You deserve to know what—"

"Jo deserves to be alive," Finn snapped. "How dare you, of all people, tell me what I deserve? You basically killed her."

"I did not—"

"If Jo hadn't gone with you, she would still be alive. I told her you were trouble. She assured me you were fine. She said you were reformed and that you weren't gambling with other people's lives anymore."

"I—"

"No!" Finn yelled, turning red. "Jo was wrong. She trusted you and Xander, and look where she ended up. Dead and buried without even a proper blessing from a priestess."

"We gave her a proper burial," Daegal whispered. His face was paler than I had ever seen, and he clenched his fists at his side. "Finn, she wouldn't have wanted—"

The bartender's fist snapped out, connecting with Daegal's nose with a vicious snap. I gasped, raising my hands in front of my face and pushing myself against the shelf as Daegal stumbled back, pressing a hand to his nose and cursing.

Finn sneered. "Don't tell me what my sister would have wanted. I knew her far better than you ever did."

Daegal didn't respond. He didn't fight back. He just stood there as blood dripped from his nose onto the floor. My heart pounded in my chest, but neither of the males moved.

Was this what he had Seen? I wondered what the other possible outcome was. Could it have been worse than a bloody nose?

"I won't fight you, Finn," Daegal said after a moment. "Not now, not ever."

Somewhere in the tavern, someone began singing. Instead of relieving the tension in the small room, it only made things worse.

The air was so thick I could barely breathe. My lungs were tight, and my heart raced as violence simmered.

The first song ended, and another began. This one was louder than the first, a chorus that had the patrons singing at the top of their lungs.

"Damn you, Daegal," Finn snarled, his fists clenched at his side as his nostrils flared. "Can't you see I need to fight you?"

"It won't bring her back," the Fortune Elf said quietly. "Nothing will."

Silence fell in the storeroom, and time seemed to still as the moment stretched for eternity.

My heart thudded, and I clutched the shelf behind me, waiting.

The bartender took a shuddering breath, unclenching his fists as he stumbled back. A thick plume of dust filled the air, and the anger melted off his face, giving way to absolute anguish.

This was a male in pain.

His chest heaved, and he stared at us both.

"Just... just go," Finn said. "Get out of here. For Josephine's sake, I'll give you an hour before I call the Winged Soldiers. Not a minute more."

Daegal took my arm, holding me close to him.

"I'm sorry, Finn," the Fortune Elf said. "For everything."

"Go!" the human yelled.

My breath caught in my throat, and my heart pounded as Daegal led me out of the tavern. We slipped out the back door, and he pressed a handkerchief to his bloody nose as we hurried through the shadowy streets.

After we crossed through the wall again, leaving Thyr behind, Daegal broke his silence.

"Finn... he is well-meaning, but he's hurt. His sister... she shouldn't have died." Daegal shook his head. "It happened just after we found Aileana."

"What happened?"

"The Winged Soldiers were hunting Aileana and killed Jo as a warning."

A shudder ran through me.

"I'm sorry," I whispered.

He nodded, and we fell into a comfortable silence, the soft rustling sound of leaves beneath our feet adding to the symphony of the night insects chirping around us. Soon, talking would have been impossible, anyway. It was all I could do to follow behind Daegal, lifting one foot after the other.

By the time the sun pushed back the last tendrils of darkness, I could barely keep my eyes open.

"We need to stop," Daegal said, glancing at the sky. I stumbled along behind him, leaning against a tree. "With your father's soldiers crawling through the forests, it won't be safe to travel during the day. We have to make camp."

His eyes turned silver, and I waited, this time without my dagger, until the magic cleared from his eyes.

"There's a cavern a short walk from here. We'll be able to spend the day there."

It didn't take long to reach the cavern, which was just a small hole in the side of a hill. At least it was hidden and dry and out of the way. Sleep was calling my name. At that point, I probably would have slept anywhere.

Daegal dropped his pack first, sliding down against the rocky wall of the cavern and rubbing a hand over his eyes.

"You should sleep, Princess," he said, pulling out his dagger and turning the hilt over in his hands. "I'll keep watch and wake you in the afternoon so we can switch before continuing to the Indigo Coast."

A yawn slipped out of me. Perhaps I had underestimated the value of exercise because Daegal didn't seem nearly as tired as I was.

Maybe if we succeeded in our quest, I would consider adding some type of fitness regime to my routine. Keeping my clothes on in case a quick escape was needed, I rested on my stomach and placed my head on my hands. I studied Daegal through hooded eyes. Sadness radiated from him, and the air around him was heavy.

For some reason, that bothered me.

"I'm sorry about Josephine," I whispered.

Daegal put down the dagger as a heavy sigh escaped him. "Thank you, Ryllae. I hoped that Finn would be... better, but I can't hold his reaction against him. I probably would have acted the same way if it was Maiela."

"Do you have any other family?" I asked, another yawn slipping out of me.

A long moment passed before Daegal shook his head. "Not anymore."

His words echoed around the cavern. Tinged with loss and pain, they burrowed inside of me.

Not anymore.

Maybe Daegal was as broken as I was.

He leaned his head back against the wall, slipping his eyes half shut. Clearly, he did not want to answer any other questions right now. "Go to sleep, Ryllae. We have a long journey ahead of us."

I did.

No One Will Survive

AILEANA

The door slammed shut, and my body tightened. Xander was back. I knew it without even walking down the stairs.

Hours had passed since he left to go on his run.

Hours since I turned down his marriage proposal.

After he left, I showered, brushed, and braided my hair. Then, I sat on the bed and worked on banishing the greenery I'd created during our... time together. It served as a good distraction from his question.

While ribbons of magic slipped from my palms, eager to do my bidding, dozens of scenarios flitted through my mind as I wondered how Xander would react when he returned.

Would he still be angry? Would he yell at me? Throw something? Was the dragon going to come out?

Or maybe he would be so hurt and broken by my reply that he shut me out again. Of all the possibilities, that was the scenario that kindled fear in my heart.

I didn't think I could handle that. Going back to having Xander be cold and aloof would be akin to torture now that I knew what it felt like to be loved and cherished.

Running my fingers over my mating mark, I sucked in a deep breath. We needed to talk, but I didn't want to hurt him more than I already had.

I was under no false impressions about the harshness of my words. I felt his pain through the bond when I turned him down.

Hurting the male I loved was like driving daggers into my own flesh.

Why did he think I'd ever say yes? How could he believe marriage was an option? It was the very thing I had run from all those months ago.

"Aileana?" Xander's deep voice came from the first floor, and I swallowed.

This is it.

Pushing myself out of bed, I walked over to the landing. "I'm up here."

Xander looked up, and instantly, my heart melted. He was the picture of masculinity... and he was *mine*. Sometimes, I still had trouble believing that. Sweat covered him from head to toe, but somehow, he made even that look good.

"Come on down, Sunshine." He yanked his tunic over his head. I blatantly ogled his bare chest as he said, "We need to talk."

Four simple words had never sounded so ominous.

This was it.

Drawing in a deep breath, I nodded slowly. Disappearing into the bedroom, I emerged a moment later with a fresh tunic. If we were going to talk, the least he could do was cover up his distracting chest. Bundling up the fabric, I threw it down the stairs. "Catch."

The tunic sailed through the air, and Xander reached out and grabbed it as I took the steps one step at a time. I could have gone faster, but something in me wanted to stretch this out a bit longer. If Xander was going to be yell at me, then I would enjoy these last few moments of peace.

I hoped that whatever came next, we would get through it.

When we had solidified the mating bond, we called ourselves equals. Partners in everything.

Hopefully, that extended to disagreements like this.

As I walked, my magic beat a steady tune in my veins. Ever since I woke from our eight-day slumber, it was stronger than ever. Louder. More insistent. Before, my magic had been a mere hum. A sound I could tune out if I wanted to. Now it practically demanded release. It bubbled up within me, needing to come out.

My fingers ran down the railing as I walked down the stairs, and I released some of the magic bubbling in my veins. A flash of green preceded the trail of bright purple flowers that erupted in my wake.

Xander chuckled softly. "You are amazing, Aileana."

My core twisted. Surely, that meant he understood where I was coming from... right?

Even though I loved him, I couldn't marry him.

As soon as I stepped off the last step, Xander tilted his head. The ghost of a smile danced on his lips, and I felt a fraction more at ease.

He was smiling. That was good. It *had* to be good.

"Come. Sit." Xander pulled out a chair, and I slipped into it. I expected him to sit on the other side of the table, but his warm hands landed on my shoulders instead.

He rubbed, his large hands pressing out knots that had somehow gathered in my shoulders while he was gone. For a long moment, neither of us spoke. The air grew thick with nervous energy, and every passing moment felt longer than the last.

The only sound was the occasional mewl that escaped me as Xander worked on my shoulders and upper back. I melted into Xander's firm touch. His familiar scent washed over me, filling my senses as we just... were.

Together.

Bonded mates. Earth Elf and dragon shifter. Lovers.

But not husband and wife.

Eventually, when I could bear the silence no longer, I drew in a deep breath. "Xander, can we—"

"I have to say something—" he said at the exact same time.

We both laughed, the sound breaking some of the tension.

Xander bent, pulling aside my hair before his lips brushed the back of my neck. I sucked in a breath at the gentleness of his touch.

He should have been yelling at me and telling me how much I hurt him.

This would have been the moment for him to remind me he was the White Death. He should have used this moment to remind me he was a male feared across the Four Kingdoms, and I had dared refuse him.

I knew what he was capable of, this mate of mine. The anger that ran through his veins. The dragon that resided beneath his skin.

He should have been angry, but instead, he was being kind.

My heart wrenched. I did not merit kindness. Not right now.

Xander's fingers trailed the back of my neck as he whispered, "Go ahead, Aileana. I'm listening."

Drawing a deep breath, I leaned my head against him. Letting his warmth seep into me, I closed my eyes. "Elyxander, I love you."

"I love you, too," he whispered a mere moment later, his palms rubbing out my shoulders once more. "Aileana, I'm sorry about what happened before."

Wait.

Why was he apologizing to me? He had nothing to apologize for. This was all me. *I* was the problem.

The scars on my back were nothing compared to the ones on my soul.

"Don't be," I murmured. "I'm the one who should be sorry. The one who *is* sorry. I'm sorry that our conversation ended the way it did. I'm sorry about my response." His hands stilled, and I twisted in the chair, meeting his gaze. "I'm sorry for causing you pain."

Pushing myself up, I reached out and clutched Xander's hands. "I can't marry you, Xander, but you are *mine,* and I will never leave you."

Without him, I was nothing.

I hoped I would never find out what it was like to live without him. Having an argument like this was bad enough. But being separated?

I was fairly certain I would break in half.

Xander squeezed my hands, and the air thickened. Barely a foot separated us, and our breaths came in synchrony as every moment felt longer than the last.

He was the first to move. Xander raised a hand, pulling down the sleeve of my green tunic. Tracing my mating mark, he murmured, "You think I'm going to leave you?"

"I..."

"I will *never* leave you," he said gruffly as an animalistic growl rose in his chest. "You are *mine.*"

Warmth ran through me at his possessive words, and I shuddered as my core twisted.

"I'm yours," I murmured.

My words seemed to placate him. He continued to run his hand over my mating mark before placing a kiss on my forehead.

"What did you want to talk about?" I asked.

Xander's fingers stilled for a moment before they continued their path on my arm. "The proposal." I stiffened, but he continued. "I shouldn't have asked you like that. Aileana, I should have known... I'm sorry."

"No, I—"

"Shhh," he said in an authoritative tone. "Not yet. I'm still talking."

Part of me wanted to talk back and remind him I wasn't a weak female who was incapable of making decisions for myself. The other part of me, the one that could happily stare at his well-defined muscles and sculpted chest for hours, was delighted to play the simpering female and make my core twist in delight when faced with my bossy mate's antics.

That part of me really liked it when Xander took control. When Xander took charge, it made me feel warm. Protected. Loved.

The simpering female won out. Instead of talking back, I groaned and slammed my lips shut.

Xander chuckled darkly. "I shouldn't have asked you today. Things are too fresh. I understand that. With the raven and everything else..."

"It's already been a long week." I finished his sentence.

He nodded, pulling me to him. I pressed my head against Xander's chest, and his hand moved to rub my back. "I need you to know, Aileana, that I will never stop loving you. I will never stop wanting you. You are mine. Because of that, I will always be ready. Wanting. Waiting. One day, when you are ready, I will be standing at the altar, waiting for you."

This time, the groan made it past my lips. This infuriating, insufferable, vexing male. He did not know how to take a hint, did he? I had been more than clear about my stance on marriage.

I sighed, trying to pull back. "Xander, I can't—"

"Don't," he whispered, putting his finger on my mouth. "I know what you're going to say. But... think about it. For me. I'm not expecting you to say yes today or even in a year from now. I'm just asking that you consider it."

How could I say no and crush his spirit more than I already had?

"Alright," I murmured after a moment, keeping my voice low. "I'll think about it. I—"

A loud knock came from the door, and a cold front swept over me as Xander stepped away. Giving me a warning glance that told me to stay back, he marched toward the door and wrenched it open.

Tiaesti's small, leafy form danced in the doorway as she hopped from one foot to the other. The Spirit didn't seem to be capable of remaining still. "Myhhena has sent me. She says it's urgent."

"What's happened?" Xander asked.

Tiaesti's eyes widened, and she swallowed. "It's the shifter. The raven has awoken, and it is demanding to speak to the hidden daughter of Thelrena."

THE RAVEN SAT in a golden cage. Its black wings were outstretched as it glared at us through the gilded bars. The room, if it could be called that, was a circular courtyard covered in vines and ivy.

There was no roof, but ancient trees lined the sides, spreading their branches overhead. Beneath our feet, packed dirt made up the floor. The scents of falling leaves and bitter traces of the coming winter were in the air. If the cold wind and goosebumps on my arms were any sign, it would be here soon.

Armed as though he was going to war war, Xander stood before me, his legs spread wide as he glared at the captive shifter. Power and strength radiated from him. Clenching his fists at his sides, he appeared every bit the warrior I knew him to be.

Twin daggers rested against my thighs, ready to be used at a moment's notice. Kydona only knew how much safer I felt when my blades were within reach.

On my other side, Myhhena stood beside a male entirely made of water. Xander had greeted him like an old friend when we'd entered the courtyard. They met earlier while Xander was out on his run. The two Spirits—one of the Waters and one of the Woods—were discussing the raven with animated gestures in low tones.

From the bits and pieces of their conversation I overheard, it sounded like Myhhena had neglected to inform the other Spirits of the raven shifter's presence until now.

Why would she do that?

Maybe she should have just let Xander kill it.

Now, the raven paced the interior of the cage. I couldn't help but stare at it. Matted dried blood was on its black feathers, and it looked like a creature of death.

I shuddered at the sight, and the bird's black, beady eyes met mine. I shrank beneath its malicious glare. For a moment, it felt as though I was staring at death itself. Standing before such a hateful creature, my magic strained to be released. I shoved it down, trying to listen to Myhhena and Castien.

"... sent from High King Edgar," Myhhena growled. "How did it get through your defenses?"

The male made of water shook his head. "I don't know, Eldest. I have sent three of my males to search the wards for cracks. So far, we haven't found anything. Perhaps if you had told us about this earlier, we could have solved the problem by now."

My thoughts exactly.

"The situation is complicated," the Spirit of the Woods said.

"How complicated can it be?" Xander snapped, crossing his arms in front of his chest. "This is a massive problem. What good are your wards if creatures can just fly in?"

His words echoed around the courtyard, and both the Spirits turned to look at him.

Myhhena raised a brow. "You dare question me about this, dragon? We took you in when you were dying from poison. I didn't have to help you, but I did."

A growl rose within me. How dare she speak to Xander like that?

The male in question moved towards Myhhena, his skin rippling as the dragon made its presence known. "For your *help*, we are grateful."

Tension simmered in the air as Xander glared at Myhhena. She opened her mouth as though to speak, but Xander shook his head. "If you cannot guarantee our safety, what good is this place? Aileana requires rest and a place to learn how to control her magic."

"And she can do that here," Myhhena said forcefully.

"Can she?"

"Yes," Myhhena snapped. She crossed her leafy arms and turned back to the Spirit of the Waters. "Triple-check all the wards. You know the history—"

"Don't you lecture me on history!" Castien growled. My eyes widened as the watery male grew, his liquid form expanding until he towered over Myhhena. "My people have been guarding the Sanctuary since the gods created this sacred place."

Myhhena flicked a leafy wrist, and the wind blew. Leaves swirled, and dark clouds drew near as the air crackled with violent energy. "You would dare shout at—"

A rough, maniacal laugh cut Myhhena off. Everyone instantly stopped, shifting their attention to the raven shifter.

"You lot are all idiots," the bird hissed. "Complete and utter fools. You argue over trivial matters such as wards?" The raven laughed again, the malicious, cruel sound sending shivers down my spine. "Don't you understand?"

"Understand what?" Xander snarled. Moving toward the cage, he grabbed the gold bars and glared at the shifter. "What are you talking about?"

The air in the room shifted as the bird cackled. A bitter taste filled the air as it became as thick as soup, and a heaviness descended upon us.

The raven shook its head, growing larger and larger. A flash of white light filled the courtyard. When it cleared, the raven was gone. My mouth fell open, and my heart thudded as I took a stumbling step back.

Xander and Castien cursed, and my dragon shifter moved back. The twang of metal filled the air as Xander came to stand in front of me as though to block the cage from my sight.

Withdrawing my dagger, I came to stand *beside* my mate.

I was perfectly capable of defending myself. Maybe Xander needed a little reminder of that. My fingers twitched around the hilt of my dagger, and the smallest of smiles danced on my lips as I remembered the first time we met.

"Aileana," Xander growled my name in warning.

"I'm not moving," I snapped. "Get over it."

Thank the gods he did not push the issue.

The cage, which had appeared large enough before, now appeared painfully small. A tawny male was crouched where the raven had been. His back was bent, and his arms wrapped around his legs. His knees pushed against the golden bars.

I squinted. There was a red mark on his chest, but I couldn't make it out.

The raven shifter laughed, and the mark *moved*. Moments later, a blinding red light reminiscent of Death Elf magic flashed from the shifter's chest.

167

My eyes widened, and my hand slickened around the hilt of my dagger.

What is happening?

Xander snarled beside me, and the hairs on the back of my neck rose as the red light dimmed.

"No one will survive High King Edgar's wrath." The raven shifter turned, his black eyes widening as he glared at each of us. "No one in Ithenmyr is safe. Not the daughters of Kydona and Thelrena. Not this so-called 'Sanctuary'. Not a single person."

Myhhena gasped. "You dare threaten Thelrena's own?"

The shifter laughed. "You should be more concerned about what is happening next, *Spirit*. Once the illustrious High King marries the Southern Queen and they participate in the blood pact, you will all perish. There will be none left in Ithenmyr who can stand against him."

The shifter's warning fell like shards of ice all around us, and an ominous silence filled the courtyard.

I shivered, rubbing at the goosebumps on my arm as chills ran down my spine. When I could take the silence no longer, I asked, "Why would you tell us this?"

I tried to take a step forward, but Xander's arm shot out in front of me.

"Don't even think about it, Aileana," he said through clenched teeth. "Something is wrong here."

As if I wasn't aware of that fact. Wrongness tainted the air, lingering like a faint scent of sulfur. It was a weight pressing down on my lungs, making it hard to breathe as a sense of foreboding filled the air.

A macabre chuckle came from the raven.

He turned his eyes back to me, and I shuddered. His eyes weren't black anymore. Flashes of red ran through pupils that shouldn't have been familiar but somehow were.

OF ASH AND IVY

Dread surged through my veins, and the thrum of my magic grew stronger as my stomach churned. My mouth dried, and my throat tightened as I stared at the raven.

Those eyes.

I knew those eyes.

"Who are you?" I breathed.

This was so incredibly wrong. Alarm bells rang in my head, and my breath came faster and faster.

"Why, my pet, don't you know me?" The male in the cage laughed, and my breath caught in my throat.

The shifter's voice changed. Deeper now than before, it was edged with scorn, greed, and pure *evil*.

It was the voice of my gods-damned nightmares.

This was all the confirmation we needed.

The Crimson King was still alive, and somehow, he was speaking through the shifter.

Beside me, Xander snarled. He shoved me back against one of the pillars, and this time, I didn't fight him. My hands clenched at my sides, the cool white marble of the pillar soothing beneath my fingers.

How was this possible?

A whimper escaped me as I tried to form words. "But... you... the tower?"

I wished I could have said that courage ran through my veins at that moment. But even my magic seemed to hide at the sound of the king's voice.

"It was a valiant attempt to kill me," High King Edgar said through the shifter. "Luckily, I survived."

That was not the word I would have chosen.

Beside me, Xander snarled. He ran towards the cage, his dagger raised. Before he could reach the shifter, Myhhena held out her hand. A gust of wind and leaves erupted from her palm, and Xander slammed into the wall of her magic.

"We *do not* kill in this place!" Myhhena yelled.

Xander roared, struggling against the Spirit's magic. From the corner of my eye, I saw the Spirit of the Waters saying something to Myhhena, but my entire being was focused on the shifter in front of me.

"I *will* find you, my dear." Flecks of red filled the shifter's eyes, and violence radiated off him. "You belong to me."

"No!" I screamed.

He cackled. "This isn't a warning. This is a vow. For the scars your bonded mate gave me, I will kill him. When I marry Queen Sanja on the Winter Solstice, there will be no stopping me. My power will be unmatched, and you will be *mine*."

Bile rose in my throat, and Xander *roared*. He stopped fighting the wall of wind, instead turning towards the Spirit of the Woods.

"You will let me pass," he snarled, brandishing his sword. "Let me end this bastard here and now."

"You will *not*. It is forbidden." Myhhena's face twisted in a way I had never seen before, and her voice deepened. "This is my land, dragon. Not yours."

For one long, eternal second, Xander and Myhhena glared at each other. Violence pulsed in the air, and my magic begged to be released.

Then, a strangled cry came from the shifter.

Everything seemed to come to a halting stop. My heart. The wind. Even the rustling of leaves.

The only remaining sound was the eerie wail coming from the shifter.

I turned, my hand on my throat, as I stared at the shifter. The whites of his eyes were completely gone, leaving two bright red orbs staring back at me.

Myhhena hissed, and Castien shouted, but I could barely hear them over the roaring in my ears.

The shifter shuddered, and a choked sound came from his throat. My legs trembled, and my mouth fell open as a red sphere of magic tinged with black erupted from the mark on the raven shifter's chest.

The male screamed, his eyes black once more as they opened wide. He shuddered, blood spilling from the cavity in his chest before his body convulsed. His head slammed into the bottom of the cage, a sickening *crack* filling the air, and he screamed one last time. Blood poured out of the wound, and bile rose in my throat as red sparks erupted out of the place where his chest used to be.

A sphere of red magic shot toward the sky, and then there was silence.

Sickening, horrifying, heavy silence. No one spoke. No one moved.

Crimson blood dripped from the cage, pooling on the floor.

Red.

It always came down to red.

"Oh my gods," I moaned as blackness edged my vision. My entire body shook, and the roaring in my ears grew louder.

Xander turned, shouting at me, but I couldn't understand his words.

Every part of me was focused on those drops of blood.

The earth called to me frantically, and this time, I didn't fight it.

Green ribbons escaped my outstretched hands as I fell to the ground on all fours. Casting my dagger to the side, I gasped for breath through aching lungs. My fingers dug into the dirt, the soil cool beneath my touch, and I succumbed to the call of the earth.

The moment I gave in to the urgent summons of my magic, everything else faded away. The bleeding corpse of the raven shifter, High

King Edgar's warning, even Xander's concern. Nothing else mattered except for the *life* flooding my consciousness.

The ground rumbled as I sent my magic through it. *Keeper of the Earth*, it cried out. Its voice echoed through me, and I stretched my awareness further.

There was no death here. No blood.

Here, there was only *life*.

The earth needed me, and I was coming to realize that I needed it, too.

The Protectress of the Woods has returned to us.

In reply, I sent more and more magic into the earth. My ribbons danced over the first tendrils of frost seeping into the ground. They wound around the minuscule insects and larger animals, preparing themselves for the coming winter.

With every passing moment, the earth around me flourished.

And I...

I was still aware. Alert.

I was still myself.

The green marks on my hands glowed as ribbons slid out of my fingers. Xander crouched before me, but I couldn't move. My mind was connected with the life around me. Hundreds of voices filled my mind at once.

Many were familiar—the elks that brought us to the Sanctuary cried out, their voices mingling with the trees, plants, and insects living near Nonna's cottage.

But there were other voices.

I didn't know them yet, but I would.

Keeper of the Earth. Old and new, fresh and ancient voices all called out my name simultaneously.

My lips twitched.

I don't know you yet, I said to them. *But I will. Each and every one of you, I will know.*

The promise echoed through me, and my skin tingled. I stretched my awareness further as the magic in my veins flooded out of me, pulsing into the earth.

I pushed my magic into the earth until all the traces of fear within me were gone. And then I kept going.

Eventually, a feeling of *rightness* filled me. A sense of peace pulsed through my body as the earth poured reassurances into me.

No matter what High King Edgar threw our way, we would be okay. I wasn't alone any longer. I was out of my tower. My Maturation had begun. Not only that, but I had a bonded mate who loved me more than anything.

That feeling of rightness expanded, and I poured more magic into the land. Surprisingly, when I checked the pool of my power, I found it nearly full.

Beneath my touch, new life grew in Ithenmyr. Trees burst out of the autumnal ground. Roots expanded. Flowers erupted out of the earth. Late-season crops grew stronger. They would yield more than ever before as they flourished beneath my touch.

The earth hummed contentedly, and even now, I was still myself.

My body was my own.

I curled my toes, relishing the feeling of being connected to the earth but still in control. My magic thrummed in my veins, the beat of my power like a steady drum as it rushed through my blood, but I wasn't lost.

If anything, I felt stronger than before. It was as though the earth was feeding off my fear, taking it away and giving me strength in its place.

The earth bounced with the energy of a young child beneath my fingertips.

You are ours, Protectress of the Woods.

When my magic no longer felt like it was going to explode out of my veins, I breathed out a sigh of relief. The earth still sang beneath my touch, and somewhere outside of my body, I heard Xander talking to the Spirits of the Woods and Waters. Their voices were muffled, but they were there.

My bonded mate's presence was calming in a way that nothing else was.

As I remained connected to the earth, I thought about what the raven shifter said. High King Edgar was going to wed the Southern Queen. They would complete the blood pact, whatever that meant, and he would become stronger.

Not only that, but he knew where we were...

A cold thread of fear threatened to erupt within me, but I shook my head. I would not let it take over. That was what High King Edgar wanted.

In sending the raven shifter, he probably hoped to intimidate us.

He could not have been more wrong.

I wasn't intimidated.

The Crimson King made a mistake in coming after us, and it would cost him his life.

Thanks to him, I now had a goal. An objective.And perhaps most importantly, a timeline.

Winter Solstice was coming.

Finding the fiery bond within me, I wrapped my hands around it. With a final goodbye to the earth, I followed the warmth of my mate back to my body.

I had a king to kill.

Practicing Magic and an Unexpected Arrival

XANDER

A few minutes ago
I glared at Myhhena as rage pulsed through me like an all-consuming fire. Crouched at my feet on all fours, Aileana gripped the soil as green ribbons slipped from her hands.

I would protect her because no one else was up to the task.

The Spirit of the Woods stood firm against a pillar, her mossy eyes never leaving mine as I tightened my grip around the hilt of my sword. Behind me, rippling water came from the cadre of four Spirits of the Waters who had appeared moments after the shifter died.

He should never have been here.

"This is all your fault," I snapped. "If you had let me kill the damned raven, he wouldn't have had the chance to deliver its message."

"You are mistaken, dragon." Myhhena didn't even blink. "I had nothing to do with this. Thelrena herself created the laws that govern the Sanctuary. They were created to protect us all."

"Damn you and your laws," I snarled. Inside me, the dragon writhed, fighting to get out. I shoved it down, gesturing to Aileana as she fed her magic into the earth. "They did nothing to protect my mate. You should have let me kill the shifter days ago." My blood boiled, and fire burned beneath my skin.

"Xander," Aileana said softly from the floor.

My gaze flickered over to her, and I crouched, placing my hand on her back. "Yes?"

She looked up at me, the green sheen of her skin dimming as her emerald eyes flashed. "There's so much blood." She shuddered. "It always comes down to blood."

"I know," I whispered.

I hated that I knew precisely what Aileana meant. Once again, the Crimson King injected himself into our lives.

But this time, there was someone else to blame.

Myhhena was at fault here. The Spirit of the Woods was hiding something. I wasn't sure what, but I could feel it in my core.

Kill her, the dragon urged.

That sounds like an excellent idea.

Pushing myself to my feet, I stepped around Aileana and prowled toward Myhhena. "Give me one good reason why I shouldn't destroy you right now before I take my bonded mate and leave."

We would find the last piece of the map and figure out how to defeat the Crimson King ourselves. This place was no safe haven.

"You speak of destroying me?" Myhhena scoffed. "What will you do if you leave? How will you protect the Keeper of the Earth? She hasn't finished Maturing yet."

"I can protect my mate," I growled. "You dare insinuate otherwise? This is not my fault. This was *your* fault. You are the reason there is blood staining this place. You should have let me kill the shifter days ago."

I didn't even know if I could kill a Spirit of the Woods, but I would give it my best shot. Even if doing so doomed me for eternity, it was a small price to pay.

The encounter with the raven had shaken Aileana. Someone needed to pay for that.

Myhhena seemed like the perfect option. Besides, she had hated me from the moment she first saw me.

"Enough!" Myhhena grew before my eyes. "Watch your words, dragon. I have allowed you to speak to me in such a fashion out of respect for your bonded mate, but that only goes so far."

I snarled in response, my skin rippling.

"Spilling blood in a sacred place such as the Sanctuary is against all the laws of this land," the Spirit of the Woods said. "To do so will result in retribution from the gods themselves."

"That's a damn flimsy excuse, and you know it," I snapped.

Myhhena sucked in a breath, her twiggy face twitching. "Flimsy or not, it is the truth."

I stared at her. Castien edged away from the other Spirits.

"Does she speak the truth??" I asked of the male made of water.

Castien nodded slowly. "She does. The laws of the Sanctuary are ancient and complex."

I cursed.

Would I really be willing to break the laws of this place?

Even as I asked myself the question, I knew the answer. Of course, I would. For Aileana, I would do anything.

"Xander, it's okay." Aileana's voice came from behind me, and I turned as she put her hand on my arm. Her red hair was in disarray, and her face was flushed, but other than that, she seemed fine.

"It's not okay," I growled. "This place is no sanctuary. We have to be on our guard, Aileana. Always."

To my surprise, she didn't fight back or argue. She simply bent and picked up her dagger where it lay discarded on the floor. Slipping it into the sheath, she said, "I agree."

A splash came from in front of me, and the four Spirits of the Waters disappeared, taking the body of the shifter with them. Myhhena and Castien stood nearby, watching us carefully.

Aileana *agreed* with me.

Good. That should make things easier.

The problem was that there was no safe place for Aileana. There wasn't a single place in this cursed country where she would be completely free. Not while High King Edgar still lived.

But if we were going to stay here, things needed to change.

Stepping towards the Spirits, I raised a brow. "*If* Aileana and I are going to remain here, I need some assurances."

Myhhena raised her brow. "What do you need from us, dragon?"

Not relinquishing my grip on my sword, I told them exactly what I needed.

The Spirit of the Woods pursed her lips, tapping her hand on her thigh before nodding. "It can be done."

Myhhena opened her hands, and golden ribbons slipped from her palms. They swirled in the air, forming a shimmering oval. The magic crackled in the air, and Aileana stepped closer to me, sliding her hand into mine as a familiar face appeared in the air in front of us.

"Greetings, young ones," Nonna said. Her reflection was hazy, her face rippling as though it was in water, but it was her. My chest warmed at the sight. "I was wondering when we would hear from you."

My lips tilted up. "Hello, Nonna. How are you?"

She tilted her head. "I'm fine."

"What about the others?" Aileana asked.

My grandmother smiled. "Kysha and Maiela are right here." The two females' voices rose in a chorus of hellos, and their heads appeared in the ripples behind Nonna.

Brows furrowed, I asked, "Where are Daegal and Ryllae?"

Pursing her lips, Nonna frowned. "They're not here."

"What?"

Maiela's voice popped up. "They left days ago for the Indigo Coast. They're trying to—"

Her voice trailed off, and the oval shuddered.

I glanced at Myhhena, whose mossy eyes were wide as she shook her head. "Dark magic is interfering with my spell. I can't hold it for much longer."

Castien stepped forward. "I will find the Fortune Elf and deliver a message for you after I check the wards."

I grunted my thanks.

Nonna's face reappeared. "Be safe, young ones. I love you."

I replied moments before the oval shattered into a thousand golden pieces, scattering like ash on the wind.

Myhhena cleared her throat. "Both of you should go home. Eat. Rest. We will check the wards."

That was literally the least she could do. I opened my mouth to reply, but before I could speak, Aileana yawned. Yelling at Myhhena would have to wait.

Wrapping my arms around my bonded mate, I carried her back to our stone house. She fell asleep within moments.

Later, Castien came and reported that the wards were stable. When I was satisfied that it would be safe enough if I went to sleep, I barricaded the door before heading upstairs.

I stayed awake long into the night, haunted by the things I could have done differently.

All night long, the sword remained by my side.

The Sanctuary was not safe.

A LOUD SCREECH pulled me out of my sleep, and my eyes flew open. A roaring sound filled my ears. Something was wrong.

Without a second thought, I flung myself upward into a sitting position. Instinctively, my eyes flew to my side to check on my bonded mate.

A roar escaped me, and my fists clenched. Fire rose to the surface, bubbling below my skin, and fear pulsing through my body.

The bed was empty.

A rumpled quilt was all that remained beside me. Aileana was gone. Placing my hand on her side, my fingers came away cold.

"Dammit," I growled. Far more colorful curses escaped me as I jumped out of bed, pulling on my trousers. I did not scent fear, but that didn't mean something terrible hadn't happened.

Extending my senses, I tried to find my mate. Last night, she barely made it into bed before falling asleep. After she connected to the earth yesterday, I expected her to sleep for an entire day.

Evidently, I was wrong.

My ears perked up. A rustling sound came from outside, followed by hushed whispers.

What is that? My dragon stirred within me as fear pulsed through my body.

Something is wrong, I told it. *Aileana is gone.*

Find her, he ordered.

I would do just that. After yesterday's tumultuous events, I would never be able to let Aileana out of my sight again.

Yanking my tunic on from where it lay in a crumpled heap on the floor, I grabbed my sword. Stumbling over the vines that Aileana had grown in her sleep, I ran out of the room.

"Aileana?" I called out as I took the stairs three at a time.

No response.

My heart raced, and my breaths came in shallow gasps as panic set in my bones.

This couldn't be happening.

What if the Crimson King had come back?

Vaulting over the lower half of the stairs, I landed in a crouch as another shout came from outside.

"Hold on, Aileana, I'm coming!" Rushing around the table, I grabbed my scabbard, hurriedly strapping it around my waist. It needed to be tightened, but I didn't care.

Shoving the door with my shoulder, I sucked in a breath as a frigid, wintery wind slammed into me. The brilliant sun illuminated the abandoned city, but my bonded mate was nowhere in sight.

Another scream came from behind the house. I sprinted down the mossy path, the trees providing a leafy canopy as I raced toward the sound of Aileana's distress.

A feminine shout came from the forest, and a snarl ripped from my chest.

I would kill whoever dared touch my mate.

The dragon waited beneath my skin, ready if I needed to shift. Racing around a corner, my feet skidded on a frost-covered cobblestone. I teetered, nearly toppling to one side but never stopped running.

There.

I spotted a flash of red hair in the thick pine trees up ahead.

Running into the forest, I reached within myself and tugged desperately on the bond. If I could get her attention, at least she would know I was coming.

I needed Aileana to know I would always come for her.

There came no response. Panic pounded in my veins, red tinged my vision, and I rushed through the forest. Vaulting over fallen logs and under low-hanging branches, I hurried towards the spot where I'd seen her hair.

"Aileana!" I roared her name.

Nothing.

Panic surged through me.

I ducked beneath a pine tree, and finally, honey and earth filled my nose.

She was close. I could sense her, and my mating mark tingled on my arm.

A rabbit ran in front of me, and I followed Aileana's scent over a small stream.

Moments later, a high-pitched laugh came from nearby.

Instantly, I knew it belonged to my mate.

Spinning, I turned as Aileana appeared from behind a thick pine tree. She panted, putting her hands on her knees. A forest green cloak fluttered around her as she grinned at me.

Grinned. As if nothing was wrong. As though she hadn't woken me with her screams and was now running through the woods.

"Morning, dragon boy," Aileana said. Her tone was light and playful. Nothing like it should have been, given the circumstances. Someone was chasing her, and she was... smiling?

Who smiled while they were being chased?

For that matter, where was the person chasing my mate?

"Aileana, what's going on?" I snarled, tightening my grip on the hilt of my sword.

She raised a brow, looking around. "Why, I'm practicing."

"Practicing?" Primal fear still coursed through my body, but slowly, it shifted. Fear for her safety gave way to confusion. My brows furrowed as I lowered my sword until the tip rested against the dirt. "What do you mean, 'practicing'? Your scream woke me up."

The infuriating female I loved lifted a shoulder. "I asked Tiaesti and her friend Erwen to help me practice." Aileana's tone made it clear she thought her explanation was more than adequate.

It was absolutely, unequivocally, not adequate.

I blew out a low breath, tamping down the snarl rising within me. It took every ounce of patience I had in me not to scream at my mate.

My voice was surprisingly cool and did not betray the rage within my veins as I asked, "What in the name of all the gods are you talking about?"

"I told you we were practicing."

My brows furrowed. "*What* are you practicing? Why were you running?" My voice grew louder, and a frustrated huff escaped me. "For Kydona's sake, I thought someone was chasing you!"

I thought someone had taken you again.

The words didn't make it out of my lips, but Aileana must have felt something through the bond because she paused. She stepped towards me, placing her hand on my chest.

"Xander, I didn't... I'm sorry." She sighed. "I didn't mean to frighten you. Tiaesti and Erwen are helping me with my magic, that's all. They are chasing me, it's true, but only so that I can practice using my magic."

It was only then that I looked at my mate. Beneath her cloak, she wore a pair of forest-green leggings and a matching tunic. Her red hair was braided tightly against her head, and her cheeks were flushed, highlighting the grin on her face. A wreath of flowers rested on her head, and her bare feet dug into the mossy soil.

She looked... happy.

"I see," I growled. "You were... practicing."

She nodded. "Exactly."

Reaching down, I captured Aileana's much smaller wrist in my hand. Running a thumb over the swirling green tattoos on her hand, I pulled her close.

Lowering my lips until they hovered above hers, I murmured, "And why wasn't I invited to practice with you?"

Those emerald eyes widened. "I thought you would want to rest," she whispered. Biting her lip, her heart sped up as uncertainty pulsed through our bond. "I didn't think—"

"Sunshine, when will you learn?" I interrupted Aileana, letting go of her wrist to slide my hand behind her neck. Keeping my eyes locked on hers, I pressed a hard kiss against her mouth. "I will *always* want to be right by your side. Whether it's today or five hundred years from now, I want to be with you. It's always you, Aileana. It's *only* you."

She drew in a deep breath. Behind us, leaves rustled, and a brisk wind blew past.

"I want you by my side, too." Aileana rose on her tiptoes, clutching the fabric of my tunic as she pressed herself against me. Her deep desire pounded through the bond, and my anger melted away as her lips claimed mine.

The world faded away as we kissed, our mouths clashing as I poured all my fears and worries into this moment. Aileana took everything I had and handed it back to me. Our hearts beat to the same rhythm, and I released my grip on my sword, pulling Aileana tight against me. My tongue swept into her mouth, and she moaned.

My skin sparked everywhere she touched me, and time melted away as we kissed.

A high-pitched shriek filtered through the trees.

"Don't look, Erwen! The Protectress of the Woods is kissing the dragon!"

Tiny laughs that sounded like leaves falling from the trees came from behind us, and I stiffened.

Breaking our kiss, Aileana stepped back. A soft chuckle escaped her as she turned in my arms, her back pressed against my chest. Amusement splashed through our bond, and I wrapped my arms around my mate as a familiar Spirit of the Woods walked out of the trees backward.

"Hello, Tiaesti," Aileana said, clearly trying to tamp down a chuckle.

Even I found the situation rather humorous. Tiaesti was hunched over as though she was trying to hide something. Her bark-like dress rose above her knees as she asked, "Is it safe to look, Protectress?"

"Yes, Tiaesti. You can look now. It's safe, I promise."

The small Spirit of the Woods turned, unfurling herself and revealing an even smaller bundle of leaves and twigs that had been hiding within her arms. This one was barely two feet tall, and she was made primarily of bark.

The smaller Spirit's mud-brown eyes were wide as she stared at us. It was definitely a "she". Like Tiaesti, this Spirit's body was made of the woods. Unlike Myhhena's propensity to do away with all notions of clothing, this newest Spirit wore a tiny dress made of bark. Long tendrils of grass extended from her head all the way to her hips.

"Dra-dra-dragon," the tiny Spirit stammered, pointing a twiggy finger at me.

Sighing, I ran a hand through my hair. What was it with these Spirits of the Woods? They all harbored something against me. It was exhausting.

A memory slammed into me so hard I nearly lost my breath.

I clutched Saena's hand, her black hair flying out of her braid as we followed our mother down the worn path toward the village. "Momma, why can't I go to school with Lian?"

Stopping in the middle of the dirt path, Momma crouched. I tugged Saena to a stop, and the two of us stood in front of our mother.

Momma sighed, her lips tilted into a small smile, but it didn't reach her eyes. "Lian is different from us, sweetheart."

I furrowed my brows. "Because he is an elf?"

Lian had small black horns and green wings that sprouted from his back. One day, we would fly together. But he wasn't old enough to fly yet.

Momma blew out a long breath, and something I didn't understand flashed across her face. "Do you remember what I told you about our village, Elyxander?"

Drawing my lip through my teeth, I shuffled my feet. "Yes, Momma, I remember. We are different from other people in the Four Kingdoms. Dragon shifters weren't made to be with others."

"You're a good boy, Elyxander." A soft, sad smile crossed Momma's lips. Ever since Pa died last year, she only seemed to have those smiles. "Why do dragon shifters live separately from others?"

I thought about her question, but before I could speak, Saena jumped beside me. Her blue and white bracelet jingled on her wrist, and she shook it around, exclaiming, "Because dragons are the best! They're powerful and full of fire."

She let go of my hand and laughed as she ran in circles around us. Her small dress, black like her hair, billowed behind her.

"Your sister is right, Elyxander." Momma let out a long breath. "For many centuries, dragon shifters have paid the price for the sins of the draken. There are those in the Four Kingdoms who don't take the time to get to know others. They fear what might happen if we give into the beasts living beneath our skin."

Draken were dragons who lost control. All they wanted were riches, and they were willing to do anything to get it.

"But we aren't draken, Momma." *I frowned. "They're wrong."*

"*I know, Elyxander." She ran her hand down my face, cupping my cheek softly. "But still, they fear us. The best thing we can do is show them kindness and hope they will one day change their opinions of us."*

Kindness.

My mother's words echoed in my mind as I lowered myself to the small Spirit's level. So many things had changed. My mother was dead. My village was destroyed. Saena was gone.

But I was still here.

This bridge could still be mended.

I had to try. If not for the past, then for the future. For my bonded mate. For me.

And perhaps most importantly, for the future children I hoped to have with Aileana.

Holding out a hand, I tilted my head and met the tiny Spirit's gaze. "While it's true that I am a dragon shifter, I actually prefer Xander."

My hand rested in the air between us, and Tiaesti sucked in a breath. She poked the smaller Spirit in the side. "Erwen, he wants to shake your hand."

In response, the young Spirit stared at me, her mouth opening and closing as I waited.

And waited.

Every second seemed to drag on as my hand rested between us. My heart beat in my chest, and Aileana and Tiaesti were statues as we all waited for the smallest Spirit of the Woods to move.

I was about to withdraw my hand when the tiny Spirit inched forward. Her brown eyes were filled with trepidation as she extended a twiggy hand. I didn't move, barely breathing, as she placed her hand in mine. Her fingers were extraordinarily small, and her entire hand was as big as two of my fingers.

Gently—far more gently than I'd ever moved before—I shook the Spirit's hand with the care of someone holding a newborn as I tried to make myself as small as possible. "It's a pleasure to meet you..."

My voice trailed off, and I looked at the Spirit patiently.

The small two-foot creature watched me with enormous eyes, her free hand fluttering at her side.

Tiaesti poked the other Spirit in the back. "Your name," she hissed.

"I'm sorry!" the smallest Spirit of the Woods gasped. "My name is Erwen Liliana Morcan. I am the first offshoot of Farryn, the Second Spirit of the Woods."

Offshoot. I wondered if that meant daughter.

I coughed. "That is quite the title. Is it alright if I call you Erwen?"

A long moment passed, and I could feel the child-like Spirit's assessing gaze.

Eventually, she nodded. "It is."

"Thank you, Erwen." I released her hand, making a show of bowing in her direction.

A sparkling laugh that sounded like rustling leaves filled the air, and my lips twitched. Even Aileana chuckled, and the taste of sugary amusement came through the bond.

Erwen turned to Tiaesti, exclaiming, "The dragon shifter doesn't seem scary at all! I don't know what you were talking about."

Tiaesti grumbled under her breath, mentioning something about danger and fire as I pushed myself to my feet. Huffing a quiet laugh, I pulled Aileana against my side.

In the way that only children seemed capable of doing, the two Spirits looked at each other and laughed. Seemingly content to ignore us now that they had determined I was safe, the Spirits of the Woods darted into the nearby trees and started a game of chase.

I bent, picking up my discarded sword and sliding it into the scabbard on my hip. "Now that we are alone once more, Aileana, could you explain exactly what you were practicing?"

"Magic." She blinked. "Didn't I say that?"

This female. The glimmer in her eye and the twitch of her lips made me think she was being deliberately obtuse.

I groaned, running my hand through my hair and pulling it into a knot at the back of my neck. "Sunshine, I got that. I didn't exactly think you were practicing a high level of mathematics out here with those chil —young Spirits."

They weren't young, at least Tiaesti wasn't, but they acted like children.

A shriek of laughter came from the woods nearby as if in response to my thoughts.

A pang went through me. The two young Spirits reminded me so much of Saena. My little sister had been the night to my day. She had long black hair, wide blue eyes the color of clear ice, and skin as pale as the moon. Her dragon was blue, smaller than mine, but still powerful.

For a time, we were inseparable.

But now, she was gone.

"Xander?" Aileana's voice pulled me back to the present. She stared at me, her hand running over our mating mark. "What's wrong?"

"Just the call of the past." I shook my head, sighing. Saena was gone. But Aileana was not. She was right here in front of me, and she was mine. "Tell me, Sunshine, what kind of magic were you doing that required being chased through the woods?"

Aileana shifted from one foot to the other, pulling her lip through her bottom teeth. "I thought that maybe if I was scared, it might help... speed things up."

"Speed things up?" Raising a brow, I put my hands on her shoulders. "What in Kydona's name are you talking about?"

She held up a tattooed hand. "Maturing."

Understanding engulfed me.

"I see." Sliding my hands down her shoulders, I laced our fingers together. "Aileana, I don't really think that's how this works."

Maturing wasn't something that could be forced. At least, I didn't think so. When I Matured, it came on fast. My dragon emerged when I was three, but I didn't Mature until much later in life.

Every being Matured differently. For dragons, it occurred overnight, whereas elves had three stages to their Maturation.

Aileana groaned, tugging her hands out of mine. "I know that, Xander. At least, I was fairly certain. But I needed to try. You heard the raven."

"I *hate* that gods-damned raven," I growled. "If he weren't already dead, I would kill him for the way he spoke to you."

In a way, the raven's message was well-timed. It was a good reminder that we couldn't sit on our laurels playing house in this so-called Sanctuary.

Staying here wouldn't prevent the Crimson King from marrying the Southern Queen. He was already the most powerful Death Elf in all of Ithenmyr. Ryllae herself had confirmed that if her father completed the blood pact, he would be practically unstoppable.

The Four Kingdoms would fall under his red fist.

"I know you would," Aileana whispered. "But he mentioned the Winter Solstice. I can smell the winter in the air, and it'll be here sooner than we think. I just... I don't want to waste a single second of it."

"I understand, Sunshine. You want to be strong and train."

"I do. I can't sit around and wait for him to attack. It's not in my nature."

I knew it wasn't. That was one of the many reasons I loved her.

A burst of childish laughter came from the forest. Tiaesti and Erwen returned, their bellies shaking as they shared a private joke.

"You're right," I said.

"I am?" She looked surprised.

I nodded. "You should train. Why don't you show me what you were working on? Preferably without the screaming."

Aileana grinned, a spark entering her eyes as she stepped back. I leaned against the trunk of a nearby tree, crossing my arms. The bark was rough against my back, the orange and red leaves nearly translucent as the sunlight shone through them. A cool breeze brushed up against me, and a deer ran through the forest as Aileana prepared herself. A few feet away, the two Spirits of the Woods whispered excitedly to each other.

Extending her hands at her sides, Aileana turned her palms towards the sky. She met my gaze and grinned. "Watch this."

As if I could tear my eyes away from her for even a moment.

"I am." I would watch her every second of every day if I could. It didn't matter what she was doing or where we were.

She was my world.

Aileana's lips twitched, and she blew me a kiss before shutting her eyes. Moments later, a vibrant green glow erupted from her skin. Dozens of ribbons, some thick and others thin, flew out of her outstretched palms. They swirled in the air as though they were dancing to a tune only they could hear. The magic twisted around my mate in a cyclone of her own making. Soon, I could barely see her through the thick curtain of magic that separated her from the world.

Tiaesti and Erwen watched nearby, their hands clutched together.

"Incredible," Erwen breathed. "The Protectress is so powerful."

Tiaesti shushed the smaller Spirit as Aileana closed her palms.

For a moment, everything was still. The wind stopped howling. The leaves stopped crinkling. Even the birds, who had been singing just a few moments before, ceased their songs. The ribbons of magic hovered in the air, as though they were frozen in time.

Aileana exhaled. The sound echoed through the otherwise silent forest, and the ribbons dashed toward the ground in unison. Moving like a multitude of snakes, they slithered over the fallen leaves and pine needles, spreading out in all different directions. One by one, they disappeared from sight as they sank into the earth.

When the last ribbon was gone, a weighted silence fell upon us.

Standing in the middle of the clearing, Aileana had a small, knowing smile on her face. The Spirits held their hands in front of them, and their excitement was palpable as they watched my mate.

My heart pounded, and my skin prickled as the air grew heavier.

Then I heard it.

Thunder rumbled in the distance, and the world around us shifted. The trees grew, the vibrant color of their leaves intensified, and the bark behind my back shifted. Beneath our feet, purple flowers erupted, covering the entire forest floor. Birds sang once more, and their voices were louder than before. The sun seemed to shine brighter, and the air was warmer.

My bonded mate grinned.

A smile crept onto my face, and I took a step forward. "Aileana, that was—"

A branch cracked nearby, and I tensed. Drawing my sword, I turned toward the source of the sound.

"Is that—" Tiaesti asked, her voice filled with awe.

"Are you seeing this, Tiaesti?" Erwen squealed.

"I am."

"The Eldest needs to see this!" Seconds later, Erwen disappeared in a puff of autumn leaves.

My heart pounded as a sense of being watched filled me. The hairs on the back of my neck prickled, and I backed up until Aileana was right behind me.

Leaves crunched, and twigs cracked as a sense of eager anticipation filled the forest.

Widening my stance, I prepared to protect my mate.

The boughs of the largest pine tree shook, and the air seemed to quiver.

The first thing I saw were its legs. Four massive legs ended in thick hooves that shook the forest floor as the creature walked.

I swallowed.

I may need you, I told the dragon.

It nodded.

"Do you see that?" Aileana whispered from behind me.

"Yes, I most definitely do."

The pine tree shook, and then the creature revealed itself.

It was a deer... or at least, I thought it was. This creature was not alive, not in the truest sense of the term. It had bark for a body, and its eyes were bright green, mossy orbs. Standing at more than double the size of a regular woodland creature, its long brown antlers were sharpened into razor-sharp points.

The creature was a warrior through and through.

The deer raised its head, meeting my gaze. For a moment, there was nothing else. We met, beast to beast. Male to male. I let my dragon rise to the surface as fire ran through my veins. My muscles tightened, and an animalistic growl rumbled through me.

"She. Is. Mine," I snarled at the deer.

As though it understood my words, it bowed its head ever so slightly.

Behind me, Aileana scoffed. "Overprotective alpha male. I can take care of myself."

She pushed against my arm, but I didn't let her pass. Not now. "Be still," I ordered.

"You can't tell me what to do," she snapped.

"Right now, I can."

She huffed. "Xander—"

The wind swirled all around us, cutting Aileana off. Seconds later, Myhhena and Erwen stood before us. The Spirit of the Woods stared at the creature, an expression of awe on her face before she turned to Aileana.

Myhhena asked, "You... Did you do this?"

"I think so?" Aileana's eyes widened. "I was sending out my magic into the earth when the deer appeared."

Myhhena turned toward the creature, dropping to her knees and prostrating herself on the ground. "Greetings, Kethryllian, Guardian of the Appointed Ones."

Kydona has No Place Here

DAEGAL

Thick, dark clouds covered the sky, and the smell of rain hung heavily in the damp air. Lightning sparked in the distance, and I knew the storm would be here before the day was done. Seven days had passed since we left Thyr for the Indigo Coast. There had been a few close calls with Winged Soldiers, but I Saw them with enough time to hide. Once we were far enough from Thyr that we no longer ran into the soldiers, we switched to traveling during the day. It was safer, and we could move faster.

The first few days, Ryllae and I barely spoke. She was quiet, lost in the past, and I kept replaying the encounter with Finn. Even though it hadn't gone well, I would still do it again. Finn had deserved to hear about his sister's death from someone who witnessed it.

I didn't blame him for his reaction. I knew all too well the horrors of losing one's family. It tore a hole through your heart, one that couldn't be easily mended.

The difference between Finn and me was that the only person I could blame for my mother's death was myself.

A branch snapped behind me, and I jolted out of my thoughts. Glancing over my shoulder, I glimpsed Ryllae's dark crimson aura as it pulsed around her. Her blond hair hung in a long braid down her back, and she drew her cloak around herself.

"What did you See this morning?" she asked, offering me a handful of autumnal berries from the handkerchief in her palm.

"There is a storm coming," I said softly, popping a few berries in my mouth. Glancing at the sky, I wrapped my own cloak around myself as we walked. "It will be here soon. In an hour or two."

We walked in silence for a few more minutes, and I knew Ryllae was lost in that incredible mind of hers. Each day, she was opening up to me more.

Yesterday, Ryllae shared a little about her childhood with me, and I told her about the time Maiela and I went hiking in the Weeping Woods. Our mother had always warned us away from the woods, but we ignored her. We had been thirteen and thought we knew everything there was to know about life. Until the night fell. At that point, both of us were certain we were going to die. The howling of the wind coming through the trees resembled that of a mourning female, but thankfully, the night had passed without incident.

The Death Elf had laughed.

Today, though, Ryllae wasn't laughing. Her face was drawn, and I could tell this was one of *those* days. The ones where the Death Elf walked precariously close to the edge of sanity. She was having them less often now that it was just the two of us, but I worried about her.

She nodded. "And we're... close?"

I paused, trying to remember what she was referring to.

"To the Indigo Coast? Yes. We should be there in a few days. It will probably be four days, although we might make it in three if we hurry.

There's a stream up ahead. We can stop and fill our canteens before continuing."

"That sounds great." Popping the last berry in her mouth, Ryllae chewed thoughtfully as running water grew louder.

Stepping around a fallen log, Ryllae opened her palm. Her fingers twitched as though she was summoning magic.

I watched her silently, wondering if perhaps *this* would be the moment her magic returned.

Ryllae struggled, her hand opening and closing, but nothing came from her pale skin. Not even a few stray red sparks. She kept trying until the small stream was in sight.

Letting out a frustrated huff, the princess shook her head. "The sooner we get there, the better. I need my magic."

"I understand. I can't imagine what it would feel like to be cut off from the future."

Sometimes, my magic was the only thing that kept me sane. Seeing the future was not for the faint of heart, and more than a few Fortune Elves had collapsed under the burden fate handed them.

Dropping to her knees in the dewy grass by the stream, Ryllae cupped her hands and dipped them into the water. She drank her fill, splashing her face before disappearing behind a tree to relieve herself.

When she came back, the heaviness was still about her.

My brows furrowed, and I stood, drying my hands on my tunic. "What's wrong?"

Pausing, Ryllae ran her hands through her hair as she mulled over my words. "Daegal, I don't know how... but I need to... this burden I bear... it's so heavy."

Her words confused me, but that was Ryllae. I learned that it was best to encourage her to talk. We could sort through her words later.

"What is it?" I asked. "Princess, I want to help."

A beat went by, and she inhaled sharply.

"Sometimes... sometimes I don't feel like a person anymore." Ryllae's voice was barely louder than the water behind her as she whispered, "I don't know who I am. What I am."

"What do you mean?"

The Death Elf, this dark princess whose very presence spoke to that broken part of me, sighed. "I mean, I don't know what I am anymore. I don't know what anything means!" Her voice grew louder, and she yanked down the collar of her dress roughly.

I swallowed, forcing my eyes to stay on Ryllae's face even as all of my instincts demanded I let my gaze drop.

"Look at me, Daegal," she demanded.

Kydona help me.

I did what she asked.

The usually high neckline of Ryllae's dress now rested about the swell of her breasts. Her fingers were tangled in the fabric as she exposed her skin to me.

My mouth dried. "I'm looking," I rasped.

At this point, even if I looked away, I would never forget this sight.

Ryllae ran a finger over her skin. "Do you see these?"

Red swirls and whorls covered the majority of her body. Starting as a necklace around her collarbone, the red tattoos followed the curves of her body. They painted her upper chest in brilliant color and covered the supple mounds of her breasts before disappearing beneath her dress.

"I do," I said hoarsely. I could barely find the words to say. Good gods, I would *definitely* be dreaming about this. Pointing to the whirls, I asked, "What are those?"

"I don't know." She huffed, releasing the fabric. It rode back up, covering the markings as Ryllae crossed her arms over her chest. "I got them when I Matured."

"Interesting," I murmured.

When I Matured, I received a similar mark. Mine was on my back, a silver whirl between my shoulder blades. Maiela's was on her thigh, a similar silver swirl that ran the length of her hand.

I had never heard of someone with markings like this, though.

As if she read my thoughts, Ryllae bent. Yanking up her skirt, she showed me her left leg. The same bright red whirls covered the skin as she kicked out her leg toward me. "They started around my ankles, but by the time the final stage of my Maturation hit, they covered my entire body."

"You mean..." I blinked as a mental image of Ryllae without any clothes appeared unbidden in my mind.

"I have them all over, Daegal," she confirmed. "From the tips of my toes to my neck."

I groaned. "Oh, gods."

How in Kydona's name was I supposed to think of anything except for this? I could picture it now, my dark skin against her much paler one, the red markings a stark contrast to our two bodies, sweaty and...

Running my hand over my hair, I looked at the gray sky and inhaled sharply. I needed to think of something else. Anything else.

The faint scent of salt permeated the air, providing a welcome distraction to the mental image of Ryllae's naked body writhing beneath mine.

"I have these markings, Daegal, and yet they mean *nothing*. I have nothing. Who am I without my magic? I was born to be queen, and yet I cannot summon a single red ribbon." Anxiousness filled Ryllae's voice, and I looked at her.

"You're the same person you've always been," I said. "Beautiful. Courageous beyond belief. Strong. You're Ryllae."

She scoffed. "I'm none of those things, Daegal." Letting go of her skirt, her hands clutched at her cloak as frantic energy radiated from her. "I have these markings, but no one knows what they mean. I told my father about them when the last ones appeared, and less than a day later, I was in prison. For what? Why? Nothing makes any sense. Who am I? Why am I here? If I don't have my magic, I'm afraid..."

Ryllae's voice trailed off, and she trembled. I took a step toward her, keeping my hands outstretched. The air between us thickened, and I slowly reached out and placed my hand on her arm. When she didn't pull away, I kept going until there was barely a foot between us. The wind blew around us, and the leaves of the nearby trees rustled.

I sucked in a breath. "What are you afraid of, Princess?"

Her wide eyes met mine, and a long moment passed.

I wasn't sure she would answer. When she did, her voice was so quiet I had to strain to hear it.

"I'm afraid I'm nothing but a wisp on the wind. You have the future. Xander has his dragon, and Aileana has the earth. I have *nothing*. No throne. No magic. I don't even have a family anymore."

A choked sob escaped her, and a crack appeared in my heart. I wanted to do nothing more than wrap Ryllae in my arms, but I knew that she wouldn't accept it from me.

Not yet.

I needed her to know that she had me. In every way, I hoped.

"Ryllae—"

"I am nothing!" she screamed, stomping on the damp grass. "For the gods' sake, people forgot about me."

"I will never forget about you," I said fiercely.

Her lips tilted up in a sad smile. "I am their princess, and they don't even know I exist."

My heart squeezed tightly as I studied this incredible female before me. She might not have been a warrior, but she was amazing in her own right.

And she thought she was nothing.

Shaking my head, I held onto Ryllae's arm. "You're wrong," I whispered.

"What?"

"You're not nothing. You exist, and you have a purpose. Never let yourself believe otherwise. You. Are. Amazing." Stepping toward Ryllae, I kept my movements slow as I wrapped my arms around her. Her head tucked beneath my chin, and I pressed her against my tunic. "I'm so sorry, Ryllae. For everything that has been done to you. For anyone who made you feel like you were nothing."

For a long moment, neither of us spoke. I wanted to tell this princess that everything would be alright. That I would look after her and protect her until we both Faded. I wanted to promise that we would get her magic back and that we would kill her father.

There were so many things I wanted to say to this dark princess, but I had Seen the future.

I wouldn't lie to her.

Darkness was coming, and no one was safe.

So, instead, I held Ryllae, and I let her feel how much she meant to me. As a friend. A companion.

And perhaps, if I was right about the connection between us, as something more.

One day.

I wasn't sure how much time had passed before Ryllae mumbled, "I feel safe with you, Daegal." She raised her head. "Will you continue to keep me safe?"

My chest constricted, and this connection between us, the one that had existed since I first carried her out of Nightstone Prison, grew.

"Always." I squeezed Ryllae tightly, letting her feel everything I wasn't ready to put into words. "I will never let any harm come to you, Princess. Not as long as I am alive. Your trust in me means more to me than you know."

Her cheeks reddened. "I... thank you, Daegal. You... I'm not frightened of you."

My lips tilted up. "I'm glad."

Our eyes met, and the air between us thickened. The urge to kiss her slammed into me so hard I almost lost my footing. My hand moved of its own accord, and before I knew it, I was gently cupping her chin.

"Ryllae," I breathed. "Do you—"

The air shifted, and the small stream darkened. A bird screeched. My heart pounded as every part of me urged me to pay attention.

"Get behind me," I hissed, drawing my sword and widening my stance.

Ryllae obeyed instantly, tucking herself behind me. "What's going on?"

"We're about to get a visitor," I said.

I had not Seen this.

That wasn't entirely out of the ordinary. The future was strange like that. It played games with us and changed with a moment's notice.

"A good visitor or a bad one?" Ryllae paused, and a morose chuckle escaped the Death Elf. "Who am I kidding? It's always bad."

Ryllae's tone was dark. I didn't want to leave her alone, but I needed to See what was coming.

I threw myself onto the silver plane and flicked through the future far faster than usual. Nothing looked out of place, but I knew something was coming.

Mere moments had passed when I returned to myself. Blinking as my soul resettled within my body, I shook my head.

"I don't know who is coming." I lowered my voice. "But whether they are good or bad, I will always keep you safe, Princess."

"I know you will." She twisted her hands in the back of my cloak.

Every single part of me urged me to protect Ryllae. My heart thundered, and I tightened my grip on my sword. Thank the gods, we were armed.

The stream churned, and I stepped back, bringing Ryllae with me as the waters darkened. Every second felt like it was an hour as the water expanded.

I thought I had seen everything in my two hundred years, but I was wrong.

I had never seen this.

A head emerged from the water, followed by a torso, then legs, until an extremely muscular soldier stood before me. Made entirely of water, the male was at least half a foot taller than me. His glistening blue eyes were hard as he stared down at us. His aura shimmered with gold, which was new, and his hair hung in long strands around his face.

"Who are you?" I growled, shifting my grip on my sword. I wasn't sure that metal would do anything against a male such as this, but I would try.

The being made of water bowed at the waist. "My name is Castien. I am a Guardian of the Sanctuary and Spirit of the Waters." His voice was deep, and he radiated strength and power. "I come to you bearing news of the Protectress of the Woods and her bonded mate."

Aileana and Xander. I Saw their path this morning, and everything looked fine...

But Myhhena said the future could be manipulated.

My palms slickened, and my heart quickened as I stepped toward the male. "Are they all right?"

"They are fine," Castien said gruffly. "They are... safe within the boundaries of the Sanctuary and send you their greetings."

My eyes narrowed. The tone of the Spirit's voice brought me pause. There was something dark and dangerous between his words.

"This Sanctuary," I asked. "Where is it?"

"In the west," Castien replied evasively as his watery form dripped.

I narrowed my eyes. "Where in the west?"

He shook his head. "I can't... They are safe. But there are laws... the magic allowing me to speak to you is precarious." The male held out his hand, and a golden ribbon slipped from his palm. The water bubbled, and it started reclaiming him as the ribbon twisted, transforming into a small, round golden pin. He looked over my shoulder at Ryllae. "This is for you, daughter of Kydona. Take it and keep it on you."

Ryllae jolted. "Me?"

Castien nodded, sinking into the river. "Yes. Hurry."

"What is it?" Ryllae reached around me, plucking the pin from Castien's palm.

His legs disappeared into the trickling stream. "A gift from the Spirits to contact the Protectress and her bonded mate." His torso was half gone when he shouted, "It is activated by blood and can only be used once. You must use it wisely."

Ryllae clutched the pin. "Thank you."

The wind rustled, and a cold breeze blew by as Castien sank into the water.

His head was barely visible as I met his gaze. "Thank you. For everything."

The Spirit of the Waters opened his mouth, but before he could say anything, he disappeared into the stream.

Within moments, the water returned to normal.

Ryllae turned, raising a brow and holding up the pin. "That was different," she said, stepping toward me. A beat passed, and she turned it over in her hands. "I think you should have this, Daegal. It came from your friends."

My brows furrowed. "Castien said it was for you."

"I know," she whispered. "But I would feel better if you kept it safe for us. I am... my mind... I don't always trust myself, Daegal."

"I trust you, Ryllae." I sucked in a breath. "But if it will make you feel better, I'll wear the pin."

"It will," the princess said. Closing the distance between us, Ryllae's fingers held my cloak as she slid the pin into the interior of the fabric. When it was on, she didn't step away.

Ryllae's fingers ran down my neck, tracing the line of my skin from my ear to my collarbone. Her touch was light, but it sent sparks through me.

I sucked in a breath, and my heart drummed a steady beat in my chest. Ryllae's movements stilled. Her blue eyes darted up to meet mine, and her lips parted.

Now that I knew those red tattoos were hiding beneath her gown, I couldn't stop my eyes from darting down and seeing the first few lines of her tattoos.

The Death Elf sucked in a breath, her fingers starting their perusal once more.

I barely breathed, my lungs too tight, as she traced my upper body. Her fingers ran over the scar that stretched across my left shoulder, and she frowned.

The air was thick with tension as Ryllae continued to run her hands over me. Something had shifted between us, and I wasn't sure how to address it. If I should address it.

Eventually, Ryllae sucked in a sharp breath. She pulled her hand back as though it was on fire, clutching the offensive limb to herself.

"We should go," she whispered.

I blinked, nodding as I tried to get my thoughts in order. "Whatever you want, Princess."

She held my gaze for a long moment before turning and walking.

What was I getting myself into?

A FEW HOURS LATER, a companionable silence stretched between us as we hiked through the forest.

Ryllae walked ahead of me, carefully picking her way over roots and humming a wordless tune. That now-familiar reddish-black haze hung around her as she hiked, and I couldn't help but admire the view.

By the time the sun had passed the midway point in the sky, we came to another small stream cutting through the forest. I eyed the water, looking for another Spirit. The water looked normal, and I didn't think we would get another message today.

"Let's take a break." Crouching at the stream, I grabbed our bottles from the pack, rinsing them out before filling them with fresh water.

Ryllae knelt nearby, washing her hands and face before sitting back on her haunches. Digging through her bag, she withdrew an apple. Turning the red orb around in her hand, she eyed the flesh dubiously before bringing it to her nose and sniffing. A small smile danced on her face.

"It's a little bruised, but it smells good." She bit into it, letting out a small moan as juice dribbled down her chin. "Tastes good, too."

Reaching into her bag with her free hand, Ryllae grabbed another apple and tossed it at me. I caught it and took a bite. The tart juices flooded my mouth, and I swallowed before asking, "Tell me again what you know about the merfolk."

She glanced at me, raising a blond brow. The way she sat on the green grass, her horns glinting in the sunlight, drew the eye instantly. She could never blend in, this strange, dark princess.

"I don't know too much about them," Ryllae murmured. "Only that their king lives in Coral City, and he is extremely powerful. My father,"—she paused, shuddering in a way that made me want to murder High King Edgar for the things he had done to his daughter— "took me to the coast once. He met with the king... or at least, he tried to."

"What happened?" I asked.

"The merfolk didn't acknowledge his power. They refused to grant him entrance into their city."

"He must not have taken that well."

Ryllae shook her head, her eyes taking on a far-away look. "They were the first beings I ever saw who disobeyed him and lived. Their ruler blocked my father's magic somehow." Her voice took on a wistful tone, and her eyes darkened as she walked closer to that edge of sanity. "If they could do that, then maybe they know what's wrong with me. I can feel my magic, Daegal. It's there, but something dark is keeping it from me."

I was familiar with darkness. It was everywhere in the future. Death and destruction covered the silver planes. No matter where I turned, darkness was there.

Sometimes, if I spent too long on the silver planes, I could feel it edging along my soul, pulling at me.

If I wasn't careful, it would take over everything I had.

Maybe that was why Ryllae and I got along so well.

Darkness was a part of us both.

The Death Elf took the last bite of her apple and threw her core into the forest. "What about you?"

"Me?"

"Have you ever been to the Indigo Coast?"

The question was innocent, and yet it took me off guard. Once again, Ryllae was surprising me. I should have seen this question coming, but I didn't.

Memories flashed through my mind, ones that I had long since forgotten. A Light Elf with dark eyes, begging for information about his future. The scent of salt in the air. A pack of werewolves coming to me late at night. Deals done under the table. Silver paths tinged in darkness.

Death.

So much death.

And I caused it all.

"Once," I said. The word slipped out before I could even stop it. What was I doing? Even Xander didn't know my entire story.

Something about the princess made me want to tell her my deepest, darkest secrets.

She looked at me, her eyes wide. "What happened?"

"It's a long story." Sighing, I rubbed my temples. "Fifteen decades ago, right before the Winter Solstice, I was Seeing the future for a pack of—"

A branch cracked nearby, and my ears pricked up. The hairs on the back of my neck stood, and I shivered.

I might not have had Xander's senses, but I knew something was wrong. Shoving the past back where it belonged, I leaped to my feet, leaving my pack on the grass as I drew my sword. "Get behind me, Princess."

Once again, Ryllae complied. The Death Elf was a lot of things, but a skilled warrior was not one of them. That much had been made clear when I watched her drop a knife and then grab it by the blade.

Tightening my grip on the sword, I stared into the wall of trees all around us. Nothing looked out of the ordinary, but I *knew* something was off. My entire body was on high alert, my nerves tingling as my mind screamed.

We really needed to stop talking at streams.

Making a mental note not to be so careless, I scanned the forest.

If it didn't mean leaving Ryllae defenseless, I would check the future. But I couldn't. Not right now. A thick sense of foreboding filled me, and I knew that Looking ahead would be the wrong move right now.

A strange bird song came from the forest. A heartbeat later, an eerily similar call came from behind us. Moments later, a third came from my right.

A breeze rustled the leaves, and the air was heavy with the scent of pine and damp earth.

Something was wrong.

I could feel it in my bones.

For a long moment, nothing happened.

I was beginning to doubt myself when a flash of bright purple fabric caught my eye. Red leaves rustled, and moments later, bright colors assaulted my vision as a dozen beings dropped from the trees. They landed on silent feet, staring at us both.

Elves.

They slinked out of the trees, their hands clenched around weapons made of steel and wood.

"Dammit," I cursed beneath my breath.

By their auras, it appeared most of them were Light Elves. Some were winged, others were horned. I spotted the red aura of a Death Elf, and another whose aura was purple, like Kysha's. A halfbreed, then. The elves were lithe, their frames little more than skin and bones. A mixture of males and females, their skin ranged from the palest of whites to as dark as the night sky.

And their faces...

Some of them looked at us with so much hostility that it felt like they were tearing us apart from the inside out. Others eyed us with unabashed curiosity, their brows raised as they eyed us.

The leaves rustled, and even more of them emerged from the forests. Werewolves, by the looks of them, and maybe a shifter or two. They all held weapons and wore tunics and leggings designed to blend into the forest.

This was not good.

As if realizing the same thing, Ryllae groaned. "We're surrounded."

There was nothing to say. She was right. Frail states or not, there were too many of them. There was no way we could fight our way out of this. Maybe if Aileana and Xander had been with us, this might have been a different story.

But they weren't here, and I had to make the hard decisions.

Right now, Ryllae was my only priority. She couldn't fight, and I needed to keep her safe, no matter the cost.

Knowing when to pick my battles, I kept my movements slow as I bent, placing my sword on the grass. Keeping my eyes on the elves, I straightened, lifting my hands in the air. My heart thundered against my chest, and everything in my body was too tight.

My magic thrummed in my veins, urging me to Look into the future, but I forced it down.

A female elf with a light purple aura stepped forward. Gripping a sharpened staff in her russet-brown hands, her long brown hair ran in an intricate braid down her back. Her clothes marked her as a warrior, her mouth was set in a firm line, and she radiated authority.

Deciding to take my chances, I cleared my throat.

"Greetings." Hoping that my voice didn't reflect the racing of my heart, I dipped my head in a show of respect. "My companion and I are seeking the merfolk who live off the Indigo Coast."

The whisper of the wind brushing past me was the only reply.

Remembering the words of old, I continued. "Our bodies are cold, and our stomachs are empty." Not exactly true. "All we ask for is a night of Kydona's hospitality, and we will be on our way."

A long moment passed, and the air quivered with tension.

The Light Elf took a step forward. Her voice was like steel as she snarled, "Kydona has no place here."

She dropped her staff, opening her hands wide before muttering under her breath. Violet ribbons escaped her palms, swirling in the air before rushing toward us.

They pricked my skin, and fire erupted beneath my veins.

Beside me, Ryllae screamed.

SOMETHING sharp poked me in the side. I shifted, trying to get my eyes to open, but everything was black. Slowly, far too slowly, things came back to me.

Being in the woods with Ryllae. Stopping at the creek. The ambush. A request for hospitality. Being denied. Then, the magic....

"I think he's waking up." The speaker sounded young, but I couldn't see them. Why couldn't I see them?

My eyes were open, or so I thought, but darkness was everywhere. A pulsing wave pounded through me, and I reached up to rub my temples. Except, my hands wouldn't move.

They were bound together.

"Shit," I muttered. Or at least I tried to. In reality, my words came out as more of an inarticulate mumble.

Pushing myself up, I shuffled backward until my back hit something hard. A thousand curses ran through my mind. My head felt heavy, as though it was too big for my body. Forming words was suddenly a task far too difficult for someone whose life was as long as mine.

"Yeah," the voice said again. "He's waking up. Go tell the Old One that the male is awake."

The scurrying of feet was the only response.

Reaching up with my bound hands, I tried to touch my head. My hands were tingly, and they took far too long to respond. Running my fingers over my rough stubble, I kept going until I hit something rough and unnatural.

"It's a blindfold," the voice said, as though I were an idiot.

Yes, this was not good.

I groaned into my hands. "I got that, thank you."

At least those words came out relatively clearly.

A searing pain flashed across my cheek. "Don't talk back to me, you Kydona-worshiping piece of shit."

Choosing to keep my mouth shut, I nodded. The speaker huffed but didn't say anything else. Moving slowly so they wouldn't notice, I grabbed the sides of my cloak—thank Kydona, I was still wearing it— and ran my fingers up the inside. When my fingers brushed up against the cool metal of the pin, relief ran through me.

At least I still had the pin. Maybe once I found Ryllae, we could use it.

If only I knew where she was.

The only thing I needed to do was keep Ryllae safe. Instead, I got us kidnapped.

Some Fortune Elf I turned out to be.

I failed. *Again.*

I couldn't even stop to Look into the future. Not right now. I couldn't afford to leave my body defenseless as I walked on the silver plane. I'd heard horror stories of Fortune Elves being cut down in the past while they sought knowledge of what was to come.

The sound of murmured conversations came from behind me. I stilled, lowering my bound hands and clenching them into fists.

"What do you want from us?" I asked my unseen captors. The words sounded better this time. They were still a little slurred, but far more like myself.

That was an improvement. Good.

A female laugh, tinged with echoes of pain and age, came from in front of me. "Want? There are many things I want. But first of all, I want to know who you are."

"Why would I tell you that?"

A rustling sound, then the scent of cardamom grew stronger. "Because I know who your companion is," the female hissed.

My eyes widened beneath the blindfold, and I sucked in a breath. This was probably a ploy. An act. No one knew who Ryllae was. Not anymore.

Still, I had to know.

Hoping my voice did not betray me, I asked, "Oh? Who is she?"

The female laughed. "Many do not recognize her. But I have seen many moons. Centuries have come and gone beneath my watch. The moment the Forgotten One was dragged into camp, I knew her to be the Princess of Ithenmyr."

My entire body felt too cold. Everything screamed at me to get up. To run. To look for Ryllae. My magic thrummed within me, begging me to use it.

I denied its call. If I left myself, even for a moment, they might kill me. Ryllae needed me alive.

Forcing myself to take deep breaths, I sorted out my words carefully in my mind. These people were dangerous; that much was clear. "Will you take off the blindfold so I can see you?"

A tittering laugh came from the elderly female. "No. You should be grateful you aren't bound to a stake right now. We don't take lightly to the followers of Kydona here."

I had so many questions. Flexing my fingers beneath their bindings, I tilted my head. "I see."

"You don't, not yet. But you will."

A sense of dread grew in my stomach, and my spine tingled. This was far worse than I could have imagined.

Something dripped nearby, and I tried to catalog every sound. Every smell. Maybe then I would figure out where we were.

The female clucked her tongue, and her words were tinged with impatience. "Tell me your name, male."

I remained still. This wasn't the first time in my life I'd been captured, although I'd never been interrogated by a female before. I didn't know what they wanted from me... or why I was still alive.

If I wanted to remain that way—which was definitely the preferable option—I had to tread extremely carefully.

My life wasn't the only one on the line.

Shutting my eyes—a pointless movement considering the black material covering them—I drew in a breath. "My name is Daegal. Son of Braern of the House of Videntis."

"There, that wasn't too hard, now was it?" A rustling of fabric came from nearby, and the female sighed. "Now... Daegal, right?"

She said my name like *dee-gull*, her accent one that I had never heard before. It sounded like she came from everywhere and nowhere.

Storing that information away for later, I cleared my throat. "Yes, Daegal. That's correct."

The female made a sound that was close to approval. "Imagine how surprised I was when the Fortune One showed up in my camp with no one but a measly Fortune Elf by her side.

"What do you know about Ryllae?" I asked, curiosity shoving aside common sense for a moment. "Where is she?"

"Ryllae, is it?" the female asked. "Familiar with the Death Elf Princess, aren't you?"

I cursed myself for my stupidity.

"Where is she?" I asked again.

The female clucked her tongue once more. "I didn't say you could ask questions, Daegal."

A growl rumbled through me. "Tell me where she is."

"What is going on here, Crystenn?" a deep male voice roared. "Why are you talking to the prisoner?"

My spine stiffened.

The female who had been interrogating me—Crystenn—snapped, "I'm dealing with him, Orrin. *Obviously.*"

Orrin growled. "You can't just parade around and do whatever you want! These two are my prisoners, and I am the one in charge—"

"Quiet!" Crystenn shouted. "You dare speak to your elder in such a fashion? You know as well as I do that balance needs to be restored. The world is in disarray. This male might know something—"

"Enough!" the male shouted. "We need to discuss this outside. *Alone.*"

A tense moment passed before Crystenn said, "Fine. Lead the way."

Footsteps filled the air, and their voices faded until they were out of earshot.

Time went on. My stomach growled, and exhaustion pulled at me.

No one ever returned.

The High Lady

AILEANA

My eyes widened, and I stared at Myhhena. As was becoming a typical response for me, I had no words. Or at least, none came to mind.

Guardian of the Appointed Ones.

What did that even mean?

The deer made of bark took a step forward, the ground quaking beneath his feet. Was it a "he?" I thought so. Myhhena had addressed him by name.

Although I probably should have felt fear in the presence of such a magnificent, enormous creature, an unearthly calmness washed over me instead.

Moving toward the buck, I side-stepped Xander's arm as he reached to stop me.

"What are you doing, Aileana?" he hissed between clenched teeth. "Get behind me."

This was becoming very old, very fast. Xander knew I could take care of myself.

"You want me to hide?"

"Yes," he snarled. "I want you to pretend at least to think about your own safety, for once."

I huffed. "Xander, I'm not a coward. I want to talk to him. That's all."

"Insufferable female," he growled.

I lifted a shoulder and took another step toward the deer. He still had not moved and was watching me carefully.

I wasn't even sure it was possible to speak with such a creature, but I was going to try. If I had summoned him, as Myhhena thought I did, then it must have been safe.

Right?

Firm in the thought that the deer probably, almost certainly, wouldn't hurt me, I held out my hand and approached him. Behind me, leaves shook, and from the corner of my eye, I watched as Myhhena pushed herself to her feet. The two smaller Spirits of the Woods stood near her, their faces painted with a mixture of fear and reverence.

"Be careful, Protectress," Myhhena breathed, her voice as quiet as the wind that caressed my cheeks. "Kethryllian is a Guardian, but he is also dangerous."

Kethryllian.

The name echoed in my mind as I approached him.

When I was close enough to touch the deer, I turned my hand, palm facing up. My heart thundered in my chest, and I counted the beats as I stared into the creature's mossy eyes. He was tall—far taller than any other woodland creature I'd ever seen—and he seemed sentient in the same way the stags had felt *alive.*

Kethryllian was as beautiful as he was large. Majestic roughness radiated from him and part of me felt intrinsically called to him.

"Aileana," Xander cautioned, his voice low and rough. "Be careful."

Without removing my gaze from the deer's green eyes, I nodded. "I will be."

The air was thick as I slowly placed my hand on the deer's head. The moment my fingers connected with the rough bark, magic thrummed in my veins, and the earth rumbled beneath my feet.

An ancient, ethereal voice echoed in my head. *Greetings, Aileana of the House of Corellon, Earth Elf, Last daughter of Uhna, and Granddaughter of Niona.*

"Um... Hello?"

The deer chuffed beneath my hand, and instinctively, I reached up and scratched behind his ears.

Gasps came from the others, but I ignored them. "It's Kethryllian, is that correct?" The syllables sounded strange on my tongue. *Keth-reh-lee-yan.*

It is, the deer replied. *I am the Guardian of the Appointed Ones. Thelrena herself sent me to guide you.*

"What does that mean? Guardian of the Appointed Ones." My brows furrowed, and I dropped my hand to my side, stepping back. "I mean, I understand the words, but I'm not... I don't... Why would Thelrena..."

Warmth enveloped me, and the scent of smoke, ash, and pine filled my senses as Xander's hands landed on my arms.

Golden ribbons of godly magic slipped from the deer's flank.

The three Spirits gasped as the golden ribbons spun to a silent waltz, creating a beautiful tapestry against the autumnal forest. Their presence called to the magic within me. Without even thinking, I opened my palm. A flurry of green magic escaped me, joining the golden cords in their dance.

All around us, the air hummed. The ground trembled, and the

purple flowers I had created earlier glowed. The magic danced, gold and green like my mating mark, before scattering into the woods.

When they were gone, Kethryllian took a step forward. The deer spoke, and this time, his voice was audible. "It means exactly what you think."

My mouth fell open as Kethryllian knelt before me, dipping his head so low that his antlers practically touched the ground. The ground shook, and Kethryllian's eyes shone a vivid green. "As the last surviving elf of your lineage and the granddaughter of Niona, you are the High Lady of Life."

Frozen in place, all I could do was stare at the deer kneeling before me. Tiaesti and Erwen gasped, but I had no words.

High Lady.

Xander, on the other hand, always seemed to know what to say. His hands moved to my hips, his firm touch a warm reminder of his presence.

"What exactly are you saying?" he asked.

"The triad of living power exists in your bonded mate's veins." Kethryllian's green eyes met mine. "You are the Protectress of the Woods, the Keeper of the Earth, and the High Lady of Life. Thelrena has blessed you."

A shiver ran through me at the creature's words. A piece of myself I never knew existed suddenly fell into place. Questions I had never voiced were being answered.

"Why?" I breathed. "Why me?"

The Guardian tilted his head, his antlers glinting in the sunlight. "You are the daughter of Thelrena. Chosen by blood and by birthright to rule the life in Ithenmyr."

His words echoed around the clearing, settling upon us.

I stared at the deer for a long moment before laughter bubbled up inside me. It started as a small giggle, but soon I erupted into absolute mirth. I laughed and laughed, my stomach cramping, as I waited for the Guardian to tell me he was joking.

I half expected Xander to join in with the laughter, for the Spirits to tell me it was untrue, but they didn't move.

Why didn't they move?

This was a joke. It had to be a joke.

I was nobody. An Earth Elf, yes, but I had no family. High King Edgar kept me to breed, but...

The laughter died down as realization slammed into me with the weight of a falling tree. My lungs tightened, and breathing became difficult.

He kept me to breed. Why would he do that unless...

"Oh, my gods." My hand flew to my heart, and my legs shook. If it weren't for Xander's hands around my hips, I would have collapsed to the ground. "Is this true?"

"It is," Kethryllian said roughly. "You are the High Lady of Life. Chosen by Thelrena herself. Meant to rule beside Kydona's daughter. This was the way of the world until the Death Elf disturbed the balance."

I wanted to deny Kethryllian's claims, but his words rang with truth. My chest hurt, and a coldness washed over me.

I was frozen. I didn't breathe. I didn't move. All I could do was stare at the Guardian.

Pieces of my life that hadn't quite seemed to fit fell into place. Questions I'd had since escaping my tower were answered. Things that never made any sense suddenly became clear.

I had never understood why High King Edgar wanted *me* specifically. Why had I been spared when all the other Earth Elves were slaughtered? Why was my magic so strong after completing just one step of the

Maturation process?

Why was *I* the Protectress of the Woods?

As though he read my mind—which, to be fair, perhaps he could—Kethryllian nodded. "You are strong, High Lady, because royal magic flows through your veins."

Royal. Magic.

That was the tipping point.

All of this was too much.

My feet shook, and my vision blurred. Xander called my name, but I couldn't stop the darkness from pulling me under. My legs finally won the battle they had been waging, and despite Xander's grip on my hips, I fell into darkness.

WARMTH SURROUNDED ME, and a familiar pair of golden eyes greeted me.

"Hey there, Sunshine," Xander said, his deep voice laced with concern as he ran his hands up and down my arms. "How do you feel?"

That question, which should have had such a simple answer, wasn't so simple anymore.

I was...

Shaken.

Off-kilter.

Confused.

I was the High Lady of Life.

Royal blood ran through my veins.

What did that even mean?

Panic threatened to overtake me, to push me back into the darkness where reality did not exist, but I refused to let it happen. Focusing on the leaves above me and the cool autumn breeze that blew red strands of hair on my face, I breathed in deeply.

"I think I'm in shock," I whispered as my heart pounded against my chest.

My bonded mate clutched me tighter to him. "I gathered as much from the way you fainted."

That explained how I ended up in Xander's arms. Not that I was complaining. At all. Being held by him was like getting a warm, fiery hug from all sides.

"Kethryllian.... Is he still here?"

A coughing sound came from nearby. "He is."

Blood rushed to my cheeks as I shifted to face the Guardian. The three Spirits of the Woods stood nearby, their twiggy hands clutched in front of them as they all watched me. "Oh, I didn't realize—"

Kethryllian shook his head. "Not to worry, High Lady. Admittedly, this is a lot for anyone to take in. You should have been raised knowing what you were..." The creature's voice trailed off, and he shook his head. "What has been done is done."

"I'm sure you and your bonded mate have much to discuss, my lady." Myhhena stepped forward, gesturing for the smaller Spirits to follow her.

Tiaesti walked past me, sliding her twiggy hand over mine. "High Lady of Life," she said in awe.

When the two small Spirits stood in front of her, Myhhena decreed, "Restoring the balance will not be an easy task. We shall discuss what this means at a later time. Ladies?"

Tiaesti and Erwen raised their twiggy hands, and together, the trio of Spirits disappeared in a flurry of leaves.

When the wind settled down, Kethryllian bowed once more. "I will be waiting. When you need me, all you need to do is call."

Golden ribbons swirled all around the creature, and the bark that made up Kethryllian's flesh slowly faded into the forest. He was almost gone when a question popped into my mind.

"Wait!" I called out, pushing myself out of Xander's grasp and coming to my feet. "Before you go, I have a question."

The deer chuckled, his form solidifying once more. "Yes, my lady?"

That new title was so strange that for a moment, I didn't respond.

Kethryllian looked at me expectantly, and beside me, Xander stood. He laced his hand through mine, and he squeezed gently. "The question, Sunshine?"

"You said you serve Thelrena's Appointed Ones?" I asked.

"I do." The deer nodded.

"That's plural, so... does that mean there are others like me?"

Deafening silence filled the forest, and time slowed. The wind blew around me, and a low, keening wail echoed through the earth beneath my feet.

Regret painted Kethryllian's face, and a pit grew in my stomach.

"There were," he said sadly.

My stomach pinched, and my legs wobbled. "Were?"

"Now, there is just one." He shook his head. "You are the last remaining elf of your line."

A deep sense of sadness welled within me at his words, and a part of me fissured. I had known early on in my life that I was alone. A hole had always existed within me that should have been filled with love from my family.

I knew I was alone, but hearing it confirmed out loud was different. It made it real.

My heart cracked, and my vision blurred. "Oh."

Kethryllian dipped his head. "I am terribly sorry for your loss. The earth and Thelrena weep with you."

"Thank you," I whispered. My legs shook, and I stumbled back a step. Xander's arm wrapped around my waist, holding me up.

They were all dead. My parents. Grandparents. Siblings, if I'd had any. They were dead, and I was alone.

A single tear ran down my cheek.

Kethryllian faded into the forest, and this time, I didn't stop him.

Once Xander and I were alone, a deep, shuddering sob escaped me. Then another. I crumpled to the ground, my knees digging into the purple flowers as salty tears ran down my face.

Xander pulled my hair back from my face, running his hand over my back as my tears flowed.

There is just one.

Me.

I wept.

For myself and for my family. I wept for all the elves who came before me.

I wept for all those whose lives were lost too soon. For those I would never know.

I wept for Saena and for all the females in Ithenmyr.

I wept for my mate's family and friends. For the peaceful future that had been stolen from us.

I wept until the sadness within me shifted. It grew, giving way to something bright and hot and vibrant.

I wept until anger flowed through my veins. I wept until I ran out of tears. My shoulders shook, my heart tightened, and I made myself a promise.

This would be the final time I wept. These were my last tears.

High King Edgar had already stolen so much from me. My family. My childhood. But he would not take this.

I would cry now because, after this, I would not cry again. I was far stronger than I had ever been.

I was Aileana of the House of Corellon, Bonded Mate of Elyxander, Protectress of the Woods, Keeper of the Earth, and the High Lady of Life.

I would restore the balance in Ithenmyr if it was the last thing I did.

High King Edgar would rue the day he crossed me.

Death Knocked on my Door

⤬

DAEGAL

My teeth chattered, and shivers ran from my head to my toes. Curling into a ball, I tried to remember what it felt like to be warm.

The effort was futile.

Cold was my new reality. The air smelled of winter, and the crisp, bitter wind tasted of snow and ice. It reminded me of my travels to Eleyta, where snow and ice reigned. Beneath me, the hard ground was uncomfortable.

Hours had passed since my captors left, and no one had come back. Not wanting to be defenseless, I resisted the call of my magic.

Now, it was night. Silence filled the air, and I knew this was my best chance—perhaps my only chance—to See what was to come.

Shutting my eyes seemed futile, considering the blindfold still tied around my head, so I didn't bother with it. Instead, I simply gave into the call of magic in my veins and left this plane of existence.

A dark cloud hung over the future, casting shadows over the wisps of silver that filled the air. Bending, I searched through the paths and checked on those closest to me.

Nonna, Maiela, and Kysha were still at the cottage. Their future was steady, and I did not See any harm coming to them.

Next, I sought out Xander and Aileana. Flames and vines intertwined on their path, and I ran my fingers over them. Their future was hazy and fluid, with many different paths coming to head in the next few days.

At least they were still alive. I had to move on. Concern for Ryllae welled up within me, pulsing as it urged me forward.

Wandering through the silver plane, I batted away wisps of visions as they flew toward me. Unrest was building. Riots were taking place in the Southern Kingdom. Females were being executed in Vlarone. Slaves were being taken from human villages and forced into labor.

I Saw something else that had taken place a few weeks ago. Running my fingers over the silver wisp, flashes of a union between Ipotha and Eleyta appeared in my mind. A human in a golden gown walking through a crowded room of vampires. The vampire known as the Prince of Darkness binding himself to her.

Interesting.

Blood coated their dark path, but I couldn't Look further.

The need to See Ryllae's future was a pounding force within me.

Leaving the vampires to their own devices, I swept dozens of paths away until I found the one I sought.

Edged in crimson, Ryllae's path lay before me. Crouching, I ran my hands over her future. Dozens of visions flashed before my eyes, one after the other. Faceless elves surrounded her in the coming days. I Saw her eating and drinking. She looked tired, but she was alive.

When I looked further into the future, ribbons of red magic

surrounded Ryllae. Someone unseen spoke, and Ryllae *laughed*. A brightness filled her eyes that I had never before seen.

All of these visions had one thing in common: I was nowhere to be found.

Releasing my grip on Ryllae's future, I stood on the silver plane and ran my hands through my hair.

Sorrow welled within me, and my lungs tightened. For a moment, I could barely breathe.

I could not See my own death. No Fortune Elf could. Although part of me wanted to argue that I was not present in Ryllae's future simply because I left her and went down my own path, I knew that wasn't true.

I would never leave her. Not intentionally.

That thing that rested between us was too strong.

I was going to die.

It wasn't entirely surprising. After all, being held captive by a group of armed elves wasn't conducive to survival.

A single, salty tear slipped down my cheek.

Having Seen enough, I withdrew from the silver planes.

Darkness surrounded me once more, and I shifted, seeking a comfortable position as I ran over everything I had learned.

Ryllae was safe here. She would survive.

I would not.

Leaning my head back, I tried to ignore the chills sweeping through me as I sent a prayer to Kydona.

When I die, please keep my family safe.

Thoughts of death and doom plagued me as I fell into a restless sleep. Blood-soaked memories I had long since pushed away forced their way to the surface. Long nights spent in gambling dens. Debts piling up. Desperation. Fear. Wolves howling. Blood-soaked floors.

They haunted me all night long.

Sometime later, I woke up. My stomach ached, and my hands were still bound in front of me. The smell of urine assaulted my senses, and the fabric between my legs was damp.

Shame curled in my stomach, and I burrowed my face into my arms.

No one came to see me.

Hours went by. Days? I lost track of time. My throat dried, and hunger was my constant companion. My captors didn't poison me. They didn't need to.

My own body was betraying me. I might have been Mature, but I still needed food and water.

If I didn't get any soon, I was going to die.

Waking and dreaming were closer than ever, and it was difficult to recognize the difference between them.

I tried to walk the silver planes, but my magic was not responding. It was a trickle in my veins, a barely there presence.

I could not move. I could not see.

The end was near.

"He needs to eat and drink," a female said. The voice sounded vaguely familiar, but I couldn't recognize it.

Everything was foggy. My mind struggled to understand what was happening.

I attempted to look up, but everything was black. My hands were so heavy tgat I could barely move them.

A moan escaped my dry, chapped lips.

She hissed, "I won't tell you anything if he dies."

Rough hands landed on my head. Someone cursed. Pain flashed through my body. My head was yanked up. Stars filled my vision.

"Stop!" the female cried out. "You're going to kill him. He needs food and water!"

"Anything else, your royal bitchiness?" the male said sarcastically, dropping my head. It banged against the wooden pole, and I groaned.

"Yes, actually," she said. "A cloth to clean him up, a new pair of trousers, and a chamber pot. If you don't help me, I'll tell Orrin you're the reason I'm refusing to speak. I'm fairly certain you do *not* want me to do that."

A long moment passed as the sound of heavy breathing filled the tent.

"Wait here," the male ordered. "*Don't* talk to him. Or else."

The threat of violence hung in the air as footsteps stomped on the ground. The male went outside, barking orders.

An awkward silence stretched between me and the female I couldn't see. It felt like she wanted to say something, but fear scented the air. Beneath it, though, she smelled like the darkest night. Like the crisp wind and stars and the moon.

It was an achingly familiar scent, and something within me calmed at her presence.

The footsteps returned.

"Well?" she asked.

Something landed on the floor near my feet. "Do it yourself, princess."

The female inhaled a sharp breath, and her scent flooded through me. Gentle fingers landed on my cheek.

"Don't worry," she said softly. "I won't look. I'm just going to help you."

I blinked, my mind trying to understand what she meant when fingers hooked into the sides of my trousers.

A coldness came at me from all sides, and my teeth chattered.

"I'm sorry. I got here as soon as I could." She pulled the new trousers on me, the entire situation awkward as she tugged them over me. I tried to help, but my body was so weak I could barely lift my hips from the ground. Eventually, she tied them around my waist.

"Hurry up!" the male barked from outside.

"Bastard," the female whispered.

That brought a smile to my face as gentle fingers ran down my cheek.

A rough rim landed on my mouth, and I groaned. Everything hurt, and even drinking seemed too difficult right now.

"Come on, Daegal," the female said softly. "Drink. You need to survive. I need you to survive."

Her soft fingers rubbed my cracked lips, and she murmured soft encouragements until my mouth opened.

Lukewarm water dribbled into my mouth and down my throat. I swallowed reflexively, the water trailing a path to my stomach.

"More," I whispered, licking my chapped lips.

I heard a smile in the female's voice when she said, "Good."

The rim of a cup was placed on my lips again, and this time, I opened my mouth eagerly. The female was gentle, and she didn't laugh, even though I was certain more than half the water had ended up down my tunic. When the cup was empty, she fed me bits of stale bread until my stomach was full.

Heeding the mysterious male's warning, she didn't speak to me, but I couldn't help but feel a connection with her.

When she left, a part of me went with her.

"Wake up," a gruff voice demanded from somewhere above me.

My head pounded, and I groaned. "What do you want?"

A rough hand landed on my arm, yanking me to my feet. "I have no time for questions, and neither do you."

Cruelty edged the male's voice, chasing all traces of sleep away.

Pay attention! my instincts screamed.

"What's going on?"

"That's for me to know and you to find out," he snapped.

Seeming to decide that he had spoken enough, the male dragged me behind him. I stumbled along, my feet catching on the ground as a freezing cold wind slammed into me.

My teeth chattered.

The person yanking me scoffed. "Pitiful."

They continued to drag me over the rough, hard ground. My foot bumped into something, and I bit back a curse as I stumbled forward. The male let go of me, and my face slammed into the dirt. A burst of pain erupted on my cheek, and I tasted blood.

The rough hand grabbed me, yanking me back to my feet with a curse. "Gods-dammit," he said.

Rough fingers grazed against my head, and the blindfold was ripped away from me. Bright light assaulted my vision. I winced.

The redheaded male dragged me as I tried to take in my surroundings.

Low murmurs of conversation and shrieks of laughter spoke of children somewhere in this camp, but I couldn't see them. Behind me was the small tent where they had held me for the gods-only-knew how long. In front of me was a thick forest.

I stumbled behind the male. His hair was tied in a knot at the base of his neck, and he wore a mud-colored tunic and trousers. One sword was strapped to his back, and another was on his hip.

He didn't need the weapons.

The male's aura pulsed bright red around him, and I recognized the Death Elf from our encounter at the stream.

Shit.

Death was definitely on the horizon for me. Why else would they have sent this male to deal with me?

My stomach sank. I kicked at the Death Elf, but my movements were far too slow.

The lack of proper food made me a walking target.

The elf pulled me into the forest, skirting fallen logs and low branches until we were deep in the woods. My hands were still tied in front of me, and the Death Elf was at least three inches taller than me.

He could have been a giant, but it wouldn't have mattered. I was going to fight until the last breath left my body. I just needed to bide my time.

Branches whipped at my face as the Death Elf pulled me deeper into the woods.

Even the animals were silent and watchful as the male dragged me to my death.

When we finally stopped moving, he shoved me. Holding out my bound hands, I tripped toward the gnarled brown trunk. My muscles were weak after spending so much time on the rough, cold ground. My captors had given me food and water a few times since the mysterious female had first arrived in the tent, but she had never come back.

When was the last time I ate and drank? A day ago? Maybe two? By the burning in my throat, I thought two was most likely.

"I need some water," I rasped, leaning against the tree's rough bark.

Pine needles covered the forest floor, and evergreen trees mixed with tall birch and maple trees loomed above me. It was eerily quiet, and there were no other voices.

I knew what kind of place this was.

The pit in my stomach widened into a chasm.

My captor chuckled darkly. "You won't be needing water much longer."

So this was it. Death finally found me. I'd successfully evaded it for over two centuries, but now, death was knocking on my door.

I stared at the male standing before me. His skin was tanned and freckled, as though he had spent a long time in the sun. His hands were extended at his sides, and though he appeared relaxed, I could sense violence in the air.

As if in response to my thoughts, he smirked. A ribbon of red magic slithered from his palm, spinning around his leg lazily as it eagerly awaited his command.

"So this is it?" I rasped, clearing my dry throat. "You're going to kill me?"

The elf walked around me in a slow circle. He didn't seem like he was in a hurry, and his demeanor was at odds with the urgency he had displayed, yanking me through the forest.

"I might," he said cryptically.

"Might?" I echoed. "You brought me out here so you 'might' kill me? What kind of brutish practice is this?"

My mother always said I had a mouth on me. It turned out that she was right. Even when faced with the male sent to kill me, I couldn't remain silent.

The Death Elf smirked. "That's what I said."

Reaching into his pocket, he withdrew something round and threw it at me. He missed, and the sphere landed with a splat, rolling a few feet away from me. I recognized the red fruit immediately.

My stomach growled, and I snatched up the rain berry with my still-bound hands, shoving it in my mouth. The juices dripped down my chin, and the gnawing hunger in my stomach stopped feeling like a jagged knife spearing into my middle, becoming more of a dull sword. It was present but not agonizingly painful.

I tensed as the Death Elf withdrew the sword from the scabbard at his hip. My back clenched, and I was preparing to run when the male threw the sword at my feet. It landed a foot from me, and the metal gleamed as sunlight filtered through the leafy canopy.

"What is the meaning of this?" I asked as I bent, grabbing the hilt of the sword with my bound hands. It was heavy and awkward, but I felt a sliver of hope for the first time in days. "You would arm me, then kill me?"

The Death Elf raised a brow. "You might think us brutes—"

I scoffed. "You've been keeping me blindfolded and barely fed. It seems pretty brutish from where I'm standing."

"But we're not," he said. "I'm not a murderer, and I won't kill you in cold blood."

"No? What do you call starving me for days and dragging me into the woods?"

There went my mouth again.

"I call it giving you a chance to live." A wolfish grin appeared on the Death Elf's face, and I shuddered. "The Forgotten One told us about you. She said you're a powerful Fortune Elf. That you can See the future. So, given your gifts, I'm sure you know that your life most likely ends within the next few minutes."

Unless you play this game with me.

The unspoken words hung in the air, and I stared at the male.

After a long moment, I sighed. "So this is it?"

"Yes." He nodded. "Take the sword and *run*." The Death Elf

snarled. "You have a day, Fortune Elf. Best me and I will let you live. Lose, and your blood will coat the forest floor."

I exhaled slowly.

I had no other choice.

Holding the sword awkwardly, I sawed through the rope binding my hands. "It seems like we are still... unbalanced. You have Death magic, and I don't."

The elf eyed me as the frayed rope fell to the ground. "You're right. To make it fair, I won't use my magic." He met my gaze. "Now run."

My blood chilled, and I obeyed.

A Multitude of Distractions

XANDER

Aileana stood a few feet in front of me with her arms outstretched as green ribbons flooded from her open palms. Aileana's skin glowed, and the swirls on her hands shone brightly. Even the mark of our mating was brighter as she pulled on her magic.

The ribbons swirled, dancing in the air before diving into the trees around us. The ground rumbled beneath my feet, and Aileana smiled.

"Did you see that?" she asked as joy filtered through the bond.

"I did." Crossing my arms, I leaned against a tree. "You are incredible."

"The earth is singing to me." Grinning, Aileana bent and placed her palms against the cold ground.

I smiled. "I'm glad."

Giddiness filled Aileana's voice as she connected to the earth once more. "There is so much magic, Xander. I can feel it overflowing... The life in Ithenmyr is giving back to me as much as I give it.

We were alone in the forest, having come to practice near the edge of the Sanctuary. The two of us were far enough from the shimmering wall of magic that I knew we were alone, but near enough that gods forbid, if something did happen, we could get help.

Mostly, I was just happy that Aileana was training. The faster she got her magic under control, the better.

Two weeks had passed since the Guardian of the Appointed Ones had first arrived. Over that time, Aileana and I had spent most of our time training with magic and swords. Every evening, once the sun fell, we retreated to our small stone home. We ate dinner, talked, and spent long hours in bed. Then, after a few hours of sleep, we did it all over again.

Day in and day out.

Castien assured us that the borders of the Sanctuary were safe, but even so, a sense of foreboding niggled at me.

Something was coming.

Yesterday, I thought I spotted another raven flying above the Sanctuary. When I investigated further, I couldn't find the bird. I convinced myself it was in my head.

Aileana was growing stronger with every passing day. She was incredible. Even though I knew her muscles burned and exhaustion plagued her, she never once complained. She was willing to work hard and push herself as far as she could.

Her resilience only made me love her more.

Kethryllian's announcement hadn't surprised me. I had always known Aileana was magnificent, and that incredible power ran through her veins.

Now, I knew why.

She was the High Lady of Life.

The dragon hummed contentedly within me. It had been quiet these past two weeks, only surfacing long enough to comment on

Aileana's increased magic before going back to watching things quietly.

Her powers were stronger than ever, and her control had increased exponentially. With every passing day, she could maneuver the green ribbons with greater ease. They did whatever she asked, moving like extra limbs.

Aileana was incredible, and I couldn't believe I ever doubted her.

Even now, as she worked with the Earth Elf magic, I felt her tugging on the bond between us as she fed magic into the earth.

Walking toward her, I bent, placing my hands on Aileana's hips before resting my chin on top of her head. She hummed, pressing her backside against me.

"I love how your hands feel on me," she whispered.

A rough chuckle escaped me as Aileana lifted her palms from the ground, the green ribbons fluttering around us both. They swirled as though caught in a wind only they could feel.

I pressed my lips against the pointed shell of Aileana's ear, and she sucked in a breath. "Xander," she chided. "I'm trying to concentrate."

A rumble ran through me as I licked her flesh. "Am I being distracting?"

"Yes," she gasped.

Desire pounded through the bond, and Aileana's need for me was so strong it nearly bowled me over.

She was insatiable, this mate of mine.

My hands slid from her hips, sliding towards her core. Aileana moaned, pressing herself against me as my fingers slipped beneath the hem of her leggings, and I found the warmth I was looking for.

A rumble slipped from my chest. "Is this distracting?"

Green ribbons slipped from Aileana's palms with increasing intensity, swirling around us and hiding us from any prying eyes.

She groaned, and the sound sent shivers down my spine as she twisted beneath my touch. "Gods, yes."

Kissing her neck, I whispered, "Good. Try to use your magic now."

"What?" she asked breathlessly. "Why?"

"Distractions happen," I smirked and pressed my fingers harder. Aileana panted, squirming beneath my touch. "Consider this... training."

Aileana spread her hands on the ground, writhing beneath my touch as the green ribbons bent to her will. They wove around us, and the rest of the world faded away as I concentrated on the way my mate moved against my touch.

Holding her close, her ass pressed against me, I provided *ample* distractions.

When she reached her peak, the ribbons dove into the frost-hardened dirt as she screamed. The earth rumbled as in thanks, and the forest, which was firmly in the grips of the coming winter, brightened.

Dark gray clouds covered the previously blue sky, and thunder rumbled in the distance.

Aileana looked up at me as I slid my hand out of her leggings, her eyes still glowing. "How did I do?"

Brushing my lips over her temple, I murmured, "You were amazing."

The green glow receded from Aileana's eyes as she pulled herself from the earth. When it was gone, I pulled her to her feet, drawing her toward me for a kiss.

She tasted like the earth, and sparks flew between us as our lips moved together. With every claiming kiss, I told Aileana how much I loved her and how proud I was of her.

I showed her that she was mine.

A rumble of thunder came from above. The wind picked up,

whistling through the trees, and the ground shook as the storm approached.

What started as a few drops of rain quickly became a torrential downpour. Water streaked down us both, plastering our hair and our clothes to our bodies.

Aileana laughed, breaking our kiss and looking up at the sky. "I think we should get out of the storm." Even as she spoke, she lifted the hem of my tunic and slipped her fingers beneath the fabric.

"Gods, Aileana!" I jolted, shivering. "Your hands are like ice!"

A dark chuckle came from my mate as she splayed her fingers. "Is that so? Do you find them... distracting?"

An inarticulate mumble escaped me. Words were harder to come by as those deft fingers slipped lower and lower.

Her icy touch trailed down my stomach even as frigid drops of rain pelted us from above. When she slipped her hand into my trousers, I reached out and grabbed her wrist.

"Not here," I growled.

She pulled her hands from my grip, continuing down her tortuous path. "I thought you like distractions, Xander?"

"I fear you may have misunderstood," I growled. "I enjoy being the cause of your distractions, Sunshine."

In response, she slipped her hand beneath the waistband of my trousers.

I cursed.

Grabbing the back of Aileana's thighs, I lifted her and pulled her against me. She wrapped her arms around my neck, capturing my mouth with hers. We kissed, our bodies pressed together in all the right ways, and I walked.

"Where are we going?" she asked against my lips as rain pelted us through the trees.

"Somewhere dry," I said, my legs eating up the length of the forest.

"Good." Aileana's mouth trailed a path down my cheek.

I tightened my grip on her thighs, taking the opportunity to appreciate her muscular, lithe form. Her clothes were soaked, providing me with the ability to see *everything*.

A growl rose within me as I pressed Aileana tighter against me. Suffice it to say, I would have to kill anyone who saw my mate in such a state.

I hurried through the forest, the autumnal breeze blowing past us as thunder rumbled again. The storm carried hints of winter. The rain pelting us was freezing, reminiscent of shards of ice as they fell on our skin.

Aileana shivered, and I drew her wet form tighter against me.

She asked, "Where are you taking me, Xander?"

Reclaiming her lips with mine, I infused as much warmth into the kiss as possible.

"I found a cavern earlier this week while you were talking with Myhhena," I said against her mouth. "I want to show it to you."

She laughed. "Why do we always seem to end up in caves?"

Chuckling, I wrapped my arms tighter around Aileana as I stepped over a fallen log. "I don't know, but I don't mind." Pausing, I glanced at her. "Do you?"

"No. They're our special place."

The cavern was close by. Hidden by a large evergreen tree whose boughs dusted the ground, it was tucked away and out of the elements. Releasing my grip on Aileana's legs, she tightened her thighs around my middle as I brushed the boughs aside and walked us both inside. The cavern was dim, the air chilly, but at least it was dry. Aileana slid down my body until she stood before me.

"Th-this cave is pretty small," she said through chattering teeth, rubbing her hands over her arms.

Reaching out, I ran my fingers down her cheeks. If I thought Aileana had been cold before, now she was like pure ice.

"Hold on," I said, reaching for my scabbard. I laid it and my sword on the ground near the cavern entrance before pulling my tunic over my head. I was halfway through pulling off my trousers when disbelief washed through the bond.

Looking up, I met my mate's incredulous gaze. "What are you doing?"

Letting my trousers fall to the floor, I stepped out of them as a breeze blew in through the entrance of the cave. "I'm going to warm you up."

"How?"

"I have my ways." I waggled my eyebrows. "Do you trust me?"

A roll of thunder boomed above us, and the trees blew, their branches rattling as lightning lit up the sky.

"With my life," she breathed.

"Then lift your arms, Aileana."

She did as she was told.

She must be freezing, the dragon remarked. *Your mate is usually a terrible listener.*

Shut up, I grumbled.

The dragon snorted.

Within a few minutes, we were bare except for the necklace hanging around Aileana's neck. I spread out our clothes under her watchful eye. The rain continued to pour outside, but other than a small trickle of water near the entrance, the ground was dry.

Crouching, I ran my fingers over the rocky floor. "Sunshine, do you think you might do something about the ground?"

"The ground?" she echoed, staring at the rocky floor for a moment, her brows furrowed.

"It's not very comfortable right now." I tilted my head. "I was wondering if you could help with that?"

"Oh!" Aileana laughed, and my insides warmed. I loved that sound. "Of course."

Green ribbons slipped from her hands, sinking into the ground. Seconds later, dark green moss carpeted the interior of the cave, and a small rain berry bush sprouted in the back corner.

"Is that better?" she asked.

I knelt, pulling her down to lie in front of me as I pressed my body against her back. Running my hands over Aileana's icy skin, I tried to infuse as much heat into my touch as possible.

"It's perfect." Pressing my lips to the back of her neck, my hands wandered over her stomach before traveling lower. "Now, let me warm you up."

THE STORM RAGED FOR HOURS. By the time the thunder abated and the rain stopped pouring from the skies, the day had given way to evening. Gray clouds continued to fill the sky, and the scent of snow was in the air.

Our clothes were dry, but we had yet to put them back on. The cavern was warm enough, our bodies having heated the small space thoroughly. Aileana was silent, her head resting against my shoulder as she twisted a strand of my hair through her fingers.

The setting sun filtered through the evergreen boughs at the front of the cavern, and I basked in the warmth and joy coming through our mating bond.

This was good. Happiness was good. Amazing, even.

It would be enough... right?

People were happy even if they weren't married.

Since accepting our mating bond, Aileana had proven time and time again that she was mine in every sense of the term. What we'd just done proved that.

I didn't need her to be my wife. Marriage didn't really mean anything. The problem was, even as the thought entered my mind, a pang ran through me.

I would be happy even if we never wed. Wouldn't I?

Aileana shifted, moving to rest between my legs. She placed her chin on my chest, those stunning green eyes blinking up at me.

"Penny for your thoughts," she said.

Cupping her cheek, I rubbed my thumb on her soft skin. "I was thinking about marriage."

As soon as I said the words, I knew they were the wrong ones. The mood shifted in the cavern, and Aileana's mouth pinched in a thin line. Her eyes grew heavy, and a long-suffering sigh escaped her.

"This again?" She pushed herself up, reaching over and drawing her tunic over her head. Kneeling on the mossy ground beside me, she crossed her arms and glared at me. "I thought we talked about this."

"We did." I pushed myself up until my back rested against the wall.

"What was so hard to understand? I said 'no'."

"I understand that you're not ready yet—"

"Ever," she snapped, those green eyes blazing. "I won't *ever* be ready for marriage."

Sighing, I pulled on my tunic. I was not in the mood for an argument. "Aileana, I wasn't suggesting that we—"

"What about the word 'no' did you not understand, Xander?"

"Gods," I groaned. "Do you really want to do this right now? I thought we were having a good day."

A great day, to be honest. Distracting Aileana had been fun, and I enjoyed spending time alone with her.

But now, all the nice feelings were gone. The air between us was charged as though the lightning from earlier had moved inside.

"You're the one who brought it up," she said.

"You asked!" Running my hand through my hair, I shook my head. "Do you think there is a chance that you might change your mind one day?"

"Never," she replied, venom dripping from her words. She pulled on her leggings, her movements stiff. "Xander, I will never get married. I won't."

She *won't*.

Before, when she said no, it felt different. It had still been a refusal, but her words had felt softer.

Now, though, they were like a dagger through my heart.

I loved her. She loved me. She showed me that time and time again.

But now, it seemed like that didn't matter. I pulled on my trousers, doing up the buttons before crossing my arms.

"Is it marriage you don't want, or me? Is this because of the White Death?"

Aileana stilled. "No," she breathed, shaking her head. "I told you, Xander. I chose you." Her eyes widened as she stood in the cavern, her fists clenched at her side. "I will *always* choose you."

Rolling up the sleeve of my tunic, I held up my mating mark. "You chose this, right?"

"Yes." She nodded, running her hand over her own mark.

I thought I had accepted her refusal, that I could live with not marrying her until I could prove I was her equal in every way. But apparently, it meant more to me than I ever imagined. "Then why won't you marry me?"

"Because I can't!"

My eyes widened. "Can't"

"That's what I said," she snapped.

"From where I'm standing, it sounds an awful lot like an excuse."

She gasped, her hand flying to her heart. "Excuse me? What in Thelrena's name are you talking about?"

"We're already mated. That is an eternal commitment, Aileana. There is *nothing* that can break this bond between us. And yet, for some reason, you were fine with mating me, but you won't marry me?" I shook my head. "You just don't want to marry me because you're afraid."

"Yes!" she screamed. Shoving her feet into her boots, Aileana ran her hands through her hair. "I am *afraid*! I would have to be an idiot not to be! Do you know what marriage is, Xander?"

I stared at her. "Of course, I know what marriage is. It's a ceremony where two people vow to spend the rest of their lives together. For royals, it includes a blood pact—"

"You horrible, insufferable, vexing male! I didn't ask you for the dictionary definition of marriage." She balled her fists at her side, stepping toward me as her eyes blazed with fury. "Marriage is not a choice. It is not something nice to be shared between two people. Marriage is a gods-damned cage!"

"A cage?" My heart thundered in my chest. "Do you think I would do that to you?" I spread my hands wide. "Of all people, you dare accuse me of doing something like that?"

She seethed. "Then why do you want to marry me if not to trap me?"

"Because I gods-damn love you, you ridiculous, aggravating, stubborn female!" I yelled. "I love every single part of you. The fire inside you, your strength, your propensity to violence, even the way you don't listen to anything I say. I have so much love for you that it feels like it is burning through my skin."

She stared at me with wide eyes.

"I want to marry you because I want to shout from the rooftops that you are mine. I would do anything for you. I would burn the entire world down. Destroy anything and anyone who would dare come between us. My love for you is a fiery inferno, and I want to marry you because we are partners. Equals in every way."

A long moment passed as my words settled between us.

"Marriage in Ithenmyr isn't about equality." Her voice was as cold as the breeze blowing through the trees. "It never has been and never will be."

Her words knocked the breath out of me. "Aileana, love—"

She held up her hand. "Xander, the rain has stopped."

It stopped over an hour ago, but this didn't feel like the right time to point that out.

"And?" I asked through clenched teeth.

"And I'm hungry. Let's go home and grab something to eat before going to bed. We can talk about this more in the morning."

She turned, crossing her arms, and stood at the front of the cavern while I buckled my scabbard around my waist.

We walked back in complete and utter silence.

Gone

AILEANA

The soft sounds of Xander's snores filled my ears, and I groaned. I had spent the past few hours in an exhausted state somewhere between sleeping and waking. It was nearing the middle of the night, and I was no closer to finding rest.

Eventually, I gave up on sleeping altogether. Xander and I hadn't exchanged a single word since our fight in the cave. When we returned, I showered and braided my hair. By the time I was done, he was already asleep.

Rolling out of bed, I pulled on a shawl over my nightgown. Standing by the door, I looked over our room. The moon shone brightly, casting a soft glow over the bedroom. Vines crawled over the wall, and Xander's naked sleeping form was sprawled over the mattress as his silver-white hair spread out like a halo all around him.

Warmth swelled within me at the sight. Even though we were fighting, he was still my mate.

My feet carried me over to him, and I bent, brushing his hair back from his face. I kissed his forehead and whispered, "I love you."

With one last glance at the top of the stairs, I headed down.

Xander didn't understand why I couldn't marry him. The scars on my back, the things that were done to me... they all happened in the name of marriage. Thanks to Kethryllian, I understand why High King Edgar wanted me to marry Remington.

Wives had no rights in Ithenmyr. None. If I said yes to Xander, I would be handing him my freedom.

To be fair, females didn't have many rights either. But at least right now, I wasn't anyone's property. I belonged to myself. I did not have a father or a brother—the High King had made sure of that.

If I married Xander, I would give up my last rights.

No matter how much I loved him, I couldn't do that.

Xander was my whole world. My other half. My reason for living.

But I couldn't give him the keys to my freedom. Not when I was so focused on liberating the females in Ithenmyr.

How could I do that if I married Xander?

I just needed to think of a way to explain this to him. Preferably one that would not destroy our relationship.

However, this was not the time. No good ever came from having a conversation in the middle of the night. Considering that our discussion in the cavern had resulted in an explosive argument, I would rather wait until I was well-rested to tackle the marriage discussion again.

If I was awake, I might as well take a walk.

Pulling on a pair of fur-lined black boots resting by the front door, I slid a dagger into the sheath on my thigh and opened the door slowly. A *creak* sounded, and I stilled. My heart pounded in my chest, but the soft sounds of Xander's snores filled my ears. Letting out a low breath, I slipped out the door and slid it shut behind me.

The air was frigid, and the moon was bright as I stood beneath the night sky. Clouds hid most of the stars from view, but every so often, one of them would pop through. Taking a deep breath, I relished the freedom of being outside. I loved the crisp night air and the way the wind ruffled my hair and kissed my cheeks.

It was beautiful. Quiet. Still.

My feet took me down the moss-covered cobblestone path, my destination aimless as a brisk wind blew by. I had not been outside long when something small and wet landed on my cheek. Another quickly followed it. Then another.

I gasped, looking up.

Small white drops fell from the sky, their descent leisurely as they floated towards the mossy cobblestones. Night insects called out, and I thought I heard a raven caw somewhere in the distance. But I looked at the sky and didn't see any birds at all. The only thing I saw were snowflakes falling like a million moonlit dancers.

I put out my hands and let the snow fall on my outstretched palms. The droplets were cold but dissolved almost instantly upon contact with my skin.

I had never touched snow. Never held it.

When I lived in my tower, I used to watch snowflakes fall from the confines of my room. I wasn't even allowed to sketch the winter landscape. Not after my tutor Orvyn was killed.

Watching something from afar and taking part in it were two very different things.

Laughter bubbled up inside of me. From afar, the snow was beautiful. Up close, it was breathtaking.

Soon, the cobblestones were covered by the white material. I danced along to the tune of the wind, my shawl thoroughly soaked. Another raven cawed in the distance, and I waltzed down an empty street. Eventually, my toes grew cold as water seeped through my boots. It didn't dampen my spirits, though.

This was why I couldn't marry Xander.

There was still so much I had to do. So much I needed to experience. How could I ever risk giving away my freedom?

When dancing in the streets grew tiresome, I opened my mouth and caught a snowflake. It burst into cold, crisp nothingness as soon as it touched my tongue. I loved it. I caught snowflake after snowflake, twirling beneath the night sky until my limbs burned with exhaustion.

Only then did I retrace my steps, walking back to our home.

Pushing open the door, I shrugged out of my shawl and dropped it on a chair. "Xander, wake up! It's snowing!"

The silence was deafening as I waited for a reply.

A heavy sense of foreboding slammed into me, and I furrowed my brows.

"Xander?" Hurrying up the stairs, I took them two at a time.

My heart raced in my chest, and my eyes widened as I tried to understand the scene before me.

Too much.

This was too much.

My nose burned at the astringent scents of sandalwood, lemon, and cedar. My stomach twisted, and bile rose in my throat.

Destruction reigned.

Shutters banged against the wall, letting in lazy snowflakes through the open windows. The wardrobe was open. What used to be clothes were now scraps of destroyed fabric. And the vines that used to cover the walls...

They were lying on the floor in piles.

I picked one up, running my finger over it. A clean slice ran through the top as though someone had taken a sword through it.

A choked sob rose in my throat as I turned.

Beside the bed, less than a foot from me, was the decapitated head of a Winged Soldier. His dead eyes stared at me as he lay in a pool of black blood. His headless body was a few feet away. Jagged tear marks were visible, as though someone had ripped his head from his body.

Bile rose in my throat. I swallowed, forcing it back down even as it burned.

The dead soldier wasn't the worst thing in my room.

Not by a long shot.

The worst thing was on the bed. The pillow, to be exact.

A crimson dagger pierced the fluffy material, pinning a slip of paper in place. A small beaded bracelet hung off the hilt, the opaque blue and white beads at odds with the death and destruction all around me.

My lungs tightened to the point of pain, and breathing became impossible as I strode over to the bed. Yanking the dagger from the pillow, I ran the bracelet through my fingers and picked up the note. My eyes swept over it, reading it once. Then twice.

My stomach twisted into a knot.

New game, pet.
My bride wants to meet you.
Come get him.
—JKE

In the middle of the paper was a single drop of crimson blood. I knew, without a shadow of a doubt, it belonged to Xander.

Holding the paper in my hand, I looked down.

Really looked.

Beyond the black blood streaming from the Winged Soldier's corpse, blood droplets were all over the room. They were on the bed, the vines, and even on the pillow.

Red was *everywhere.*

"Oh my gods," I moaned as I struggled to draw in a breath.

Red.

There was so much red.

And Xander wasn't here.

Gone.

He was *gone.*

He'd been taken while I'd been dancing in the snow.

All of a sudden, the reasons for our fight seemed so distant. Marriage didn't seem so problematic anymore.

Not now that I was faced with a problem like this?

I was here, and he was gone.

And he was injured.

The paper fluttered to the floor, and the dagger fell to the ground with a *twang.* Blackness edged my vision as my legs shook.

Dozens of green ribbons slipped from my fingers, flying out the open window. My heart stuttered. Everything was brighter. Louder. I could hear everything. The wind blowing in through the open window was a trumpet. The leaves crackling were like booms of thunder. The yipping of foxes and the hooting of owls were like drums in my ears.

And my heart?

The thundering *lub-dub* was a roaring boom.

I kept seeing the words on the paper. They played on repeat in my mind, over and over again, until I knew them by heart.

New game, pet.

Pet.

Clenching my fists at my sides, my heart felt like it exploded as I *screamed.*

I screamed and screamed and screamed. My voice was ear-piercingly loud as my screams rang out, filling the air around me.

Magic exploded out of me, and I screamed.

I screamed even as the wind blew and leaves swirled around me. Myhhena appeared in my peripherals, a frown on her leafy face. Castien came next, his watery gaze filled with deep concern as he stood before me.

Still, I screamed.

My voice grew hoarse, but I did not stop. Magic poured out of me in droves. The well within me seemed endless as I pushed my power to its limits. Something within me clicked into place, and I felt a stretching, but I ignored it.

I ignored everything.

I had nothing left. Nothing at all except Xander, and he was *gone*.

He wanted to marry me, and I refused him.

Still screaming, I reached within myself and grabbed our bond. I yanked with all my might.

Emptiness reigned within me.

I couldn't feel Xander. I couldn't find him.

He was *gone*.

I screamed.

I thought I knew pain. I thought that all those years in my tower and all the abuse I'd suffered taught me the depths of agony. I thought I knew what it felt like to be broken.

I. Was. A. Fool.

The pain I had known was nothing compared to the absolute anguish and torment currently ripping through my body. From my head to my feet, everything hurt. My mating mark burned with the fire of a thousand suns.

The green swirls on my hands flashed, writhing on my skin. Fire coursed through my body, and my heart fissured. I was broken and reborn. My body was made new. I hadn't known heartbreak could be so visceral.

Still, silent screams escaped me.

He was gone.

I was broken.

One by one, Spirits paraded through the house. Their faces blurred together as they read the note, offering condolences. One of the Guardians said something about black magic. Another mentioned an attack on the wards. They said darkness was on the horizon.

They spoke, but all I could think of was that line.

Come get him.

Every time I thought of those words, I screamed.

The earth trembled with fury. The ground in the Sanctuary shook, and cracks appeared in the walls. Shouts of shock and horror filled my ears.

Green ribbons continued to flood out of my palms, and the air in the empty house became too much to bear.

I ran outside, dropping to the ground. Digging my hands into the snow, I reached for the earth.

"He's gone," I cried out.

We will find him, Protectress. The earth's promise rang through me, and tremor after tremor ran through the ground.

As one, the life in Ithenmyr turned its gaze to me. The trees, the roots, the animals, and the insects—every living thing looked at me.

As one, they shuddered and screamed and withered as they felt my pain.

We will find him.

The ground quaked. Cobblestones crumbled before me, and the earth shook. Green ribbons flowed from my hands, and trees rattled as the earth trembled.

I knew that this was felt all through the Four Kingdoms.

I reached for my bond again. It was still present, still burning strong within me. Grabbing the bond, I yanked as hard as I could.

There was no response.

"I'll find you," I vowed. "No matter what."

Holding tight to the bond between us, I sent Xander my love. My hope. My peace. My strength.

I sent him everything I had.

And then, when it was all gone, I screamed once more.

Magic *ripped* through me. My arms tingled, and I pulled back the collar of my nightgown. Green swirls stretched from my fingers, up my arms, all the way to my collarbones.

I glanced at my well of power.

It was deeper than ever.

Earlier, this would have been a cause for celebration.

Now, I had nothing left.

The Forgotten One

RYLLAE

"What else do you know about your father's soldiers?" The question came from a male called Orrin.

He clasped his hands behind his back as he prowled on the other side of the large wooden table separating us. The tent was big, and even though there was a table between us, Orrin was using his height to intimidate me.

Dawn was a few hours off, and a lantern rested on the middle of the table, its flickering light illuminating my interrogator. A brown jug of water sat on the table, just out of my reach. Dark shadows covered the tent's walls, and a cold wind blew in beneath the canvas walls. We had been at this for hours.

Perhaps, at one point in my life, Orrin's tactics might have succeeded in frightening me. Perhaps, at one point in my life, I was capable of feeling fear.

I was no longer that female.

Now, all I felt was anger.

It pulsed through my veins like a raging fire. I was angry that this

258

group of rebels felt like they had any power over me. Angry that they took Daegal away.

On top of that, I was angry that I was, once again, being held prisoner.

Orrin and I had been at this for days. At first, I refused to speak until they took me to Daegal. When they finally let me see him, I almost fainted. He looked horrible. The stench in that gods-damned tent had nearly bowled me over. Thank the gods, he hadn't been too far gone. After that first visit, they assured me he was being looked after.

I didn't trust them.

"I've told you and your friends everything I know." I groaned into my hands.

The male shook his head, snarling as he displayed his blackened teeth in my direction. "Look, Forgotten One—"

"Ryllae," I snapped, slamming my hands down on the table. The jug of water shook, and Orrin drew in a breath. If I had my magic, I would have destroyed this male ten times over for how he spoke to me.

If I'd had my magic, I wouldn't be in this situation.

I seethed, "My name is Ryllae. What is it with you people and calling me the Forgotten One? I have a gods-dammed name. Use it or don't speak to me."

Violence flashed in the horrible male's eyes. "Look, *Forgotten One*, I have already explained to you who we are."

I groaned. This was nowhere near the first or even the tenth time we'd had this conversation. "Yes, you and your merry collection of outcasts call yourselves the Resistance. Well, that's all well and good, except you're parked in the woods doing the gods-only-know-what instead of fighting for people who need you!"

Orrin had the audacity to snarl at me as if I wasn't the gods-damned princess of this entire country. "Watch your tone, *Ryllae*."

"Or what?"

He raised a brow, smirking as though he knew something I didn't. "Or you'll never see your friend again."

Cold trickled down my spine, and I straightened, my eyes narrowing. "What did you do with Daegal?"

Orrin didn't respond.

"Tell me!" I couldn't help the increased pitch of my voice. "If you hurt him, so help me—"

Before the last word could make it out of my mouth, the entire world shook. The table trembled, and the tent poles cracked. Water sloshed over the sides of the jug as screams came from around the camp. The ground quaked beneath our feet, and somewhere in the distance, trees splintered.

Orrin's eyes widened, and he cursed. "Wait here," he ordered gruffly. "If you want your friend to live, you won't move a muscle."

I stared at him. I was a princess, for the gods' sake. Raised in palaces far finer than this male had probably ever seen in his entire life, if his lack of manners was any indication. Did he dare order me around?

A shout came from outside the tent. "Orrin, come quickly!"

The male in question cursed, pinning me with a final glare before high-tailing it out of the tent.

The screams continued. The ground's unnatural rumbling grew louder and louder, and chaos reigned.

An itch came to life within me. It had been so long since I felt it that it took a moment for me to realize what it was.

My magic *called* to me. For the first time since the prohiberis had come off, I felt it.

I gasped, quickly reaching within myself to where my power resided. The moment the pool of my magic came into view, a sob ripped out of me.

A strange black mist still covered it from sight.

A tree cracked, and a flash of lightning lit up the sky, visible through the tent canvas. Moments later, someone screamed, "Fire!"

"Help!" another yelled.

"The world is ending!"

A sob. "Why is this happening?"

"The gods are angry."

Footsteps and screams and chaos were all around.

"Get Ammath!" another yelled.

A baby wailed somewhere in the camp, and I sucked in a breath. Whatever was happening was not normal. It was not good. Nor was it safe.

When yet another minute passed, and no one returned to check on me, I made up my mind.

I would not sit here, waiting for the world to end.

I might not have been a proficient warrior, but two hundred and fifty years in prison taught me a thing or two about self-preservation. The first lesson was that when presented with opportunities, one did not shove them aside.

In his rush to help with the emergency, Orrin forgot to escort me back to my "quarters." That was a rough term for the small shack on the edge of camp where they'd shoved me when they'd first brought us here.

I would not let this opportunity slip me by, and I stood. Another tremble ripped through the ground, and I swayed, nearly toppling over. Grabbing onto the table, my gaze darted wildly around the dark tent. My heart raced, and I knew I had to move quickly.

There wasn't much in the way of weapons here—not that I knew how to use them, anyway. The porcelain jug in the middle of the table would have to do. Keeping one hand on the table to maintain my balance, I set the lantern on the floor before grabbing the jug and flipping it over. Water poured out on the other side of the table, landing on the ground with a splash.

The shouting outside continued. Everything was so loud. My ears rang, and my head pounded as the noise encroached upon me. I could feel the madness calling my name like a distant friend, but I shut it out.

I couldn't waste any time.

Grateful the yelling would cover the noise I was about to make, I gripped the jug. Some people would probably have prayed to Kydona that this would work and that they could escape.

I did not.

The gods had shown time and again they did not care about me.

Releasing my grip on the table, I held the jug above my head with both hands before heaving it down on the edge of the wooden surface. A crack ran down the side, marring the once-smooth brown porcelain, but it remained in one piece.

More screams. It sounded like the fire was getting worse.

Grunting, I slammed the jug down again. And again. My arms burned, but I didn't stop.

The fifth time, the jug finally broke into a dozen pieces. Sifting through the shards, I grabbed the largest piece. It was triangular, with a jagged edge that ran along two sides. I gripped it tightly, wincing as the skin broke on my palm. The scent of blood filled the air, but I ignored it.

I had to go.

Creeping over to the tent flap and listened. The rumbling was no longer as loud, but the ground still shook. Dozens of elves ran around the moonlit camp like chickens with their heads cut off. There was so much noise that I couldn't sift through the sounds to make out individual words.

It was chaos.

A thick plume of black smoke rose to the sky from the direction of the middle of the camp, and heavy coughs intermingled with the screams.

No one was taking charge. No one was telling them what to do.

Scoffing, I shook my head. "And these people call themselves the Resistance."

They were lucky my father's guards hadn't found them yet. If a little rumbling and a small fire scared them, what would they do when faced with a Winged Soldier? Or worse, the Crimson King's red magic?

He would have them choking on their blood in seconds. There were dozens of elves in this camp. Entire families. But I hadn't seen anyone wield the kind of power my father did.

The kind the Earth Elf seemed to hold.

The kind that I used to have access to.

A cry of frustration escaped me, and I huffed.

I had to get out of here.

Slipping out of the tent, I ran towards the edge of camp. I might not have been great with weapons, but I was good at memorizing paths after taking them once. A benefit of growing up in maze-like castles, I supposed.

An elderly female named Crystenn had insisted Orrin let me take a guarded walk every day to "stay fresh."

Thanks to her, I knew the layout of the entire camp. They were keeping Daegal in a small tent on the outskirts, far from where they'd been holding me.

I needed to find Daegal. I felt a connection to him. A trust that was unmatched. A loyalty that I had never felt before.

Something within me ached at the very thought of leaving him.

I wouldn't do it. I couldn't.

Clutching my shard of porcelain, I weaved through the camp.

Ducking in the shadows as people ran towards the flames, I hurried to the edge of camp. The tent they had thrown him in was little more than scraps of fabric billowing in the wind.

Shoving aside the flap, I hissed, "Daegal!"

The wind blew past me, but there was no response. I hurried inside the tent. My eyes widened, and my stomach dropped. It was empty.

Where is he?

Orrin's words echoed in my mind.

You'll never see your friend again.

My breath came faster as realization slammed into me.

They were going to kill him. Maybe they already had?

Even as the thought entered my mind, I shook my head. No. I knew he was alive.

That *thing* inside of me would know if the Fortune Elf died.

I had to find him.

Not wanting to waste a moment, I exited the tent and looked around me. Where would they take Daegal if they were going to kill him?

I glanced towards the middle of the camp.

Not there, I decided. These people were horrible, but unlike my father, they didn't seem to be the type to revel in a public execution.

No, the forest was my best option.

I hurried into the dense woods, leaving the rebels' camp behind me. Thick trees surrounded me, and the only source of light came from the moon shining through the canopy of leaves.

Another tremor ran through the earth—where in the gods' names was this coming from?—and my foot bumped into a fallen log. I careened toward the ground, barely avoiding cutting myself with my shard as I slammed face-first into the dirt. Cursing, I got to my feet and dusted myself off.

My thigh burned, and I limped as I ran once more. Screams kept rising from the direction of the camp, but I knew they would soon turn to cries of outrage when Orrin realized I left.

I didn't have long.

I went deeper into the woods. With every step, I looked for any sign of Daegal.

An owl hooted above me as I darted beneath a tree. My lungs burned, and my muscles protested my quick movements. Running was hard, and my entire body ached.

Another tremor. I grabbed onto a tree to wait it out.

As soon as it ended, I kept going. I couldn't stop. My heart pounded, and branches slapped me in the face, but still, I ran.

"Daegal, are you out here?" I didn't dare raise my voice louder than a forceful whisper as I called his name repeatedly.

The silence of the forest became oppressive, and with every passing moment, I feared the worst.

I ran for so long, I thought I would be lost in the woods forever.

Eventually, the strange rumbling stopped.

Still, I didn't find him. Worry bloomed in my stomach.

Either I was going in the wrong direction or...

He was dead.

Maybe I was wrong, and that thing between us didn't exist. Perhaps it was all in my head.

Why wouldn't the one person I trusted die on me?

Everyone else had.

A crazed laugh threatened to escape me. Of course, something was wrong. Nothing in my life had ever been right or easy.

I was so busy feeling sorry for myself that I almost missed the low groan coming from nearby. The hairs on the back of my neck prickled, and I crept toward the noise. It grew louder, and the sound was tinged with echoes of pain.

Gripping my porcelain shard in my hand, I hurried towards the noise.

"Hello?" I whispered, my eyes darting through the brush. "Who's there?"

A moan came from my left.

Holding the porcelain shard so tightly that it nearly cut my hand again, I rushed around a massive maple tree.

I gasped, and my shard fell to the ground as I dropped to my knees.

"Oh, my gods." Reaching out, I took Daegal's hand in my own. It was wet with blood, and my eyes widened as I looked him over. A sheen of sweat covered his forehead, and his breathing was labored. But he was alive. "What happened to you?"

"I'm fine," he lied.

"I've seen corpses that looked better than you," I retorted, running my eyes over him as I searched for an injury. "You're not fine."

A hoarse laugh escaped Daegal as he cradled his arm against his chest. "If you think this is bad, you should see the other guy."

My visual inspection found nothing wrong, so I reached out and ran my hands over Daegal's torso. He stiffened beneath my touch, but he didn't pull away. I wasn't even sure what I planned to do when I found his injury, but I knew I couldn't leave him here.

Daegal groaned, and despite his protests, I knew he was hurt. Trying to distract him, I asked, "What other guy?"

The Fortune Elf laughed softly. "The one they sent to kill me."

He tilted his head to the side, and the glimmer of metal caught my eye. A bloody sword lay beside Daegal, half-covered in fallen leaves.

I continued to feel for wounds on his torso, but everything felt okay. Moving to his shoulders, my hands slowly ran down his arms. Daegal's left arm was fine, but when I reached his right, I only made it about halfway before he hissed through clenched teeth.

"Shit. That hurts," he said.

Moving around him as carefully as I could, I rolled up his sleeve. My eyes widened. A cut about three inches stretched along his upper arm's muscle. "You call this fine?"

"Yep." He raised a brow. "I'm alive. Therefore, I'm fine."

I wasn't so sure about that. This did not look good. "Can you lift your arm?"

Daegal inhaled sharply. Grabbing the hilt of his sword with his good hand, he used the weapon as a crutch to push himself to his feet. "I think so."

The Fortune Elf wobbled, leaning against the tree as he drew in breath after shallow breath.

Standing, I put a hand on his arm. He sucked in a breath, staring at where our flesh touched, but he didn't say anything.

My brows furrowed. "Daegal, are you sure you're going to be alright?"

Pushing himself off the tree, Daegal clutched his sword in his left hand before offering me a wry smirk. "I have to be. We have no other choice."

I swallowed. He was right. The wind still carried screams toward us, a reminder of the rebels we were fleeing.

"Okay," I said, frowning. "Let's go."

Leaves crunched beneath our feet as we left the tree. It wasn't long before I noticed a lump lying in the middle of a clearing. It was bent in half, and something smaller lay a few feet away.

Bile rose in my throat, and I barely kept it down. "I take it that's the other guy?"

A hoarse chuckle escaped the Fortune Elf.

"It is," he said. "Hold on a second."

Daegal walked over to the headless corpse and grabbed something from his middle. He buckled a scabbard around his waist, sliding the sword into the sheath.

When the weapon was put away, Daegal extended his left hand. It hovered in the air in silent invitation, and I stared at it for a single moment before slipping my hand into his. He exhaled, his fingers squeezing mine lightly, and we walked once more.

I kept thinking about the rebels we were leaving behind. If I thought they were going to be angry when they learned we escaped, now I was sure they would be furious to know Daegal killed one of their own.

Trying to take my mind off it, I asked, "What happened?"

A beat passed before Daegal shrugged. "The Death Elf wanted to kill me 'properly.' Apparently, he had some form of perverted morals. He took me into the woods, armed me, and then hunted me."

"What?" Disbelief ran through my words, and I blinked. "He *hunted* you?"

"For sport."

"Gods." A rage, unlike anything I had ever felt before, ran through me. How dare they? They called themselves the Resistance but were no better than my father. "If he weren't already dead, I would kill him for that."

For a moment, Daegal didn't respond.

I worried I had scared him with my intensity, but then he laughed. "I know you would. You're dark, Princess. I like that."

We stepped over some logs, walking through a cluster of thick birch trees. "How did you survive?"

"I found some late-season berries nearby. I ate them, found some water, and Looked into the future. Once I Saw the perfect moment, I waited him out." Daegal shrugged. "It was him or me."

"And you chose yourself," I whispered.

We walked silently for a few more minutes. The sky showed the first hints of sunrise before Daegal spoke again. "Does that bother you?"

"That you killed someone?"

"Yes."

I tightened my grip on his hand, thinking it over. Did it bother me? Perhaps most people might have found death frightening.

I wasn't "most people." I was a Death Elf and the princess of Ithenmyr. Even though the majority of the country didn't even remember I existed—something which I was determined to fix—I was still here.

"No," I said as a small cavern came into view a few hundred feet in the distance. I moved us towards it. We both needed to rest. "It doesn't bother me. Does knowing who my father is bother you?"

This time, it was Daegal's turn to be silent. His brows furrowed, and his mouth pinched in a firm line. Whether he was in pain or lost in thought, I wasn't sure. We went into the cavern, which turned out to be little more than an opening in the hill.

Every passing moment felt longer than the last as I waited for his answer.

But I would not push him. I had to know.

We slid down the rocky wall beside each other, and Daegal took out his sword. He placed it within arm's reach before he gestured for me to come closer. I sat next to him, our thighs touching, as the sun crested the horizon.

"Ryllae?"

"Yes?" I murmured, leaning against him.

"I know who your father is, and that doesn't change how I feel about you. We are not our family members, nor are we the mistakes of our past." He sighed, sliding his good hand into mine. "I was... my mother is dead. Did I tell you that?"

"No," I whispered. "But I know how it feels. My mother is dead, too."

"I'm sorry." A long moment passed before he spoke again. "My mother... she's dead because of a mistake I made."

My heart cracked as he gathered his thoughts, and I didn't dare speak or move.

"A pack of werewolves near the ocean sought me out. They wanted me to See the future for them. They weren't good people, Ryllae. I didn't know it then, but they were working for your father. I shouldn't have worked for them, but there was... I was... I had debts." He shook his head. "Before... I used to gamble. The werewolves knew this and were willing to pay a lot."

He shuddered, and I squeezed his hand. "It's okay," I whispered. "I'm here."

Daegal pressed his head against mine. "Thank you. I Looked ahead for the pack, but I made a mistake. The paths changed, but I was cocky. The pack... they killed my mother because of my mistake." He shuddered. "That Death Elf wasn't the first person I killed. He probably won't be the last, either. But my mother's death is the only one that remains on my conscience."

His anguished words echoed around the cavern. They were tinged with so much guilt and pain that all I could do was hold him.

So I did.

Time went on, and the sun rose as the heaviness of Daegal's story hung over us.

Eventually, I whispered, "I killed my mother, too."

That was the first time I said those words out loud. The first time, I acknowledged the painful truth.

Daegal shifted, pulling his good arm over me. He drew me against his chest, hugging me as he pressed a feather-light kiss against my forehead.

We were both broken.

"Sleep," he whispered.

I did.

Happiness Had No Place Here

AILEANA

E very single second without my mate felt like an eternity.

Every.

Single.

Moment.

Hurt.

My chest ached with the sorrow of a thousand heartbreaks. Agony was my new reality.

Everything felt like too much. The bond within me burned, and my mating mark itched like it never had before.

I had nothing left, and inside... I was empty.

He was *gone*.

The absence of my mate was a hole in my heart. I had nothing left. I was nothing without him.

Two hours had passed since Xander was taken. Two hours since my heart shattered into a million pieces. Two hours since my world ended.

The pain in my heart made the whippings I'd endured seem like a walk in the gods-damned park. Every breath that I took, every time I glanced within myself and felt that fiery bond, was a knife being thrust into my heart.

I stood on the snow-covered cobblestone streets outside the home I had shared with Xander, running the small beaded bracelet the king left through my fingers. I should have been cold, but I had nothing left with which to feel the sharp, bitter wind as it swirled around me.

What was the cold when one's mate had been abducted by a maniacal king?

I couldn't move. I could not feel anything at all. My magic thrummed persistently in my veins, trying to get my attention, but everything hurt too much.

He was gone.

The snow had stopped falling, but the sky was still a dark gray as the dawn pushed away the darkness of this horrid night.

"My lady?" Tiaesti's small voice caught my attention, and I looked down.

The small Spirit of the Woods stood at my feet, wringing her twiggy hands in front of her. "I heard about what happened. I'm so sorry."

Sorry.

As if that could bring him back.

But it wasn't her fault he was gone.

It was mine.

The High King took Xander to get to me.

Come get him, pet.

I forced a "thank you" out of my throat.

Tiaesti nodded, and tears shaped as flower petals fell from her eyes. She sniffled. "The Eldest has requested your presence in the Great Hall."

"What for?" My voice was monotone.

Tiaesti wiped a finger beneath her eyes. "There is a meeting to deal with the... situation."

"Xander is gone," I said softly.

"I know." The Spirit shook her head. "We all know. Myhhena asked that I help you prepare."

Glancing down at myself, I realized my nightgown was soaked and clinging to my body. My skin was white and wrinkled, and my toes were numb.

I didn't even notice.

The leafy Spirit reached out, wrapping her twiggy fingers around mine. "I will help you."

Moving as though I were underwater, I followed Tiaesti into the stone building. Standing in the middle of the main floor, my hand traced over the back of the chair as the Spirit hurried up the stairs. A few moments later, she reappeared carrying a bundle of clothes. She must have found an intact set underneath all the destruction.

Tiaesti took one look at me and hurried into the bathing room. The sound of running water filled my ears, and she popped her head out of the small space. "You need to shower. The water will help."

I didn't think anything would help.

Walking into the bathroom, I stripped and tugged on the bond.

Nothing.

Keeping my necklace with the pieces of the map on, I stood under the shower head as lukewarm water fell on me.

Gone.

He was gone.

Not even the scent of my favorite soap helped pull me out of my numbness. Wrapping a towel around myself, I turned and glimpsed of myself in the mirror.

Clutching the sink, I stared at my reflection with wide eyes.

I barely recognized the person looking back at me. The green of my eyes was darker, as though a grassy storm was caught within them.

Swirls and whorls the color of the forest ran down my arms like sleeves, starting at my collarbones and running to the tips of my fingers. The green and gold markings of my mating bond stood out among these new tattoos, a reminder of everything I had lost.

The markings confined what I had already suspected.

I was one step closer to finishing the Maturation process.

I should have been happy. Xander would have wanted me to be happy. But I couldn't even force myself to smile. I couldn't force myself to do anything.

I dressed mechanically, barely noticing the soft material of the tunic and leggings as they slid over my body.

At least now, I wasn't screaming.

That was better.

Right?

I knew this couldn't last. I needed to make a plan. To fight back.

The door slowly creaked open. A small hand tugged on my sleeve, and I looked down.

Tiaesti's eyes were wide, and she looked forlorn. "We must go, my lady."

I followed her out of the bathing room, and she stood by patiently as I strapped every single weapon in the home onto my body. I hid three daggers—including the one the High King had left upstairs—on me, and I strapped Xander's sword to my back before yanking on my boots and cloak.

When I found my bonded mate alive—because I refused to believe that anything else would happen—I would give it back to him.

~

Tiaesti led me through the stone city, our feet leaving prints in the rapidly melting snow as we walked. She chattered on and on, talking about everything and nothing, but I remained silent.

All my thoughts centered around my mate.

I felt for the bond, the fiery living thing that connected us, and I tugged.

Again and again, I tugged.

Xander was still alive. I could feel him.

But a response never came.

Tiaesti's voice was the only sound. The atmosphere was somber in this so-called Sanctuary. The animals were silent, and the usual birdsong was absent, as though the creatures of the woods mourned alongside me.

Good.

Happiness had no place near me. Not right now. Not while my bonded mate was in the hands of the Crimson King.

Soon, Tiaesti's steps slowed, and her chatter ceased as we approached a massive structure. Built into a large hill, the building was made of black marble. Two dozen steps led up to the entrance, where four massive trees with gnarled bark acted as columns supporting the front of the obsidian building. This building was different from the rest of the Sanctuary. Darker.

An air of ominous foreboding settled upon me, and I shivered.

Tiaesti led me up the black steps, stopping at the large wooden doors. She frowned, her hands twisting together in front of her. "I cannot go any further."

A pang went through me. Something about this felt like a goodbye. This was the end of the way things were. Change was in the air. Xander was gone. Nothing would ever be the same.

Tiaesti was tiny in stature, but she had cared for Xander and me over the past few weeks.

My knees cracked as I bent, hugging the Spirit. Tiaesti stood still for a moment before wrapping her arms around me. They barely made it around my waist, which made my heart ache even more.

I squeezed the leafy child tight. "Thank you, Tiaesti."

The Spirit stared up at me, her wide eyes. "For what?"

My lips tilted up into the smallest smile. "For being kind." Running a hand down Tiaesti's leafy face, I sighed. "There are few beings who have extended me kindness in my life, and I appreciate your friendship."

Tiaesti's eyes welled, and fresh flower petals fluttered down from her cheeks. "That's the nicest thing anyone has ever said to me, my lady." She squeezed me tightly. "Thank you. I shall pray to Thelrena every moment of every day that your bonded mate will return to you."

Standing, I squared my shoulders and straightened my back. It was time.

Running my fingers over the hilt of High King Edgar's dagger, I walked to the large double doors. Drawing in a deep breath, I pushed them open. They swung with vigor, slamming into the walls with a *bang*.

Instantly, a dozen pairs of eyes turned to me, and I halted. Twelves Spirits—six each of the Woods and the Waters—sat around a large slab of black marble that served as a table. They wore various pieces of clothing made of their elements, ranging from long robes and dresses to armor.

I recognized Myhhena and Castien, but I did not know the other ten Spirits.

The room was vast, filled with large, rectangular stained-glass windows. The marble table and wooden chairs with carved backs were the only pieces of furniture in the room, their form imposing in the otherwise empty space.

As one, the Spirits of the Woods and the Waters moved. Leaves rustled, twigs cracked, and water splashed softly as they stood in unison.

Myhhena stepped away from the table, her leafy form nearly a head taller than the other Spirits.

"My lady, welcome to the Great Hall." She moved toward me like she was walking on air, her feet barely touching the tiled floor until she reached me. Her twiggy hand landed on the small of my back, guiding me to an empty spot at the table. "Come. The Council has been waiting for you."

My booted feet squeaked softly as I walked across the hall. The Spirits were still standing. Their gazes were trained on me until I stood in front of the empty seat at the table.

Once there, I paused. My fingers tightened around the hilt of the dagger as I stared at them.

What should I do?

No one had ever trained me for this. No one had ever taught me how to be a High Lady. I was raised with one sole purpose: being Remington's wife.

Gods, I wish Xander were here.

He always knew what to do.

Clearing my throat, I rubbed my mating bond. "Thank you for having me."

Myhhena stood beside me, her leaves rustling as she dipped her head. "You are always welcome here."

She pulled out the chair in front of me, and I noticed it was a little more ornate than the others. Dark green velvet covered the seat, and trees were carved into the back.

The Spirit of the Woods leaned toward me, her breath tickling my neck. "Please, sit."

Despite my discomfort at the obvious place of honor I was being given, I slipped into the seat. The sword rubbed against my back, reminding me why I was in this building.

Xander was gone. There was no time for discomfort. No time for personal requests or questions. The only thing I had time for was finding my bonded mate before it was too late.

New game, pet.

A shiver ran through me.

Chairs scraped on the tile floor as everyone, but Myhhena sat.

Instead of taking her seat, the Spirit of the Woods opened her leafy hands at her sides. Golden ribbons slipped from her fingers, coating the table's marble surface. She murmured under her breath, and the ribbons shifted. My eyes widened as mountains, trees, and rivers erupted out of nowhere, covering the black surface.

Based on the passive expressions of near-boredom gracing the faces of the eleven other Spirits, I assumed they had seen this before.

Raising a hand, I touched the nearest tree. It looked solid, but my finger went right through it.

Myhhena stopped speaking, her mossy eyes meeting mine. "It's a living map of Ithenmyr, my lady."

"I see." Standing, I placed my hands on the edge of the table as I studied the map. Far to the west, near what I assumed was the border of Ipotha, a stone city stood. Pointing to it, I asked, "Is this the Sanctuary?"

"It is." Pride infused Myhhena's voice. "But that is not why we are here. I want to welcome you, Aileana of the House of Corellon, to your first Council of the Twelve. Thelrena has appointed us—"

"Stop, please." The words were quiet as they left my mouth, but instantly, Myhhena stopped.

"My lady?"

"I don't need to know any of this," I said wearily. "My bonded mate is gone, and you want to tell me about this council? I don't care."

I didn't need to know any of this. Not right now. The only thing on my mind was my missing mate.

Silence filled the room, and one of the Spirits of the Waters awkwardly cleared their throat.

"What do you want to know?" Myhhena asked.

"I want to know how this happened." I huffed.

A long moment passed, and Myhhena didn't say anything.

With every passing moment, frustration bubbled up within me.

Did Myhhena ask me to come to this meeting to tell me about their history? To show me a map? I didn't need any of this.

I needed my mate.

And he was gone.

Still, Myhhena was silent.

My shoulders tensed, and I balled my hands into fists at my side. "How was Xander abducted from this so-called 'Sanctuary'?"

The Spirit of the Woods pursed her lips, and her eyes were wide. "If you would just let us—"

"There is not the time for pleasantries!" I shouted. Magic pulsed in my veins, and a roaring filled my ears. "You assured us both this place was safe! But it wasn't! Xander is gone. He was stolen from under my nose, and you said the Sanctuary was safe! It wasn't safe. Nowhere is safe."

Castien stood, his watery hands braced on the table. "My lady, the Guardians are investigating what happened. It appears as though the wards were breached—"

"Appears?" My mating mark burned, and anger ran through my veins. I slammed my fist on the table. Green sparks flicked off my tattooed hands. "Xander is gone!"

"We are searching—" Castien tried again.

"Enough!" I yell. The call of my magic became too much. Green ribbons slid from my hands, coating the living map as I snarled, "It's gods-damn clear that the wards were breached. What I want to know is, how? Why wasn't there a warning?" My voice rose, and the flurry of green ribbons increased. The entire room glowed from my magic as I seethed. "How did High King Edgar's soldiers get in here with dragons-bane? How come no one stopped him when he took my mate?"

The last words escaped me with a moan, and I clutched the table as power flooded out of me.

None of them moved. They sat there as the ribbons erupted throughout the room in an array of fauna. Greenery filled the large space, but I didn't even look at them.

"You told me this place was safe! And yet, here I stand. *Alone.*" My voice cracked at the last word. Gripping the table, my knuckles turned white as I repeated, "I am *alone.*"

No one spoke. The only sound was the crinkling of leaves and rustling of water as the Spirits of the Woods and the Waters breathed.

"Well?" I asked. "Does anyone have an answer for me?"

The silence was deafening, echoing the hole in my heart.

"Anyone?" I turned in a circle, meeting their gazes one by one. "Where is my mate?"

Myhhena turned to me. "That is what we have gathered here to discuss. If we choose to go after the king—"

"If?" I screeched. I tightened my grip on the table as red filled my vision. "What in Thelrena's name do you mean by 'if'?"

The Spirit of the Woods regarded me carefully as though weighing her words. "Aileana, my lady, there are certain things—"

"No. There aren't." My voice was as hard as ice as I withdrew the Crimson King's dagger from a sheath. Slamming it and the bracelet on the table, I snarled, "There is no *if*. No questions. I won't hear them. I *will not* stand by while my bonded mate is in Edgar's bloody hands. You have no idea what he is capable of. None. But I do. I will not remain here while my bonded mate is in danger. Either you agree to help me, or you will get out of my way."

Myhhena protested. "You need to train—"

"I'll do it on the road." I crossed my arms, glaring at the leafy Spirit. Up until this past day, I thought Myhhena was my friend. But I was beginning to see things more clearly.

Xander was right. She was not to be trusted.

"It's not safe," she protested.

"Being here is not safe!" I yelled. "Your 'Sanctuary' is not safe! My magic is a part of me. I will learn how to control it. But I swear to you, Myhhena, I will not allow you to keep me here. I will go after my mate, whether you agree or not."

A long silence ensued before Myhhena dipped her head ever so slightly in my direction. "Alright," she said. "We will find him."

A wave of tension left my body. "Thank you."

The Spirit of the Woods studied me for a moment longer before waving her hand. A golden tube appeared in her grasp a moment later, and she eyed me carefully as she extended it toward me. "Before we go any further, you may want to see this."

Accepting the offering, I twisted off the top. My eyes grew large, and my heart thudded against my ribs as I stared at the contents.

Raising my eyes, I asked accusingly, "Where did you get this?"

Racing Against Time
❦

DAEGAL

"If something happens to me, you must get to the coast." I looked at Ryllae, trying to ignore the searing pain running through my arm. When I woke up a few minutes ago, I could barely move the limb.

This was not good.

As soon as I had verified that Ryllae was safe, I checked the silver planes.

To say the future was dark would have been an understatement.

Now, Ryllae sat across from me, braiding her blond hair as we prepared to leave the cavern.

She furrowed her brows. "What?"

I continued, "Just follow the scent of the ocean, and it will lead you there. No matter what, Ryllae, get to the merfolk."

"What are you saying?" She frowned. "Is something going to happen to you? Did you See something?"

I had Seen many things, each one darker than the last.

I ignored the question, not wanting to lie to Ryllae and tell her everything would be alright. "You will have to stick to the shadows. Don't risk traveling by day on your own, and make sure you drink enough water. Only eat the berries you recognize, and don't talk to anyone. We're two, maybe three, days away from the ocean. You can get there if you keep heading east. Just follow the direction of the sun."

"No." She shook her head. "I don't understand what you're saying, Daegal. I'm not going anywhere without you." She reached out as though to touch me. "If this is about your arm—"

"It isn't," I lied, even as fire ran through the limb in question. "I just want to make sure you know how to look after yourself. Just in case."

We were racing against time. I wasn't a witch, but I had seen injuries like mine before. Time was running out. Soon, the throbbing in my arm would get worse. Then, it would make moving impossible.

Not long after that, I would be dead.

By my best estimates, I had three days.

We had to move fast.

"Just in case." The Death Elf huffed, her expression disbelieving. "And people say I'm strange." Ryllae stomped out of the cavern. "Come on then, let's go."

Sliding the sword into its scabbard, I followed Ryllae. With every step, I prayed that we might make it in time.

Together, we had a chance at survival.

HOURS SLIPPED by as we picked our way through the forest. Guided by the moon's light, we moved towards the Indigo Ocean.

The scent of salt in the air grew stronger with every passing hour, and soon, it was all I could smell. My arm throbbed with every step, providing me with a constant reminder that our time was short.

Ryllae barely spoke, but I caught her casting worried glances in my direction through the night. The silence between us was comfortable, as though we had known each other for years and not months.

I was happy to remain quiet. It was easier to hide the pain this way. As it was, putting one foot in front of the other became more difficult as the night wore on. By the time the sun crested the horizon, exhaustion plagued me. Heat ran beneath my clothes, and sweat covered my body despite the bitter, cold, salt-laced wind battering us from all sides.

I knew it was odd and probably a reason for concern, but my mind was sluggish. I didn't know what it meant. Maybe my estimates had been off. Maybe I had less time than I thought.

"We should stop for the night," Ryllae said, breaking the silence. Her blue gaze ran over me, and she frowned. "You need to sleep."

I would have argued, but at that moment, my toe caught on a stump, and I barreled forward. Catching myself on the trunk of a nearby tree, I just nodded.

Ryllae threaded her fingers through my left hand. "Come on. There's a tree up ahead where we can spend the night. It should be safe enough."

Trees were not great shelters. I probably should have argued with her. But I could barely get my mouth to work.

She led me over to the tree, and we huddled beneath it as dawn approached. I could taste the salt in the air, mixing with the scent of damp earth. Shifting, I tried to get comfortable despite the rough bark at my back.

Beside me, Ryllae shivered.

Raising my good arm, I reached over and pulled her closer to me. I thought she might protest, but she snuggled up against me instead. Her horns curled, brushing just beneath my chin, and a sound of contentment escaped her as she pressed herself against my chest.

For a moment, there was nothing else in this world except for her. Something within me mended as Ryllae pressed her head against me, and I forgot about the pain in my arm. The fog on my mind lifted just long enough for me to realize that the way our bodies were reacting to each other meant something. I just didn't know what it was.

Ryllae reached up, running her hand over the stubble on my cheek. "Is this okay?" she asked sleepily.

It had been years since I'd held a female close like this. I'd forgotten how good it felt.

"It's wonderful," I said earnestly.

She hummed, and within moments, her breathing steadied. My fingers moved of their own volition, tucking her hair beneath her pointed ear before my eyes slipped shut.

If I was going to die, there were very few people in the world I would rather die beside.

Life and Death Would be Torn Asunder

〜〜

AILEANA

"This is the last piece of Xander's map." My voice was flat as I ran my fingers over the parchment. Tracing the black lines, I tried to wrap my mind around this new development. "Why do you have this?"

Myhhena's leafy hands rubbed together in a whisper as she shifted from one foot to the other. Her mouth was pinched in a tight line, and she avoided my gaze.

None of the other Spirits looked at me, either.

"Tell me where you got this!"

Myhhena cleared her throat, staring at the floor. "A... concerned citizen placed it in our care."

"What do you mean?" Ice dripped from my words. "How long have you had this?"

My fingers tightened around the piece of parchment and sucked in a breath.

I couldn't let anything happen to it. This was the last piece. Pulling out my necklace, I slipped this piece of the map with the others before I could do something foolish like rip it.

Once it was safely away, I turned towards Myhhena. "You knew this was important to Xander and didn't say anything!"

The silence was so heavy that I felt like I was suffocating. My lungs tightened, and fury pulsed through my veins. My numbness was forgotten, pushed aside by the anger that took over when Myhhena handed me the missing piece of the map.

I stepped toward the Spirit. "You *lied* to us!"

"We didn't lie," the treacherous Spirit insisted. "We just... We weren't sure if it was time."

"Guess what," I snapped. "It. Was. Time."

The Spirit of the Woods had the decency to look ashamed as she said, "A long time ago, long before you or your bonded mate were born, a prophecy was foretold."

Of course, there was a prophecy.

As if my life couldn't get any more complicated.

"Explain," I demanded through clenched teeth. Magic pulsed in my veins, and green sparks flicked from my fingers, but I shoved it down.

I wasn't ready for it. Yet.

Myhhena sighed. "Five and a half centuries ago, a Fortune Elf named Wynter Lovelace lived in the Southern Kingdom. In those days, the borders between the kingdoms were open. People traveled to and from Ipotha, Eleyta, Ithenmyr, and Drahan easily. Even the fae would come from across the sea."

"I don't need a history lesson," I snapped. "What did Wynter want?"

"She traveled a great distance to seek an audience with this council."

All around the table, the Spirits nodded their agreement.

A Spirit of the Waters with long seaweed for hair picked up the story, her voice high-pitched and bubbly like a brook. "The Fortune Elf came to us and spoke of a time to come. One where males and females were no longer equals. She warned of great darkness that would fall upon the Four Kingdoms. Wynter said it would start in Ithenmyr and that once it began, very little could be done to stop it."

I turned toward the female made of water. "I see... I'm sorry, what is your name?"

The Spirit's lips tilted up. "Firana, my Lady. I am the Third Spirit of the Waters. My mother's waters feed into the Niphil River."

"Thank you, Firana." I sighed. "What else did the elf say?"

This time, Myhhena spoke. "In the future, during a time she could not yet see, there would be a great unbalance in the Continent."

"Unbalance?" I echoed.

Firana twisted her watery hands through her green hair. "Wynter Lovelace predicted that Life and Death would be torn asunder and the Four Kingdoms would be thrown into disequilibrium. No one would be safe—not human, elf, witch, werewolf, vampire, mer, or dragon. No creatures above or below the earth would escape the destruction that was to come. The only way to repair the balance would be to rid Ithenmyr of the darkness and restore things to how they once were."

Disequilibrium.

That was a very long word to describe the current horrors I knew people faced throughout Ithenmyr.

"What does this prophecy have to do with the map?" That was the part I couldn't figure out. Something Xander had said in passing was niggling at me. Why were *we* mated? Of all people, of all species, why the two of us? Why now? And the map... we knew it was necessary, but we couldn't figure out its purpose. "Why did Wynter have a piece of the map?"

Myhhena shook her head. "I don't know, my lady."

"You don't know." I resisted the urge to roll my eyes. "Of course not. You've just held onto this for over five centuries, not knowing why."

"Five centuries for a mortal is a blink of an eye for us."

I had so many questions. Everything felt like it was leading up to something, but I didn't yet know what it was.

"I see." Clenching my fists at my side, I tilted my head. "You've had this the entire time?"

Myhhena opened and closed her mouth. "My lady, we didn't know if it was safe to share—"

"The whole time." Each word escaped my mouth like a hammer, slamming into the empty air. Red filled my vision, and my blood boiled. "The. Whole. Time?"

"You were safe here, and we thought we had time—"

"You do not control me!" I screamed.

Opening my palms, I released the magic pounding through my veins. Ribbons of green escaped my palms, and they slithered around Myhhena. To her credit, the Spirit of the Woods didn't fight back. She let me encase her in my magic.

"You knew about this," I seethed. "What else do you know about?"

Myhhena didn't move, and her mossy eyes were wide as she stared at me. That was too bad. If she thought she could feign ignorance now, she was mistaken.

Any trust that had been built between us was gone.

A long moment passed, and a sigh came from one of the other Spirits. "I told the Eldest that keeping the prophecy to ourselves was unwise."

I turned, my eyes sweeping over the council members, but I didn't see who spoke. My veins burned, and a tremor ripped through the ground as a dark desire rose within me.

I tasted revenge on the tip of my tongue.

At that moment, I realized how easy it would be to give into the darkness within me. I was a step closer to Maturing, and power flowed through my veins. I could destroy these Spirits for what they had done.

They played games with me. With Xander.

Why? Because of some prophecy?

I could kill them all.

I saw the entire scene unraveling before me in my mind's eye.

Xander's sword hung on my back, but I didn't need weapons to cause destruction. The dark green ribbons that pulsed in my veins could draw life and create. I could drain them all and scatter the leaves, twigs, and water that made up their bodies.

I could rip this Sanctuary to shreds, summon the earth to swallow this place whole.

They hid behind the golden wards of the Sanctuary while others suffered. For that alone, I could destroy them.

I could have my revenge.

Darkness existed within me.

I always knew it was there, ever since I killed those Winged Soldiers when they were trying to harm my mate. It was dark green, almost black, pulsing like a somber beacon within my soul.

Their deaths could be mine, and they would be justified. Their lives as payment for their failures. Their lies. Their secrets.

As I lifted my hand, my mating mark burned.

Xander wouldn't want this.

My lungs tightened, and I struggled to breathe as I fought with the darkness within me. It would be far too easy to seek my revenge.

But it would be wrong.

Shutting my eyes, I exhaled. Shoving thoughts of revenge aside, I pinned Myhhena with a glare and walked toward her. The Spirit's eyes were wide, and her mouth was pinched in a firm line as she stared at me.

"Did you know he would be taken?" I asked as green ribbons poured from my hands.

Every second that passed felt like an eternity.

"No," Myhhena breathed, shaking her head. "We had no idea. Black magic broke the wards. That is what we came here to discuss." She raised a leafy hand, pressing it against her heart. "I swear upon Thelrena's holy name that did not know Edgar would take your bonded mate. And I'm—we're—sorry it happened."

As if "sorry" could bring Xander back.

I studied Myhhena a moment longer before taking a step back. Opening my palms, the ribbons of magic dissolved into thin air. "I believe you."

I didn't like what she had to say, but I did not sense any lies in what she had to say.

But belief was not the same thing as trust.

Myhhena lost my trust, and earning it back would be incredibly difficult.

I slipped back into my seat, the sword pressing against my back once more, and I asked, "What was this about black magic?"

Over the course of the morning, Myhhena and Castien explained what they believed took place the night before.

I rubbed my temples, trying to take it all in. A witch had broken through the wards, allowing High King Edgar and his gods-damned soldiers to break into the Sanctuary. They dosed Xander with dragonsbane before moving him.

"How did they get out so quickly?" I asked at the end.

Castien ran his hands through his watery hair. He looked as worn out as I felt. "I believe they have a Walker among them, my lady."

"A Walker?"

"Very few Walkers have ever been recorded in the history of the Four Kingdoms," Firana said. "They can traverse large spans of distance in the blink of an eye."

"Like a vampire?" After the incident with Valeria, Xander explained more about the beings of the night who lived in the Northern Kingdom. Some could move through the shadows, moving from one place to another.

"Not exactly," Myhhena said. "Vampires can only shadow places where they have already been. Walking is... not like that."

Of course not.

"What is it like?"

The Eldest Spirit of the Woods cleared her throat, spreading her hands from her sides. "Magic requires balance. Walking requires... sacrifices."

"What kind of sacrifices?"

Myhhena sighed. "For everything, there is a price. When Walkers move, they disrupt the balance. The greater the distance they travel, the greater the cost. Sometimes, if they Walk across long enough distances, they leave trails of death in their wake."

My eyes widened. "Trails of death?"

That did not sound good.

"You should probably prepare yourself," Castien said, glancing at me.

Around me, the council members pushed their chairs away from Myhhena as though they didn't want to get too close.

A knot twisted in my stomach as the Spirit of the Woods waved her hand, and a ribbon of gold appeared in the air.

Moments later, something large and black landed at Myhhena's feet.

My breath stuttered as I saw two large, black wings extending from what was, at one point, a body.

The soldier's helmet had been torn off, and his skin was wrinkled. Black lines ran down his face, and his entire body looked like a husk of what it once was.

"What happened to him?"

The Spirit of the Woods waved her hand, and the body disappeared. "Balance." She lifted a shoulder. "The soldier's life was given in exchange for the magic the Walker used."

Why couldn't anything ever be simple? Xander was gone, I had all the pieces of the map, Daegal and Ryllae were going to the ocean to try to unlock her magic, there was a prophecy, and now we had something called Walkers to contend with.

I buried my face in my hands, groaning. "Now what? How are we going to find Xander?"

Another member of the council—a Spirit of the Woods—stood and bowed. "High Lady of Life, I am called Krinth."

"Krinth." Remembering my manners, I forced a slight smile on my lips that I did not feel inside. "Nice to meet you."

"I know how to find your bonded mate."

My eyes widened. "Why didn't you start with that? Let's do it. Whatever it takes. I need to know where Xander is."

Rounding the table, Krinth came to stand before me. "If I have your permission, my lady. A drop of blood should be all we need to find your bonded mate." He extended a twiggy hand, the palm facing up. I sucked in a breath.

It always came down to blood.

"Alright." Drawing a deep breath, I shut my eyes and steeled my nerves. "Do it."

For Xander, I would do anything.

Krinth rolled up my sleeve, and a sharp sting pierced my skin moments later. I opened my eyes as the Spirit of the Woods pulled a sharpened tip out of my arm. The claw retracted into his wooden body as he gripped my forearm.

A single bead of blood swelled above the small cut, and Krinth swept a finger over the wound, balancing the blood on the tip of his finger.

He carried it over to the map, murmuring under his breath. Golden ribbons slipped from his hands, and he turned his finger, releasing the drop. It fell towards the table so slowly that I knew its movements weren't natural.

The moment it landed in the middle of the living map, it sizzled. The drop of blood bloomed into the size of a coin before moving around on the map like a hound seeking a scent.

The entire room was thick with tension. I gripped the edge of the table, and my heart pounded in my chest as I prayed to Thelrena that this would work.

Time dragged on, and for a moment, I thought it was a lost cause.

What if this didn't work? What if I couldn't help Xander? What if—

The drop of blood came to a stop.

Myhhena turned to me, her mossy eyes shining brightly. "We know where he is."

Absolute Darkness

XANDER

Horrible pain coursed through my entire body, starting in my head and running down to my feet. A throbbing ache tore my body apart from the inside out. It was like a thousand daggers were being shoved beneath my skin.

It felt like how I always imagined death would feel.

And yet, that pain was nothing compared to the emotional torment I was experiencing.

It was as though my heart had been torn out of my chest, stomped on, set aflame, and then thrown into the depths of the deepest, darkest sea.

I knew that being separated from one's bonded mate hurt.

But nothing could have prepared me for this.

Was Aileana feeling the same way?

Gods, I hoped not.

Groaning, I rolled my head back against the stone. It was so dark that even with my enhanced eyesight, I couldn't see a single thing. The air was frigid and smelled of snow, but other than that, I did not know where I was.

The bastards who abducted me had surprised me while I slept, injecting me with dragonsbane and sending the poison directly into my veins.

Even when the poison flooded through my veins, I fought them tooth and nail. Even with the burning, searing pain that had taken over my senses, I had fought.

Every single step of the way, I had fought them.

And then they threw me down here.

I did not know how much time had passed since I last saw Aileana. The burning pain caused by our separation grew with every day.

The thought of my red-headed Earth Elf cut me to my core. I could barely breathe as an image of the infuriating female who held my heart flashed before my eyes.

At least Aileana was still in the Sanctuary. She was safe and nowhere near this hellhole. I would endure this torture forever if it meant that she would remain out of the king's clutches. Better it be me than her.

Hours passed. All I did was replay memories of my life. Aileana's laughter mixed with loving memories of my parents when I was a child. Time spent in Nonna's cottage intermingled with memories of flying through the skies with Saena's blue dragon as we weaved through the clouds.

Every time, no matter where the memories started, they always came back to Aileana.

My bonded mate.

My love.

I had nothing else to do but relive memories. I couldn't hear or see anything. I couldn't even move without being in agonizing pain.

Before throwing me down here, four Winged Soldiers clamped thick iron manacles around my wrists. They stretched from my hands to my forearms. Matching chains were secured around my waist and neck.

Their efforts to keep me contained might have been amusing if the iron hadn't been soaked in dragonsbane.

Every so often, the soldiers dropped a canteen of water and moldy bread through a small hole. They always landed on the other side of my cell, and I had to crawl to reach them.

Every inch across the dark cell was a lesson in agony as the dragonsbane sank deeper into my body. I couldn't hear my dragon. I couldn't even feel it.

Aileana was the only thing that kept me going.

I tugged on that bond between us and prayed. I prayed more than ever before. Beseeching any gods who would listen, I asked that they would keep her safe. That she would remain hidden. I prayed that Myhhena would force Aileana to stay in the Sanctuary.

With every fiber of my being, I prayed that for once in her life, my beautiful, fierce, stubborn mate would listen to common sense.

The last thing I wanted was for Aileana to come storming after me.

I wanted—I *needed*—for her to be safe. Nothing else mattered.

Gripping the bond, I begged her to hear me. To be careful. To stay hidden.

Even as I pleaded with her to stay away, I knew I was being a hypocrite.

I was asking something of her that I would never do. I would fight for Aileana until my lifeblood was running out of me. I wouldn't stop until she was safe.

But maybe I was wrong. Maybe she would listen to reason and put herself first.

Maybe there was a small chance that she would go on without me.

I needed to believe that because I needed her to survive.

Curses and Nightmares

RYLLAE

"You will never be the queen of Ithenmyr." My father raised a blond brow, sneering as he glared at me from his throne.

"What are you talking about?" I stood in front of him, my crimson gown fanned out around me as I stared at the throne that was my birthright.

Or so I thought.

Father's eyes flashed as he prowled toward me. Red ribbons slipped from his hands, hovering menacingly in the air around him as he drew near.

I wiped my free hand on my gown, the red cloth of the House of Irriel mocking me as I stared at the king. In my other hand, I gripped the Opal Scepter. A gift from the gods to the heir to the throne of Ithenmyr, Kydona's priestesses had given it to me at my birth.

And now my father wanted to take it?

"Isn't it clear?" he asked, his tone mocking. "You have failed me, Ryllae. Repeatedly, you have proven you are not worthy of this throne."

No.

How could he be doing this to me? I had worked my whole life for this. I was born for this.

My eyes widened, and I sucked in a shaky breath. "What are you saying?"

My voice wobbled on the last word, and I hated myself for that. Why couldn't I be strong in front of him?

Why was this happening today, of all days?

Magic still coursed through my veins from the final stage of my Maturation, and I felt renewed. Invigorated. Strength ran through my veins, and I was fairly certain I could take on an entire army and win.

I was the second-most powerful Death Elf in all the land, yet here I was, shaking in front of the king.

"Why won't you tell me what these new markings mean?" *The tattoos covered my body, and no one seemed to be able to explain them.*

I asked Father about them, but he dismissed me, saying he didn't have time for my questions.

I received his summons less than an hour later, and now, here we were.

Father laughed, the sound bone-chilling as it rang through the throne room. Dozens of Winged Soldiers, my father's black-blooded guards, lined the walls of the otherwise empty room.

"Ryllae, Ryllae, Ryllae." *he tutted.* "Haven't you learned anything yet?"

He waved his hand, and more red magic filled the air. My stomach twisted, and a feeling of dread filled me. A voice in the back of my head told me to arm myself, to pull on my magic to defend myself, but this was my father.

He might not have loved me, but he would never intentionally hurt me.

Right?

"What are you talking about, Father?" *I asked again.*

"*Don't call me that.*" *He snarled, his face contorting into a blanket of pure rage.* "*You are no longer any daughter of mine.*"

His words slammed into me like a wave, and I gasped. "*What?*"

Father looked over my shoulder, making eye contact with someone, before tilting his head. "*You see, Ryllae, I have a plan.*"

"*A plan?*" *I echoed as confusion roiled through me.*

A wolfish grin painted my father's face, and right then and there, I knew.

I should have listened to my gut. Reaching within myself to grab a spool of red ribbon, I barely heard my father as he said, "*Today is a special day.*"

Light footsteps came from behind me. A female murmured, and I went to turn around when a thick, black mist enveloped my feet. My mouth opened to scream, but all of a sudden, my body stopped obeying my commands.

My eyes widened, and horror swept over me as the black mist rose above my feet. Even my magic refused to obey me. I struggled against the bonds, but it was no use.

I could not move.

A female wearing a black robe and heavy hood appeared at the edge of my vision, and the mist came from their hands.

A scream crawled up my throat, but I could make no sounds.

The mist continued to rise until it was all that I could see. Inky blackness covered my vision, and then two rough hands grabbed onto my arms. They tore the Opal Scepter from me, and it clattered on the throne room floor, rolling away.

Seconds later, thick, heavy weights appeared on my wrists.

The moment they touched my skin, everything felt... off. Wrong. It was like a part of myself had been taken away from me.

I could barely breathe.

Wrong.

This was so wrong.

"It is done," the female voice said.

There was a jingle of coins, and then my father grunted. "You may go."

"Thank you, Your Majesty."

Hurried footsteps filled my ears as I continued to struggle.

They were in vain. No matter how much I tried, I couldn't even move an inch.

Doors banged, and then, the black mist evaporated.

The second it was gone, I reached for my magic.

Only...

It wasn't there.

My magic was gone.

My heart raced in my chest as I raised horrified eyes to meet the king's gaze. "What did you do to me, Father?"

"I took care of a problem."

Was that what he thought of me?

"I'm your daughter. Your heir. You think I'm a problem?"

"You were a problem," he said. "I had this perfect plan. Everything was working, and then you had to go and Ma—ruin it. Now, you won't be a problem anymore."

"What do you mean?" I cried out.

He smirked, waving a hand, and a dozen Winged Soldiers peeled off the walls. They approached me from all sides, their expressions fierce as they drew near.

One of them grabbed me and yanked me backward.

Heavy, ominous silence filled the throne room as I screamed, "Father, what did you do?"

The guards laughed, and I yelled, "Father!"

They dragged me through the streets of Vlarone like I was a common prisoner. My screams echoed off the walls of the cavernous city. Down, they dragged me.

I screamed the whole way, right up until the moment when they threw me into a cell like a discarded piece of trash.

And then I screamed until my throat was raw.

Gasping, I jolted upright. My breath came in short bursts as I tried to remember where I was. It was dark, but the air smelled fresh. This was nothing like the prison where I'd spent decades of my life.

Running my hands over the ground, I picked up a long, thin needle and snapped it in half. The strong scent of pine grounded me, and I rubbed my back against the tree bark behind me. It was hard, the scratchy texture nothing like the smooth prison walls. The scent of salt in the air was almost overpowering, and if I concentrated hard enough, I thought I could hear the crashing of waves.

I was not in Nightstone Prison. My father had tried to break me, but he lost.

I was free.

Slowly, my breathing steadied, and my mind cleared as the remnants of the memory left me.

Rubbing my eyes, I blinked away the last vestiges of sleep.

"Evening, Daegal," I mumbled, taking in the low light filtering through the low evergreen boughs. "We must have slept the entire day."

There was no reply.

My brows furrowed, and I pushed myself up. "Daegal?"

Nothing.

I turned to the side. "Shit!"

A dozen curses, each worse than the last, escaped my lips. Daegal leaned awkwardly against the tree, and his head lolled to the side, hanging at an unusual angle. His usually dark skin was frighteningly pale, and even his lips had a chalky tinge to them.

Ice-cold terror surged through me.

Grabbing his shoulders, I shook them, avoiding his injured arm. "Come on, Daegal, wake up."

He didn't move.

"Wake up!" I shouted.

Nothing. I moved closer to him, taking care not to jostle his injury. Placing my hand on his neck, I felt for his pulse.

I wasn't sure exactly what I was looking for, and it took me a few moments to get it right, but eventually, I felt a flicker of movement.

His heart was still beating.

Then, a breath that was little more than a rattle escaped his lungs.

"Daegal?" My voice cracked as I ran my hand down his cheek. "Wake up."

A shaky breath was his only response.

I closed my eyes, pressing them against his good shoulder. "Please wake up," I whispered. "I need... If you die on me, I'm going to be so angry. It's not every day I meet someone I can trust. Especially not someone who might be my... please, just wake up."

Unsurprisingly, he did not listen to me.

Shifting, I moved around him until his injured arm was directly in front of me. The sleeve of his tunic must have fallen while we were sleeping because the cut on his arm was fully exposed.

"Oh, gods," I moaned.

The skin around the laceration was bright red, and an unnatural white liquid oozed from the cut. A smell I was far too familiar with assaulted my senses, overpowering the scent of pine and salt in the air.

In Nightstone Prison, most people stayed there until they Faded. But every once in a while, my father's guards went too far. They pushed the prisoners, inflicting injuries on them that refused to heal. Those festered without medical attention until it was too late.

Injuries like this only had two outcomes: healing or death.

From the sickly sweet smell of Daegal's arm, I knew he was almost out of time. This was probably the time that most people would have resorted to prayer. Maybe they would have begged the gods to listen.

I was not like most people, and praying was out of the question.

I hated the gods. They hated me.

With my luck, they would probably smite Daegal where he lay to spite me.

No, the only way he would get out of this alive was if I could figure out a way to help him.

A glint of metal caught my eye, and I lurched forward, grabbing the gilded pin from the lapel of his cloak.

"Just a drop of blood," I repeated the Spirit's instructions, grateful I had committed them to memory. "That's all it takes."

Holding the pin tightly, I spread my hand and pressed the sharp point against the tip of my index finger. A quick burst of pain was quickly followed by a bead of blood. I smeared it on the golden pin, holding my breath.

We had one chance. That was it. I would have preferred to use this when Daegal was awake, but beggars couldn't be choosers.

My heart pounded in my chest, and I smoothed invisible wrinkles on my dirty dress as I waited for the magic to work.

The air in front of me shimmered, the pin vibrated, and a breath whooshed out of me.

"What's wrong, Ryllae?" Aileana's green eyes were wide, and lines bracketed her mouth. She did not look well. "Where is Daegal?"

"He's injured," I said urgently. "We ran into some trouble."

I filled her in on the overarching details of what happened to us.

The trip to Thyr, going to the coast. Being abducted by the Resistance. Daegal's injury. I kept the attraction between Daegal and me a secret. It did not seem important right now. Reaching the end of my story, I sighed. "That's it."

A long moment of silence passed before Aileana swore. "Thelrena, help us all."

The way she spoke... I knew that tone of voice. It was the one I had far too often in my life. One edged in violence and pain and hurt.

Something had happened to them.

"What's going on?" I asked.

Aileana sucked in a breath. "Xander was taken." Her eyes hardened, and her voice turned steely. "I'm going to get him back. Look, Ryllae, I'm sorry, but I don't know what else to say. Daegal needs you to be strong. You need to figure this out. Once I have Xander, we need to meet. There's so much..."

Her voice trailed off, her image flickering in and out before it disappeared altogether.

I opened my hand, letting the pin tumble to the floor.

Be strong.

I snorted.

What a waste of time. I couldn't just sit around and wait for help.

Resigning myself to having to leave the injured elf alone while I found a solution, I drew his tunic back up his arm as best I could. Before I realized what I was doing, I leaned forward and pressed my lips to his damp forehead.

Running a hand over Daegal's chest, I whispered, "Try not to die on me."

Grabbing the sword with both hands, I backed out of our makeshift shelter. The branches of the evergreen tree were low, hiding Daegal from sight.

Sword in hand, I walked through the woods. Even with my good sense of direction, I didn't trust myself not to get lost. Using the sword, I notched every fifth tree. The evening was cool, but a warm, salty breeze came through the forest. It ruffled my hair as though encouraging me to continue. The coast was near. I could feel it in my bones.

I just needed to figure out a way to help Daegal.

I had just made my tenth notch when I saw something wooden and decidedly unnatural tucked beneath a pile of fallen leaves. My breath caught in my throat, and I walked toward it slowly.

Lifting my dirt-covered dress, I gingerly extended a foot and prodded the wood. When nothing terrible happened, I dropped the sword on the ground and bent, brushing off the leaves. My movements grew more frantic as I uncovered my find.

When the leaves were gone, I sat back on my haunches.

A door.

I had no idea what it was doing here in the middle of the forest, but to be frank, I did not care. Made of wood, it was aged but still in one piece. Bending, I grabbed the top and pulled. It moved fairly easily, and it was lighter than it appeared.

Satisfied that it would do what I needed it to, I maneuvered the door and the sword back the way I came. I followed the marks, moving significantly slower now that I was dragging a large object behind me.

I'd reached the sixth notch when I looked up and frowned. A groove remained on the forest floor where I'd walked, a clear indication of my path.

"Dammit." I couldn't leave such an obvious trail. I knew better than that. Dropping the door, I backtracked and scuffed up the dirt. Once the groove was gone, I grabbed the door and began my trek again.

Night had completely fallen by the time the pine tree was in sight. Stars shone through the trees, but still, I could barely see. I tripped over dozens of roots, and branches snapped at my face. My eyes stung as many minor lacerations covered my arms and face.

Even so, I did not give up.

Dropping the door next to the tree, I ducked back down.

Daegal hadn't moved.

I got him onto the door with a mixture of rolling and pushing. His chest still rose and fell, but his color was worse.

It only served to propel me to move faster.

Unbuckling his sword belt, I slipped it around my waist before sliding the weapon into the sheath.

Probably should have done that before going out in the first place.

Practiced soldier, I was not.

Finally, it was time to go. Reaching down, I grabbed the corners of the door and pulled. And pulled. My muscles strained under the weight, and the door groaned, but it did not move.

If he was too heavy, this was it. I had nothing else. No other ideas. No other plans. The coast was so close. I knew within my heart that if I could get Daegal there, the merfolk would be able to help him. They were renowned healers, and that was exactly what he needed.

Tightening my grip on the door, I groaned.

"Don't give up now," I told myself out loud.

The sound of my voice spurred me on, and I pulled. The door moved a fraction of an inch. "Gods-dammit. You didn't come all this way to fail now. Pull!"

With my words as encouragement, I reached into myself for a strength I didn't know I had. This time, the door moved an entire inch.

"Do it for Daegal." Another inch. "For yourself." It moved again. "For all the gods-damned times that Father treated you like you were nothing."

This time, the door moved an entire foot.

Inch by torturous inch, I pulled Daegal through the forest. Within minutes, I was a sweaty, stinky mess, and my hair was plastered to my face, but we were moving.

Time slipped by as I dragged the injured Fortune Elf through the forest. Soon, the sound of crashing waves grew louder. What started as a whisper of water became something more powerful.

Eventually, it was all I could hear.

Then, I saw it through the trees, lit by the rising sun. My heart pounded, and a cry of relief escaped me at the sight.

Water.

Absence Makes the Heart Ache

AILEANA

"Are you certain we can't convince you to remain in the Sanctuary?" Myhhena's leafy arms were crossed, and she frowned.

I sighed. "No, you cannot. As I have stated multiple times over the past day, I will not stay in this place a minute longer than necessary."

Twenty-four excruciating hours had passed since Xander was taken. With every passing hour, the ache in my chest grew worse.

I was leaving now, whether Myhhena liked it or not.

The pillars that served as the gates of the Sanctuary were at my back, the shimmering gold ward brighter than ever. Thick snowflakes fell from the gray sky, dusting the ground as the chilly air blew around me.

Stepping over a large puddle that probably housed a hidden Guardian of the Sanctuary, I ran my hand over the ward.

"I will not stay here. Xander is in Breley, and I must go to him." Turning to Myhhena, I raised a brow. "Surely you can understand that. My bonded mate is my life. My other half. I need him."

Already, his absence was a hole in my heart that was growing larger by the day.

"I know he is yours," Myhhena said slowly. "It's just that there's so much risk and—"

"I will not discuss this anymore. Anything I need to do to get him back will be worth it. No cost is too high."

The Spirit looked like she was going to talk back, but thankfully, Tiaesti chose this moment to yell, "My lady!"

I looked away from Myhhena. My eyes widened as the small Spirit ran down the cobblestone path carrying a large mound of fabric. She slowed as she approached, her load tipping precariously. "My lady—"

"Aileana, please," I requested.

The twiggy Spirit nodded. "Aileana. Erwen and I wish that we could come with you on your journey to Breley—"

"Absolutely not," Myhhena interjected, shaking her head. Her leaves rustled as she stepped forward, grabbing Tiaesti's shoulder and pulling her back. "Neither of you is authorized to leave the safety of the wards."

Tiaesti sighed. "Yes, Eldest. I know. But we have a gift for the High Lady." She looked up at Myhhena. "Certainly, you would permit me to give it to her?"

Myhhena studied the shorter Spirit before giving a terse nod.

Visibly relieved, Tiaesti stepped forward and thrust the bundle of fabric in my direction. "Erwen and I stayed up all night making this for you."

I took the bundle from her arms, appreciating the heavy weight as I unfurled the material.

"You made this?" I asked, studying the dark green, almost black material.

"Yes!" she said proudly.

"It's beautiful." I ran my fingers down the long, fur-trimmed hooded cloak. A matching pair of gloves tumbled out of the cloak, and I picked them up off the ground, slipping them on my hands. They fit perfectly, and already, I felt warmer. "Thank you."

Tiaesti shifted from one foot to the other as pride came off her in waves. "We infused the material with our magic. It will protect you from harm as you venture towards the northern border."

Breley was in the province of Midena, near the northern edge of Ithenmyr. I assumed the weather would be far worse up north if it was already snowing here. I couldn't imagine how cold the Kingdom Of Eleyta would be, where it snowed nearly every month of the year.

Sliding my pack to the ground, I slipped the cloak over my fur-lined leggings and long-sleeved tunic. It fit perfectly, creating a cocoon of warmth around me. My fingers went up to my neck, finding a clasp made of two silver leaves. The intricacy of the cloak astounded me.

"This is beautiful," I said. "Please tell Erwen how grateful I am for this gift. I will not take it off."

"Of course." Tiaesti's cheeks flushed, her bark-like skin becoming a shade darker, and a pang of sadness went through me. I would miss the Spirits of the Woods and the Waters.

But I couldn't stay here.

Shouldering my pack containing all my supplies, I patted my body. The reassuring hilts of my various daggers greeted me, and Xander's sword hung from a belt at my side.

Swallowing, I turned to Myhhena. "Well, I suppose this is goodbye."

She nodded solemnly. "You are always welcome to return to the Sanctuary."

"I appreciate that. I do. But after what happened here, I don't think I will ever return."

"I understand," Myhhena said softly. "Hopefully, one day, you will change your mind."

I did not think that would happen, but I didn't want to start an argument. For all her deception, Myhhena had assisted us in our time of need.

Instead, I turned my attention to the land beyond the shimmering wards. Raising my palms, I concentrated on the pool of magic within me. Green ribbons slid from my outstretched hands, slithering out of the ward and into the forest like tiny snakes.

A few seconds passed before the clopping of hooves filled my ears. The forest floor trembled, and the leaves shook as Kethryllian approached me.

The deer was every bit as majestic as I remembered. Looking at him, it was hard to believe he came because I called him. Kethryllian emanated godly power with every movement.

When the Guardian was close enough that I could see the shimmering points of his razor-sharp antlers through the ward, he dipped his head.

"High Lady of Life." Kethryllian's ancient voice echoed through the forest. "You called?"

"I need your help."

"Anything."

Fingering the hilt of Xander's sword, I explained my plan. I was acutely aware that if the Guardian turned me down, I would have to make the trek on foot. It would not be ideal, but I would make it work.

For Xander, I would make anything work.

When I finished, I sat back and waited. The Guardian seemed to mull everything over, his eyes shrewd as he thought.

Eventually, he nodded. "I will do it."

Relief flooded through me. "Thank Thelrena." I placed my hand on the shimmering ward and looked back at the Spirits. "Myhhena? A little help?"

The Spirit of the Woods sighed behind me, muttering under her breath as she held out her hands.

I narrowed my eyes. Her attitude was getting on my nerves.

Despite Myhhena's obvious displeasure, she did as I requested. The ward brightened, becoming almost blinding, before disappearing with a flash of gold. The moment it was gone, I stepped through the space where the wall had been.

With another flash of gold, the ward was back in place.

Tiaesti watched me through the ward, flower petals falling freely from her eyes while Myhhena stood behind her.

Kethryllian nudged my hip. "My lady, are you ready?"

I nodded and turned to the deer whose head came up to my shoulder. The sooner we left, the sooner I'd get to Xander. "I am. Are you sure it's alright if I..."

Saying "ride you" to a Guardian who came from the gods themselves seemed almost blasphemous. Not that I cared about what the gods thought, but it still gave me pause.

The deer shook his head. "Climb on, my lady. It is an honor to attend to you on this quest."

Well, I wasn't going to argue with that. Once I was settled on Kethryllian's back, I leaned forward and hugged his neck. "I'm ready."

This time, the Guardian's voice echoed in my mind. *Hold on tight.*

I did.

Xander was in Breley, and he needed me.

HOURS PASSED in relative silence as Kethryllian's hooves pounded on the forest floor. The snow-covered trees were little more than white blurs as Kethryllian ran by them.

When I told Myhhena I would train on the road, I wasn't lying.

I spent every spare moment digging into the well of magic within myself and pulling on threads of power. Drawing it out like a spool, I released green ribbons into the ground. They moved with us, giving life to the forests as we passed. Bark darkened. Trees grew taller. Plants burst through the snow. Briars and thorns retreated into the ground.

The earth sang as Kethryllian's feet pounded on the ground, *Protectress of the Woods. You have returned to us.*

Not all my ribbons went into the forest. Some stayed with me, weaving in the air and pulsing as they awaited my command.

The breeze caressed my cheeks and ruffled my hair, *Keeper of the Earth. You are welcome here.*

We kept moving north.

Kethryllian didn't speak much, nor did I. All I could think about was Xander.

Would we make it in time?

Every time I thought of him—which was often—I drew on our bond. There was no response, but I kept trying.

It was all I could do.

THE NEXT FEW days were a blur of aching muscles, burning limbs, and exhausting attempts at learning the depths of my magic. Kethryllian seemed to have endless energy, and he continued to carry me north. The bond within me burned, a constant reminder of my missing mate.

Snow pelted us from all sides as winter took Ithenmyr firmly in its grip. Gratitude for Tiaesti and Erwen filled me as I drew the cloak tightly around myself. I remained warm despite the heavy snowfall, and no matter how much snow fell on me, my tunic and leggings remained dry.

I probably would have been more appreciative of remaining dry if it weren't for the acute pain in my heart.

Each day that passed without Xander, the ache in my chest worsened. His absence was breaking me apart from the inside out.

I needed him like I needed air in my lungs. He was my everything. My reason for existing.

Our bond was the only thing keeping me going. Every night before I slept, I pulled off my gloves and ran my fingers over the green and gold swirls of our mating.

I'm coming, Elyxander. Don't give up.

Every day, as we rode further north, I dug into the well within me, trying to find a bottom.

No matter how far I went, I couldn't find one.

EARLY IN THE afternoon on the fourth day, the snow increased in intensity. The flakes cycloned around us until the whole world was white. The wind howled, sounding frighteningly similar to a screaming female, and the scent of ice was thick in the air. Danger coated my tongue, and my entire body was on high alert.

Beneath me, Kethryllian slowed.

Regret tinged his voice as he said, "I apologize, my lady, but we must stop. The storm is getting worse."

I bit my tongue, internally groaning.

I didn't want to stop, but Kethryllian was right. We couldn't stay out in a storm like this. If we got lost, it could cost us days that Xander didn't have.

"There is a tree up ahead," the Guardian said after a moment. "It will have to do."

His hooves no longer made any sound on the snow-covered ground, and I held on tight. My back was tense, and my shoulders were firm as the howling wind picked up speed.

"Here we are," he said.

I slipped off Kethryllian's back, murmuring my thanks as I ducked beneath the low-hanging evergreen boughs. I bumped into a branch, causing a small avalanche of snow to fall on me. Beneath the tree, however, the ground was surprisingly dry.

"Kethryllian?" I called out. "Are you coming in?"

There was a pause, and the Guardian's voice came to me through the snow. "I will be. One moment."

A flash of golden magic filled the air, and the boughs rustled.

I raised my brows. "Oh. I didn't know you could do that."

The Guardian of the Appointed Ones, sent by Thelrena herself, was no longer the size of a magnificent steed. Instead, he had shrunk to the size of a small dog. Kethryllian came to sit next to me, curling his legs beneath him.

I couldn't help but reach out and scratch behind his ears. A sound that was awfully close to a purr came from the mighty Guardian, and I laughed. No sooner had the sound escaped my lips than a horrible knot appeared in my stomach.

Xander had been abducted, and here I was, laughing.

Guilt rose within me, coating the back of my tongue in bitterness, and I felt like I was going to be sick.

Withdrawing my hand, I rested my head against the scratchy bark of the tree. It hurt, but I didn't seek a more comfortable position.

There would be no more comfort. No more laughter.

Not until Xander was with me once more.

A Summons and a Healing

RYLLAE

The crashing of the dark blue water against the rocks was so welcome after the endless trees that the ache in my muscles disappeared for a moment. A joyous *whoop* escaped my lips before I glanced over my shoulder, remembering our precarious position.

We were alone on the edge of the Indigo Ocean, and we were on the run. Kneeling beside Daegal, I sucked in a breath as I pressed my hand against his cheek. His skin was clammy, and a sickly green pallor had taken over his complexion. The cut was in such bad shape that his arm was barely recognizable.

Groaning, I sniffled as tears rushed to my eyes. I pressed my forehead against Daegal's and whispered, "You need to live. If you die, I'll never forgive myself. I won't be able to survive that."

Already, I was dancing on the precipice of madness. This male before me made me feel things I never thought possible.

If Daegal died, I would dive headfirst into the terrifying pit of insanity waiting for me.

318

And this time, I didn't think I would come out.

Pulling the makeshift stretcher as close to the water as I dared, I placed it gently on the ground. The Fortune Elf did not wake despite my less-than-smooth movements.

Hoping that I was right, I knelt by the lapping shores. The rocks cut into my knees as a cool breeze approached me from the water. Next to the crystal clear liquid that seemed to stretch to the end of the world, my dress's torn and filthy remains seemed almost laughable.

Bending, I placed my hand in the water. An intense tingling sensation started at my fingertips, the cold so jarring that my heart skipped a beat. At another time, when Daegal's life wasn't on the line, I probably would have given up. The pain would have made me turn around.

But today, I would not give up. Gritting my teeth against the cold, I pulled up my sleeve and lowered my arm in the water.

Kneeling at the shore, I begged and pleaded for someone to come and help us.

My hand grew numb beneath the cold water, but the only response was the constant crashing of waves against the rocks.

It wasn't working.

Think.

There had to be something I was missing. Closing my eyes, I tried to remember *how* my father's soldiers had summoned the merfolk in the first place.

Pushing past the barrier I had erected around my past, I forced aside memories of curses and pain and torture. I searched through my childhood memories, seeking a specific moment.

Everything was blurry. My memories were old and tainted by time.

But somehow, with Daegal nearby, it was easier to look through them.

I sifted through my memories until I found the one I sought.

Dirhinth, one of my father's lieutenants and a powerful Death Elf in his own right, knelt by the crystal-clear water. His head was bent, and he spoke slowly, moving his hand in a circular motion through the water. "People of the Sea, merfolk, bearers of the Coral Scepter. We request an audience with your ruler."

The air thickened, and I looked up at Father. "Is that it?" I asked.

My father raised a brow. "Yes, Ryllae. Now we wait." Red ribbons flicked from his hands, forming a red scepter. "How long, Dirhinth?"

"Not long, Your Majesty," the elf replied.

He was right.

Soon, the water rippled.

They were here.

Pulling myself out of the fog of memory, I opened my eyes.

That was it. The missing piece.

Ignoring the rocks digging into my shins, I plunged my hand back into the water. Moving it in the same circular motion I had seen Dirhinth do, I said, "People of the Sea, merfolk, bearers of the Coral Scepter. My name is Ryllae—formerly of the House of Irriel—and Princess of Ithenmyr. I request an audience with your ruler."

The words rang with power as they escaped my lips. Withdrawing my hand from the water, I waited.

And waited.

I waited for so long that my hold on my fragile mental state slipped.

Nothing was happening.

The wind stopped blowing. The birds stopped chirping. Even the animals seemed to stop moving as I waited.

A sob threatened to overtake me.

Of course, nothing was happening.

Nothing ever happened.

Memories of things I had no desire to relieve flashed before my eyes.

Each one was worse than the last. Darkness. Screams. Being taunted and tortured and touched in places that should have been sacred.

The water continued its perilous march against the rocks. Over and over again, it smashed against the shore.

My heart mirrored the sound of the waves beating rapidly in my chest.

Putting my hand back in the water, I repeated the summons.

Once. Twice.

A dozen times, I called the merfolk.

I stared at the water, my eyes sweeping the horizon. Left. Right. Again.

Water glimmered. In the distance, a fish jumped in a smooth arc.

No one came.

Of course, no one came.

Why did I think it would be different this time? I had called for help countless times before.

Rubbing my damp fists against my eyes, I groaned.

It would be so easy to give up. To stop and just let things go. Daegal was so close to Fading, and maybe that was a blessing. Maybe I should have let him go.

Perhaps ignoring the tugging in my soul would have been in his best interest. This world was a horrible place. A dangerous one. Maybe death would be a kinder fate than what was in store for us.

But even as the thoughts appeared, I shook my head. I couldn't let him die. If I was right about what Daegal was—who he was to me—how could I let him go? He couldn't fight right now, so I needed to do it for him.

I couldn't give up. Not yet.

And so, with one last look at the male behind me, I did something I never thought I would do.

I knelt on the grassy shore, clasping my hands in front of me, and I prayed.

"Please, Kydona, let someone come. If you ever cared about me at all —if you're even real—let this work. I haven't been... I'm not good. But he is. Beneath it all, Daegal is a good male who needs help. So even if you don't care about me, help him. Please."

As my prayer filled the air, I returned my hand to the water. Repeating the summons from before, I moved my hand through the liquid.

This time, I didn't stop. Even as my hand numbed and my arm ached from the cold, I kept calling for help.

The sun rose, burning away the early-morning frost, and I kept going.

When my skin was wrinkled, and my voice was hoarse, I saw something in the distance. A flutter of excitement came to life within me, and I gasped.

Pulling my frozen hand from the water, I wiped it on my dress as I stared at the rippling surface.

A flurry of color moved towards me, far faster and more graceful than any fish. When they were near the shore, I glimpsed a dark green tail moments before a bright pink head broke the surface. "Greetings, Ryllae, Forgotten Princess of Ithenmyr."

"You came," I breathed.

The mermale nodded. "Your call for aid has been heard."

The speaker's hair was long, with shades of pink ranging from coral to magenta and everything in between. The handsome male's violet eyes paired well with his long cheekbones and straight nose.

He wore a sleeveless tunic made of quilted seaweed, the material highlighting his muscular form. His tawny skin shone in the sunlight, and he gripped a large, golden trident.

Stepping forward until the water lapped at my shoes, I dipped my head and clasped my hands. "Thank you for answering my call for aid. What may I call you?"

He raised a brow, dipping his head. "I am Erthian, Captain of the High Queen's Guard."

My brows rose. "Oh, I thought... What happened to the High King?"

When I was young, a High King ruled the Indigo Ocean.

Erthian made a reverent sign across his chest. "The High King Faded a few years back and joined his ancestors. His daughter Mareena and her bonded mate now rule Coral City."

Interesting.

Yet another thing that changed while I was in prison. A pang went through me at the reminder that entire centuries of my life had been stolen from me, and for a moment, I retreated into my mind.

A throat cleared, and the mermale raised a brow. "You called for aid, Princess?"

His question jolted me back to reality.

"Yes," I said hurriedly, looking over my shoulder at Daegal. "My... friend needs help. He's injured."

The mermale's gaze followed mine. "I see." Erthian swam closer to the shore, tilting his head as he studied Daegal.

Drawing my lip between my teeth, I sucked in a breath. "Can you... will you help him?"

"What happened?" he asked.

"He was attacked a few days ago. The wound on his arm is festering, and it looks like he doesn't have long."

"Do you not have healing magic?" The mermale's brows furrowed. "Our tales tell of the Death Elf princess and her incredible powers."

At another time, I probably would have been flattered that the mermale knew who I was. Gods, before I'd been imprisoned, I would have preened over his comments.

But now, I had no room for compliments. Worry gnawed at my insides for Daegal, and everything I had was focused on him.

"My father stole my magic," I murmured. "He cursed me."

That was the first time I said the words out loud, but I knew them to be true. Ever since I'd had that dream-that-wasn't-a-dream, I couldn't get the thought out of my mind. A curse explained everything.

"I understand." Erthian looked Daegal over once more. Then, without saying another word, he turned and disappeared back underwater.

"Wait!" I cried out. "Come back!"

But he didn't.

Not right away. Not as the sun rose. Not even as I kneeled on the shore weeping, running my hands through the water and begging him to return.

"No, no, no!" I yelled.

Behind me, Daegal remained in the same near-death state.

The sun rose to the midpoint in the sky, and sweat dripped down my neck. I called out to the people of the sea, and I prayed.

The rocks grew black and hot beneath me, but still, I remained at the water's edge.

I did everything I could, refusing to give up.

By the middle of the afternoon, Daegal's breathing was worse, and worry twisted within me.

If this didn't work, I had nothing left. No other options.

Just as I was about to give up and drag Daegal into the woods to find shelter for the night, I saw something in the distance.

At first, it was just a flash on the horizon. A glimmer of something bright beneath the water.

A splash. Then two.

Soon, I saw many tails swimming beneath the water.

Hope fluttered to life within me, and I gasped. Hurrying over to Daegal's side, I crouched beside him as they approached.

"Hold on." Clutching his clammy hand as I sent the gods thanks. Daegal did not move, but a small moan left his lips. I murmured, "Help is coming."

As one, a dozen heads broke the surface.

Thank all the gods.

The merfolk formed a triangle, with Erthian at the front. Some wore bands around their chests, while others were nude from their tail up. Two wore tunics woven from seaweed. Each wore their hair long, the vibrant colors ranging from the brightest gold to the deepest purple and every color in between.

Erthian swam forward. "I have spoken to Her Majesty." He raised his hands, and coral ribbons escaped his fingers. "Princess Ryllae, you may have been forgotten by your people, but the people of the Seven Seas welcome you and yours."

The coral ribbons laced around me and Daegal, sniffing us both like dogs before sinking into our skin. I remembered something from long ago. The merfolk had magic that allowed beings from the Surface to breathe beneath the water. Their magic, like mine, was a gift from the gods.

More coral ribbons escaped Erthian's fingers, pulling the makeshift stretcher towards the water. I pushed myself to my feet, following quickly. The door dipped into the water, floating effortlessly, and Erthian swam over to Daegal. He placed his hands on Daegal's chest, and coral ribbons slipped from the mer's fingers.

Not wanting to leave Daegal behind, I took one last look at the forest before kicking off my shoes. Leaving them on the shore, I ran and jumped.

My lungs seized as the cold water surrounded me. Pinpricks assaulted me all over as the water enveloped me.

For a singular moment, I thought I made a mistake, but then my body adjusted. The water felt slightly better. Pulling my head out of the frigid liquid, I flicked my hair back and out of my face. Without even looking at me, Erthian extended a hand in my direction. More coral ribbons enveloped me, sinking into my skin and warming me from the inside out.

I thanked him, and he returned to helping Daegal.

Treading water, I looked around. My dress billowed around me, but it did not impede my movements. The other merfolk watched me warily, keeping their distance as though they weren't sure what I would do.

Neither was I, to be honest, so their reaction was probably warranted.

A splash alerted me to someone approaching, and I turned just as a mermaid drew near. She had bright blue hair, and a smile danced on her face.

"You're the princess," she stated matter-of-factly.

"Yes," I whispered, my eyes trained on Daegal and Erthian.

Hearing people using my title when addressing me was strange, but it wasn't bad.

It felt... right.

The mermaid grinned. "I'm so happy I got to meet you. Erthian is the best healer in Her Majesty's guard. You are lucky he found you." Barely pausing to breathe, the mermaid continued. "I am his sister. Younger, if you couldn't tell. I always had big shells to fill, with Erthian as my older brother."

"Oh?"

Erthian swam around Daegal, and I raised a brow. Daegal's skin looked better. Less green. The knot that had been present in my stomach for the past two days began to slowly unravel.

I kept treading water as the mermaid swam closer to me. She dropped her voice as though she were imparting a vital secret. "He isn't allowed to heal just anyone. I'm sure you understand. Erthian had to get permission first before he healed your friend."

"Perhaps luck is on our side after all," I murmured. "And you are..."

"Tinix," the blue-haired mer said, a laugh sounding like wind chimes filling the air. I glanced down, watching Tinix's dark violet tail move effortlessly through the water. "It's a pleasure to meet you."

"And you as well," I said, keeping my eyes on the Fortune Elf.

Tinix began telling me about the merfolk swimming around us, but I wasn't paying attention.

Erthian had stopped pouring magic into Daegal's chest, and now he was swimming in circles around him.

"Princess?"

I turned. "Yes?"

Tinix smiled softly. "I asked if you have any siblings?"

"No," I said forcefully, shaking my head.

I never considered Remington a sibling. The Red Shadow had delighted in torturing me, and besides, he was dead.

"That's too bad," Tinix said woefully. Apparently, she had no understanding that some people might like to keep things to themselves when first meeting others because she kept talking. "My brother and I are forty-seven years apart. We are rather close in age for merfolk, but—"

A groan came from Daegal, and my heart leaped in my chest.

"I'm sorry," I said, interrupting the mermaid with a quick shake of my head. "I need to see him."

Tinix moved aside quickly as I swam toward Daegal. I grabbed onto the wooden door, carefully kicking my legs to remain afloat before taking Daegal's hand in mine. His dark skin was warmer than before, and the green pallor was gone. I glanced at his arm, looking for the cut, but all that remained was a slightly pink scar.

Thank the gods.

Daegal's head turned, and his eyes blinked open. "Ryllae," he said, a grin overtaking his features.

"Hey," I whispered. I wasn't sure what possessed me to do it, but I pulled myself onto the door, causing it to shake wildly, before brushing the lightest of kisses over Daegal's mouth. "You're alive."

He raised a brow. Whether it was because of my words or my kiss, I did not know. "I know. I'm rather shocked, to be honest."

"But happy, I hope."

He reached out, running a hand over my cheek. "Definitely happy."

Our eyes locked, and for a moment, nothing else existed.

I saw myself through Daegal's eyes. He understood me like no other. That piece within me shifted and grew stronger than ever.

"Daegal, I—"

A shout came from the woods, and moments later, Erthian turned to us with wide eyes.

"There are armed elves approaching. Unless you wish to face them, we need to leave."

Daegal shook his head. "I think that's our cue to leave."

I raised a brow. A few minutes ago, he looked like he was moments away from Fading. I said as much, but Daegal just shook his head, pushing himself onto his elbows.

The door rocked beneath him as he shifted his weight, reaching out and taking my hand. "I feel fine. Honestly, I haven't felt this good in a long time." He paused. "How are you?"

My bones were weary, and my limbs were sore, but beneath all that was a deep-seated sense of relief. We made it to the Indigo Ocean.

Even the anger and frustration that fueled my revenge weren't as strong today. Maybe it was because of the male beside me, or maybe it was the hope blooming in my chest, but either way, right now, I felt a little more like... myself.

Whoever that was.

"I'm tired," I said after a moment. "But I'll be okay."

Erthian cleared his throat. "We have an outpost in a village near here. We will take you there, and the two of you can rest before we journey to Coral City tomorrow."

Then, before any questions could be asked, more magic slipped from Erthian's palms and wrapped around us. It tingled as it sank into my skin.

"Come," the mermale said. "You will be able to breathe underwater. Just kick your legs like normal, and our magic will aid you in moving swiftly."

A splash came from beside me as Daegal rolled off the door into the water. His lips tilted up, and he shook his head like a dog before nodding at Erthian. "Understood. Let's go."

With one last look at the surface, we slipped beneath the surface.

Alone Once More

AILEANA

The snow kept falling.

At first, it was beautiful. Then, the sun gave way to the moon, and it was *still* snowing.

Now, morning came once more, and I was officially over winter. The novelty of being outside in the cold snow had worn off surprisingly quickly.

I was ready for the summer again. Ready for late nights, sunshine, warmth, and beds.

In my opinion, beds were *severely* underrated.

This week of sleeping in caverns and beneath trees reminded me I was taking simple things like mattresses for granted.

I wouldn't do that again.

The pain in my heart was worse today. A churning feeling of dread and agony twisted within me, a constant reminder of the mate who should have been by my side.

Come get him, pet.

Kethryllian had slipped away at dawn, telling me he would be right back.

Enough time had passed that the sun was firmly in the sky, and he still hadn't returned. Resting against the rough bark of the evergreen tree, I listened to the earth's hum as I drew pine needles through my hands.

It appeared Kethryllian was about as good at telling time as Xander was with direction.

Cocooned in my cloak, I leaned back against the tree and waited. And waited.

When the sun had risen substantially, burning off the last bits of darkness, and Kethryllian still hadn't returned, irritation bubbled up within me. I finished off the dried fruit and nuts passing as my breakfast, and I grumbled, "Next time, I'm going to insist on coming along."

More time passed, and the deer didn't still return. Eventually, I slipped the necklace containing the pieces of the map off from around my neck. If I was going to be waiting beneath this tree all morning, I might as well do something useful.

Pulling my gloves off with my teeth, I removed the necklace and withdrew the five pieces of parchment.

Five.

It was still hard to believe that I had them all here, in my possession.

If I had any tears left in me, I would have shed one now. Xander should have been here to see the map and put it together. It was his, after all.

I missed the infuriating male so deeply that I would do anything for him.

I would even marry him.

That realization slammed into me with the weight of a thousand trees, and for a moment, I forgot to breathe.

I would even marry him.

Being placed in a gilded cage wouldn't be so bad if it meant I got to spend my days with the male who loved me. After being apart from Xander and feeling the hole his absence created in my life, I never wanted to feel this way again.

Xander was a lot of things, including angry and often irritating, but his love for me was as vast as the forests in Ithenmyr.

Gingerly, I stretched out my legs. The shelter provided by the tree was large, and no snow fell on me. I spread out the pieces of parchment on my lap, my dagger easily within reach. The edges were jagged, as though someone had ripped the map in a moment of desperation.

Laying the five pieces side by side, I narrowed my eyes as I studied them. Something was off. One of the pieces wasn't quite fitting.

Drawing my bottom lip through my teeth, I rearranged them until the five pieces were somewhat connected. At first glance, the map looked like it was detailing Ithenmyrian scenery. Hills, mountains, forests, and rivers covered most of the parchment.

That didn't surprise me. The terrain of this country was anything but flat.

The more I studied it, though, the more I realized that this couldn't be a map of Ithenmyr. For one thing, there was a massive mountain right in the middle. According to Myhhena's living map, no such mountain existed in Ithenmyr.

Furrowing my brows, I ran my finger over the ancient script that sprawled across all five pieces of the map.

I'd seen scrawling writing like this before. As a child in my tower, my tutor forced me to memorize the *Ballad of the Light Elves*. At the time, it had seemed like a pointless activity, but I was beginning to see its usefulness.

I read the tight cursive slowly, my mouth moving silently as I committed the lines to memory.

When great darkness is woken,
And the balance is broken,
Only then will those with pure intentions and hearts of gold,
Find the object they seek in the mount of old.

Tapping the mountain in the middle of the map, I pursed my lips. I narrowed my eyes, staring at the drawing. Something was off about this mountain, though. A river of fire surrounded it.

But that couldn't be right. Rivers were made of water, not fire. Everyone knew that.

Even so, it looked rather imposing.

More important, however, was the location of this mountain. Where was it, and what did it contain?

Drawing my lip through my teeth, I continued to study the map, committing it to memory before gathering the pieces and sliding them back into the tube around my neck. As I tightened the lid on the cap, the evergreen boughs rustled.

Flakes of snow fell gently on me as Kethryllian's head popped into the shelter. He said, "It is time."

Nodding, I armed myself before drawing my cloak around my body and following the deer out of the tree.

When my head popped out from beneath the boughs, I paused. Yesterday, a light dusting of snow covered the trail, but I could still see the canopy of leaves all around us.

Today, they had disappeared.

Everything was white, providing a stark contrast to the cloudless blue sky. I stepped out from beneath the tree, and my boot sank until the snow was halfway up to my knee.

Somehow, I hadn't realized snow could be this expansive.

"I'm glad you're here, Kethryllian," I said, tossing my pack onto my back and adjusting Xander's sword. The tip dragged in the snow, and already, I could see that walking through this would have been impossible.

The deer dipped his head. "I'm happy to be of service. The path is clear, and the sun is shining. If we hurry, we can be in Breley by this time tomorrow."

"Then what are we waiting for? Let's go."

KETHRYLLIAN'S GODS-GIVEN magic propelled him through the snow, and he ran for hours as I trained. With each passing day, my control over the power in my veins increased.

Endless green ribbons streamed from my palms as the Guardian ran. I fed them to the earth, which sang a grateful song in reply.

By the time the sun was in the middle of the sky, the forest was changing. Trees were thinning, and the air was colder. Soon, the sound of rushing water filled my ears. By the time we passed through the last layer of trees, I saw the source of the sound.

A massive raging river rushed through the middle of a large clearing, the water churning as though in anger. Chunks of ice bobbed in the water. Some were as big as a person. Snow edged the banks, and on both sides, large trees loomed nearby.

Icy talons took hold of my heart, squeezing tightly. I tightened my grip on Kethryllian's neck as memories of another river flooded my mind.

Gasping for air. My head dipping underwater. Tightening lungs. My clothes dragging me down. No air, no matter how much I tried. The only reason I survived that first river was because Xander saved me.

He wasn't here to help me now.

A shooting pain went through me at the reminder of his absence.

"Hold on," Kethryllian said.

As if I would ever let go.

He snorted, digging his feet into the ground, before taking off toward a bend in the river. Instantly, I saw what he intended to do. Wrapping my arms around his neck, I readied myself for a jump when, suddenly, Kethryllian came to an abrupt stop.

I flew off his back, barely missing being impaled on the Guardian's antlers as I sailed over his head and landed in a snowbank a few feet from the river. The fall knocked the breath out of me, and for a moment, I just blinked.

Pushing myself to my feet, I turned and glared at the deer. "What was that?"

Kethryllian looked at me, his eyes filled with confusion. "I don't know." He took a step towards me before his head reared up.

He cursed, a word escaping his lips that sounded far filthier than anything I'd ever heard from Xander or Daegal. The Guardian shook his head, his antlers knocking against... something. He walked down the river before turning and coming back.

His expression was sorrowful as he shook his head. "I was afraid of this."

"Afraid of what?" A frigid wind blew by, and I rubbed my arms. "What's going on?"

"Black magic is at play. There is a barrier blocking me from coming any further." The Guardian grunted, and his voice was strained. "Even now, the black magic is eating at me and forcing me away from here. I cannot stay for long."

Now, it was my turn to curse, loudly and colorfully.

"But you're a Guardian," I sputtered when I ran out of curse words. "Sent by Thelrena herself. You have godly magic! Can't you counter this?"

Kethryllian met my gaze, shaking his head sadly. "My magic is strong, but there are limitations, even for me. All magic has a limit, my lady. Even yours and mine. There is always a price that must be paid. Balance is always required."

Crossing my arms, I paced at the riverbank.

I couldn't stay here. I wouldn't.

Glancing up, I studied the Guardian. "What if I summoned you from this side of the barrier? Maybe that would—"

"It won't work," Kethryllian said. "Black magic like this is dangerous, even for beings like me. If I attempt to cross, there is a chance the dark spell will destroy me from the inside out. The spell must be dismantled."

"So that's it." I shook my head. "From here on out, it's just me."

Alone again.

I turned back to the river, frowning. It seemed bigger. More imposing.

This crossing would not be easy. Right now, it seemed nearly impossible.

As if he could read my thoughts, Kethryllian spoke. "I have faith in you, Aileana. You are worthy of the power running through your veins. Believe in yourself."

I brushed past the comment about worthiness. Xander had been taken because I was out playing in the snow. I did not feel worthy of anything.

Shaking my head, I twisted my hands together. "Let's say I get across the river. What should I do?"

"Breley is nearby. A few hours' walk at the most. The path through the forest should be easier to traverse, and the snow won't be as deep. Head north." The deer pointed his head in the direction of the city. "I am confident you will find it."

I paced in front of the water. "Do you think there's a smaller point in the river that will be safer to cross?"

"Unfortunately not." Kethryllian shook his head, but a brisk wind came from behind him before he could say anything. The bark forming his body began to dissolve, and his eyes widened. "Thelrena is summoning me. You must go!"

A gust of wind blew by, and he was gone.

I was alone once more.

"What am I going to do?" My voice rang out over the snow, and a bird tweeted in reply.

Not exactly helpful.

By my best estimates, an hour had passed since Kethryllian abandoned me on the edge of the river. The sun was setting, and the bitter wind held the promise of more snow.

Since the Guardian left, the only thing I accomplished was wearing a track through the snow. Now, the ground was turning icy where I walked, my frozen footprints glistening in the setting sun.

"Come on, Aileana, think. *Think*. You can't stay here forever."

Unsurprisingly, nothing came to mind.

One thing was certain: I was *not* going to get into the water. Not today. I might not have had much experience with snow in the past, but I knew that submerging oneself in freezing water was a foolish idea, especially if one wanted to live a long life.

Going in the water was not an option. I had to figure out how to get around the water.

Frustrated, I let some of the magic out from beneath my skin. Ribbons slipped from my palms, and I stepped back from the riverbank, leaning my forehead against the bark of a nearby tree.

What is the matter, Protectress?

The earth's voice echoed through me, that strange mixture of vitality and ancient life.

"Xander was stolen from me," I whispered.

We know. We felt your pain.

Of course. How could I have forgotten the earthquake?

"He's in Breley, but I can't figure out how to cross the river."

The earth hummed beneath me. *We can help you.*

My brows raised. "How?"

A rumbling came from the earth as though the land was... chuckling. This time, when it spoke, a definite tinge of amusement filled its voice. *Many years have passed since a High Lady of Life walked among us. You have done so much for us these past few days. You fed us and gave us new life. Allow us to do something for you.*

"What do you need from me?"

The wind brushed against my skin in a warm caress. *Magic.*

That I could do. I seemed to have an ample supply of magic these days.

Reaching into my well of power, I spooled dozens of ribbons. Pulling them out, I released them into the bitter air. They swirled around me, dancing in the wind before sinking into the snow.

A tremor ran through the ground, and dozens of thick brown roots burst out of the riverbank. Twisting together like strands of a rope, they expanded slowly until they covered the width of the river. I watched with wide eyes as the gnarled roots sank into the snowbank on the other side of the raging river, anchoring themselves into the ground.

"I... wow." This was unexpected.

I probably should have tried my magic before wasting an hour of daylight stomping around.

I probably would have known that my magic was capable of something like this if I had been taught how to use my powers.

Thanks to High King Edgar, there wasn't anyone like that anymore.

Trial and error was the only way I could learn what my magic was capable of. I only hoped I would be able to learn fast enough.

The tree shook beneath my fingers. *Do you like it, Protectress?*

"I love it," I said earnestly.

Hoisting my pack on my back and double-checking the sword hanging awkwardly around my waist, I walked toward the river. Keeping my arms extended at my sides, I put my foot on the roots and gingerly tested my weight.

The makeshift bridge held firm. It was small and extended less than a foot on either side of me. It wasn't much, but it would be enough.

I hoped.

"Please, Thelrena, let this work."

Knowing I had no time to waste, I gathered all my courage and took a single step onto the bridge. I wobbled, shaking precariously above the water.

I stopped moving instantly, holding still until I found my balance.

Exhaling slowly, I inched my foot forward. Then I moved the other one. Shuffling along, I slowly made my way across the bridge. Keeping my eyes on a large birch tree on the other side of the river, I stared at the white bark as I inched my way across.

I was nearing the halfway point of the bridge when I heard a splash. My heart caught in my throat, and my eyes dropped to the rushing waters.

That was my mistake. As soon as I caught sight of the white-tipped waves as they carried ice downriver, my legs shook, and my heart raced.

"Oh my gods," I moaned.

I *definitely* shouldn't have looked down.

The water rushed beneath me, looking more and more like a grave the longer I stared at it. Droplets of chilly water landed on my cheek, and panic squeezed my lungs like a vise.

There was no question in my mind. If I fell into the water, I would die. And if that happened, Xander would never know what happened to me. He would never find out that I came for him. That I was willing to do anything for him.

He would never find out that I would marry him.

I couldn't let that happen.

This couldn't be the end.

Forcing myself to take one breath after the other, I dropped to my knees. My pack hung awkwardly on my back, and Xander's sword dangled off the side of the bridge, but at least now I could grip the roots. Grabbing onto them with my gloved hands, I half-pulled and half-crawled across the bridge.

Every inch was a struggle, but eventually, the other side of the river was within touching distance.

"Thank Thelrena." Scooting down the last few inches of the bridge, my breath escaped me in a ragged exhale when my hands touched the fresh snow.

I made it.

I crawled onto the snow, leaning against the nearest tree, and I caught my breath.

The hum of my magic grew more persistent, and without conscious thought, I let it out. Green ribbons seeped into the snow, disappearing as the earth drew them in, and the bridge burst into a flurry of brown bark that floated away in the water.

"Thank you for helping me," I whispered to the earth.

Surprisingly, using so much magic hadn't drained me. If anything, I felt more energized than before.

You are ours, the earth murmured in reply. *You give us life, and in turn, we will do all we can for you.*

"Balance," I mused.

Balance, the earth echoed.

Invigorated by surviving the crossing, I let a few more ribbons escape my hands before pushing myself to my feet and dusting off the snow. There was no time to waste.

I needed to find my bonded mate.

A Myriad of Problems

⌒~⌒

XANDER

"Not so mighty now, are you?" The jeering voice came from above me, and I lifted my head slowly. Searing pain flashed through my neck as the poisoned iron came into contact with my flesh. Sucking in a breath, I slammed my fist against the stone and cursed.

The male laughed, the sound of his amusement filtering down the dark hole.

"Leave me alone," I rasped.

The agony of our separation had given way to deep, persistent pain. My entire body felt like it was being ripped apart from the inside out.

Time had no meaning anymore. Not without Aileana.

Pain was my constant companion, and I could barely remember a life without it.

I did not know how many hours had passed since I'd last smelled the honey and earth that was Aileana's unique scent. Days. Weeks. Maybe even months.

It didn't matter. I would gladly suffer centuries of torture and pain if it meant she was safe.

Please, Kydona, let her remain in the Sanctuary.

I yanked on the bond, but there came no reply.

That didn't surprise me.

I was completely and utterly alone.

Last time, Nonna saved me with her magic.

But this was different. I could feel it in my bones. There would be no saving me.

A grating sound came from above, and I looked up just as a shard of bright light shone on me. I winced, curling into a ball as the same voice laughed.

"Unfortunately for you, I can't leave you alone." A thump came from beside me, and I lifted my head to see a pair of black wings looming above me. "You see, there's someone who wants to see you."

"Who?" I asked weakly.

In response, a fist slammed into the back of my head.

Everything went black.

A LOW GROAN escaped me as I slipped into consciousness, the never-ending pain from the dragonsbane greeting me like a horrible friend. My flesh seared as I shifted, but I pushed past the pain, reaching for the bond within me.

As soon as I touched the fiery connection to my mate, I knew she was alive. Our life forces were tangled together, pulsing despite the distance separating us.

Stay away, I begged her silently. *Please.*

I would burn the world to ash before I let the Crimson King lay a hand on my bonded mate. Wife or not, she was *mine*.

My fingers stretched out slowly, my every muscle screaming as I shifted on the ground, assessing my position. The cold stones were gone, and something rough and grainy was beneath my fingers. Wood, probably.

My senses came back to me one at a time.

Sandalwood assaulted my nose, the strong scent pushing past the lemons and cedar that had been with me from the moment they took me from Aileana's side. It was so strong that I nearly gagged.

That wasn't all, though. Other smells flooded through me all at once. The scents of iron and decay intermingled with a strangely familiar scent that pushed at the edges of my mind. No matter how much I concentrated on it, I couldn't figure out what it was.

I shifted, lifting my right hand. A clanging sound filled my ears, and my flesh sizzled.

And then I heard it.

A low chuckle, tinged with evil and madness, came from behind me. A shiver crawled up my spine, and I swallowed.

"What do you want with me?" I asked.

That chuckle came again.

I lifted my face off the ground, and darkness greeted me. Blinking, I sought a source of light. Anything. Slowly—far too slowly—my vision adjusted. Tiny pinpricks of light came through thick black fibers.

The weight on my head suddenly made sense.

I groaned. I *hated* being blindfolded.

"What do you want with me?" I asked again. This time, my voice sounded stronger. Louder. More like myself.

That was good. If they wanted to kill me, I was going to fight them until the very end. I needed my strength for that.

Footsteps approached, and I tensed, clenching my fists.

My captor said, "You dare ask me what *I* want? *You* who are the scum of the earth?"

I cursed at the sound of High King Edgar's voice.

"Don't talk to me about scum," I snarled through clenched teeth. "We both know who the genocidal maniac is in this room, and it isn't me."

"You dare speak to your king in such a manner?"

Something cracked in the air, and moments later, a line of fire burst on my back.

I curled in on myself as pain forced the breath from my lungs.

"You are no king of mine," I rasped as soon as my body cooperated.

"Insolent fool," the Crimson King hissed.

Another crack.

More pain.

Half a dozen times, the whip landed on my back, sending searing pain down my back.

Still, I did not cry out. Thoughts of my red-headed Earth Elf kept me going. I would not give up or let the king know he caused me pain. I would submit to anything if it would keep her safe.

My back clenched, and blood dripped onto the floor.

He called me every name in the book. As if those could hurt me.

I had endured far worse than this.

"I am going to kill you," I vowed breathlessly after the whip slashed down again.

He laughed, and I wanted to throw up. I hated this male with every fiber of my being.

"The only one in this room who will be dead soon is you," he snapped. "Everyone in this kingdom belongs to me. Every living being bows before me."

Not me. Not Aileana.

Biting my tongue, I remained silent.

Footsteps filled my ears once more as High King Edgar walked in circles around me.

"Do you have nothing to say?" he taunted. "You're not so mighty now, dragon."

Pushing myself to my knees despite the irons clamped around me, I snarled, "Why don't you take off these manacles and talk to me, then? Fight me, male to male. Let's see who will come out on top, then."

A beat passed, and I could feel the king's assessing gaze.

A grim chuckle escaped him. "Do you take me for a gods-dammed fool?"

I pinched my mouth shut. The Crimson King was a lot of things—bastard, genocidal maniac, and a powerful Death Elf—but he was no fool. One couldn't bind the five provinces and keep Ithenmyr together without possessing at least a modicum of intelligence.

But I would not give him an iota of praise, so I remained silent.

That strangely familiar scent continued to plague my senses. Wildflowers mixed with... ash? I couldn't quite place it, but it triggered something in me. Something dark and old, and so far in my past, I couldn't place it.

I focused on that as the king paced. He didn't speak, seeming content to see me on the floor before him. Every so often, he kicked me, and the iron would sizzle when it came in contact with my skin.

I didn't let him hear me moan.

Time slipped by.

Without my sight, it was difficult to keep track of. The hard floor dug into my knees, and I focused on that instead of the male in front of me.

Eventually, he spoke once more. "You asked what I want?"

"Yes," I growled. "Do you have hearing problems?"

He laughed. "No. Not at all. My hearing is pristine."

"Good to know," I snapped. "So tell me then, what is your problem?"

"I have a myriad of problems, dragon. They begin and end with you and your bonded mate."

My chest swelled with pride. "Good."

The whip cracked in the air, and my back clenched, but the pain never came. High King Edgar laughed cruelly. "When the redheaded bitch comes back to me, we're going to deal with you both once and for all."

Comes back.

Intense relief flooded through me at the confirmation that Aileana wasn't anywhere near here.

I sagged against the floor. "Thank the gods."

High King Edgar snickered. "Oh, believe me. When we're done with the two of you, you won't even have a voice with which to thank the gods."

"We?" I asked without thinking.

"Oh, that's right." He clucked his tongue against the roof of his mouth. "How foolish of me."

A sense of dread unfurled in my stomach as footsteps approached. "Allow me to introduce you to my fiancée. She was most intrigued when I told her you were the Last Dragon in Ithenmyr. She insisted on meeting you before our wedding and even left a present for Aileana. Isn't that nice?"

"Bastard," I growled.

A hand landed on my head, wrenching off the blindfold. Light slammed into me, and I blinked. When my vision finally cleared, my eyes widened.

I was on a dark wooden floor, lying a few feet before a large black dais. On it sat two gilded thrones beneath a crimson canopy. One of them—the larger one—was empty. But sitting on the other one sat...

My heart stopped. My mind blanked. I had no words. I froze.

All I could do was stare at the throne.

Surely, I was mistaken. Hallucinating. The dragonsbane must have been eating away at my mind. This couldn't be real.

The Southern Queen sat on the golden throne, staring at me. She was an achingly familiar sight, her black hair twisted into an elaborate knot on top of her head as she tapped her fingers on the side of the throne.

If this was real...

It couldn't be real.

"What?" I stuttered as visions of blood, death, and anguish flooded through me. Memories that I had suppressed years ago rose to the surface, followed quickly by an intense feeling of loss and pain.

The High King laughed maniacally.

I ignored him, staring at the smaller throne.

"How?" I asked quietly. "You were..."

Gone.

Dead.

Ripped from this life.

My last link to my past, torn away from me.

Queen Sanja sat on the throne, staring at me.

High King Edgar crouched before me, his horns stretching above his head as wings unfurled behind him. But his skin... burn scars ran down half his face, from his hairline to the edge of his collar. He followed my gaze, smirking as red magic sparked between his fingers.

"Thank you for these, by the way," he said, tracing the scars.

"Without them, I might not have been able to convince my bride of your existence."

My gaze darted between the Crimson King and the Southern Queen.

"I need an explanation," I growled at Queen Sanja. "Tell me what you're doing here. *Please.*"

She remained silent.

Laughing, High King Edgar extended his palms. Red ribbons tinged in black swirled in the air around him. I stared at them. His magic was wrong.

All of this was wrong.

"I see you recognize my new queen." Edgar smiled, and it was one of the most horrifying sights I'd ever seen. "We can't have you telling the world who she is, now can we?"

The red ribbons shot toward me, diving into my body with a painful punch.

"Take him away," the Crimson King commanded the Winged Soldiers lining the walls. "The magic will ensure he cannot speak or think of the truth about my bride's identity. Lock him up. I don't want to see him again until my wedding."

The queen didn't say a word. Winged Soldiers grabbed my arms, dragging me out of the throne room as I stared at the Southern Queen.

She never said a word.

The High Tide Waits for No Fish

DAEGAL

"How much further is the village?" I asked the mer swimming nearest to me. It felt strange to speak underwater, but whatever coral magic the mer had used meant we could speak and breathe as normal.

We had been swimming for some time, and though I wasn't tired, I was worried about Ryllae. Bags hung beneath her eyes, and she looked like she hadn't slept well in days.

The mer turned, his aura blue like the water around us, as he tightened their grip on his trident. "An hour or so. Maybe a bit less if the currents are in our favor."

He turned, engaging the mermaid beside him in conversation. I eyed their weapons. All the merfolk around us were armed with tridents and swords. I couldn't help but wonder if they were guarding us or escorting us to a watery grave.

Ryllae seemed to trust them, but something about this entire situation felt a little strange. However, the pink-haired mermale had healed me. He probably wouldn't have bothered doing that if they planned on murdering and feeding us to the sharks.

The princess's hand brushed against mine, and I glanced at her. Despite her exhaustion, her blue eyes were wide open as she looked around in awe. I didn't blame her one bit. The sea was nothing like I'd expected. From above, it looked like a plain blue sheet of water. Beneath the surface, it was an entirely new world.

Bright blues, greens, and pinks swirled together, weaving a tapestry of life that stretched as far as I could see. Fish of every size swam around us, and in the distance, I could have sworn I saw massive sharks racing through a swirling current.

Maiela would have loved this. She always appreciated the beauty of our world far more than I ever did.

Maybe it was because I tended to see the darkness in things... or maybe it was because life taught me at an early age that even beautiful things could kill.

That was the difference between me and my twin.

She saw beauty and hope in the world. Mai believed that with a little love, things could flourish even in darkness. That was what drew her to her wife in the first place.

I did not see beauty or hope or love. Not anymore.

Those were stolen from me on the day I caused our mother's brutal murder.

No, when I Looked into the future, I did not See good things.

I Saw death and darkness and pain.

That was why Xander and I got along so well. From the moment we met, I recognized him as a kindred soul.

He was darkness, and I knew it intimately.

Walking on the silver planes as I did, I knew that darkness was at the core of most people's hearts. Many hid it or ignored its presence until it destroyed them from the inside out.

Not Xander.

Ryllae didn't either. She had a darkness deep within her that she didn't even try to hide. I respected that far more than she probably knew.

The Death Elf's arm bumped against mine again as the waters deepened. The grainy sand was the same color as Ryllae's hair, and dozens of green plants fluttered in the current. "How are you feeling?"

Shrugging, I reached up and touched my arm where the sword had cut my skin, expecting to still feel pain. "I'm feeling... fine."

"Good." She smiled. "I'm glad to hear that. When I... this morning... I wasn't sure you would survive."

I sucked in a breath. Swimming closer to Ryllae, I brushed my hand against her arm. "You saved me," I whispered. "I will be eternally grateful for that."

"Technically, the Captain of the Guard saved you," the princess pointed out. "I just got you here."

"Let me say thank you, Ryllae," I murmured. Reaching out, I took her hand and raised it to my lips. Brushing my thumb over the back of her palm, I squeezed her fingers. "You could have left me to die, but instead, you risked everything to save me. Thank you."

A long moment stretched between us before she whispered, "You're welcome."

After that, a comfortable silence stretched between us as we swam hand-in-hand, following our escort deeper into the sea. The merfolk's scales shimmered in the water. They moved as gracefully as the schools of fish that passed us by.

The sheer amount of life we passed was incredible. Fish of every kind—some as big as horses, others as tiny as my hand—intermingled with dozens of plants that I had never seen in my entire life.

When the brilliant sunlight faded into the purple and reds that spoke of the impending night, small buildings dotted the sandy horizon. Dark green plants grew from the sandy bottom, their long, thin arms stretching towards the fading sunlight filtering through the surface of the water. Small gardens stood in front of homes made of coral, where lumps of green, blue, and purple rock were interspersed with various sea vegetables.

Ryllae's grip tightened on my fingers as we approached the village, and she swam so close to me that our thighs brushed against each other with every kick of our legs.

That thing within me, the one we had yet to acknowledge, swelled at the way that she was coming to *me* for safety and protection.

If we survived this, we would have to talk about what this meant.

I rubbed my thumb over the back of her hand as a high-pitched voice squeal came from nearby.

"Erthiannnnnn!"

Ryllae tensed as a dozen small merlings swam out of a nearby building and approached us at high speeds. Their tails ranged from dark blue to bright purple, and they all wore brilliant smiles. The small creatures swarmed the male who had healed me, and he somersaulted backward as half a dozen merlings slammed into him all at once.

"Oomph," Erthian muttered, returning upright. "Be gentle with me, all right? I'm not as young as I used to be."

A child with navy blue hair shorn close to his head laughed. The sound was infectious, and I chuckled.

Ryllae was silent, her grip growing even tighter around my hand. I wasn't sure if it was the children or the village making her nervous, but she was finding solace in me, and I was happy about that.

One of the merlings pointed at us, their bright green eyes matching their vibrant hair. "Erthian, who are they?"

The Captain of the Guard leaned toward the children, waggling his brows. "These are two very special guests." He mock-whispered, "They came from the Surface to see High Queen Mareena."

The merlings gasped.

"Is that true?" a young boy asked.

His question must have inspired the others because all the merlings spoke at once.

"From the Surface?"

"Momma says an evil red king lives up there."

"And bloodsuckers!"

"When I grow up, I want to be a member of the Queen's Guard, just like Erthian," another declared.

"They look funny."

The last comment came from one of the oldest merlings. She had long yellow hair, and a turquoise band was wrapped around her breasts. By my best estimates, she was around thirteen.

Erthian turned slightly, raising a brow. His gaze swept over us. "Yes, I suppose they do." His voice deepened, and a stern quality overtook his features. "But Linthi, you know that the gods and goddesses put many types of people on our planet. They don't all look like us, but that doesn't make them wrong or bad. They're just different."

I raised a brow. I couldn't have said it better myself.

Suitably chastised, Linthi dipped her head. "My apologies, Erthian. I spoke out of turn."

"Apology accepted," Erthian said. He raised his voice. "Now, all of you, go and play."

A chorus of laughter filled the air as the merlings dispersed. The Captain of the Guard shouted, "Tinix!"

One of the mermaids broke apart from the escort. "Yes, brother?"

"Escort the guests to the Reef House for the night," Erthian commanded. "We will leave for Coral City at first light. I'm going to find my husband."

He murmured something about needing a stiff drink under his breath as he turned, swimming in the opposite direction from the merlings.

"Right away," Tinix said.

With a swish of her tail, Tinix gestured for us to follow her. We had no choice but to go along. We swam behind the mermaid, and Ryllae clutched my hand the whole time. Tinix led us through the coral village, coming to a stop in front of a small building made of soft pink coral.

"This is where you'll be staying," the mermaid said. She swept an arm, showcasing the two thin stone beds and the small table as if it were a suite made for royalty.

At least there were beds.

Tinix pointed out the bathing room, pulling leafy greens and dried crackers from a cupboard. Assuring us that the magic allowing us to breathe underwater would work for the length of our stay, she took her leave. Ryllae and I ate silently, taking care of our personal needs, before lying on the cots.

I should have been tired, but all I could think about was how Ryllae's lips felt when they brushed against mine. I could still taste her on my lips, and even now, a surge of protectiveness filled me.

Hours passed as I pondered the way I felt about her.

Ryllae slept.

I never did.

Instead, after I was certain the princess was in a deep sleep, I walked the silver planes. Lost to the depths of my magic, I pushed through the wisps that made up the time to come.

I found Aileana and Xander's trail and ran my fingers over their future.... or at least, I tried to. A thick black mist surrounded their path, blocking nearly everything from sight. I could See that they were alive, but nothing else was visible.

Worry gnawed at me for the bonded pair, and I prayed to Kydona for their safety.

Next, I checked on my sister. They were still at Nonna's, and the three females were preparing to celebrate the Winter Solstice. An aura of safety and warmth enveloped the trio, and I smiled at the vision of Kysha and Maiela dancing in Nonna's living room.

They were safe.

Thank the gods. At least someone I loved wasn't in imminent danger.

After that, I ran my fingers down Ryllae's path. Visions of the next few days flashed before my eyes. The possibilities were endless, and the future shifted so quickly it was hard to grasp what was to come.

When I was certain I had Seen all that I could, I slid back into myself.

Turning to my side, I rested my head on my arms and studied Ryllae.

Sleeping, she looked almost... peaceful.

Her chest rose and fell as her blond hair floated in the water around her like a veil. Her horns were poking into the pillow, somehow managing to be both endearing and a reminder of the power that rested beneath her skin.

She was the most stunning elf I had ever met.

Gods.

I couldn't believe she *kissed* me.

More than that, I couldn't believe I was still thinking about it. I was acting like a youth who had experienced his first kiss.

Get a hold of yourself, Daegal.

Apparently, I was destined to act like a youngling, though, because I couldn't get the thought of her lips out of my mind. What would it be like to kiss her again? Preferably in a more intimate situation.

Thoughts of Ryllae's soft lips and those red tattoos occupied me until a knock came at the door. It swung open a moment later, revealing the same mermaid from yesterday. Her violet tail was covered in shadows as the moonlight shone through the depths of the water.

Recognizing another morning person when I saw one, I greeted the mermaid. Tinix grinned, her tail flicking eagerly behind her.

"The high tide waits for no fish!" she exclaimed in a chipper voice. "It's time to get up!"

Reaching over the small gap between the cots, I gently shook Ryllae's shoulder. "Hey, Princess," I whispered. "It's time to wake up."

Ryllae blinked, her lips curving into a soft smile. "Hi, Daegal."

Gods, my name on her lips was the best sound I'd heard in days.

"Hi," I murmured.

"Morning!" Tinix said in a voice that was too loud, even for me.

"Oh my gods," Ryllae groaned, her eyes widening as her dark crimson aura pulsed around her. "What time is it? Why are we awake?"

I chuckled. The princess was definitely not a morning person. I stored that knowledge away, eager to learn even more about her. Did she prefer sweet or salty foods? What was her favorite color? Did she have dreams? What were they?

I wanted to know it all.

Tinix laughed, ignorant of the thoughts running through my mind. "It's a little past four in the morning."

"Four in the morning?" Ryllae grumbled. "This is akin to torture." She pushed her head back into the pillow. "I would know."

The mermaid's eyes widened. "But Princess, we must go! The High Queen is waiting for you!"

Ryllae pulled her head out of the pillow. "The High Queen?"

Tinix grinned. "Yes! Your ride is waiting. If you leave now, you will be in Coral City by dinner. Erthian says Her Majesty is anxious to meet the Forgotten Princess."

Gods, I was not a fan of that title. It rankled me. I drew in a breath, ready to tell Tinix not to use the name, but my irritation vanished when I glanced at Ryllae.

Throwing her hair in a bun—a feat considering our watery surroundings—Ryllae grinned. "All right," she chirped. "Let's go."

"It's a seashell," Ryllae said from beside me. "A bright orange seashell."

"Did I forget to mention that?" Tinix laughed as if this was an inconsequential fact. "My apologies! This is the fastest shell in Her Majesty's fleet."

"I see," I said, eyeing the pointed vehicle. It spiraled outward, opening at the back where handrails made of coral lined the shell. "And the sharks are..."

"Don't worry," the mermaid said. "Brutus and Silver are tame."

I raised a brow. The two massive silver sharks harnessed to the shell did not look "tame."

Tinix must have seen something in my face because she continued, "Erthian is a fantastic driver. All the two of you have to do is hold on tight."

Her words did nothing to calm the knot growing within me.

"Morning, Tinix." A booming voice came from behind us, and I turned to see the pink-haired mermale from yesterday.

Tinix swam over, whispering to the Captain of the Guard.

Beside Erthian was a mermale with skin as dark as mine. His aura was a deep indigo, a few shades from black, and he gripped a trident.

I had never seen an aura like this before, and instantly, I was on high alert. The unknown was rarely good, especially when it came bearing a trident.

Swimming closer to Ryllae, I slid our fingers together once more. This time, it felt like second nature, and I squeezed her hand tightly.

"Stay close to me, Princess," I whispered as we approached the three mer.

Ryllae quirked a brow, twisting so she was swimming in front of me. "Was that... Did you just give me an order?"

Until then, I hadn't even considered that it might not be a good idea to boss around the Princess of Ithenmyr.

But I already said the words, and there was no taking them back.

"Yes," I said, running my thumb over the back of her hand as I stared into those blue eyes. "I did."

Ryllae sucked in a breath, and her eyes widened. Wrapping her hand in my tunic, she pulled me close. My heart felt like it was going to burst out of my chest.

The princess smirked, and a playful glint entered her eye. "You must be feeling comfortable with me, Fortune Elf, to be ordering me around."

"I am, Princess." The words slipped from my tongue, filling the water around us. "Very comfortable."

The air thickened between us, and I watched her closely.

Ryllae's tongue darted out, wetting her lips.

"Good," she said after a moment. "I am also finding that I am becoming more comfortable with you."

Thank the gods. Knowing what I did about her past, I would *never* force her to do anything.

We were going to move at whatever pace she set. If there was any movement at all.

I would not gamble with this.

Heat pulsed through me as I studied this dark princess. Squeezing Ryllae's hand, I pulled her towards me. She moved effortlessly in the water, and soon, there was barely an inch between us.

Lowering my head so my lips hovered above hers, I whispered, "Ryllae, we need to—"

"It's time to depart!" the Captain of the Guard called out.

The moment shattered, blowing away like grains of sand in the current.

Pressing my forehead against Ryllae's, I groaned. "We'll finish this conversation later, okay?"

"Okay," she whispered.

The next few minutes went by in a blur. Erthian introduced us to his husband Shamis before we boarded the shell, and we bid Tinix goodbye before the sharks moved.

The ocean passed before us, and Ryllae was silent at my side. This female, who had appeared out of nowhere and wormed her way into my heart, held all my attention. Even in the quiet, I found more comfort in her presence than ever.

Erthian and Shamis spoke quietly between themselves, and the shell drove smoothly.

When it became clear that this journey would take most of the day, I retreated to the silver planes and checked the future.

What I Saw concerned me.

There were two possible outcomes. A fork lay in the proverbial road once we arrived at Coral City.

Down one path, I Saw Ryllae laughing.

But down the other...

Tears ran down her face.

In both, I stood by her side.

No matter how much I prodded the paths, I couldn't See the cause of her tears. The pivotal moment of choice was hidden from me.

For now.

All I knew was the next few days in Coral City would change our lives. One way or another, after this, nothing would ever be the same again.

They're Going to Kill Me

AILEANA

"I hate the snow," I grumbled under my breath, tucking my gloved hands into my armpits.

The white flakes falling from the sky were the bane of my existence. In the few hours since I had crossed the river, it started snowing *again*. Every time one of those damned white flakes had the audacity to fall on my cheeks, I cursed them. Everything, from the tip of my nose to the toes tucked within my boots, was cold.

The cloak Tiaesti and Erwen gifted me was keeping me alive, but it didn't stop the perpetual chill of the winter from setting in my bones. My boots, while dry, were heavy on my feet. I yearned to take them off but knew that if I did, I wouldn't be able to get them back on. Already, they were blistering where the boots had rubbed the skin of my ankles raw.

At least the cold took my mind off the pain of being separated from Xander.

Breley lay before me. Hundreds of buildings were crowded together in the city center. Like Thyr, a thick stone wall surrounded the city.

However, this one was nearly double the size of the wall surrounding Thyr. From here, I could make out the silhouettes of Winged Soldiers patrolling the wall.

Beyond the wall, in the very center of the city, was a massive white castle.

The wind carried faint sounds of male conversation to my ears, and somewhere nearby, a baby wailed.

I leaned against a tree trunk, my magic begging to be released as I studied the city. Green ribbons slipped from my palms, slithering down the tree trunk and disappearing into the snow.

What do you need, High Lady of Life? The earth sounded energized, and it shook beneath my feet. Ever since I asked for help with the bridge, it was more eager than usual.

Perhaps the earth and I were coming to a truce of sorts. It no longer seemed to want to keep me for itself, and in exchange, I fed it my magic.

Sighing, I pressed my cheek against the tree. "I need to find Xander. He's here somewhere, but the city is massive." I shook my head. "I don't know where to start."

Even though the white castle was just ostentatious enough to belong to High King Edgar, I didn't think he would keep Xander there.

But where else could he be? I didn't have time to sweep through the entire city, going from one building to the other. There had to be a faster way.

Already, I was risking everything by being here.

When I entered Breley, I would be doing so alone. The moment I stepped foot into the city without a male, I would be breaking the Accompaniment Law. Castien had offered to come with me, but I turned him down.

I played by the Crimson King's rules long enough.

Now, he was going to play by mine.

No more accompaniment. No more dresses. No more feeble female who did what she was told.

I was the High Lady of Life, and he had underestimated me for the last time.

Running my fingers over the necklace, an idea struck me. I pursed my lips, running through the various components.

It was... good. Brilliant even.

And hopefully, it wouldn't get me killed.

Taking a quick look around and confirming that the trees hid me from prying eyes, I gathered a spool of green magic and bent. The green ribbons slipped from my palms, disappearing into the snow. When the spool of magic was almost gone, I dug my gloved fingers into the ground. My consciousness flowed with the magic, and within moments, I heard echoes of the life all around me.

I was still Aileana... but I was more.

The earth called to me, and I dove into its embrace.

Pouring myself into the earth, the life in Breley brushed up against me. I felt them all. The trees, the roots, the grass, the flowers, and the plants growing in gardens throughout the city. All of them spoke to me, but I didn't stop there.

Further and further, I dove into the earth. I found the roots that ran deep below the city, the mice and rats that scurried along floorboards and in alleys, and the insects that called the earth their home.

I let even more green ribbons slip from my hands.

The well of magic within me was deep, and the earth sang as I fed it my power.

Soon, I was *everywhere* in Breley.

There wasn't a single living thing, plant or animal, that didn't recognize my touch.

As one, they paused and *saw* me.

The ants crawling through the dirt stopped their movements. The roots running beneath homes and through the city tightened their grip on the ground. Even the spiders living in ceiling cracks ceased weaving their webs.

For one singular moment, all the life in Breley turned to me.

Thousands of voices echoed through my mind at once. *What do you need, High Lady?*

I sent a mental image of Xander and described him as best I could. I waited as my army of life scoured the city for my bonded mate.

Time had no meaning as I fed my magic into the earth. I ignored the pain in my knees as I pulled up more power from the well within me and fed it into the earth. Stars shone through the clouds, illuminating the night sky, and I waited for my army to find something. Anything.

As I was beginning to think it might have been for naught, an image flashed before my eyes.

A prisoner with long silver-white hair was curled in a ball, lying motionless on a stone floor. Irons were clamped around his wrists and ankles, and blood seeped from his back. It was incredibly dark, but the moment the vision flashed before my eyes, I knew.

This was Xander.

My heart thundered in my chest, and my hands grew sweaty in my gloves.

"Where is he?" I demanded of my army.

The response came to me swiftly, carried by a black ant that had seen him recently. Delivering my thanks, I retreated from the earth. My hands withdrew from the snow, and I sat back, panting.

If the information was accurate, I wouldn't even have to go into the city to retrieve my mate.

I allowed my lips to tilt up into the smallest of smiles. Dusting myself off, I glanced at the sky. The moon shone, and its dim light cast dark shadows all around me.

Good.

The cover of darkness was exactly what I needed.

THE ANT'S directions were rather difficult to follow. Perhaps that was what I got for asking a creature the size of my fingernail for help.

Unfortunately, I didn't have any other options.

I walked through the trees, staying away from the city walls until I saw the stout black building the ant had described. Shrouded in darkness, it stood far enough away from the city wall that the light from the Winged Soldiers' torches did not reach it.

I circled the building, taking careful stock of the structure. It was windowless, and the single wooden door appeared to be the only way in or out. It looked like it was unguarded, and there were no signs of life.

Reaching within myself, I pulled hard on the bond.

A deafening silence was my only response, but I wouldn't allow myself to give up. The image from the ant had been clear. This was the place they had seen Xander.

Knowing this could be a trap, I slipped two of my daggers free from their sheaths.

"Here goes nothing," I muttered.

Keeping my grip on my daggers, I crept towards the door under the cover of darkness. Standing outside the door, I paused and held my breath. Night insects chirped, and the bitter wind howled, but I didn't hear any noise coming from inside the building.

Shifting my blades, I gripped the handle and pressed my ear to the door.

The only sound was the thudding of my own heart.

I'm coming for you, Xander. I sent the message down the bond, hoping he could hear me. *Hold on.*

Twisting the handle, I pushed against the door. I expected it to be locked, but it swung open with ease.

My eyes widened, and alarm bells rang in my mind. Something about this felt wrong. Who left doors unlocked? It was almost too good to be true.

Even so, I could not leave. Xander needed me.

Slipping into the windowless building, I closed the door behind me and walked into...

An empty space.

There was nothing here.

I turned in a slow circle, my daggers still tight in my grip. Four walls and a roof. A dark wooden floor was beneath my feet, but that was it.

There was nothing here.

No people. No furniture. There weren't even any signs that life had been here.

It was just... empty.

My daggers clattered to the floor, and I gasped, dropping to my knees.

A sob welled up within me, and my lungs tightened. "Where are you, Elyxander?" Pounding my fist on the floor, far too aware of the Winged Soldiers in the city, I whisper-yelled, "Where are you?"

The wind howled in response.

Again and again, I repeated the question, slamming my fist into the floor.

The wood splintered beneath my touch.

And then I saw it.

A crack. A piece of wood broke apart, and something beneath it caught my eye. Pulling up the sliver, my mouth fell open.

The floor was hollow.

Sucking in a breath, I hurriedly grabbed a dagger. Slipping the blade beneath the wooden floorboard, I jiggled. As soon as I could, I shoved my hand beneath the plank and yanked.

The board came loose, and I threw it to the side. A curse that Xander would have been proud of slipped out of me as I looked down.

They kept him in a *hole*.

The air stank of unwashed bodies and other unpleasantries, but beneath that was a scent I would recognize anywhere.

Smoke and ash and pine wafted up to my nose.

Xander had been here.

Grabbing onto the next floorboard, I pulled it up. I tore up the planks one by one and threw them to the side. When the opening was big enough for me to fit into, I took my pack and Xander's sword, laying them on the ground.

Sliding my daggers back into their sheaths, I took a deep breath, and then, before I could talk myself out of this, I dropped into the dark hole.

Landing in a crouch on the cold, hard ground, I sucked in a breath as a silent sob threatened to escape me.

Inky darkness surrounded me, and Xander's scent permeated every part of this horrible cell.

He wasn't here.

Falling to my knees, I slumped against the wall.

My muscles ached with exhaustion, but I couldn't rest.

I needed to find my mate, but every turn was just another dead end.

That ache within me from our separation twisted, sharpening as I sat surrounded by my mate's scent.

I needed Xander like I needed air to breathe.

This couldn't be the end.

Slamming my palms onto the stone beneath me, I *screamed* as I reached into the pool of magic and let all my power flood out of me at once.

It came out in a rush of green ribbons, sinking into the ground as I dove into the earth.

No longer was I concerned about my well-being. I left my body behind as I threw myself into the earth.

The leaves, the trees, the roots, the insects, and the animals all turned toward me. As one, they sang to me. *The High Lady of Life is here.*

I didn't respond. I couldn't.

Diving into the earth this quickly was literally stealing my breath. Even though I was pouring out my magic, I could still feel everything happening to me.

Back in that dark hole that smelled of my mate, my body was changing. Glowing a vibrant green, my skin stretched. My body molded and remade itself as I poured my magic into the earth. My gums ached, and something sharp poked my tongue. Blood filled my mouth. Something snapped within me.

Everything felt... new. Right. Whole.

It felt like it was always meant to be this way.

Drawing in a deep breath, I tasted the particles of the earth all around me. Seeking my pool of magic, I was surprised to see it was full.

Now, beneath Xander's scent, I caught something else.

Fear.

What had they done to him?

Anger pulsed through my veins, and I poured myself deeper into the earth.

With every passing moment, I felt stronger than ever.

Remain with us, High Lady, the earth cried out in its loud, ethereal, ancient voice.

I shook my head. *I cannot.*

I had a purpose. A reason for being here.

A renewed sense of life filled me, and I searched for that fiery bond that lived within me. The moment I laid eyes on the pulsing, writhing cord of my mating, I yanked on it harder than I ever had before.

A searing pain ran through my hands, but I ignored it.

"Where is he?" My voice was unlike anything I had ever heard. Power reverberated through every single word, and it felt as though my body was burning from the inside out. "Where. Is. He?"

Pouring every ounce of energy into finding Xander, I tightened my grip around the fierce cord and yanked again.

This time, I did not stop. I kept pulling on the bond, ignoring everything else around me, until finally, I felt something.

I felt *him.*

A thick, hot haze surrounded him, but still, I *felt* Xander.

He was there. Here. Wherever our bond had brought me.

And then the haze cleared.

My heart squeezed, and a scream crawled up my throat.

"Oh my gods," I moaned, those treacherous tears threatening to escape despite my unwillingness to cry.

Kneeling in a dark cell barely big enough to contain his large body, Xander looked like he was moments away from Fading. His veins were black, a stark contrast to his pale skin, and his eyes were closed as his head rested against the iron bars. He yelled over and over again, "Let me out!"

There was no reply. There was no one else here. The entire cell block was empty except for him.

My heart broke in a way that I hadn't known was possible.

"Xander?" I whispered.

He didn't move.

The scent of lemons and cedar was almost overpowering as it wafted toward me. Xander's knuckles were white as he clutched the iron bars, and our mating bond was barely visible through the dirt and blood coating his skin. Iron manacles were clamped around his wrists and his neck, filling him with poison.

I could barely breathe. Barely think. All I could do was stare at my mate.

That twisting, aching pain from our separation mended itself, morphing into red-hot anger.

They were *killing* him.

Lurching forward, I grabbed Xander's hands. They were as cold as the snow falling through the small window at the top of the cell.

"Xander," I hissed urgently.

He jolted, his golden eyes flying open as he looked around frantically. "Aileana?"

Hearing my name on his lips was like tasting honeyed wine after days without a drink.

I needed it more than anything else in my entire world.

I squeezed his fingers. "I'm here."

"Where are you?" he asked.

My brows furrowed. "I'm right here." Shifting forward, I brushed my lips over his. The feeling was strange, and something was off. "Can't you see me?"

"No." His eyes widened. "Is this.. am I dreaming?"

I shook my head. "No. At least, I don't think so."

"You're not making any sense, Aileana. Please tell me you're not here."

"What? No, I am. I'm here. I came for you." I drew in a deep breath, tightening my grip on his fingers. "Xander, I found the place where they were keeping you."

"No." He paled impossibly further. "Tell me you're safe in the Sanctuary with Myhenna and the other Spirits. That I just wanted you so badly that I dreamed you were here."

My insides churned as a wave of anguish ran through my entire body. Why was he acting like this was the worst thing in the entire world?

"It's not a dream, Xander. The hole... I'm there right now. I don't know how I got here, I just... looked for you."

A look of pain and horror crossed his face. "What have you done?" He slammed his hands against the bars. "You need to leave, Aileana."

What?

He must have been delusional. Clearly, they had done something to addle his mind. There was no way I was going to leave him here.

"No," I hissed, tightening my grip around his fingers. He might not have been able to see me, but he could feel me. I pressed my lips to his white knuckles, uncaring of the grime. "I'm not leaving you. I will find you, Xander, and then we will get married."

He blinked. "What?"

I nodded eagerly. "I'll do it. I'll marry you," I breathed. My words came out of me in a rush, "Elyxander, I need you like my body needs air. Like the sun needs the moon. I need you like the earth needs me. I don't care anymore if marriage puts me in a cage. If you're by my side, I'll survive anything."

"You'll marry me," he said, his tone oddly flat.

"Yes." The words didn't feel like enough. I leaned forward, pressing my head against the bars. "Elyx, my love, I swear to you, I'm going to find you, and then I'll marry you."

For a long moment, neither of us spoke.

Our chests rose in synchrony as our breath mingled. My mouth hovered near his—not touching, but so close, I could feel his breath on my lips.

"Xander," I breathed. "Say something."

His golden eyes flickered, and then his face hardened. He tightened his grip around my fingers to the point of pain.

"No," he hissed.

I gasped. "What?"

"You aren't going to find me."

"I'm close," I insisted. "I can feel it."

"Listen to me, Aileana," he snarled, masking the anguish in his voice. "You need to leave."

"Never," I hissed in return. "I will never leave you. I chose you."

"Get out of here," he growled. "Run back to the Sanctuary. Leave me."

My heart thundered in my chest. Breathing, which hadn't been a problem moments before, suddenly became impossible.

This was wrong.

He wasn't supposed to fight me on this. He should have been celebrating. I was coming to rescue him. To save him, just like he had saved me countless times before.

Didn't he want to be rescued?

Forcing my mouth to open, I whispered, "What are you saying?"

"Leave!" he thundered, pulling his hands back and smacking them against the iron bars. The shackles around his wrists clanged against the iron, and fresh blood dripped down his arms. "Forget about me."

"No." I shook my head, staring at the blood. "I can't. I won't... you're *mine.*"

He reared back. "Aileana, you don't understand. It's not safe for you here. Queen Sanja is—" He gasped, his hands rising to his neck as a choking sound came from his throat. His eyes widened, and though his mouth moved, no sound came from it.

"What about the Southern Queen?" I asked hurriedly. "Do you know something?"

"I can't... it's stopping me... you need to *go*," he said hoarsely. "Save yourself. Let them kill me. I would die hundreds of deaths for you if it means you will be free."

Tears rushed to my eyes. "Elyxander—"

"Go." His voice cracked. "*Live*."

His words were like a dagger through my heart. I could never do what he was asking of me. To live without him would be to exist without my other half.

"I will never leave you," I vowed.

He slammed a hand into the bars. "Gods damn it, Aileana! For once, just listen to me. It's not safe for you here. If you come, they're going to—"

Footsteps came from behind me, and I stiffened.

"What in the seven circles of hell is going on here?" The deep voice came from behind me, sending shivers up my spine.

I turned, my eyes widening at the sight of a Winged Soldier standing in the hallway above me. As customary, he was dressed in all black, and his wings were outstretched behind him. The male's eyes were hard, and violence ebbed from him as he glared into the cell.

He held out a taloned hand, waving it in our direction. "Talking to yourself again, dragon scum?"

Xander glared at the male, pinching his mouth shut.

The Winged Soldier approached the cell. I slammed my back against the bars, but the soldier didn't even look in my direction.

Thank the gods.

My thankfulness was short-lived, however, as the guard snarled.

"Answer me!" Spittle flew from his mouth, landing less than a foot from where I was pressed against the bars.

My heart thundered in my chest, and I shoved my fist into my mouth to stop myself from crying out.

"Yes," Xander sneered. "I have to entertain myself somehow. The gods only know you lot are a bore."

The Winged Soldier looked at my mate, tapping his foot. "It's entertainment you want, is it?"

The tone of his voice made my insides curl. I was going to be sick.

Xander just nodded. "A male's got to do something to pass the time."

The guard crouched, his expression almost gleeful as he glared at my mate through the bars. The Winged Soldier was so close to me that I could smell the rotten meat on his breath.

"Don't you worry. I hear you'll be quite *entertained* during the king's wedding in two days. After all, he's requested that you witness the momentous occasion. It's not every day our monarch binds himself in matrimony to such a powerful female."

Xander cursed, and the guard laughed.

The soldier stood, clearly enjoying himself. "Yes, it's all planned out. The king will be wed in two days, and on the dawn of the third day, the entire city of Breley will be present to witness the execution of the Last Dragon."

I sucked in a breath, my heart pounding frantically as my vision swam.

Execution.

"Enjoy the next few days because they're all you have left."

My bonded mate roared as the Winged Soldier disappeared.

Two days.

Once the guard was gone, I turned to Xander. Urgency filled my voice, and I gripped the bars once more. "I have to get you out of here. Quick, tell me everything you know about your prison. Where are they keeping you?"

Seconds ticked by. Long, eternal seconds. Why wasn't he talking?

"Xander," I breathed. "Tell me."

He shook his head, and the movement jostled the iron around his neck. His skin *sizzled* as the dragonsbane leached into his skin.

My eyes watered. "My love, please. Tell me where you are."

One of Xander's hands reached out from the bars. He moved it through the air slowly as if searching for something.

For me.

I placed my cheek in his hand, breathing in his unique scent.

Xander pulled me close to him, his hand wrapping around the back of my neck. He drew me toward the bars, and I let him pull me. I slid my hands through the iron, ripping up the bottom of his tunic to run my hands over his chest as our lips came crashing together.

Desperation filled our every move as our hands explored each other. Everywhere he touched felt like it was on fire, but it wasn't enough. It was never enough. At that moment, I didn't care about the dirt or the blood covering my mate.

I needed him.

He kissed me like it was the last time he would ever see me. His mouth moved urgently against me as if...

He was saying goodbye.

"Elyxander, I need to know where you are," I murmured against his lips. "Tell me."

A long moment passed, and his chest heaved before he pushed away from me.

"No," he said.

I blinked. "No?"

"No, I won't tell you."

Jolting back, my eyes widened. "Why not?" I breathed.

"You need to leave," he snarled. "Get as far away from here as you can. Cross into Ipotha. Go to the universities. They care for refugees there and will shelter you."

"You want me to run away to the Western Kingdom?" I couldn't believe my ears. My entire body was numb. "I'm the last Earth Elf, your bonded mate, and you just want me to... leave?"

"Yes," he breathed. "Things are worse than we ever imagined. Did you hear the guard, Aileana? The king is marrying the Southern Queen. In two days. And then they're going to kill me."

Despair filled his words and the look in his eyes...

He was giving up.

My heart stopped beating, and my lungs squeezed. Breathing was no longer important. Nothing else mattered. Not anymore.

"That's it?" I stared at him. "After all this, that's *it*?"

"That's it," he snarled. "Get out of here. Go."

My ears burned, and my blood boiled as I glared at my mate. It didn't matter that he couldn't see me. I was here, and he was telling me to run away like a coward.

"You're giving up?" I asked incredulously. I didn't even bother telling him about the map or the prophecy. Our time was short, and he wanted me to *leave*. "You want me to just... pack up and leave you to die?"

My words hung between us, and his eyes widened.

"Yes," he said on an exhale.

I clenched my fists around the iron bars.

How dare he kiss me like that? How dare he make me love him and need him and want him only for him to turn around and say something like this?

He was mine, and I was his.

Yanking up my sleeve, I snarled. Even though Xander couldn't see me, I shoved my mating bond in his face.

"Well, too bad, Elyx," I spat. "I'm not going to leave. I promised to fight for you, and I will, whether you like it or not."

Reaching into the cell, I grabbed his face. Drawing our lips together for one last scorching kiss, I whispered, "I will find you. This isn't goodbye."

Before he could say anything else, I reached within myself.

Take me back, I commanded the earth.

I wasn't sure how I knew it would obey, but it did.

The moment my eyes slipped open again, I stared at the dark stone wall in front of me.

A plan formed in my mind.

Xander didn't want to tell me where he was, but it didn't matter.

I knew where he would be in two days.

Invitation or not, I would be at the wedding, too.

I had a king to kill.

Coral City

RYLLAE

"Do you know who the best creatures are in Ithenmyr, Ryllae?" Father's tone was pleasant enough, but a spark in his eye made me pay attention.

He sat on the other side of the long formal dining table, balancing a red sphere of magic in his hands. He turned it over thoughtfully as he studied me. The servants had already cleared the remnants of our dinner, but Father ordered me to remain.

I didn't know what I'd done wrong. When he commanded me to stay, I frantically thought over my day but couldn't figure it out. I hadn't even broken anything with my magic today.

"N-no, Father," I said, twisting a blond lock of hair through my fingers. "I don't."

He slammed a fist on the table, and I drew in a sharp breath. Glasses shook, and the red sphere pulsed in his hand. "Death Elves, you stupid, ignorant child. How will you be a strong queen when you don't even know that?"

He stood, shoving back his chair so hard it smashed into the ground.

The scent of sandalwood grew stronger until he stood mere feet from me. His magic continued to pulse in his hands.

"No one else in the Four Kingdoms is comparable. Not a single person. No other elf, werewolf, vampire, witch, shifter, fae, or human. No one can compare to the might of the Death Elf. Do you understand?"

I stared at him, willing my face not to betray my racing heart. "Yes, Father."

A long moment passed before the red sphere of magic shifted into a scepter in his hands. "Good," he snarled. "Now get out of my sight."

"Ryllae?" Daegal's voice came from beside me, and his hand gently nudged mine.

Drawing myself out of my memory, I shook my head. "Sorry, I'm paying attention."

We were standing in the back of the seashell carriage. The two mermales escorting us talked as Erthian directed the sharks.

Daegal's lips tilted up, the smile reaching his eyes. "Good. I don't think you want to miss this."

I raised my eyes, drawing in a breath as I looked at the expansive ocean. "Oh," I whispered. "It's beautiful."

After we left the village, much of the ocean appeared barren. Sand dotted the ground, and while there were sporadic reefs and forests made of seaweed and kelp, we hadn't run into any other signs of life.

That was no longer the case.

The shell slowed at the top of a large hill, and in the center of the valley was an enormous, colorful city that stretched as far as my eyes could see. From one point on the horizon to the other, hundreds of colorful structures emerged from the sand. Made from coral, it quickly became clear where the city got its name. There were hundreds of buildings, some short and others tall, but all of them paled in comparison to the massive palace in the center of the city.

Merfolk filled the crystal blue waters. Young and old, with skin ranging from the palest of whites to the darkest of blacks, their tails shimmered in the sunlight.

An air of lightness filled the atmosphere.

Was it possible that these people were... happy?

The thought brought me great joy.

Maybe there was hope for me. This morning, when I woke, I felt further from the edge of madness than I had in years.

It was Daegal's presence. I was certain of it.

He brought me peace.

Erthian made a clicking sound with his tongue, and the sharks continued down the hill toward the city. At first, the buildings were spread out, but they grew more compact with every passing moment.

If Ithenmyr was a study in green and brown, then Coral City was a lesson in vibrancy. Brilliant blues, pinks, greens, and purples were scattered throughout the city. Hundreds of plants grew, some small and others large, as they claimed this thriving underwater metropolis for their own.

I leaned over the side of the ride, reaching out towards a green plant with red flowers on the tip. I almost had one in my grasp when the shell went over a bump. Crying out, I stumbled back.

"Careful, Ryllae," Daegal said in a deep voice as his arm went out, catching me before I could fall.

He held me while I regained my footing. "Thank you," I whispered.

The Fortune Elf smiled, and his blue eyes shone brightly. "I will always catch you, Ryllae."

The way he said my name made my insides twist. Our gazes locked, and everything else faded away. The mermales driving the shell, the city we were approaching, the animals, they all disappeared into the background.

"Daegal, I... I dreamed about you last night."

The words slipped out of me, hanging in the air between us.

He moved towards me, my breath catching in my throat as he raised a hand, running it down my cheek. "Good dreams, I hope."

"Very good," I whispered, squeezing my thighs together as memories flashed through my mind.

Daegal moved closer to me, our chests brushing against each other as he stepped into my space.

If it had been anyone else, I would have felt afraid.

But it wasn't. I trusted this male with my life.

Leaning in close, I sucked in a deep breath.

Daegal tilted his head. "You make me feel things, Princess." His eyes searched mine as he brushed his thumb over my cheek. "Things that I probably shouldn't be feeling about you."

I knew exactly what he was talking about.

This connection between us was growing stronger by the day. Soon, we wouldn't be able to ignore it. "I feel the same way."

A spark lit up in his eyes, and he stared at me. His mouth opened, and he dipped his head to kiss me. His lips hovered over mine when something slammed into the carriage.

Daegal jolted, pulling me to his chest just as a green ball of kelp sailed over the carriage.

"Careful!" Erthian shouted. He looked over his shoulder at us, shrugging. "The merlings are always getting into trouble when they're not in school."

As if to prove his point, yet another ball of kelp sailed over the shell, narrowly avoiding us. I turned, my back pressing against Daegal's front, and looked behind me. A dozen merlings swam in the middle of the road, throwing three kelp balls between them in some sort of game.

Laughter filled the air, and my insides warmed.

There was no laughter in Nightstone Prison. There hadn't been much laughter before that, either.

According to my father, Death Elves did not laugh.

No, they just killed.

But here, the people laughed. There was joy in this underwater kingdom.

My heart swelled.

"It's incredible, isn't it?" Daegal's breath tickled the back of my neck, and I hummed.

I did not know what I was doing with this male.

This didn't feel like any of the dalliances I had partaken in when I was younger, but that didn't bother me. That link between us, the one I was pointedly ignoring at this particular moment, hummed in contentment.

"It really is," I replied.

I stood there, my back against his front, as we rode toward the city center. Soon, other shells pulled by sharks and eels joined us on the road. The merfolk cast a few curious glances in our direction, but they didn't feel malicious. Perhaps the most surprising thing was the voices rising in the sea around us. Males and females alike spoke, their conversations filling the water.

Seeing all the happiness sparked something within me. The broken parts of me, the ones that had been fractured from my extended stay in my father's prison, were knitting themselves together.

It didn't just start today. I realized suddenly that I had been feeling better for days. More like... myself.

Not the female I used to be.

The female I was meant to be.

Every day with Daegal, I felt stronger, and a sense of rightness filled me.

THE SHELL STOPPED in front of the looming, large white coral palace, and Daegal's arms tightened around me. Dozens of spires rose towards the surface of the water, and hundreds of windows dotted the front.

Erthian turned to us. "If you'll excuse us, Princess, I shall inform Her Majesty that you have arrived." He raised his voice. "Vinali!"

A tanned mermaid with white hair swam up to the shell. "Yes, Captain?"

"These are our guests. Keep an eye on them."

"Of course, Captain," Vinali said.

Erthian and his husband gathered their tridents, swimming towards the entrance of the castle. The guard swam back, but I could feel her eyes on us.

It was a little ridiculous. After all, it wasn't as though Daegal and I were going to leave. We needed the High Queen's help. Besides, where would we go?

Once the mermales were gone, I leaned against the side of the shell and studied the city. My dress swirled around me, the fabric oddly soaked but not sodden, but I didn't care.

For the first time in years, I wasn't angry. I wasn't even frustrated.

I was happy. My lips twitched, and before I knew it, a grin slid onto my face.

I. Was. Happy.

For a long time, I thought happiness was nothing but a fairy tale told to children to appease them. Then, in prison, I decided happiness was a lie told to placate the masses.

But now, I knew the truth.

Happiness was not a singular thing. It was not something that could be bought or traded. Happiness was safety and love and being cared for. It was sharing moments of life with others who valued and cherished you. Happiness was finding reasons to live despite the horrors of everyday life.

Daegal made me happy. He looked at the broken part of me and didn't shy away from it. He saw me for who I really was and wasn't scared.

Daegal made me happy.

"Why are you smiling?" His voice was soft in my ear, and I leaned against his chest. He hummed in approval, his arms running up and down mine as he pressed me against him.

"I'm happy." The admission stole my breath.

"Me too," Daegal whispered. He twisted me in his arms so that my chest lined up with his. As we looked into each other's eyes, the sounds of Coral City faded away.

Open affection filled Daegal's gaze, and warmth twisted in my core. My heart raced, and the water around us grew thick with anticipation.

Cupping my chin, Daegal's voice was husky as he asked, "Can I kiss you?"

There wasn't even a moment of hesitation before I breathed, "Yes."

Daegal's head bent, and his eyes never left mine as he clasped the back of my neck. He pulled me towards him, pressing our bodies together as he swept his lips over mine.

He tasted of salt and darkness and a moonlit night. It was strangely delicious, and I couldn't get enough of it. This kiss was everything I knew Daegal to be. Kind. Gentle. Caring in all the best ways.

And it was far too short.

Daegal pulled away after just a moment, and I whimpered.

He chuckled, the sound distinctly masculine, as he pulled me against him for a hug. "I hope that means you'll let me do that again."

I murmured against his chest, "Probably."

He snorted.

I settled into his arms, and we waited for Erthian to return.

FROM THE OUTSIDE, the palace looked large. From the inside, it was grander than my father's palace in Vlarone.

He would hate this place, which only made me love it more.

Erthian led us through a maze of hallways, up a set of stairs, and down multiple corridors until we were deep within the palace.

Eventually, the Captain of the Guard stopped before a dark green door carved with a tree. Clearing his throat, he clasped his hands behind his back. "This is an enchanted suite. Beyond these doors, you won't require any magic to breathe. It was created many years ago for visitors from the Surface, although it has remained unused for quite some time. Her Majesty hopes you'll be comfortable, and she will send a servant to attend to you shortly."

The three of us exchanged a few pleasantries, and then, with a graceful swish of his tail, Erthian swam down the hallway.

We were alone.

As soon as Erthian rounded the corner, Daegal squeezed my hand. "Hold on, Ryllae. I'm going to See what is coming and make sure it's safe."

As soon as the last word was out of his mouth, Daegal's features stilled. I studied him, his short curly hair moving slowly in the current as his eyes glowed silver. His lips were parted, and I touched my own, remembering the feeling of that too-brief kiss. I could still taste him, this Fortune Elf who had quickly made himself the most important person in my life.

But I knew we needed to take this slow. To really think about what this meant. I didn't want to rush things. Not if what I suspected about our connection was true.

It was different.

We were different.

Whatever was growing between us, I did not want to ruin.

Once the silver faded, I asked, "Well?"

"It's... fine," he said, sounding surprised. Reaching around me, Daegal opened the door and gestured inside. "After you, Princess."

A small *pop* rang through my ears as I stepped into the space. Warm air enveloped me like a hug; my lungs expanded, and I breathed in fresh air for the first time in over a day.

I had never appreciated the beautiful sensation of my lungs expanding and retracting until this moment. Breathing as though I had never tasted air before in my life, I surveyed the room.

Erthian had called this room a suite, and it did not disappoint. We stood in a sitting room fit for a king. Settees made of gold and wrapped in dark blue velvet sat in the middle of the room while three massive golden rugs covered the coral floor. Each one was resplendent in its design. Gilded frames hung on the walls, and a large mirror the size of three males covered one wall.

Three doors—all of them golden, following the obvious theme—were on the other side of the room.

Beside me, Daegal cleared his throat. "Should we... explore?"

His voice sounded tentative, and something about that endeared him further to me.

I laughed, gesturing to the nearest piece of furniture. "You mean you don't want to sleep on the golden settee?"

He chuckled. "Somehow, Princess, I don't think I will quite fit."

I snorted. Daegal reached over, lacing our fingers together before pulling me towards the first door. I didn't stop him. If anything, a twinge of excitement went through me.

If anyone had asked me a year ago if I would ever feel safe alone with a male, I would have laughed in their faces. The very idea of that happening was ridiculous.

But here I was.

Alone with Daegal.

And never, in all my years, had I ever felt this safe.

The three doors hid two bedrooms of equal size—one decorated in a deep green like the kelp outside and the other in a purple so dark it was almost black—along with a bathing room four times the size of my cell in Nightstone Prison.

White and gold marble tile covered the floor, and a sunken tub that looked like it could hold five fully grown males stood invitingly in the corner. A large counter ran along the other wall, showcasing a variety of soaps and shampoos.

In short, these accommodations were stunning.

Trailing my hand along the top of the counter, I avoided looking in the mirror. I knew what I would see—someone who was broken, who had spent far too long trying to keep the pieces of herself together.

But after today's events, I thought I might be ready to look in a mirror soon.

"Ryllae, we should talk about the—" Daegal started, but a knock came from the front door of the suite. "Dammit."

Why did these interruptions always seem to come at the worst times?

A voice called out from the main room, "Hello?"

Daegal groaned, shaking his head as he went to answer the door. "Never mind. We can talk later."

Sliding the door shut to the bathing room, I took care of my needs before washing my hands.

When I came out, Daegal was leaning against the door, holding a woven basket made of kelp. A small smile was on his face as he studied me. "The queen will see us at dinner in half an hour."

Walking up to Daegal, I nudged him with my shoulder as I tried to peer in the basket. "Why are you smiling?"

He grinned, reaching into the basket. Pulling out a long, crimson dress, he handed it to me as he waggled his eyebrows. "I've Seen this dress."

I ran my fingers over the material. "Oh?"

"It's *very* nice," he said.

His gaze followed me the entire way back to the bathing room.

I didn't mind one bit.

RUNNING my fingers over the red markings that covered me from my neck to my toes, I slipped the crimson dress over my head. It hugged my body, sliding down my curves and fitting me perfectly. Keeping my back to the mirror, I brushed my hair and arranged my blond locks around my shoulders.

"Here we go," I murmured.

Pushing open the bathing room door, my eyes automatically sought out Daegal.

Dressed in a crisp black tunic and matching trousers, he stood with his back to me as he studied a painting on the far wall.

"Are you ready to go?" I asked softly, standing on the other side of the room.

Daegal turned, his mouth falling open as he ran a hand through his hair. "Ryllae... you look.... that dress... wow."

My lips tilted up as I glanced down, taking in the red fabric that hugged my curves. This gown would definitely be considered scandalous by the measures of my father's court. Long, tapered sleeves fell to my wrists, and the bodice ran in a deep V far below my bust, ending just above my navel. My swirling red tattoos peeked out, providing a tantalizing glimpse of the whirls that had marked me ever since the day I Matured.

I had never worn anything like this before, but I loved it.

It made me feel beautiful, strong, and confident.

Until this very moment, I did not know that clothing could carry this kind of power.

Crossing the room in three giant strides, Daegal's eyes darkened with desire as he bent and slid his hand behind my neck. My heart pounded, and the air thickened as he drew me towards him. He was so close, I could feel his breath on my lips. But still, he did not move.

He was waiting for me, I realized.

My heart fell wide open, and any reservations I had about this—about us—fell to the wayside.

Closing the distance between us, I pressed my lips against Daegal's. He groaned, the sound purely masculine, as his tongue swept into my mouth.

Our lips slanted together, and my core tightened. This kiss was *everything*. It was gentle and powerful, a claiming kiss and soft. Our lips and tongues and teeth said the words neither of us was able to say out loud. Not yet.

This kiss spoke of things to come. It held the promise of conversations to be had.

This kiss was the beginning of the rest of my life.

Warmth flooded through me, and I pressed my thighs together. I wanted nothing more than to press myself against this male and lock ourselves away for the night. Unfortunately, the High Queen was waiting for us.

Daegal must have had the same realization because he broke the kiss, panting as he rested his forehead against mine. His voice was husky as he said, "My vision did not do this dress justice."

I raised a brow, brushing a hand down the dress. "Did you See the kiss too?"

"No, I did not." He pressed a quick kiss to my forehead. "But I can say that without a doubt, it's the best surprise I've ever experienced in my life."

Butterflies fluttered in my stomach as Daegal led me to the door. His hand was tight around mine, and the press of his palm against mine was comforting as he pulled the door open.

This was it.

We had a dinner to attend. A queen to meet.

And most importantly, a curse to break.

Running Out of Time

AILEANA

Two days. That was all I had to get into Breley, make a plan, and rescue my bonded mate. That ache in my heart started again, even though I just saw Xander.

I needed to get out of this gods-damned hole and save him.

There was so much that could happen in two days. Lives could be irrevocably changed in two days. People could fall in love. Relationships could be destroyed. Journeys could begin. Weddings, funerals, and births could happen in two days.

In our case, I just hoped that two days would be enough.

It had to be enough.

There was no way in the seven circles of hell that I would allow the sun to rise on the third day. No way that I would stand by or run away while my bonded mate was murdered in front of an entire city.

I would die before I let that happen.

Pushing myself to my feet in this horrid black hole, I reached for the magic within me. This time, I didn't even have to look far before I found the ribbons. They were waiting, eager to be used.

Grabbing my magic, I pulled. Moments later, a handful of green magic slid from my palms, climbing up the darkened walls. With a twist of my hands, most of the ribbons became a thick set of vines. A few lingered on the stones, providing much-needed illumination. Wrapping my hands around the makeshift rope, I tugged, testing to see whether the vines would hold my weight. They didn't budge.

Using the vines as leverage, I walked up the side of the hole. As soon as I reached the top, I clambered onto the wooden floorboards.

I grabbed my pack and Xander's sword where I'd dropped them. Then, I twisted my hands. The green ribbons I'd used as light sank into the hole, joining the earth as I crept to the door. There was no time to waste. Sliding it open, I popped my head outside and glanced up at the sky. The moon was high, but traces of color were already dusting the horizon.

Dawn was coming.

I was running out of time.

Come get him, pet.

High King Edgar was going to get what he wanted. I was coming for my bonded mate. And this time, nothing would stop me.

Come hell or high water, I would be at that wedding, even if it took everything I had to get there.

Whatever game the Crimson King thought he was playing with me, I knew something he didn't. I wasn't a weak girl anymore, and he couldn't play with me.

If he wanted a game, I would give him one.

Shouldering my pack, I straightened my tunic and leggings before drawing my cloak around me. A brisk wind kissed my cheeks, and I took one last look at the small shack.

Remaining in the shadows and keeping my head down, I hurried towards a copse of trees between me and the city. From here, the black-winged guards who walked along the top of the wall were visible, along with the road into the city.

This was not going to be easy.

As soon as I was hidden by the trees, I dropped to my knees. The movement was awkward with Xander's sword on my hip, but I was happy to have his weapon. I would give it to him, and he would forget all this foolishness about me leaving.

We were equals. Partners. Mates.

We didn't give up or run away when things became difficult.

Pulling off my gloves, I ignored the cold seeping through my leggings, and I dipped my fingers into the snow. Dirt from the past few days covered my skin, and I desperately needed to feel clean.

Gritting my teeth against the cold, I gathered a snow ball before rubbing it between my hands. As the grime of the past few days left my skin, something else caught my attention.

My mouth fell open as I held my hand before my face.

Even though it was dark, I could see everything perfectly. Every line on my hand, every marking on my skin, even the dirt under my fingernails, was visible as though the sun was shining directly on me.

This shouldn't have been possible. It *wasn't* possible before I went into the hole. I thought back to everything that happened earlier. I had connected to the earth, sought Xander, and then I felt...

A stretching.

Pulling off my cloak, I pulled up my tunic, exposing my stomach to the cold wind.

I gasped.

New markings ran over my stomach, ranging from green as dark as the evergreens and as light as blades of grass in the summer. I hurriedly dropped my tunic, rolling up my leggings. There were more markings there, too. I frantically checked as much of my body as I could without freezing to death, moving more quickly with each passing second.

Soon, I confirmed what I had suspected.

Green whorls and swirls covered my entire body, from my collarbone to my toes.

I had never heard of a Maturation marking like this, but I knew in my heart that I was fully Mature.

Leaning my head against the nearest tree trunk, I clenched my fists and sought out the pool of power within me. It was so full that the magic was practically overflowing.

Placing my hands on the tree trunk, I released ribbons into the earth.

Pulling out my magic and feeding into the earth made me feel invigorated like nothing else had before.

I kept going, pulling more magic out of me. The branches above me swayed as I poured my magic into the tree.

Thank you, High Lady of Life.

At least someone was happy I was here.

Soon, I withdrew from the earth. I had to keep moving.

Cleaning my face and neck vigorously, I rubbed off as much dirt as possible before pulling my hair into a tight braid that ran down and settled a few inches behind my neck.

Tugging my hood over my hair, I shouldered my pack once more. In the time I had taken to clean myself off, a steady stream of traffic had filled the nearby road into the city. I shifted to the edge of the copse and ducked down behind a large snow-covered bush. From here, I had a perfect view of the entrance to the city. Even though it was still dark, I could see the outlines of the travelers' bodies perfectly.

Maturing had its benefits.

Some made their way into the city on foot, while others rode on horses and donkeys. Even if I hadn't seen the animals, I would have smelled them. An undercurrent of manure hung in the air, and a nervous hum came from the people heading toward the city.

Winged Soldiers guarded the entrance, and I knew as soon as I looked at them that there was no way I was getting in through the gates.

There had to be another way to get into the city.

Running my fingers over the hilt of Xander's sword at my side, I eyed the wall. Winged Soldiers walked along the top, their torches bobbing as they patrolled.

That was it.

My solution was staring me in the face. I didn't know why I hadn't thought of it before. If I couldn't go through the gate, I would circumvent the need for it entirely.

My magic thrummed in my veins as I flexed my fingers. My muscles already ached from pulling myself out of the hole earlier, but it didn't matter.

For Xander, I would do anything and go anywhere.

He was mine, and I was his.

I didn't have time to think this through. The sun was pushing away the darkness. When it rose, it would take away my chance to get into the city unnoticed.

I couldn't afford to wait until tonight.

Keeping my head down, I hurried away from the road. The conversations dimmed until the loudest sound was the pounding of my heart against my ribs.

The mating bond seemed louder than before, and it pulsed within me, urging me forward toward the wall.

I would not fail. I could not.

Creeping through the trees, I eyed the wall. The Winged Soldiers walked in pairs, and there wasn't much room between their patrols.

The road had long since disappeared from sight when I finally saw my chance. Here, the trees were closer to the wall, and there wasn't anyone nearby.

With one last glance at the forest, I ran. The necklace bounced between my breasts as I bolted towards the structure. It was a hundred feet away, maybe less. The snow softened my footfalls, covering the sound of my approach.

Thanks to my vastly improved eyesight, I could make out the individual lines of the stones, along with the cracks in the mortar and the specks of dirt stuck between them.

Thank Thelrena.

When the wall was a few feet away from me, voices came from above.

"The wedding is the day after tomorrow, Alfin, and I'm already exhausted."

Sucking in a breath, I darted forward and flattened myself against the surface. Trying to be as small as possible, I slid my hand to the hilt of my dagger and slowly pulled it out of its sheath.

If they saw me, I would fight them, but I didn't want to draw attention to myself.

A sound of agreement came before Alfin spoke with a deep voice. "You're telling me, Clark. It's going to be two days of torture. I was supposed to have the week off."

Not even a heartbeat later, the first soldier chuckled. "No one gets time off when the king gets married, you fool. That's why the number of soldiers in the city has tripled."

My heart pounded against my ribs, and my magic begged to be released. Tightening my grip around my dagger, I forced myself to breathe through the panic.

I could not let my magic out now. It would ruin everything.

Footsteps rattled the stone wall above me, and the soldiers' conversation turned toward discussing the various delightful aspects of the female form. I tuned them out. This was not the kind of distraction I needed right now.

Finally, after what felt like an hour, the soldiers continued their patrol. As soon as they were out of earshot, I drew in a deep breath. This was my moment.

Before I climbed, there was one last thing I wanted to do.

Sliding my dagger into its sheath, I shut my eyes and rested my head against the cold stone wall. I didn't know how to do this. Prayer was a foreign concept, but right now, I could use all the help I could get.

My words were little more than breath upon the brisk winter air as I whispered, "Thelrena... I have prayed so few times in my life. Honestly, I'm not even sure how to do this. But if you're there, if you can hear me, I ask that you be with me during this climb. Give me guidance. Help me get into this city and reach my bonded mate."

The moment the last words left my lips, I opened my palms. Green ribbons slid from my gloved hands, slithering up the wall like snakes. I did not have to tell them what I wanted them to do—they knew my will.

Like Xander, they were mine.

It took five seconds, maybe less, for them to reach the top of the wall. In the space of a breath, they shifted. By the time I exhaled, the ribbons were gone, and strong bands of ivy were in their place.

Adjusting the weight of my pack and the sword hanging at my side, I grabbed the ivy with my gloved hands. Tugging, I climbed for the second time in one day.

Each step took me higher off the ground. Closer to my mate.

Keep your eyes straight ahead.

This time, I would not look down. My necklace bounced against my chest as I climbed, and Xander's sword hung heavily against my hip. Despite the burn in my muscles, I pulled myself up the wall.

As soon as my feet made contact with the flat surface on the top, I clenched my fists. The ivy disappeared in a flurry of green, and I blew out a breath.

The sun was rising, and the sky was a deep purple as I crouched, looking over the city.

Winding cobblestone streets stretched within the city walls, lined on either side by tall buildings with snow-covered roofs. Smoke billowed from chimneys, and the scent of burning wood and fresh bread filled the air. From my vantage point, I could see all the way to the white castle in the middle of the city. A crimson flag flew from the top of the highest tower, a mark of red against the white cityscape.

Already, people were making their way out of their homes. Wrapped in cloaks and blankets to stay warm, the city of Breley was very clearly alive.

Xander was here.

Our bond hummed, and I pulled on it.

There was no response, but I did not let the silence discourage me.

Come get him, pet.

"I'm coming," I whispered.

Magic slipped from my fingers again, and I descended the other side of the wall without incident.

Dusting myself off from my landing, I straightened.

There was no time to waste.

After all, I had a wedding to attend.

Two Paths Ahead

RYLLAE

The sensation of walking through water and *not* drowning was going to take some getting used to. My red dress swished around me as Daegal and I followed the Captain of the Guard and his husband, Shamis, through the luxurious hallways.

The mermales were naked from the waist up, leaving their sculpted chests on display as they led us through the coral castle. If their muscles and the powerful movements of their tails gave any indications, they either exercised *a lot* or never ate anything other than healthy greens.

Probably both. That seemed like a depressing way to live.

I would know.

Their tridents were nowhere in sight, but both males oozed strength with every powerful swish of their tails.

Beside me, Daegal was quiet. His fingers were wrapped around mine, and he squeezed them every once in a while.

The message was clear: *I'm here.*

I appreciated that more than he knew.

We walked down halls lined with gilded statues that edged on being

400

ostentatious. As if the decorators knew it was nearly too much, potted plants lent a homey quality to the palace that my father's crimson castles never had.

There was so much beauty in the Indigo Ocean. So much joy. Even now, a pair of mermaids swam by, laughing.

This place was filled with *life*.

No wonder my father wanted to rule it.

He loved taking beautiful things and destroying them.

Before I was this broken shell of a female who teetered on the brink of insanity, I was beautiful, too.

My father had tried to destroy me. For years, I thought he had succeeded.

But Daegal...

He made me feel beautiful.

This dress made me feel beautiful.

"This palace is massive," Daegal murmured when we turned down another hallway.

I hummed in agreement. It truly was enormous.

On our way to dinner, we passed dozens of merfolk. Most of them were dressed like our escorts... if one could call wearing next to nothing "dressed."

The majority of the females wore bands of bright colors or shells strapped around their breasts, leaving their midriffs shockingly bare as they swam around. Others wore woven tunics that showed off a sliver of skin around their navels. Most of the males were similarly dressed to Erthian and Shamis, and none seemed concerned about showing skin.

All of them were clearly comfortable in their bodies, and I envied their confidence.

Eventually, our escorts came to a stop in front of a set of dark blue, almost black, ornate double doors that featured a carving of a massive underwater scene. It was breathtaking. I reached out and ran a finger over the smooth carving of a regal-looking mermaid.

Erthian paused. "The Ascension of the High Queen," he said, gesturing to the door. "This was commissioned right after Queen Mareena took the throne. It was installed a few months ago."

"It's beautiful."

Beside me, Daegal reached over, brushing a lock of hair over my shoulder. Butterflies flitted through me at his touch. He whispered, "She is."

My core twisted as a shuffling sound came from the other side of the doors, and I straightened. The doors swung open, revealing a massive hall.

Quiet conversations ceased immediately as dozens of merfolk turned and stared at us. The weight of their gaze was heavy, and I shifted from one foot to the other.

Daegal squeezed my hand, whispering, "It'll be alright, Ryllae."

I swallowed. It had to be.

The merfolk didn't stop looking at us, so I stared right back.

Instinctively, I reached within myself to that pool of magic, but that same thick, black fog was still there.

I huffed in frustration.

The hall was enormous. A pair of long mahogany tables laden with every kind of food imaginable went straight down the middle, and perpendicular to that one was a third table where two regal merfolk sat. My attention went right to them.

A stunningly beautiful mermaid with skin as black as ink sat in the place of honor. The High Queen of the Seven Seas wore a large coral crown. A thick band of pure, shimmering gold was wrapped around her breasts as her long black hair floated around her.

Beside her, but no less important, sat her consort. Dressed like

Erthian and Shamis, the muscular mermale had an air of violence around him. His skin was a few shades lighter than the queen's, and from the way he looked at the queen, it was obvious he adored her.

A mermale with terracotta skin swam over to us. Like the others, he was stunningly handsome with his dark brown hair and a forest-green tail. I was beginning to wonder if their good looks were a gift from the gods. There didn't appear to be a single one of them who wasn't exceptionally good-looking.

The green-tailed mermale turned, and his voice echoed through the chamber as he called out, "Your Majesty, may I present her Royal Highness, Princess Ryllae of the House of Irriel, and her companion, Daegal of the House of Videntis."

Formally of the House of Irriel, I corrected silently.

My father rejected me, and I had no qualms about doing the same.

As one, the merfolk raised their hands to their chests. Placing their fists over their hearts, they all dipped their heads.

After a moment, Daegal and I returned the gesture.

Erthian swam into the hall with his husband. "Come," he said. "Her Majesty is anxious to meet you."

Our feet made quiet sounds on the tiles, the water absorbing most of the noise from our movements. It swished around us, touching our skin but not invading our lungs. Murmured conversations rose once more as the gathered merfolk returned to their meals.

When we were about halfway down the great hall, I raised a brow and leaned into Daegal's side. "House of Videntis?" I whispered. "I didn't know that."

There were three Houses of Fortune Elves in Ithenmyr, but the House of Videntis was the oldest. I wasn't sure why, but the fact that Daegal belonged to Videntis surprised me.

He smiled slightly. "There are many things you don't know about me, Princess."

"I'd like to know everything about you," I said.

He didn't say anything for a moment, and I wondered if I made a mistake. Maybe the kisses we shared didn't mean the same thing to him.

Before I could continue down the spiral of worry, Daegal chuckled. His voice deepened, and his breath tickled my ear. "I'd like that very much."

Our escorts stopped a few feet from the High Queen, sinking into low bows before the royals. The queen exchanged a few words with them, the four of them clearly friends, before turning to me.

Her black eyes met mine, and her voice was harder than it had been moments before as she said, "Daughter of the Crimson King. We have heard a lot about you. It is an honor to have you here."

The way she said 'honor' made it sound like that was questionable.

It was fair, I supposed. After all, I knew exactly how dishonorable my father was.

Still, her reaction left much to be desired. Daegal and I were going to have to tread carefully. Every word and action would have to be weighed.

I was under no false impressions. The merfolk might have been happy, and they may have invited us here, but they had no reason to trust us.

I would have to change that.

Pulling on every ounce of training I received as a young princess, I released Daegal's hand and dipped into a curtsy. Given our current conditions, it was a feat. Out of the corner of my eye, I saw Daegal bow at the waist.

After waiting the customary period of time, I straightened. Keeping my gaze lowered respectfully, I said, "Thank you for your hospitality, Your Majesties."

The High Queen's eyes swept over us, and a small smile danced on her lips that didn't quite meet her eyes. "Please, sit."

She waved a hand in the air, gesturing to the seats on the other side of their table, and I glimpsed the mating mark on her arm. Hers was violet and coral, matching the one on her consort's arm.

That *thing* within me seemed to hum at the sight of a bonded pair as if it was giving me a not-so-subtle hint.

I didn't need it.

I had already suspected what kind of connection existed between Daegal and me. We just... weren't ready yet.

But soon, I thought we would be. I hoped.

As long as I could keep the madness at bay.

With that in mind, I smiled demurely at the High Queen as we slipped into our seats. Our hands came together beneath the table as servants came bearing trays laden with food and carrying jugs filled with dark red wine.

It was a veritable banquet. Platters of fish, clams, and other seafood were spread among various platters of dressed greens, some cooked and others raw. Deep, warming spices wafted up, and my stomach grumbled.

A servant slipped a goblet of red wine before me, and I met the queen's gaze. "This looks delightful, Your Majesty. Thank you."

I couldn't even remember the last time I partook in a feast such as this.

The High Queen waved a hand in the air. "Good gods. Everyone is so formal. 'Your Majesty' was my father. Please call me Mareena. This is Calix." She poked the male beside her, and he smiled slightly at us. "It has been many centuries since a royal elf has been welcomed into Coral City."

"I am grateful to be the first, Mareena." Glancing at Daegal, I squeezed his hand. "My... partner and I are grateful for your help. Hopefully, we can find common ground between the four of us."

"I would like nothing more than that." She gestured to the food. "Please, help yourselves. Eat. Drink. Afterward, we shall have a discussion," she decreed.

A discussion.

That was ominous. I knew what royal discussions looked like. Often filled with flowery speech and empty promises, they could either go very well or very badly.

We *really* needed this to go well. Being here in the presence of royalty was a reminder that without my magic, I was nothing.

I needed this queen and her consort to help me. Perhaps we might even build an alliance.

On the other hand, if things took a turn for the worse...

Perhaps Nightstone Prison would not be the only dungeon I would see in my life. The threat was underlying the High Queen's words, made more prominent by the powerful mermale sitting by her side. He didn't say much, but I could feel him watching us.

We didn't have any other choice. We needed them far more than they needed us.

"Eat, Ryllae," Daegal whispered.

How did he always know when my mind was wandering?

I glanced down, my eyes widening. A full plate sat before me. Daegal must have served me while I was thinking.

"Thank you," I murmured, picking up a fork with my free hand.

Every bite I put in my mouth was more delicious than the last. Sweet, spicy, sour, and salty flavors exploded against my tongue as I ate my fill. Next to me, Daegal did the same. While we ate, the high queen and her bonded mate whispered to each other, seemingly content to let us eat in silence.

About halfway through the meal, Daegal's hand tightened around mine. I glanced at him, taking in his silver eyes and white-knuckled grip on his fork.

The queen and her consort were deep in discussion with each other and didn't notice.

As soon as the silver cleared, I squeezed Daegal's hand. "Is everything alright?"

His eyes were wide, and his face was pale. A knot formed in my stomach as Daegal shook his head. "I... Ryllae... something's wrong."

That knot twisted further. "What's wrong?"

Daegal shook his head. "Aileana and Xander..." His voice trailed off, and he glanced at the royals. "We'll talk about it later. Just... pray. Pray to any gods you can because they'll need all the help they can get."

The next bite of food I put in my mouth tasted like ash. What was happening on the Surface?

When the plates before us were empty, Queen Mareena leaned back. She smiled at us, but her eyes were hard.

This was it.

The real test was about to begin.

"Would you care to join us for a nightcap?" Her voice was hard, making it clear that this wasn't really a question. She didn't even wait for an answer before tilting her head towards the Captain of the Guard. "Erthian, please show our guests to the salon."

Daegal and I stood, my dress swishing as I got my bearings. The Fortune Elf offered me his arm, and I slipped my hand into the crook of his elbow.

He drew me close against him, whispering urgently, "Your father is getting married tomorrow."

The food turned to lead in my stomach.

If Father completed the blood pact with the Queen of Drahan, his power would increase exponentially.

Even if I got my magic back, how would I be able to defeat him?

Dread filled me, and a chill ran down my spine.

"And the dragon and his mate?" I asked.

We followed Erthian around a corner before Daegal answered. "I can't See them. Their path is too dark and changing far too quickly." He cleared his throat. "But Ryllae, I need you to focus on what's happening right now."

Erthian flung open a door, and Daegal whispered, "There are two paths ahead of us tonight, Princess. One leads to life, and the other..."

His voice trailed off as we walked inside the salon, and the unsaid words hung in the air.

Leads to death.

How Had Everything Come to This?

XANDER

Fire burned through my entire body, and every single nerve felt like a wick at the end of a candle. The dragonsbane was so deep within me that I could feel it eating away at my body bit by painful bit.

The only thing on my mind was my fierce, redheaded mate. When I first heard her voice and felt her touch on my skin, I thought I was hallucinating. But then the ache in my body had eased, that pain of separation in our bond, and I knew it was real. Somehow, Aileana had visited me.

Feeling her lips on mine one last time was a memory I would cherish for the rest of my very short life.

I would go to the executioner's block willingly if it meant that my bonded mate was safe. Now that I knew the truth about the Southern Queen's identity, I would do anything to keep Aileana safe.

She needed to get as far away from this gods-damned city as she could.

If not...

I shuddered to think about what the High King would do to my bonded mate.

I still didn't understand why Queen Sanja was marrying him.

The image of the Queen of Drahan sitting on that throne with her hair as black as the night sky was seared into my memory. I would have recognized her anywhere. Even with her cold, motionless expression, there was no hiding her identity.

Not from me.

I was an absolute idiot. How had I not seen this coming?

Even as I asked the question of myself, I knew the answer.

That day in the Southern Kingdom, the one I blocked from my mind and refused to think about, the blood and gore blinded me. I was so blind, apparently, that I missed this.

And now, I would pay for that mistake with my life.

There were no options. Not anymore. Not with the dragonsbane running through my body.

Magic wouldn't save me this time.

I had cheated death too many times in the past.

It was ironic that I, the White Death, would find his end at the hands of the Crimson King.

Better me than Aileana.

My only regret was that we hadn't gotten married before this. That title, that privilege of calling her my wife, was one I would never experience. I wished that wasn't so.

These last few days, lying here in the cell, I couldn't help but imagine what our life could have been like. We would have lived in the forest somewhere far away from civilization. Our home would have been a place where Aileana could share her magic with the earth, and we would have lived in peace. In my dreams, small redheaded halflings ran around, and we taught them about their legacies. They would have been incredible, those children of ours.

I already knew Aileana would be an amazing mother. Watching her with Tiaesti and Erwen had proven that.

Our children would have provided hope for Ithenmyr. They would have been new beginnings sprouted from the darkness of High King Edgar's horrible reign.

We would have raised them well and taught them not to judge others based on their appearance.

They would have grown up to be strong, powerful beings and found their own way in this world. One where it didn't matter if they were male or female because everyone was equal.

It would have been beautiful.

But it was not going to happen.

Those were dreams and nothing more.

I would not fight. Not if it meant keeping Aileana safe.

Death was my destiny. I had avoided it for a hundred years, but now it was calling my name again.

This time, it would claim me for its own.

My dragon would probably chide me for my attitude, but it was buried so far beneath my skin I couldn't even sense it anymore.

It was just me, my thoughts, and the poison running through my body. They stopped feeding me two days before Aileana visited, and the only water I drank was from the snow that fell through the only window in my cell. Even with the extra heat of my kind running through my body, I was constantly shivering.

I had nothing left to do except wait for my death.

Laying my head against the ground, I sighed. Visions of emerald-green eyes filled my mind.

"Stay strong when I'm gone, Sunshine," I murmured.

Images of my fierce mate ran through my mind until I fell asleep.

"WAKE UP, ASSHOLE."

A boot slammed into my ribs, and I wheezed. Forcing myself to leave the comfort of my dreams, I opened my eyes and stared into the revolting black gaze of the Winged Soldier kneeling over me.

The male grinned, exposing a mouthful of rotted teeth. "Guess what time it is?"

Good gods. Why hadn't someone introduced these males to personal hygiene? The smell of this male's breath was enough to make anyone wish for death.

"Time for you to go to hell," I snapped.

The Winged Soldier's hand darted out, his talons outstretched as they raked across my face. Pain exploded on my cheek, but I didn't give him the satisfaction of hearing me cry out.

The male grabbed my collar, yanking me to wobbly feet. The shackles around my wrists seared my skin, and I sucked in a breath.

"Wrong," the Winged Soldier snarled. "It's the king's wedding day."

A sudden rush of nausea slammed into me, and my stomach dropped.

A cruel laugh filled the air. "Yes, I see you know what that means."

I found my voice and cursed at the Winged Soldier.

He ignored me, waving a hand, and four other guards materialized on the other side of my cell. "We wouldn't want you to miss the celebrations. After all, rumor has it, the Southern Queen requested your presence at the ceremony."

How had everything come to this?

The guards grabbed me roughly, jeering as their hands curled into fists.

One of them said, "Let's show the dragon scum exactly what we think about him."

A flurry of hands and feet landed on me. It was a long time before the pain became too much, and I slipped into unconsciousness's gentle embrace.

I Believe You

DAEGAL

Sitting next to Ryllae on an uncomfortable gilded settee, my back was ramrod straight as I stared straight ahead.

There were two paths, two choices in front of us.

All I could think about was that the next few minutes were possibly the most important of our entire lives.

This room was ostentatious. Filled with golden furniture and price-less artifacts, it screamed of royalty and things that a male such as myself could never afford.

Beside me, Ryllae wore a red gown that looked like it was ripped straight from my fantasies. The crimson dress hugged her every curve, the V dipping just enough to show off every incredible part of her body. Those swirling red tattoos peeked out from beneath the dress, giving a taste of what she looked like without any clothes.

I'd Seen her in the dress, but the vision paled in comparison to real-ity. She looked incredible, and I hoped that one day, I could show her just how much I enjoyed the gown.

But this was neither the time nor the place.

Right now, we needed to focus on getting out of here alive and, preferably, with Ryllae's magic restored.

The High Queen of the Sea and her bonded mate sat across from us. Power radiated off the two of them, the likes of which I had rarely seen before.

Auras of coral and gold surrounded them both, and though they tried to look relaxed, tension filled their shoulders and the lines around their mouths. Water ebbed and flowed around us as we all sat in tense silence.

We needed to be careful. Every word and gesture had the power to tip the balance. Inching towards Ryllae, I pressed my hand against her thigh gently. I wanted her to know I was here without spooking her.

The dark princess pressed herself against my touch, and my fingers stretched across her thigh. Sparks flew between us, and my heart thundered in my chest.

I had been with my fair share of males and females before, but none had ever made me feel like this. My entire world revolved around Ryllae. She was my first thought in the morning and the last at night. When I was dying from the cut on my arm, the only thing I could think of was that we hadn't had the chance to explore the connection between us yet.

Queen Mareena was the first to break the silence.

"This is interesting, isn't it?" She tapped a finger on her tail, her lips pursed. "When I woke up a few days ago, I would never have imagined that the Forgotten One would have arrived at my shores, asking for an audience."

Ryllae's thigh stiffened beneath my touch, and she whispered, "Please don't call me that."

The High Queen's brows rose. "Why ever not? Is that not who you are? The forgotten daughter of the Crimson King?" She leaned forward, resting her hands on her tail. "We hear rumors of the Surface, you know."

My ears pricked up, and it was my turn to tense. Rumors were never good.

I said as much, and the High Queen laughed. "You see, Fortune Elf, we have heard many things of late."

"Oh?" Ryllae asked, her hand slipping into mine. "I can't imagine they are all true, Your Majesty. You know what they say. We shouldn't always put stock in rumors."

"Is that so?" Queen Mareena seemed amused, and she waved a hand in the air. Her bonded mate glared at us, his expression stern, as she said, "Enlighten me."

Ryllae drew in a deep breath. "As I'm sure you know, Your Majesty, words can be twisted. You never know who might be making an accusation in hopes of turning you against someone else. I know more than most the pain that can come with falsehoods and lies."

"Do you think I'm being lied to?" the Queen asked, raising a manicured brow.

"Perhaps," Ryllae said, lifting a shoulder. "How would you know? I assume that you've spent most of your life in this castle. What do you know about life on the Surface?"

The queen's consort took offense at Ryllae's tone. He stiffened, his eyes narrowing as he glared at the Death Elf. "Watch how you speak to my wife, *Princess*."

The High Queen placed a hand on the mermale's bare arm. "It's alright, Calix." Turning her attention to us, her lips twitched. "Not many people speak their minds to me these days. It's rather refreshing."

Calix grumbled, but he did not speak again.

Hoping to diffuse the tension, I cleared my throat. "What kind of rumors have you heard, Your Majesty?"

A pair of onyx eyes turned to me as the High Queen tilted her head. She regarded me for a moment before beginning to speak. When she did, her voice filled the room, and authority rang from every word. It wasn't hard to see why she was a queen.

"Although you are correct in saying that my bonded mate and I have never been to the Surface, Princess, we have allies spread through the Four Kingdoms and beyond. From fae to human, vampire to werewolf, we have eyes and ears everywhere. We know of the vampire prince's wedding to an Ipothan human, just as we know of the Ithenmyrian king and his courtship with Queen Sanja."

No one spoke. Ryllae tightened her grip on my fingers, and I stared at the queen.

The High Queen of the Seven Seas steepled her hands in front of her, the dark shade of her skin almost glowing as a ray of sunlight filtered in from a nearby window.

"I'll tell you what else we have heard." Queen Mareena raised her hand, ticking off her fingers one by one. "Darkness is stirring on the Surface. High King Edgar is rumored to be using black magic. The vampire queen is gathering forces, and she is making alliances to strengthen her people. The Ipothan Council of Lords is watchful. Danger is awakening, and dark forces that have long since been asleep are reappearing all over the Four Kingdoms. No one is safe, above or below the Surface."

The coral and golden aura pulsed around the queen as she pushed off the settee, swimming in front of us as she continued. Her eyes sharpened, and anger leaked into her voice as she spoke. "The gods and goddesses are angry. Volatile. The balance has been disrupted for far too long."

Ryllae stiffened. "Balance," she whispered.

I immediately recognized Ryllae's tone of voice and straightened my back. The Death Elf was edging towards that madness that lived inside of her. Trying to be discreet, I slipped my thumb between our hands and rubbed circles on her palm.

Right now, I needed Ryllae to remain focused.

Our lives depended on this.

Luckily, the queen was still talking. "So yes, after hearing all these rumors, you can imagine how shocked I was when Erthian said you wanted to see us. The daughter of the Crimson King, long since forgotten by her people. It begs the question, Princess. Why are you here? Are you working for your father, or will you help us restore the balance?"

Complete and utter silence filled the room. The only sound was that of the waters slowly moving back and forth around us.

This was the moment I had Seen.

A heaviness hung in the air, and breathing became difficult as I waited.

Slipping onto the silver planes, I moved through the future quickly.

Two paths stood before me. I ran my hands down them, confirming what I already knew.

Down one path, freedom waited.

Down the other was death.

Both paths were nearly solid and surrounded by darkness. There was little we could do or say now to change them. One of these was our future.

Even as I ran my fingers down the path, I felt a pull in my soul. Ryllae was waiting for me.

Sucking in a breath, I returned to myself. When I settled back into my body, I found three sets of eyes watching me.

Ryllae squeezed my fingers, and I turned as she spoke. Her voice was strong, and there was no trace of madness as her words rang through the water.

"Your Majesties, while I cannot confirm the validity of those rumors as I have not left Ithenmyr in quite some time, I can tell you I am not here acting on my father's interests. You did not ask where I have been for the past two and a half centuries, but I will tell you.

"The day I Matured, he threw me into his darkest prison. He tortured me, took away my freedom, and stole my throne. So no, I am not, nor will I ever be, doing anything for my father again. I *hate* him more than anyone else in this entire world. When he dies, I will be the first to dance on his grave."

She took in a long, shuddering breath and sagged against me.

I pulled her against me, whispering into her hair. "You did a great job."

Across from us, the High Queen and her bonded mate stared intently at each other. It was evident they were conducting an entire silent conversation in a few seconds.

After a moment, High Queen Mareena turned back to us. "If you have not on behalf of your father, Princess, why are you here? What do you seek from me, specifically?"

Ryllae squeezed my hand. "I am here because before throwing me into prison, a witch cursed me at my father's behest. My magic is locked somewhere within me, and I cannot access it. Without it, I am helpless. We were told that you could help me lift the curse."

For a long moment, no one spoke as Ryllae's words sank in.

My heart thudded, and Ryllae's grip on my fingers tightened to the point of pain. Queen Mareena's assessing gaze looked us over. It felt like she was peeling away our skin and staring into the very essence of our beings.

The urge to squirm was strong, but I tamped it down.

"All right," the High Queen of the Seven Seas said. "I believe you."

Ryllae's shoulders loosened, and her grip relaxed enough for me to feel my fingertips again.

"You do?" she said. "I mean, thank you. It's just that... no one believes me. It's been years since my voice has been heard, and it means so much... oh my gods, I'm rambling." Letting go of my hand, Ryllae buried her face in her hands. She took a deep breath, mumbling, "Be calm, Ryllae. Don't crack."

I leaned over, pressing my thigh against hers once more. "Princess, it's okay."

Taking deep breaths, Ryllae slowly lifted her head out of her hands. "Thank you for believing me. I'm sorry, I forgot who I was talking to."

The High Queen smiled, and for the first time since we met her, the gesture reached her eyes.

"Not a problem." Glancing at her bonded mate, Queen Mareena raised a brow. "I understand not being heard or understood far more than you probably know."

Calix nodded. "That you do, sweetness."

The mermaid queen turned her attention to me. "Am I to understand you Saw the curse being broken?"

"I have Seen it, and so did my sister," I replied. "We aren't sure how it's done, exactly..."

"Don't worry about that." Mareena waved her hand in the air. "I have the most powerful sea witches in all the Seven Seas at my disposal."

"So you'll do it?" Ryllae asked eagerly. "You'll help us?"

"We will."

A swell of happiness grew within me, and beside me, Ryllae grinned. Joy radiated from her as she practically vibrated in her seat. "Thank you," she said. "Thank you so much."

"Once your magic is restored, we shall discuss our next steps." Raising her voice, Queen Mareena called out, "Erthian!"

Seconds later, the door opened, and the Captain of the Guard popped his head inside the room. "Yes, Your Majesty?"

"It's Mareena." She sighed, shaking her head. "Summon Galahad, if you will. His services are required immediately."

Erthian bowed. "Yes, Mareena. It shall be done."

The door slipped shut, and the water swirled around us. I shifted in my seat as the queen returned her gaze to us.

"Princess of Ithenmyr, I hope this is the beginning of a long relationship between us." She raised her hands, and coral ribbons escaped her palms before swirling in the water around us. "We hope that one day, balance will be restored."

Ryllae smiled, and the dark crimson aura around her pulsed. "That is my greatest desire, Your Majesty."

The four of us settled in, waiting for the sea witch.

For the first time, the future looked a little less dark.

Come Get Him

AILEANA

Bells tolled through the city as large, fluffy snowflakes fell from the sky. I huddled in the alley where I'd spent the night. My cloak protected me from the worst effects of the cold, but the snow and I were definitely not on good terms. My stomach grumbled, and I wished my rations had not run out the day before.

Even so, a little bit of hunger was not going to stop me. Not now, when I was so close.

I spent the majority of the past two days gathering information. When I wasn't snooping around, trying to find Xander—which, evidently, was not a success—I was evading the Winged Soldiers. They were everywhere in this city. Three times, they almost caught me, but each time, I evaded arrest.

Barely.

My magic thrummed incessantly beneath my skin, begging to be let out, but I refused its call.

I was conserving every last bit of power.

Now, the day was here.

High King Edgar was marrying Sanja, the Queen of Drahan.

The streets hummed in morbid anticipation. The Crimson King had declared today a holiday, and the streets were overflowing with people. Winged and horned elves, vampires, werewolves, witches, and even humans filtered past my hiding spot in the alley.

I didn't pay them any attention. My entire focus was on the massive white marble temple looming on the square's other side. There were three temples in Breley—one dedicated to Kydona, another to Ghemra, and the third to Ithiar—but High King Edgar was getting married in the temple to Kydona. Fitting.

My plan—if it could be called a plan—consisted of getting into the temple. That was all. Once I got in there, I would figure out the rest.

The temple doors had opened a few minutes ago, and streams of people were already entering the massive building. Four white columns supported the roof, and a statue of the goddess stood guard in front of the temple, casting silent judgment on all those who passed her by.

I always thought it ironic that a male who hated the opposite sex with such vigor worshiped a female goddess.

Perhaps I would ask High King Edgar about his strange attachment to Kydona before I killed him.

The sky darkened above me, and I glanced up as a Winged Soldier flew toward the temple. His wings flapped, and his form was a dark shadow against the gray, foreboding sky. The sun was nowhere to be seen on this horrible day, and the clouds cast a dark pall over the land. The damp winter air was cold, and the wind howled through the city.

All in all, it was a miserable day.

It was fitting.

The Winged Soldier landed on the temple steps, and I pulled on my gloves. The same words that had kept me company for the past two days echoed through me once more.

Come get him.

I was here. Xander would probably be angry with me when I saved him. After all, he had told me in no uncertain terms to leave.

I snorted.

When was he going to learn? I was never going to be the perfect Ithenmyrian female. Not today. Not yesterday. Never.

Because of my imperfections, I would free the other females in Ithenmyr. I was never going to fit into the mold High King Edgar created because it was ridiculous to try to shove people into small boxes and make them something they weren't.

Once I saved my mate, I was going to make the Crimson King pay for what he did to me.

I was fairly certain that in time, Xander would forgive me for disobeying his orders and saving him.

I hoped.

If not, he could hate me. I would take his hatred and wrap it around myself like a badge of honor if it meant he was alive.

I just needed him.

With that thought in my mind, I stood and dusted myself off. Xander's sword was heavy around my hip, and the weight of my various daggers was a comfort as I ran my fingers over the necklace beneath my tunic.

Dozens of male voices drifted through the air, carried by the brisk wind.

"... Happy to have the day off..."

"The Southern Queen is a beauty..."

"... I'd take her to my bed..."

"... If only Prince Remington were here..."

At the mention of my dead fiancé, I hissed. I did not need to relive any memories of the Red Shadow today.

Sending a quick thought to Ryllae and Daegal—hopefully, they were still alive—I drew my cloak over my head. Making sure my ears were hidden, I stepped out of the alley, leaving my pack behind. Some street urchin would hopefully find a good use for it. I would not need it anymore.

Either I would succeed—or I would die.

The crowd moved as one towards the temple. There were no guards posted outside. That should have put a smile on my face, but it did not.

High King Edgar's words echoed in my mind as I ran my fingers over the blue and white bracelet he had left with the dagger.

New game, pet.

Walking into the temple was far too easy. The massive white doors were open, and I kept my head down as I entered with the crowd.

Once I was inside, I saw the guards.

Dozens of Winged Soldiers lined the white walls of the enormous temple. People were packed into every corner of the structure, including on the balcony that ran the entire length of the building.

There must have been hundreds, if not thousands, of spectators here.

Standing on my tiptoes, I tried to catch a glimpse of the front of the temple. Unfortunately, all I could see were hoods, horns, and wings.

Come get him.

"Excuse me," I mumbled, dropping my voice to its lowest register as I pushed my way through the crowd. My cloak covered my tunic and leggings, but if someone looked too closely at me, I was bound to find myself in a world of trouble. Just by being here without a male, I was sentencing myself to death. "Pardon me. Coming through. Excuse me."

I was halfway through the crowded temple before a shout filled my ears.

"Halt!" a deep voice yelled. "Stop her!"

Stiffening, I sucked in a breath as the hum of conversation in the temple immediately dried up. A guard peeled off the wall, his wings tight behind him as his dark eyes swept the crowd. They came to rest near me, and I swallowed the curse that threatened to slip past my lips.

Moving my gloved hand beneath my cloak, I felt for the hilt of my dagger as I inched backward.

"What do you think you're doing?" the Winged Soldier thundered as he came nearer. The crowd parted as though it were made of water. "Where is your husband?"

Shit.

My heart raced out of control, and my lungs squeezed as I looked around frantically. The crowd was so thick that I could barely move. Although I could see the edge of the dais, I was not nearly close enough to the front of the temple.

Sweat beaded on my forehead, and my magic begged to be used.

The guard's black wings snapped out as he stormed through the crowd. "Well?"

A beat passed before a female voice squeaked out less than ten feet from me, "I-I..."

Moments later, the soldier wrenched the female to her feet. Small white horns protruded from her blond head, and ribbons of purple magic escaped her palms.

"You dare attempt to use magic against me?" the soldier roared. He was at least a foot taller than the Light Elf, and he was almost twice her size.

The female trembled like a leaf. "Please, sir—"

The soldier flapped his wings, the powerful beats stirring the air. Clutching the rough fabric of my hood, I wished I was anywhere else as the guard carried the female to the top of the temple until his wings brushed the stained-glass ceiling.

No one spoke. The only sounds in the temple were the beats of the guard's wings and the female's screams.

She dangled from the Winged Soldier's hand, her feet flailing as she wailed, "Please. I just wanted to see the wedding. That was all. My husband is sick, and I—"

"You broke the Accompaniment Law," the Winged Soldier snarled. His voice echoed through the temple, and a sick sense of anticipation filled the space.

My spine tingled, and my stomach turned.

"No," the female sobbed.

He ignored her pleas. "The law is clear. Females must be accompanied at all times."

"No!" she yelled. "Please, I just wanted—"

Her words gave way to an ear-piercing scream. She tumbled toward the ground, her body somersaulting head over heels. Purple ribbons streamed from her palms, but they did nothing to stop her descent.

I averted my eyes as she approached the ground.

A sickening *splat* was followed by a horrible silence. The scent of blood filled the air, and my stomach turned. A trickle of red appeared in the corner of my eye, staining the white tile.

Bile rose in my throat, and my stomach roiled.

A low moan escaped the female, and my eyes widened. Time seemed to slow as I turned around. Wings flapped. People whispered. The same Winged Soldier landed on the ground, and he extended a black talon. The moan ended in a gurgle as he plunged the talon into her chest.

My head spun, and all around me, females shoved themselves closer to their males.

A beat passed, and absolute horror welled within me.

The air inside the temple was thick with tension, and for a single moment, no one spoke. No one dared move.

Then, conversations rose once more. People talked and laughed as if they hadn't just seen the female be dropped to their death because she dared go out in public on her own.

Horror gave way to disgust.

This was a poignant reminder of exactly why High King Edgar had to die. I would avenge her and the countless other females who lost their lives due to the Crimson King's cruel laws.

Come get him.

I shoved my way forward until the dais was in my sights. I was close enough to see it but still far enough away that the crowd hid my presence from the soldiers.

The dais was extravagant in size and decoration, and two giant thrones made of twisted white bones—one bigger than the other—rested where Kydona's altar should have been.

Three Winged Soldiers stood before the platform, and violence radiated from their pores.

Behind them was...

A cage.

Made of iron and rounded on the top like a giant birdcage, the contraption sat to the right of the thrones. Thick bars ran up to the top while others crossed them horizontally.

The cage was empty.

For now.

My stomach churned, and nausea roiled through me.

Reaching within me, I yanked on the bond with all my might.

There came no response.

Panic threatened to overtake me, but I bit down on my lip, forcing myself to remain calm.

Come get him.

The air in the temple grew to a near frenzy as more and more people pushed their way into the space. Sweat beaded on the back of my neck as the temple grew stifling despite the winter month. Someone slammed into my back, and another shoved me to the side as everyone hunted for the best view of the dais.

Joining the fray, I shoved my way to the front until there was nothing between me and the dais except the trio of brutal Winged Soldiers.

Their eyes were as black as the blood within their bodies, and their dark wings were spread as they glared at the crowd. The Winged Soldiers sneered at the gathered spectators, their lip piercings glimmering in the sunlight as they guarded the place where the king would be. On their chests was the crimson sigil of the House of Irriel.

"They're here," someone murmured behind me.

"The King has arrived!"

A third voice came from behind me, shouting, "Move!"

The crowd obeyed instantly, parting as a cadre of Winged Soldiers shoved their way past. I twisted, looking over my shoulder as they approached. Their black wings were tight against their backs as they dragged something between them.

No.

Not something.

Someone.

People gasped and murmured. Some spat. Others shouted.

I stared.

My mating mark burned, and my magic thrummed within my veins. Red tinged my vision as I struggled to keep my head down.

Tears stung my eyes as the Winged Soldiers dragged my bonded mate across the tiled floor. Clothed in nothing more than bloodied rags and iron manacles around his wrists and ankles, Xander thrashed against his captors. He kicked and pulled as hard as he could, but there were four of them, and he was alone. The scent of lemons and cedar assaulted my nose, and I tasted bile.

New game, pet.

I clenched my fists at my side. My heart thundered. My lungs tightened. Within me, my magic churned to the point of near explosion.

The soldiers came so close to me that one of their wings almost brushed my chest. I sucked in a breath, looking down.

Golden eyes met mine, and a flash of recognition went through them. Xander's eyes widened, and the bond between us woke up. I wasn't sure if it was our proximity or something else, but I could *feel* him again. His presence, his emotions... The connection tying us together was fully awake. Tart surprise ran through the bond, followed swiftly by bitter anger and... fear.

A sob of relief threatened to rise in my throat.

Run, he mouthed. Those eyes that I loved so much pleaded for me to listen. To obey. To heed his warning for once in my life.

I shook my head. *Never.* The word echoed in my mind, and Xander's eyes widened impossibly further.

His voice rang clearly in my mind. *I can hear you.*

This was new.

I love you. Widening my stance, I sent everything I felt for Xander down the bond. *I'm here, Elyx. I will never leave you.*

Aileana—

I cut him off. *I have so much to tell you. I have the last piece of the map, and when this is over, we can find the treasure. Together.*

I told you to leave. Xander's golden eyes flashed as they dragged him up the steps of the dais. *It's not safe here. The map doesn't matter. Nothing matters. Just leave!*

No. The word echoed down the bond between us. *You should know by now I'm terrible at following orders. Especially yours.*

One of the guards wrenched open the door of the iron cage, and they thrust Xander inside. Another bent, attaching the manacles around his wrist to a chain on the floor. Then, the door slammed shut behind him. One of the Winged Soldiers slipped a key inside the lock, and it clicked with a horrifying finality.

Not even a heartbeat later, the doors to the right of the dais swung open. Silence fell over the temple. This was it.

I shut my eyes for one moment. One singular moment.

Please go, Sunshine. Xander's voice filtered through the bond.

Just wait. I clenched my fists at my side, shaking my head. *When I give you the signal, I need you to gather as much strength as you can.*

Aileana, I don't—

Xander's next words never came. My eyes flew open, and instantly, I saw the reason.

Standing at the doors to the temple, shrouded in shadows, were the bride and groom.

I swallowed.

We were out of time.

A Masterful Curse

RYLLAE

The sea witch's black hair swirled around him as he swam before me, his dark, roaming eyes assessing. The seaweed tunic covering his chest came to a stop an inch before his jet-black tail started. So many wrinkles lined his ancient face that it was difficult to see where one stopped and another began. I had never seen a being as old as Galahad.

He hummed and hawed, swimming around me in circles. I kept my hands at my sides despite the feeling of being put on display.

Daegal stood nearby, his arms crossed and his legs spread as he glared at the sea witch. I had never seen the Fortune Elf looking so protective, and he was acting this way because of *me*.

"Well, Galahad?" the High Queen of the Seven Seas demanded after this had gone on for quite some time. She and her consort sat on the golden settee across from me, a whispered conversation passing between them. "Can you do it?"

The sea witch mumbled under his breath. His brows furrowed as he swam in a circle around me once more.

"Galahad," Queen Mareena said, irritation lacing her words. "Can it be broken?"

He sighed, running a hand through his black hair. "My queen, this curse is ancient." He put his hands on his hips, running his bottom lip through his teeth. "It's masterful, really."

Exactly what every single person who was waiting to have a curse broken wanted to hear.

Why couldn't the witch have done an adequate job? Even a mediocre one? Why did this curse, the one blocking me from accessing my power even without the prohiberis cuffs on me, have to be a "masterful" one?

Galahad swam around me once more, cursing under his breath.

I wilted a little inside. The only reason I remained upright was because of the Fortune Elf standing across from me. Daegal met my gaze, and something about the way he looked at me gave me the strength to continue. Galahad swam over to the High Queen, muttering quietly about the skill of the curse-maker.

This strange dance continued for a long time. Galahad circled me, his hand beneath his chin, as he studied me under Daegal's watchful gaze.

Twice, the Fortune Elf's eyes turned silver, and twice, he nodded grimly at me when he returned to the present. The look in his eyes told me all I needed to know. There were no other options. This odd sea witch was our best bet.

After an excruciating amount of time had passed—probably close to an hour, but it felt like a lifetime—Galahad nodded.

I sucked in a breath, my heart pounding, as I whispered, "Well?"

He turned, dipping his head. "It can be done."

My breath escaped me in a whoosh. The sea witch turned, swimming over to the large wooden trunk two servants had brought in after him.

Muttering under his breath once more, he pulled open the lid and began rummaging through the interior of the trunk. His tail swished, stirring the water around him as he spoke quietly to himself.

And people thought *I* was strange.

A bottle filled with a black liquid came out of the trunk, followed swiftly by bundles of herbs I didn't recognize.

"That's not right..." Galahad sorted through the bundles, tossing one back in and rummaging some more before exclaiming, "Yes. Perfect."

Daegal moved towards me, sliding his hand into mine. Together, we watched the sea witch mutter under his breath, pulling out bottles and bundles of herbs until the floor was littered with materials.

A bottle with purple liquid landed on the floor, and Galahad straightened.

"Your Majesties, I can break the curse," the sea witch said.

He paused, and the High Queen asked, "Why does it sound like there is a 'but' coming?"

Galahad sighed. "But the magical strain will be heavy." He looked around the room. "Might I suggest we move to a location with less... expensive decor?"

Queen Mareena studied him for a moment before nodding. "I know just the place. Come with me."

"Just the place" ended up being a location far outside of Coral City. Surrounded by a contingent of the High Queen's soldiers, we were in the middle of the ocean. Remnants of old wooden ships were strewn around us as water lapped at our heels. It was late, and slivers of the dying sun filtered through the depths of the water.

Before we left the palace, the sea witch insisted I get changed. Something about the "magical strain" and how he didn't want to ruin my gown. I probably would have been more concerned about what that meant for me if I hadn't been so eager to get rid of this curse.

Now, I wore a long-sleeved black sweater that ran down to my thighs and a pair of comfortable leggings. Once again, the clothes were nothing like what I had worn at home, but I found I didn't care.

The way Daegal had glanced appreciatively at my legs when I emerged in the new outfit was definitely a positive. Maybe if this worked, I would ask Queen Mareena for more clothes like this since it seemed like her people didn't need them.

Despite the late hour, underwater life teemed around us. Dozens of fish, sharks, and eels swam around in the water, seemingly curious about what was happening. I didn't blame them. I would be curious, too.

I stood barefoot in the sand, the tiny grains sinking between my toes as the sea witch swam around me again. Servants had brought his trunk, and now Galahad was mixing up a strong-smelling potion nearby. Black fumes leaked into the water like thick ribbons of ink before he placed a cork on the top of the glass bottle.

Daegal stood a few feet away from me, his position one of a male uneasy with the entire situation. He clenched and unclenched his fists at his sides, his jaw hard as he glared at the sea witch.

Even though Galahad made me uncomfortable, a flutter of excitement was rooted in my stomach.

This was the moment Maiela had Seen. This was why we left the witch's cottage.

I needed the chains of this curse lifted so I could be free.

"I am ready, Princess." Galahad swam toward me. His ancient voice warbled with the timbre of someone who had seen many sunrises. "I will not lie to you. This will not be a... pleasant experience. The curse placed upon you was powerful, and it will take a long time to unweave the threads wrapped around your soul."

That did not surprise me. There was very little in my life that was pleasant.

"Do you agree to this?" he asked.

"Do whatever it takes," I said firmly. "I need to feel the hum of magic in my veins. You have my permission to do whatever you need to do, short of killing me entirely."

"All right." Picking up a stick, the sea witch etched a circle around the two of us in the sand. Once it was closed, he looked over his shoulder and spoke to those gathered in the cove. "Stand back. Whatever you do, whatever you see, do not cross this line. If you do, I cannot guarantee your safety."

Anticipation bubbled beneath my skin as murmurs rose all around us. My heart beat rapidly in my chest, and I took a deep breath.

This was it.

Galahad took the potion, shaking it vigorously, before twisting off the top. The contents were still churning when he handed it to me. "Drink this."

I eyed it warily. Black mist swirled above the inky contents of the glass bottle, and a putrid scent reached me.

Whatever the cost.

Wrinkling my nose, I pinched the bridge with my free hand. Raising the jar in Daegal's direction, I drank it all in one go.

It tasted worse than it smelled, which was definitely saying something. In all my years in Nightstone Prison, I'd never tasted something as horrific as the black concoction currently oozing down my throat. It moved sluggishly, leaving a bitter aftertaste in my mouth. I winced as it slid down into my stomach, burning a path through my body.

The bottle fell from my fingers, landing soundlessly on the sand, and Galahad chanted. Lilting words left his lips, and endless streams of blue ribbons escaped his hands. He swam around me in a slow circle, his voice increasing in volume until it was all I could hear.

Water swirled around me as the blue ribbons sank into my skin one by one. Soon, my entire body burned. My heart raced, my lungs tightened, and breathing became difficult.

Every single inhale hurt. Every time I exhaled, my lungs felt like they were going to explode.

Stars appeared in my vision, and Galahad's voice grew even louder. Hundreds of blue ribbons streamed from his hands, swirling around me like a cyclone.

Galahad raised his hands, and a brilliant blue light flashed from his palms. The burning within me intensified. My muscles ached, and my legs shook as hundreds of ribbons slammed into me all at once.

I screamed, and water filled my lungs before I collapsed on the ground. Daegal shouted, but I couldn't understand him.

Everything was too much.

Too loud.

Too bright.

Too painful.

The magic worked its way through me.

Darkness beckoned me as the pain became worse and worse.

I fell into its waiting arms willingly.

The Worst Listener

XANDER

My bonded mate was the worst listener I'd ever met in my long life. This aggravating female could not follow an order if her life depended on it.

Which, if it wasn't abundantly clear, it did.

One order. That was all I had given her. I'd worded it in as many ways as I could, with the hopes that she might actually listen to me, for once.

Stay away.

Run.

Get out of here.

Instead, she did the exact opposite.

I couldn't even look in her direction now. I wouldn't risk drawing the Winged Soldier's attention to Aileana.

They placed me in a cage as if I were nothing but a rabid animal. One of them dared to look back at me.

I snarled, banging my manacled wrists against the iron bars.

The bride and groom stood in the doorway, waiting to enter the temple.

My entire body strained beneath the weight of the secret I was unwittingly carrying. I knew who the Southern Queen was, and I wanted to warn them of the creature they were welcoming in their midst.

But I couldn't. The damned king had as good as tied my tongue. I couldn't even *think* of the truth of who she was.

I thought I couldn't hate the Crimson King more than I already did. I was wrong.

This entire marriage was a joke. I wished I was anywhere but here.

They thought I was rabid? Did they think that chaining me to the floor like an animal was a good idea?

I'd show them rabid. Every single part of me was in still pain. The dragonsbane was still running through my veins.

But seeing Aileana had done something to me. It infused energy into me that I had been sorely lacking. I felt invigorated. Alive. Ready to fight.

The bond between us hummed as though the magic tying us together was pleased by my mate's disobedience.

You need to leave, I insisted once more through the bond. I did not know why we could communicate like this now when we couldn't before, but honestly, I didn't care.

Never, Aileana hissed. Even through the bond, I could hear her insolence.

Moments later, a herald whistled. Everyone stopped talking as the winged male flew into the temple. He was small and lithe, his purple wings like a butterfly as he fluttered a few feet above the empty thrones.

Clad in crimson from head to toe, he gripped a yellowed scroll. "People of Ithenmyr. It is my honor to present His Illustrious Majesty,

High King Edgar of the House of Irriel, and his bride, Queen Sanja of Drahan. Please join me in welcoming them."

The herald rolled up the scroll, clapping as he flew away. Roaring applause filled the massive temple, and the bride and groom stepped onto the dais.

They came to stand a few feet from the cage, and I glared at them. Gripping the bars, I ignored the pain roiling through me as the poison-laced iron pressed against my skin.

Dressed head to toe in crimson, High King Edgar's black wings were stretched behind him. His horns curled towards the sky, and his knee-high leather boots gleamed beneath the rays of sunlight shining through the stained-glass ceiling. A black crown rested upon his blond head, inlaid with red rubies.

The sight of him made my stomach churn, even though I hadn't eaten for days.

And beside him...

The Southern Queen refused to look at me. Her long black hair hung in a thick, intricate braid down her back, and a heavy navy blue veil covered her face. Dozens of blue jewels were embedded in her hair, matching her gown. It flowed out at her hips, creating a bell-like shape. It was exactly the kind of dress Aileana despised wearing, and I knew there would be multiple petticoats underneath it.

Two Winged Soldiers followed the soon-to-be-married pair, stationing themselves near my cage.

Half of me wished the wedding to end so I wouldn't have to be subjected to this torture. The other half wanted to slow down time, to relish having my bonded mate so close to me for the last time.

The Southern Queen stood with her back straight as High King Edgar whispered something even I couldn't pick up in her ear.

She *laughed*.

The sound ran through me like a sword.

"How could you do this?" I whispered. "How could you marry *him?* After what he did?"

Queen Sanja ignored me, but I knew she could hear me. The fact that she could hear and chose not to even acknowledge me made things worse. And honestly, I didn't know things could get worse than this.

But here I was. Experiencing it.

This was definitely worse.

I thought maybe I had imagined seeing her in High King Edgar's throne room. Perhaps the dragonsbane had been playing games with my mind.

But now, there was no denying the truth.

The bitter taste of betrayal coated my mouth.

Part of me wanted to believe, even now, that the Southern Queen was bewitched. Maybe a spell had been placed on her, and she was being forced into this union. Maybe she wasn't doing this because she wanted to.

I needed that to be true because the other option was so horrifying that I couldn't believe it.

If Queen Sanja was marrying Edgar of her own volition, it meant my years of grief had been for nothing. That I'd wandered alone for no reason.

I couldn't handle that. Not right now.

Deep within me, a tug came through the bond. I could feel Aileana's confusion, but I didn't have the time to answer her.

Footsteps sounded on my left. As a priest in white robes walked into the temple, I tilted my head. The male was old, his sepia skin wrinkled and touched by age, as he came to stand near the king. His long hair and brilliant orange eyes spoke of his werewolf heritage. Even in his Maturity, he looked ancient and must have been centuries old.

The priest raised his hands, his voice echoing through the now-silent temple. "People of Breley and children of Kydona, it is the greatest honor of my life to stand before you today. We have gathered here, on this day dedicated to our magnificent goddess who gives us life, to celebrate a glorious union."

The priest paused, raising his hands as a smattering of applause broke out among the onlookers.

I gripped the bars of my cage. My heart raced, and I seethed as I stared at the priest. How dare he talk about honor as though the Crimson King wasn't responsible for the death of many?

"High King Edgar of the House of Irriel, in all his glorious wisdom, brought together the five provinces of Ithenmyr," the priest said. "In the centuries of his reign, he has kept this country running smoothly despite the numerous threats it has faced."

My eyes practically bulged out of my head.

The genocides of the dragons and Earth Elves were not "smooth." They were horrible and bloody and the thing of absolute nightmares.

Was this how history was shaped? Lies were told, and pasts were erased because people in power kept telling their narrative until everyone believed it to be true.

High King Edgar might not have wielded the weapons that killed my family, but he was just as responsible for their deaths.

The priest had to know that. He was older than the Dragon Massacre. Older than the Accompaniment Law. Older than Ryllae.

Yet he did not speak of the king's daughter, nor did he mention the dragons or the Earth Elves.

As far as I was concerned, the priest and those who worked with the king to shape these new "truths" were just as culpable as the male holding the crimson scepter.

"Liar!" I snarled, banging a hand against the bars.

A hush fell over the temple, and the air thickened as every eye landed on me.

High King Edgar turned and sneered at me. His palm raised, and a red bolt of lightning shot out of his palm. It slammed into the iron bars, sending jolts through my body.

I released the bars, landing on the ground on all fours as pain ran through my body.

I would not scream.

Not now.

I refused to give him the satisfaction of hearing me cry out.

The priest began speaking once more, but I tuned him out. He was extolling High King Edgar for his various accomplishments, and I knew if I paid attention, I would draw more attention to myself.

For Aileana's sake, I would try not to do that.

A tug came from the bond.

Don't react, Aileana said.

What? I widened my eyes, my lungs still burning from the poison. *Aileana, don't draw attention to yourself.*

She didn't respond.

Of course not.

Aileana, whatever you're doing, stop. I begged her. *Please, go.*

Nothing.

My mate was incredible. She was powerful, and I knew she was a fantastic warrior.

I also knew the Southern Queen. If this blood pact was completed, I didn't want Aileana anywhere near here.

Was I asking too much, encouraging her to run? Perhaps.

But I needed her to survive.

The priest cleared his throat, drawing my attention back to him. "This is a marriage like no other. Not only will it bind two people in the power of matrimony—a sacred union in and of itself—but it will also bring two countries together. Ithenmyr and Drahan have always been neighbors, but they have never been bound in marriage and by blood. Until today."

A strange sensation grew within me as the priest spoke. My veins tingled, and the persistent pain that had been my companion for days lessened. I remained on all fours, glaring at the crowd as something within me shifted.

I could... breathe.

My brows furrowed.

The priest turned towards the king. "High King Edgar of the House of Irriel. Bearer of the Opal Scepter and Ruler of Ithenmyr. Do you come before Kydona of your own free will?"

A long pause ensued, and Aileana's voice appeared once more in my mind. *I love you, Elyx.*

The entire congregation seemed to hold its breath. A sharp tingling, like the beginning of a fire, erupted in my veins.

I love you, too.

Warmth flooded through the bond.

Don't react, she said cautiously. *But I need you to look down.*

Confusion filled me, but I did as Aileana asked. My eyes widened, and my breath left me in a whoosh.

A thick, black liquid was seeping out of my skin. With every passing second, I felt more like myself.

The Crimson King cleared his throat. "I, Edgar of the House of Irriel, swear that I come to this union of my own free will."

I fought the urge to roll my eyes. Of course, this marriage would be the most elaborate show I'd ever seen. Most marriages in Ithenmyr never spoke of free will. Why would they? Everyone knew females in Ithenmyr didn't have free will.

But I supposed when one was marrying a queen, it was appropriate to at least *pretend* to care about their feelings.

The pool of black liquid beneath me grew. My lungs loosened, and my heart rate slowed. A cut that had been on my hand since my abduction healed.

The priest turned to the Southern Queen. "Do you, Queen Sanja, Ruler of Drahan and the Southern Wastes, come before Kydona of your own free will?"

My mating bond burned with the fire of a thousand suns, and within me, something shattered.

It was an awakening.

I drew in a sharp breath.

It was too sharp.

Another Winged Soldier turned, glaring at me. I growled at him, and he scowled in response.

"Dragon scum," he muttered, turning back to watch the wedding as the Southern Queen spoke.

"I, Sanja, Queen of Drahan and Ruler of the Southern Wastes, swear that I come to this union of my own free will. I give myself to be wed to Edgar, the High King of Ithenmyr." The queen spoke with great care, her words clipped with the slightest of accents, as her voice echoed through the large temple.

My stomach sank even as the pool of black liquid grew beneath me. The tingling became a persistent pulse that rushed through my veins.

I could *feel* the fire running through me once more.

I felt... alive.

What are you doing, Aileana? I asked, my hands slowly moving down the iron binding me to the cage. I tugged, feeling for any weaknesses.

Aileana didn't reply, but the tingling became a pulsing burn within me.

The priest stepped forward. "Then let us begin with a word of prayer. Bow your heads."

Spreading his hands wide, the werewolf spoke in the lilting tongue of the gods as he prayed.

And I...

I could feel my dragon. He was there, slumbering within me.

Wake up. I pushed at the dragon, but it didn't move.

The burning under my skin continued, and the pool of black ink beneath me was nearly as large as the cage.

I flexed my hands as power ran through my veins once more.

The iron around my wrists was strong, but without the poison, I was stronger.

Hope kindled within me.

The priest said, "Amen."

As one, the congregation repeated his words.

Smiling, the priest took a step back. I watched through the bars as he reached out, taking a hand from the king and the queen.

"Let us begin," the priest intoned. "Marriage is sacred. Do you each vow to provide for the other?"

"I do," High King Edgar said.

The priest asked the queen the same question, and she said, "I do."

"In all manners of the home, Queen Sanja, do you vow to bow before and respect your husband's gods-given authority? Will you recognize him as your rightful ruler and submit to his decisions in all matters of your home and country?"

A pause, and I sucked in a breath.

"Yes, I do," the Southern Queen said.

I snarled, and something erupted within me.

The next breath I inhaled felt different.

Better.

Whole.

Right then and there, I knew all the poison was gone. I didn't know how she had done it, but this had to be Aileana's doing.

As I inhaled, the dragon stirred to life. *I am here.*

My heart thudded against my ribs, and I clenched my fists as anger pulsed through my body.

I'm coming for you, Aileana, I said down the bond.

The priest raised his voice, looking out over the crowd. "It is time for the blood pact."

A shiver ran down my spine, and High King Edgar withdrew a dagger from the sheath on his thigh. He held the blade, poised above his forearm, when a brisk wind blew through the temple.

The earth shook, and time seemed to slow.

Aileana shouted, "Stop!"

Time for a New Game

AILEANA

My voice echoed through the temple, and a collective inhale came from the crowd at my back.

Beneath my feet, the earth awaited my call. Magic writhed within me, awaiting my call.

Soon, I whispered to the earth.

"Stop!" I cried out again.

This time, the crowd took a step back.

That was fine. I had no problem with that.

Let them step away. Let them leave.

I wasn't here for them.

This was my battle. Mine and Xander's.

I stood here on my own, just like the day I had escaped my tower.

Since then, I had tasted freedom. I had felt the sting of death and pain. I knew the burden and the beauty of love.

Because of Xander, I knew what it felt like to give myself wholly to another being: mind, body, and spirit.

Thinking of my mate, I tugged on the bond.

448

Xander jolted. *Aileana*, he hissed. *What are you doing?*

Saving you so we can get married, I replied. *I thought that was what you wanted.*

The priest took a step forward. "Who dares interrupt this union?"

Reaching up, I pulled off my hood, revealing my bright red hair and pointed ears. "I do."

The Crimson King turned slowly, and his blue eyes seared as they slammed into mine. His lips tilted into a wolfish grin as pure evil radiated from him.

Xander tugged frantically on the bond. *What are you doing, Aileana? Get out of here!*

That's not going to happen, my love.

Stepping toward the king and his bride, I threw out my arms and dipped into a mock curtsy. "You summoned me, Your Majesty?"

"Aileana," High King Edgar said my name with so much hatred that I shuddered. "How *kind* of you to make your presence known. I was afraid you weren't going to make it, pet."

The temple was so quiet that the sound of a pin dropping would have been like a clap of thunder.

Nothing but a few Winged Soldiers stood between me and the dais.

Behind them, my bonded mate's golden eyes were imploring as he watched me through the bars of the cage.

"How could I turn down such a *compelling* invitation?" I withdrew the king's dagger and flung it at his feet. The crowd behind us sucked in a breath, but the king didn't falter as the metal clattered against the marble floor.

I shook my head. "I did some thinking on my way here, Your Majesty."

"Oh?" He raised a brow.

"I think it's time for a new game."

Red sparks danced on the Crimson King's shoulders, and he sneered at me. "What did you have in mind?"

The thundering of my heart echoed in my ears, and I inhaled.

This was it.

Thelrena, if you were ever real, please be with me now.

Reaching up to my neck, I unclasped my cloak. The garment fell to the marbled floor in a heap, but I didn't stop there. One finger at a time, I pulled off my gloves until my hands were free. The fabric fell on the floor with a soft thump, forgotten as I displayed my tattoos to the world.

The air in the temple thickened, and my heart thundered in my chest.

"What are those?" someone whispered nearby.

A gasp.

"She's not wearing a dress!"

"Is that an Earth Elf? And she's armed!"

"What's going on?"

"Kydona, save us all!"

"A heretic..."

Ignoring the crowd's murmurs behind me, I rolled up the sleeves of my tunic to my forearms.

When my arms were bare, I returned my gaze to the king. The necklace containing the pieces of the map rested snugly beneath my tunic, its presence a gentle weight as I displayed my arms to the king.

Xander. The map. The prophecy that spoke of the coming darkness. It all led to this moment.

The king I planned to kill stared at my hands. I knew the moment he realized what these markings meant. His eyes widened, and his mouth fell open as he dropped the Southern Queen's hand.

"You've *Matured*," he whispered as a flicker of fear entered his voice.

The words echoed through Kydona's temple.

I didn't give him the dignity of answering.

I was not his pet, and he was not worthy of my words.

I would not speak on command, nor would I do anything he wanted.

Xander was the first to move.

The chains around his wrists clinked, and our eyes met. An entire conversation passed in the blink of an eye.

Then, he gripped the iron and *pulled*.

I turned my attention back to the king. Winged Soldiers stood between me and the dais, but I didn't worry about them.

"You're right. I have Matured." Releasing the stronghold I had on my magic, I smirked. "I've learned a few other fun tricks, too. I wouldn't want to bore you by being a 'simple female.' Allow me to show you what else I can do."

I opened my palms, and dozens of green ribbons flooded out of me. They swirled in the air around me as gasps echoed through the temple.

A heartbeat later, the air shimmered next to me. A golden flash filled the temple, and screams came from behind me.

When the gold disappeared, Kethryllian stood next to me. His head reached my shoulders, and his antlers were larger than before.

My lady. The Guardian's voice echoed in my mind. *It seems you have grown more powerful since we last met. How did you break the ward around the city?*

I shrugged, a small smile creeping over my face. *It seems that there isn't much I can't do now that I've Matured.*

After crossing over the wall and finding a place to spend my first day, I connected with the earth. The land was happy to help me dismantle the black magic that kept Kethryllian out of the city. I fed the earth while it helped me, and then, I stored my powers up for this moment.

"What is the meaning of this?" High King Edgar thundered, his face turning as red as his clothes. "I will have your head for this insolence!"

The threat, which would have had me in tears a year ago, rang empty now that I knew who I was.

"No." I shook my head as I mounted Kethryllian in one swift movement. After days of riding the Guardian, it was easy. "You won't. We both know you need me alive. The earth needs me."

My hands stretched out beside me, and hundreds of ribbons of magic slid from them. They flooded through the temple, and the earth hummed.

"You dare summon your heretical magic in Kydona's temple?" High King Edgar roared.

That "heretical" power vibrated in the air throughout the temple.

Eager to do my bidding, the earth called out to me. *What do you need, High Lady of Life?*

At that moment, I needed many things. One thing was more pressing than the rest, and I focused on that.

Focusing on the earth, I let my will be known.

Xander, I called out through our bond. *Get ready.*

His voice came back a heartbeat later. *I will always be ready, Aileana.*

Raising my eyes, I met the king's gaze once more. His bride stood silently beside him, her veil blocking her face from sight.

"You called me your pet, but you're wrong. I was never yours." My thighs clenched around Kethryllian, and the Guardian ran a hoof over the tile floor.

"I can and will claim you, Aileana. I will keep you as mine, and nothing you do will stop me. You *belong* to me." High King Edgar clenched his jaw, and red ribbons flooded from his palms, gathering around him.

"This entire country belongs to me! Do you think I did all this for nothing? Do you think I put the females of this country in their place to be bested by one *Earth Elf?*" Disdain dripped from his voice, and he sneered at me.

Kethryllian shifted beneath me, and more green magic swirled around me as I shook my head.

My voice rang out through the temple. "I don't belong to anyone."

The twang of metal being drawn filled the air, and hundreds of footsteps pounded on the floor.

People were running from the temple. Good. They didn't need to die here. Most of them had done nothing wrong.

My quarrel was not with them.

High King Edgar laughed, and shivers ran down my spine. "That's where you're wrong. You belong to me, pet."

"Don't call me that," I snapped. "Did you not hear a word I just said? I am not your pet any longer."

"No?" he sneered. "Who are you, then?"

Tell him, Xander urged.

"I am Aileana of the House of Corellon." My voice thundered through the rapidly emptying temple. "I am the Protectress of the Woods, the Keeper of the Earth, and the High Lady of Life." Clenching my fists, I stared at the High King. "And today, I am fighting back. For myself. For all those whose lives you stole. For the females in Ithenmyr. Today, I will be your reckoning."

A fierce sense of pride pulsed through the bond from Xander, and I drew in a deep breath. The ribbons I had sent into the temple twisted, and a flash of blinding green filled the massive space.

When I exhaled, the temple was no longer white. Thick ivy crawled over the walls, and moss covered the ground beneath Kethryllian's feet. Where Winged Soldiers had been, gnarled, twisted trees stood in their spots. Each one bore a sickening resemblance to the male it had been moments ago.

A single beat passed in absolute silence.

Then chaos descended on the temple.

Screams filled the air. Pounding footsteps. Calls of heresy and death.

The remaining spectators fled, but I did not move. I barely breathed, keeping my eyes on the dais.

Xander watched me carefully through the bars of the cage.

Not yet, I cautioned him.

He nodded slowly.

Returning my gaze to the High King, I smirked.

The Crimson King *trembled* on the dais, and fear leaked from his pores.

He was afraid of me.

Good. He should be.

The last time we met in the Queen's Tower, he caught us by surprise. I wasn't Mature then, nor did I understand the extent of my magic.

I was not the same female he faced then. I would not be tumbling out any tower windows today.

Fear was exactly what he should have been feeling because today, I was not some weak female he could push down and shove to the side.

Power ran through my veins, and I intended to use it all today.

The priest cleared his throat, and I remembered that he was there. The elderly werewolf stood behind the king with wide eyes, clutching a scroll. "Shall I continue, Your Majesty? All that remains is the blood pact..."

"Not now," the king snapped.

The Queen of Drahan still wasn't moving. She was oddly familiar, but I couldn't quite place her.

High King Edgar grabbed his bride's hand, storming off the dais and tugging her behind him.

When they stood at the bottom of the steps, they stopped. Red sparks flicked off the Crimson King, and he sneered. "Do you think that you're funny, pet? That your little tricks scare me? You call yourself the High Lady of Life, but do you know what it really means?"

Slipping off Kethryllian, I stood next to the Guardian. "Do *you* know what it means? Or have you been so busy playing High King that you forgot about the balance required by the gods?"

A large part of me was still confused about what, exactly, this balance was, but I knew it was important. By the High King's expression and the prophecy Myhhena had told me about, I knew I had said the right thing.

"Don't speak to me of that," the Crimson King hissed. He spooled red ribbons of magic around his hands. "You know nothing of *balance*."

Pulling my power towards myself in a similar fashion, I shook my head. "Like many things since escaping, I. Will. Learn."

Peeking within myself, I prodded my stores of magic. They were nearly full, the ribbons waiting and ready for me to use them.

"No," the High King snapped. "You won't have the chance."

Beside me, Kethryllian rumbled. "Do you need anything else from me, my lady?"

I glanced around the temple. The people were gone. The Winged Soldiers were dead. Only five of us remained.

I shook my head. "Not now, Kethryllian. Thank you for your service."

He had done what I needed him to. Without Kethryllian, I wasn't sure High King Edgar would truly understand the power that ran through my veins. And I needed him to understand. To know that the person bringing his judgment was *me*. That the same female he had abused for years was bringing his judgment.

I needed High King Edgar to know that when he crossed me, he made a mistake.

The Guardian disappeared with a flash of gold, and I stood alone.

"You forgot something, pet." High King Edgar's hands spun in the air as he pulled ribbons of magic from his hands. They formed a sphere, and he raised a brow, prowling toward me.

"I don't think so," I said.

Beneath my feet, the earth waited.

Tell us what to do, it begged. *Let us help*.

Soon, I promised the land.

"I have something of yours." The High King tilted his head toward the cage. "If you want your bonded mate to survive this day, you will surrender to me. Now." He raised a brow, a small chuckle escaping him.

Clearly, he thought himself a genius.

For one, the ability that most males seemed to have—the one where they underestimated females simply because they lacked certain parts—was working in my favor.

I let a single second pass. One moment where the king truly seemed to think he had won.

Then, a crack came from the cage.

My lips tilted up into a wry smile. "Unfortunately, Your Majesty,"—the word dripped with scorn as it escaped my lips—"I don't think you quite understand the situation yet. But you will."

Now, I said through the bond.

The High King's eyes widened. His black wings flexed behind him, and he glanced over his shoulder.

A white flash filled the temple.

A cracking sound. Fabric ripped. The iron cage twisted beneath my mate's wings. The dragon *roared*, his large green wings spreading as the cage buckled beneath him. It became nothing more than a twist of metal bars.

One enormous foot slammed into the ground. A tremor ran through the temple, and Kydona's priest cried out as a slitted golden eye met mine.

Fire erupted from Xander's maw, and my heart pounded. Seeing the majestic dragon again was just as incredible. I would never tire of this sight.

Heat filled the temple as scorching red flames engulfed the dais. The werewolf screamed, his voice reaching horrid heights before it abruptly stopped.

Ash filled the air, swirling around like black flakes of snow.

My heart swelled in my chest. My bonded mate—my dragon shifter —was out of his cage.

Death filled the air, a foreboding promise of what was to come.

I breathed in deeply.

It was time.

This was my destiny.

A Broken Curse

"It is done."

The words came from somewhere outside of myself, sounding like little more than ripples in the water, and I pried my eyes open.

My head throbbed, and my body felt different. Weightless. Testing my fingers, I ran them through the sand beneath me. The rough, grainy texture was a sharp contrast to the smoothness of the water above me.

"It is?" I rasped, forcing my eyes open. "How... how long has it been?"

The last thing I remembered was drinking that horrible inky liquid, and then darkness enveloped me.

The sea witch swam in front of me. "A half-day has passed."

"Excuse me?" I stared at the male with the swirling black hair.

"My deepest apologies, Princess," Galahad said earnestly. "Unravelling the curse was far more difficult than I had anticipated."

His eyes looked heavier than the day before, and the lines on his face were far more pronounced.

Pushing myself up, I trembled. My knees shook as my feet remembered what it was like to stand and hold the weight of my body.

When I was confident I would not tumble right back over, I extended a hand toward the sea witch. Waiting until he placed his ancient palm in mine, I kissed his wrinkled skin. "Thank you."

He smiled. "The pleasure was all mine, Princess. It is not often I have the opportunity to work on such fine art as the curse woven around your soul. I shall remember this until the day I Fade."

Clearly, the sea witch and I had different ideas about the definition of pleasure.

"Ryllae?" Daegal's worried voice came from nearby, and I jerked my head to the side. He stood just outside the ring, where a multitude of footprints in the sand told me exactly how close he'd been all night.

"Daegal," I breathed. I wanted nothing more than to run out of this ring, but the sea witch's warning ran through my mind.

"Come in, Seer." Galahad's tail lashed out, sweeping away part of the circle. "It's safe to enter. The magic is gone. You may comfort your female."

I thought Daegal might have an objection to the sea witch calling me "his" female, but apparently, he did not. Moments later, the Fortune Elf's strong arms were around me.

The hug, which was strangely warm despite our watery surroundings, was everything I needed. I sagged against Daegal, and he supported my weight with ease. He pressed my head against his chest, my horns curling under his chin as he ran a hand through my hair.

"How do you feel?" he asked.

The potion was still in my body, the black liquid oozing through my veins, but something else was present. Something new and bright and entirely at odds with how I'd felt for the past two and a half centuries.

Energy.

"I feel... different," I replied softly. "Lighter. More like... myself."

The edge of insanity felt further today than it ever had before.

Daegal brushed a lock of my hair behind my ear. "Do you... want to try your magic?"

I sucked in a breath, and the world stilled.

Did I want to try my magic?

Of course, I did.

But what if it didn't work? What if, despite this lightness within me, I was still bound? What if I was doomed to live without magic for the rest of my life? Who would I be, then? Would Daegal still want—

"Ryllae." Daegal's voice was soft as he placed a hand on my cheek. "Look at me."

I did.

His eyes were wide and filled with deep affection as he gazed at me. "It's all right." His thumb ran down my skin, and I leaned into his touch. "I'm right here. No matter what, I'm not going anywhere."

He wasn't going to leave me.

Clinging to that thought, I nodded slowly. Wrapping one hand around Daegal's tunic, I extended the other and opened my palm. Water swished around me as I reached that place where magic resided within me.

A large part of me expected that the black mist would reappear, and this would all be for naught.

After all, I was Ryllae. The forgotten princess whose birthright was stolen from her.

But my luck was changing.

I had Daegal, and he wouldn't leave me.

So I pulled on the well of gods-given power within me, and...

Red ribbons slipped from my palm. They swirled around my legs in the water, eager to do my bidding.

It *worked*.

It really worked.

"You did it," Daegal said. Angling my mouth towards his, he brushed a kiss against my lips as though it were the most natural thing in the world.

Apparently, it was because I returned the kiss with ease. That connection within me, the one we had yet to acknowledge, hummed with pleasure.

My free hand slipped beneath his tunic, and I traced the lines of his stomach as we kissed. Our lips moved, and our bodies pressed against each other as the rest of the world faded away. For a long moment, there was nothing else but this kiss and how it made me feel.

The cracks in my soul that had been there for centuries mended. This male in front of me, the one whose lips tasted of salt and cinnamon, had brought me out of the darkness.

Maybe, one day, I might be whole once more.

My magic thrummed in my veins, humming a song I had long forgotten. Power pulsed through me, and I felt... alive.

"Thank you," I whispered, breaking our kiss.

"For what?"

"For all of this." I looked around at the swirling water around us, the gentle current pulsing in time with the beating of our hearts. "For bringing me here. For believing in me."

"I will always believe in you," he promised.

"And you'll never leave me?"

"Never," he swore.

My heart warmed, and more magic flooded from my palm.

GALAHAD and a small contingent of merfolk brought us back to the palace, where the High Queen and her consort waited in the same sitting room as before. As soon as we entered, they turned towards us.

This time, though, things were different.

I stood in the doorway holding Daegal's hand as red ribbons of magic slid like eels around me. I held my head high, and my back was straight.

This time, I would not bow before anyone.

I was the princess of Ithenmyr and a powerful Death Elf.

"Your Majesties," I said, breaking the silence. "I wish to thank you for your hospitality and all you have done for us. Without you, my magic would still be locked away."

A beat passed as the royal mer studied us intently. Queen Mareena's eyes met mine, and she dipped her head ever so slightly.

Understanding passed between us.

She was a queen, and I, a princess.

Perhaps we were not equals, but together, we could do much in this world.

"Of course." Queen Mareena smiled. "Now that you are... yourself, we wish to discuss something with you."

"Good," I said, pulling Daegal into the room. "Because we have something to propose as well."

"Oh?" The High Queen of the Seven Seas raised a brow.

I nodded, squeezing Daegal's hand. "I am going to reclaim my throne," I said. "We will need allies. It is our hope that this is the beginning of a new union, one between elves and merfolk that will benefit us all."

My words rang through the room, and for a moment, the swishing of the water against the furniture was the only sound.

Queen Mareena's lips tilted up. "It seems the hands of fate are at play here, Princess, because that was exactly what we had planned to suggest. One day, Ryllae of Ithenmyr, when you restore the balance, you must not forget about us in Coral City."

When.

As if it was just a matter of time before things returned to normal.

She spoke as though she knew it would happen.

Something stirred within me, and another part of my broken soul mended.

Maybe the gods hadn't forgotten about me at all. Maybe there was a reason for all of this. For me, Daegal, Xander, and Aileana.

Maybe we were all broken so we could repair the country my father had broken.

Maybe we would have a future after this.

"I would love that," I whispered.

The High Queen of the Seven Seas extended a hand, and coral ribbons tinged with gold slipped from her palm. Recognizing what she was doing, I did the same, allowing red ribbons to slide out of me. Soon, silver and coral ribbons joined the fray as Calix and Daegal followed our lead.

The four magics twisted together, forming a tight sphere that floated in the water between us.

Keeping my palm outstretched, I said, "I, Ryllae of the House of Irriel, Princess of Ithenmyr, hereby vow on all the gods and goddesses to continue to fight until the day that balance is restored in Ithenmyr."

Daegal repeated my words, followed by the mermaid queen. The sphere of ribbons glowed brighter until the light coming from it was practically blinding.

Calix, the queen's consort, was the last to go. He repeated the vow, his deep timber echoing through the room. The moment the last words left his lips, the sphere of our combined magic vibrated. It grew larger and larger, shaking as it expanded.

All four of us kept our hands outstretched as the water thickened. Even with the merfolk's power keeping us alive, my lungs tightened to the point of pain. My heart thudded as the sphere twisted faster and faster between us.

When I thought it would all be too much, the sphere cracked. It broke apart into four equal parts, shrinking until it hovered above our extended palms.

I jolted as the magic sank into my skin. A bright silver shell appeared in the middle of my palm, nestling among the red markings of my Maturation.

Glancing up, I saw that each of us had the same marking.

The four of us stared at each other as the weight of our vows settled upon us.

Eventually, Queen Mareena cleared her throat. "Well. I must say, Princess, I have heard many things about your magic. Perhaps after some rest, you might indulge us in a little demonstration of your skills?"

"It would be my honor."

My magic was back. Daegal was by my side.

And now, I had an ally.

Nothing would stop me from reclaiming my rightful place on Ithenmyr's throne.

A Lovers' Reunion

XANDER

Black ash billowed around the temple, and the taste of bitter smoke filled my mouth. My tail thumped against the back wall, and I flexed my wings as I stepped toward the king. His back was to me as he gathered magic around him.

The High King snarled, but Aileana didn't even move.

My fierce, bonded mate.

Moss and Ivy grew all around her. Dozens of trees filled the walls of the once-bare temple, marking the spot where the Winged Soldiers had stood their last stand. Her arms were outstretched, and the green tattoos glowed. They covered every inch of her exposed skin from the base of her neck down.

I wondered if they went beneath her clothing, too.

I hoped I would have the chance to find out.

Aileana had always been beautiful. But now, fully Mature, she was *magnificent*.

Her ears were longer, the tips coming to a sharpened point. Her eyes were a brilliant emerald as they shone, and her magic was even more vibrant than before. She stood in the middle of the temple, her skin glowing green as magic poured out of her outstretched palms.

Between the tunic and the variety of weapons strapped to her incredible body, she looked like a warrior.

She looked like a High Lady of Life.

My dragon purred. *Mine.*

Still in my dragon form, my tail swished back and forth as I glared at the bride and groom. The Crimson King stood at the base of the dais with his red magic swirling around him. Beside him, the Southern Queen remained unmoving.

I couldn't help but snarl in her direction.

Traitor! Betrayer!

I was torn. A large part of me believed she deserved whatever was coming her way. After what she'd done, it was only fair that she faced the consequences of her actions.

If I were being honest, Queen Sanja deserved it all.

The other part of me, the protector I'd always been—at least where she was concerned—wanted to shift and gather her in my arms. To hide her and keep her safe from the horrors of the world. Bewitched or not, her presence here after all these years was tearing me apart from the inside out.

I did not know which side would win.

The ground rumbled, and a crack appeared on the temple floor. Aileana stepped forward, her green ribbons swirling around her protectively.

"You wanted to see me?" She smiled, showing off two sharpened canines. Heat ran through my body at the sight of those. Even while speaking with the king, who had caused her immeasurable pain, Aileana was marvelous. "Here I am."

She prowled towards the king, and for once, he didn't move.

Crimson ribbons slipped from his palms, forming his red scepter as he snapped his black wings tightly against his back.

"Stop moving, pet," High King Edgar demanded.

"Make me," she snarled, green ribbons trailing behind her like a veil.

I wasn't sure goading the king was in anyone's best interests, but I couldn't help but be proud of Aileana's bravery.

Twice now, she had faced her fears head-on.

I was male enough to acknowledge that I had underestimated her.

I was wrong, I said through the bond. *You are strong enough for anything.*

Smugness came through the bond.

At the same moment, red ribbons spun from the king's hands. "As you wish, pet." The Death Elf magic swirled in the air, aiming for Aileana's heart, as a cruel laugh filled the temple.

I roared, tinging the air with smoke and ash, even as Aileana batted the magic away with ribbons of her own.

Flames licked at my throat, but I wouldn't let them out. Not with my mate so close. I couldn't risk her getting caught in the fire.

All I could do was stand and watch as High King Edgar threw another burst of red magic in her direction.

Again, she stopped it.

They danced around each other, every movement bringing Aileana a little bit closer to me.

While the magic flew, a flurry of green and red in the air, the Southern Queen did nothing. She stood as still as a statue, but even with the veil, I felt the weight of her stare.

Aileana's hands were outstretched and more magic than I had ever seen her wield flooded from her palms. She walked backward in my direction, her eyes never leaving the king.

When Aileana was mere feet from me, the bond within me tugged.

Shift, she commanded me.

Gods, I loved the sound of her giving me orders. Sending my mate what I hoped was a smirk, I reached within myself. Pulling on the shift had never been easier. White light flared, and then I was back on two feet.

Reaching out, I drew her against me, relishing in the way she fit perfectly.

Xander, Aileana's voice appeared in my mind. *Not that I don't love the feeling of you against me, but do you think you might want to put something on?*

I was naked. Somehow, in the flurry of everything that happened, I forgot. Usually, this didn't bother me, but seeing as how we had an audience...

I eased back a step, grabbing my ripped trousers and stepping into them as quickly as I could before pressing her back against my chest. They didn't fit quite perfectly, but they would have to do.

Lowering my lips to Aileana's elongated ears, I growled, "I thought I told you to leave, Sunshine."

She stiffened against me.

"I didn't listen," she said snarkily as if we weren't currently facing down the Crimson King.

"I see that."

Now, her voice appeared in my mind. *If I had left, I wouldn't have been able to bring you this.*

Metal twanged, and I looked down.

"You brought my sword?" I asked.

She nodded. "I brought it with me from the Sanctuary. I thought you would want it."

Taking the hilt in my hands, I turned the weapon over. "I do."

Before we could say anything else, a long, slow clap filled the temple.

"Isn't this sweet?" High King Edgar crooned, his scarred face sneering at us from the base of the dais. "A lovers' reunion. A tale for the ages. Too bad it will end in death." He clucked his tongue. "Perhaps once your mate is well and truly dead, pet, you will be easier to deal with."

"The only death today will be yours, Edgar," I snarled, raising myself to my full height and attempting to pull Aileana behind me. "Once you're gone, I will deal with this." I gestured towards the Southern Queen. "Whatever hold you have on her, I will break. We will find a witch and undue these spells—"

The female in question burst into laughter, and my mouth fell open.

"You're wrong," Queen Sanja said, finally breaking her silence.

"What?" I asked.

She shook her head, and that damned veil moved from side to side. Her words were shards of ice stabbing into my heart. "I am under no spell. Did you not hear what I said to the priest? I am here of my own volition."

I gaped at the Southern Queen. "What? How could you?"

"How could I?" she sneered as pure, venomous hatred dripped from her voice. "Riches and power." She scoffed. "Obviously."

Aileana glanced between me and the Southern Queen. Her brows furrowed, and I could see her trying to work out how I knew this female.

Xander, what is happening? she asked in my mind.

I couldn't answer. The Crimson King had tied my tongue.

My heart pounded, and all I could do was stare at the Southern Queen as disbelief coursed through my body.

If she was under no spell, then it had all been for nothing. All the grief and pain I'd suffered had been for *nothing*.

ELAYNA R. GALLEA

Aileana huffed. "Will someone tell me what is going on?"

I forced my lips to open. "Sunshine, she is..." My mouth tried to form the words, but they wouldn't come out. I tried again. "This is... She..."

"This is my bride," High King Edgar snarled. "Enough of this chit-chat. Let me tell you what is going to happen. First, I'm going to kill the dragon shifter. Then, once he's dead, I'm going to take you, my little Earth Elf, and throw you in the deepest, darkest hole I can find."

"I'd like to see you try," Aileana snapped.

He laughed. His wings snapped out behind him, and red sparks flickered around his body. "Oh, pet. I'm going to do more than try. Once my bride and I complete the blood pact, there will be no one who can stop me. And then, the Four Kingdoms will be mine."

A red sphere of magic pulsed in his hand, and High King Edgar sneered. "Let's be honest, pet. This encounter has been less than delight-ful. I'm done. Say goodbye to your mate because I am not playing games any longer."

Aileana snarled, and the earth shook.

"No," she said, taking a step away from me. "That's where you're wrong. You see, Your Majesty, you're missing something here. Something that I don't think you ever took into account."

"What is that?"

"Every single time you whipped me, every time you made me witness another death, my hatred for you grew," Aileana said. "For a long time, I feared you for what you might do to me if I disobeyed you. Once, perhaps, I might have quaked at your words. But I am not that female any longer."

Her voice grew in intensity as she spooled green ribbons between her hands. "Now, I know the truth. I survived because I was strong. I know of the prophecy, and I know what power runs through my veins. Now, that strength will be your end."

A series of tremors shook the temple, a loud *crack* sounded, and the moss-covered marble split in two as a fissure ran the length of the temple.

The Crimson King laughed, forming a thick, pulsing sphere of red magic in his hand.

"Is that all you have, Aileana? I will *destroy* you." Looking over his shoulder at Queen Sanja, he said, "Let me take care of this little problem, and then we will pick up where we left off, my dear."

Snarling, I raised my sword. I would protect Aileana until my last breath. "Stay back," I warned.

High King Edgar snorted. "You have nothing on me, dragon. I will relish keeping your head as a trophy of my triumphs on this day."

He pulled back his arm and threw the sphere of magic. It pulsed as it sailed through the air, drawing closer and closer to us.

I surged forward, reaching out an arm to pull Aileana out of harm's way.

"I've got this," she hissed. "Stand. Down."

Although it went against my every instinct, I did as she asked.

If this was the moment I died, at least I would do it next to my bonded mate.

Running Out of Time

AILEANA

The earth trembled beneath my feet, and my magic thrummed in my veins. Its song was in harmony with the rapid beat of my heart. Xander stood beside me, his chest heaving as a red magic sailed toward us.

Time slowed as the deadly magic came closer.

And closer.

"Sunshine," Xander hissed through clenched teeth. "I trust you, my love, but did you maybe want to do something about this?"

I did. I was going to.

"One second," I replied, kicking off my boots. They landed nearby with a soft thud, and my bare feet dug into the moss-covered tiles.

What are you doing? he asked incredulously through our mental connection.

I need to be near to the earth.

The sphere was so close that I could make out each individual ribbon. Keeping my eyes on the sphere, I bid my time. Out of the corner of my eye, I saw the Southern Queen move. She withdrew something from her dress, but I couldn't see what it was.

"We're running out of time, Aileana," Xander said, tightening his grip on the sword.

In response, I sent a flurry of reassurance through the bond.

He snorted.

I had this under control.

At least, I was fairly certain I did.

My heart thudded in my chest as I worked on gathering as much magic as I could. The earth hummed beneath my feet, and I curled my toes, pressing them into the soft moss.

All the life in Ithenmyr waited on my beck and call.

The sphere drew nearer.

A flash of red surrounded the bride and groom, but I did not pay it any attention.

Holding out my hands, I inhaled. All the magic I had access to—this nearly endless well of power—bubbled up within me. Killing the Winged Soldiers had barely brushed the surface of what I could do.

As I exhaled, my Earth Elf magic exploded out of me like a flood. The ribbons filled the temple, and as one, they flashed a brilliant green.

The light was blinding, and for a moment, I could barely see what was happening.

Everything moved so fast.

The High King ran towards me. Xander shouted. The air was a clash of red and green. My mating bond burned, and my heart pounded.

The Southern Queen screamed. The sound of her voice was terrifyingly familiar. Glass shattered, raining down on us from above. The ground shook beneath our feet.

The earth cried out.

My lungs tightened, and my magic continued to flood out of me.

More and more until it was nearly all gone.

This was it.

Our last stand.

It would either work, or we were dead.

I had nothing left.

When the last strand of my magic left my outstretched palms, a weighted silence fell upon us. A thick, green mist swirled around the temple, blocking everything from view.

I waited to hear High King Edgar's cruel voice. Waited to see him lob another red sphere of magic toward me. Waited for him to retaliate and tell me that I wasn't strong enough.

Except...

His voice never came.

His taunts never arrived.

The only sound was the thundering of my heart and the pounding of my blood as it coursed through my veins.

That was it.

A gust of wind blew through the temple, and the thick, green mist slowly cleared. Inch by inch, it dissipated until it was nothing more than green dust on the moss-covered floor.

My jaw dropped open, and I blinked.

The ground where High King Edgar had stood was now broken in two. A deep, dark fissure ran through the center of the temple. Rising from the broken ground was a massive tree. It was enormous, and its gnarled and ancient bark stretched to the temple's ceiling.

My breath caught in my throat as I stared at the tree. Streaks of red laced through the bark, starting at the base of the roots that crawled over the cracked marble floor.

Shards of colorful, broken glass dusted the ground, and snowflakes fell through the shattered ceiling. Each tree limb, which began high above my head, bore black leaves streaked with crimson. They rose high into the sky, disappearing through the space where the stained glass had been moments before.

And at the bottom of the tree...

"I did it," I whispered disbelievingly.

The king was pinned by one of the roots, his body neatly split in two. Blood pooled beneath him as the root took up the space where his chest used to be.

There was no question. He was dead.

I did it.

A warm hand landed on my shoulder, and the scent of smoke, ash, and pine filled my senses. Xander turned me, pulling me to him and pressing a hard kiss to my lips. Pride came through the bond as he pressed his forehead against mine. "Aileana, you killed him."

"I killed him," I echoed.

This was still so new, so fresh, that I could barely believe it.

High King Edgar was dead. The male who had terrorized me for years was *dead*. There was no coming back for him. Not now. Even a Mature elf couldn't survive an injury like this.

He was dead, and I was alive.

This should have been a moment of celebration.

The king was dead.

The balance should have been restored. The prophecy said as much. High King Edgar was the reason for the darkness in Ithenmyr, and he was dead.

So why didn't I feel any different? Why wasn't the earth rejoicing beneath my feet?

Did Myhhena conveniently forget to tell me something else?

Perhaps.

After what she had hidden, I did not put it past her.

Then I heard it.

A quiet whimper came from the other side of the temple. At first, it sounded like a kitten mewling, but it steadily got louder.

The Southern Queen.

I had forgotten all about her.

Xander's ears perked up, and he cursed. His feet shifted, and I could see that he wanted to go. "Are you hurt, Aileana?"

I ran my hands over myself. I was shaken, and the magic within me was low, but I could already feel the earth feeding my power.

"No," I whispered, "I think I'm fine."

He nodded as another whimper came from around the tree. His eyes flashed as he tightened his grip on the sword. "Stay here."

Letting go of my hand, Xander jumped over the giant fissure in the ground as though it were nothing before darting around the massive tree.

Stay here.

I snorted. I had just killed a king. There was no way I was going to sit on my laurels.

Drawing a dagger, I followed Xander. My movements were less graceful than his as I picked my way around shards of broken stained glass, but I was coming with him.

I would always come with him.

When I rounded the tree, I skidded to a stop.

The Southern Queen lay on her back near what used to be a Winged Soldier. An enormous green shard of stained glass protruded from her chest, pinning her to the ground. Blood seeped out of her, staining the ground red, and her breath came in spurts. Her veil had been completely torn off, and her dress was ruined.

Xander kneeled before Queen Sanja, and his sword was discarded at his side. His eyes were wide, and his face...

A tear slipped down his cheek as deep sadness echoed through our bond.

"What's going on?" I asked.

Ignoring me, Xander reached out and grabbed the shard of glass with his bare hands.

"Stop!" I gasped, tightening my grip on my dagger as I darted forward. "What are you doing?"

Xander stilled, looking over his shoulder at me. His eyes were hard, and his mouth was pinched in a firm line. "I told you to stay, Aileana."

"You should have known I wouldn't listen." My gaze darted between Xander and the dying female. Something was wrong. Lifting my dagger, I pointed it at the Southern Queen. "Who is she?"

Xander's mouth opened and closed.

"Who is she?" I asked again, my voice harder this time. A sense of foreboding grew within me as he continued to ignore me. "Xander, tell me!"

The female on the ground moaned, and Xander stiffened. "I'll tell you, Aileana. I just... I have to do this."

"Do what?"

It was too late. He grunted, yanking the glass out of the injured female's stomach. The moment the glass was free, Queen Sanja gasped. Blood poured freely from the wound, staining everything in sight. Xander. The floor. The moss. Her gown. It was all blood red.

I wanted to be sick, but I couldn't tear my eyes away from the dying female. A rattling cough came from her, and her skin turned a horrible white as blood leached from her.

Any second now, she would die.

Except...

She didn't.

Instead, strange red magic flickered in her palms. Her lips twitched, and an odd look appeared in her eyes. They weren't... normal.

A long slit ran through her ice-blue irises. Her eyes were so pale that I could scarcely believe they were real.

The Southern Queen coughed, pushing herself up on her elbows as the wound knit itself together. "I should thank you, Aileana."

My heart stuttered.

"What?" I breathed, reaching for my magic. There was barely any left. My grip tightened around the hilt of my dagger, and I shook my head. "What are you talking about?"

"Edgar was going to be a problem." Queen Sanja coughed, and Xander stared at her with growing horror. "I was going to kill him tonight, but you took care of that little issue for me. Honestly, the male was absolutely insufferable."

My mind spun in circles as I tried to follow her words. I had no idea what she was talking about. Glancing at Xander, I could tell he was just as lost.

The Southern Queen raised a hand, and red ribbons—magic that should have disappeared with Edgar—flickered from her palms.

I gasped.

Shaking his head, Xander asked, "What are you talking about?"

"You see," the queen murmured, her voice gaining strength, "while you were busy getting ready to do this,"—she gestured to the tree—"Edgar and I sealed our union with blood. He was such a stupid male." A bitter laugh escaped her. "Always underestimating those around him. I'm sure you felt the same way, Aileana."

"Don't talk to her," Xander growled. "I saved you. Doesn't that mean—"

"Males are *so* stupid," Queen Sanja said, interrupting him. "They always discount females."

I couldn't disagree with that.

The queen shrugged, sitting up as though she hadn't just nearly died. "Now, Edgar's power is mine." She grinned, those ice-blue eyes sparking with violence. "Now that our power is linked, I will be unstoppable."

"Why are you doing this?" Xander demanded, finally coming to his senses and picking up his sword.

Queen Sanja laughed, and the sound was as cold as her eyes. "Put it down. You and I both know you won't use it."

Xander's hands trembled.

Who is she? I demanded through our bond.

I wanted to tell you, he said quietly.

Who is she? I asked again.

He trembled, staring at the female covered in blood. *I wanted to, I tried to, but Edgar cursed me. I couldn't.*

Obviously, he knew her. Something niggled in the back of my mind, something about black hair, but I couldn't quite place it.

Xander! I yelled in his mind. *Who is she?*

The Southern Queen sighed, pushing herself to her feet.

"This has been fun," she said. Raising her black brow in my direction, she tilted her head, "If you ever decide you want to see what true power feels like, Aileana, find me. Until then, I must bid you adieu."

Xander cursed as a flash of white light erupted from the Southern Queen.

Every swear word I knew ran through my lips when it cleared.

A blue dragon, the color of a cloudless sky, flapped its wings, flying towards the broken roof.

For an entire minute, I had no words.

Nothing came to me.

My mouth opened and closed, but there was nothing there. I kept staring at the hole where the dragon had just disappeared.

The *dragon*.

"Xander." I narrowed my eyes.

He looked at me as grief flickered through his gaze. "Yes?"

"Who, in the seven circles of hell, was that?"

Xander ran a hand over his face, leaving streaks of blood on his skin. He drew in a shuddering breath. "Do you remember what I told you about Saena?"

My mind flew back to the cavern where Xander and I first shared stories. As though it operated on its own accord, my hand went to my chest and gripped the map beneath my tunic.

"Your sister..." My brows knit together. "You said... you told me... she's gone."

"Many years ago, in the Southern Kingdom, we were... she was... I saw..." He swallowed. "When I left, Aileana, I thought she was dead. Her body... was covered in blood. The floor. The walls. Everything. There was so much blood... I didn't know anyone could survive something like that."

His words echoed through me.

Survive.

It took a moment, but when understanding dawned on me, it was like the world was spinning out of control. My legs shook, and I dropped to my knees. Shards of glass cut into my skin, but I ignored the shooting pain as my dagger fell to the floor.

Taking his hands in mine, I asked, "Elyxander, what are you saying?"

"I thought she died." A deep, shaking breath escaped him as his pain-filled eyes met mine. "But it turns out something even worse happened."

I didn't want to ask. I didn't want to know. But I had to. "What happened?"

"My sister... when dragon shifters lose control of their creatures, they can become something else." His voice was low, and absolute agony laced his every word. "The draken are dangerous, Aileana. They are not entirely themselves. Fed by violence, their desire for power and riches sustains them. The darkness inside of them feeds them, giving them unnatural strength."

Horror filled me, and my stomach sank as Xander's words settled on me. That blue dragon flashed before my eyes.

"Oh, my gods," I whispered as realization slammed into me. "Are you saying..."

"The Southern Queen is a draken. She will be ten times harder than High King Edgar to kill." Xander squeezed my hands, his voice hoarse as he forced out the next words. "And she is my sister."

Epilogue - Darkness is Coming

RYLLAE

Spreading my hands, red ribbons flooded from my outstretched palms. The magic danced around the great hall, swimming through the water and weaving around the gathered merfolk.

Beside me, Daegal grinned. This was the third demonstration I'd put on in many days. The merfolk couldn't seem to get enough of my magic. After so many years without my powers, I was happy to indulge them.

Laughter filled the waters, and my ribbons danced around the young merlings playing a game of chase in the middle of the room. High Queen Mareena and her bonded mate sat on coral thrones overlooking the scene.

I drew more power, intent on forming a large cat out of my magic when the doors slammed open. Erthian rushed inside, his tail flicking powerfully behind him as he hurried through the crowd.

"Your Majesty," he said breathlessly. "I have an urgent message from the Surface."

Instantly, the atmosphere shifted.

Not needing any command, the merfolk. I pulled my magic back into myself, and soon, the room was empty. The waters were thick with tension, and I *knew* something had happened.

Queen Mareena waved a hand. "Go ahead."

Erthian swallowed, turning to me. His eyes were wide, and I reached over, gripping Daegal's hand. My stomach twisted, and dread fell over me like a weight.

"Tell me," I whispered.

There was a pause before Erthian said, "High King Edgar is... dead."

My father was... dead.

The words swirled around me.

I always thought I would be the one to deal the killing blow. The one to remove my horrible father from this life.

Perhaps some children would grieve when they heard the news of their parent's death.

I would not.

Stepping towards the mermale, I asked, "Are you certain?"

"Yes," Erthian replied. "Multiple sources have confirmed it. There is no question about that."

"When?" Daegal asked.

"Five days ago, in a town called Breley."

I probably should have felt sad, but I didn't. Relief flooded every part of my body, and a smile crept over me. "That's... amazing! My throne, I can take it and—"

"No." Erthian cut me off, shaking his head. "There is... a new power in Ithenmyr."

My eyes widened. "What?"

"Explain," Queen Mareena demanded.

"High King Edgar is dead, but a new power has arisen. My spies are reporting strange things happening in Ithenmyr. Rivers are drying up.

Snow is falling where it never has before. Plants are withering. Something has changed."

My heart hammered within me, and my lungs grew tight.

A new power.

The High Queen of the Seven Seas asked more questions of Erthian, but I tuned them out. My magic was a rapid, pulsing thrum in my veins.

I turned to Daegal. "We have to go back."

He nodded. "Let me See what's happening. It's been a few days..."

His voice trailed off, and his eyes turned silver. I waited with bated breath for him to return from the silver trance of his magic.

When the glow faded, Daegal paled. "Ryllae, it's... It's worse than we had ever imagined. The future... the darkness... There is very little time."

"What about our friends?"

Daegal swallowed. "Xander and Aileana are in trouble. We must go now, or Ithenmyr will be lost forever. Darkness is quickly coming. If we don't act now, the entire continent will fall."

THE END... FOR NOW
THANK YOU FOR READING OF ASH AND IVY!

That wasn't so bad, right?

I mean, not nearly as terrible as leaving Aileana falling off a tower. Even I felt bad about that one.

But we all survived!

Reviews are so important to indie authors. It would mean the world to me if you'd leave one for this book to help other people find this story as well.

Of Thistles and Talons

The Ithenmyr Chronicles continues in Of Thistles and Talons! This book will be coming out in late spring 2023. You can preorder it here.

If you can't get enough of the world of the Four Kingdoms, I have amazing news!

My newest series, The Binding Chronicles takes place in Eleyta and occurs at the same time as Of Ash and Ivy.

Turn the page for a sneak peek at Tethered.

Tethered: An Arranged Marriage Fantasy Romance

FEBRUARY 13, 2023

Luna

"Happy twenty-first birthday to me," I muttered under my breath as I stared at the ornate double doors hiding the Great Hall from view.

For all my preparation, all my research, nothing could have actually prepared me for this moment. I was really being sold into this marriage.

Somehow, it hadn't seemed real until now. I wasn't sure why, because I could vividly remember standing shell-shocked in front of the Council of Lords two weeks ago as they told me I would be marrying the Prince of Darkness on the night of my twenty-first birthday.

Apparently, the "auspicious circumstances" of my birth were a sign. According to them, since I had been born beneath an eclipse that only took place once every eight hundred and forty-six years, I was the perfect candidate for being sold into this marriage.

Auspicious.

As if the scientific movements of the sun and the moon were enough reason to send me to my possible death. Everyone knew that along with not being able to go into the sun, the vampires were especially cruel towards humans. There was a fairly high probability that I wouldn't survive the week.

Since receiving the news of my engagement, I read as many reports about the vampires as I could get my hands on. Not only that, but over the past two weeks, everyone I knew—and some people who were little more than acquaintances—had delighted in sharing every last terrible detail they had ever heard about the people of the Northern Kingdom.

Everything I had been told could be summed up in two words: blood and death.

But the word of the Council of Lords was law. Unlike the other three kingdoms on this continent, Ipotha had no ruler. The council was, for all intents and purposes, the ruling body. One did not argue with them, especially when it came to something like this.

Still, my marriage hadn't felt real. Not when the Council of Lords had informed me of the union, and not a week later when I visited my younger brother Marius and promised to write to him as soon as I arrived in Eleyta. Not yesterday, when I supervised the packing of my trunks. Not even this morning, when I woke up and watched the sun crest the horizon for the last time.

But it was real.

The sun was setting, and tonight, I would be married to the vampire prince of Eleyta.

Footsteps came from behind me, and I turned as Papa approached. Dressed in a white ruffled linen shirt and velvet breeches, he extended his arm. I slid my hand into the crook of his elbow and leaned in pressing a kiss to his cheek. "Hello, Papa," I whispered.

"Lulu," he said warmly, somehow managing to make me feel like a child again with that one word. He patted my hand where it rested on his arm, smiling. "You look like a princess in that golden gown."

I glanced down at myself. He was right.

Somehow, that made this even worse.

After tonight, I would be a princess. But what good was being a princess when it meant you lost everything else? The moment those double doors swung open, I would lose everything. My home, my studies, and even my family. Other than my clothes, the only piece of Ipotha coming to Eleyta with me was my maid, Julieta. The Light Elf had been my constant companion since my first step-mother Kinthani died, and she was more like a best friend than a maid.

Even with Julieta's comforting presence, tonight was still changing everything.

Twenty-one years of life in Ipotha, and all it took was one marriage agreement for none of it to matter.

No one had asked me if I agreed to marry my fiancé. No one asked my opinion, because I was being sold into this marriage.

Marriage had never been my dream. Especially not an arranged marriage to a vampire prince.

"Thank you, Papa," I whispered.

My father smiled. "Did you..." He coughed. "Did you sleep well last night?"

I blinked. "I... not that well."

I hadn't slept well from the moment I found out about this match. As soon as I heard I was being married off to Eleyta, I realized all my dreams were dead.

Looking back on it, it was fanciful of me to think that as my father's last daughter, I would have been saved from the call of "duty." I should have known this would happen, but for some reason, it still took me by surprise.

Foolishly, I used to think that if I was forced to marry, my husband would probably have been a kind, hopefully young, *human* lord. After bearing him a few children, I dreamed I would be able to retire to academics where I could spend my days in sunny libraries and laboratories.

But instead, my dreams did not matter, because I was being sold.

Papa's lips tilted down. "I'm sorry to hear that, pumpkin. Maybe tonight, you'll find some rest."

"Perhaps," I said, chewing on my lip.

I doubted it. Who could sleep well when they were being sold into marriage?

Even as I thought it, I knew that technically, the term "sold" was too strong a word. The legal terms presented to the Council of Lords by Her Majesty Queen Marguerite's representative were "being brought together under the unity of matrimony."

But no matter the terms, the reality was that I was chattel and being treated like a marketable good.

The Prince of Darkness needed a wife, and Ipotha needed an alliance with Eleyta.

A shudder ran down my spine that had nothing to do with the late hour. What kind of killer was I marrying? If the rumors whispered in the darkest corners of the castle held even a drop of truth in them, my future husband was the cruelest, black-hearted vampire to ever live in the Four Kingdoms. They said he drank infants' blood to break his nightly fast and that no one, human or vampire, ever dared cross him and lived to tell the tale.

I would find out soon enough what kind of male he was.

"Do you remember the plan?" Papa whispered, straightening the lapels on his white ruffled linen shirt.

"Yes," I whispered. A knot twisted in my stomach as I met Papa's brown eyes. Like me, his skin was perpetually tanned, and we both had dark brown hair. His was short, but mine reached my waist when it was down.

Papa squeezed my hand. "Tonight, the vampires are taking you to Eleyta so you can marry the prince. Under the terms of the agreement, Queen Marguerite will send an army of her strongest soldiers to help protect Ipotha from the coming war in the east."

"And the Council of Lords is sending hundreds of pounds of grain to isolated human villages in the north of their country, right?"

"Yes." My father nodded. "The first shipment went out last week, and they will continue to be delivered on a monthly basis for five years."

That was my worth as determined by the Council of Lords.

Grain and an army.

Somehow, it didn't seem like enough.

I said as much to my father, and he let go of my hand, wrapping me in a tight hug. "You never know, pumpkin. Perhaps, in time, you may learn to love the prince. It might not be so bad."

Was that all I had to hope for? That my marriage wasn't "so bad"? That felt like such a low bar.

I frowned. "Perhaps."

Even as the word left my lips, I knew it to be a lie. I wouldn't find love, because I already knew the truth about love.

Three times in my life, I had stood witness as my father married for "love".

All it had done was teach me that love wasn't real. It wasn't quantifiable, nor was it measurable. Every time, my father said he was "in love". How could that be true?

Papa was a good man, but he didn't understand science as I did.

If something couldn't be measured or seen or touched or tasted, was it real?

I didn't think so.

Like fairy tales told to young children at night, love was a fabrication created to make people feel better about their marriages.

When I first came to this conclusion a few years ago, I tried to explain it to my current stepmother Ysabel. She just laughed me off, telling me to get my nose out of my books. Maybe then, she had reasoned, I would see love for the beautiful thing it was.

Ysabel didn't understand the appeal of books. Literature was constant. It was always there to provide a comforting hug when needed. It never judged me, nor did it ever make me feel like I was less important because I was younger than my other sisters.

Another reason that books were better than people were because books never hurt anyone. I had never heard of anyone being murdered by a book, but I couldn't say the same thing about my future husband. Even here in Ipotha, people spoke of the Prince of Darkness. They said he left dead bodies in his wake. Entire buildings and villages were found empty, the occupants nowhere to be found.

His power was unrivaled, and his heart was as black as the shadows he wielded.

That was the male I was marrying.

"I love you, Lulu," Papa whispered. "Kinthani, gods be with her soul, would be proud of you."

"I miss her, Papa," I whispered, blinking furiously as a single tear came to my eye. I straightened, wiping my finger on my cheeks as I sniffled. "I miss her so much."

For the first eleven years of my life, Kinthani was the only mother I knew. It didn't matter that she was a Fortune Elf and I was a human. Her arms were the ones that had hugged me when my sisters excluded me. Her lips were the ones that had kissed me when I got hurt. It didn't matter that we didn't share blood or we didn't look the same. I loved her, and she loved me.

When she died giving birth to Marius a decade ago, I mourned her death like I would have any blood relatives. Even now, ten years after Kinthani's death, Marius was a sickly child. He didn't have much of his mother's magic, and he needed near-constant care. He remained in our summer home, being cared for by some of the best witches in Ipotha.

It was for Marius's sake that I had spent countless hours in the university libraries and laboratories, searching for information on the wasting illness that had plagued him since birth. No matter how much he ate, he was always weak.

Papa had spoken to countless physicians and witches from all over Ipotha, and none of them knew what was wrong with Marius. They tried everything they could think of, from bleeding him to various diets and exercise, but nothing worked.

Last week when I had visited Marius, Lidya, one of the witches assigned to Marius's care, had pulled me aside and told me that things were getting worse. Marius was barely eating, and he wasn't keeping anything down. She knew someone, she mentioned, who could potentially help him. A researcher who specialized in strange illnesses. Lidya promised she would write to me if she got any information about Marius's strange illness.

Papa leaned forward, his lips brushing my cheek as he squeezed my hand. "Remember who you are," he whispered.

I knew who I was. Luna Brielle Wisethorn, fourth daughter of the Human Lord, lover of books and all things academic. And now, the bride of the vampire prince.

A heartbeat later, the doors to the Great Hall banged open with a reverberation that echoed through my entire body.

This was it.

I stared into the hall, my heart beating a rapid rhythm in my chest as I took in the darkened space. I had been here hundreds of times before, spending countless hours dancing and playing with sisters, but tonight, it was different.

This was the end of my life as I had known it.

Darkness shrouded the Great Hall in a way I had never seen before. Even on the day of Kinthani's funeral, natural light had been allowed to shine through the windows.

Not tonight.

Heavy, black curtains covered the large rectangular windows of the hall, blocking any hope I might have had of seeing the final rays of sunlight dancing across the sky. Tall white candles in golden tapers lined the thick red carpet running down the center of the stone floor. The candlelight flickered ominously, casting dark shadows throughout the Great Hall.

There wasn't even a drop of sunlight. I shouldn't have been

surprised.

Sunlight was not welcome in the presence of vampires.

Servants lined the walls, their backs rigid as they stood at attention. The Council of Lords and their families were present, and further down the hall, I spotted my three sisters and their husbands. They stood with my stepmother, Ysabel, and as expected, Marius was not present.

The air was thick with tension, as though everyone was afraid to breathe. Even Papa seemed to still, his back ramrod straight as he murmured, "You can do this, Lulu."

Dipping my head in the slightest nod, I squeezed his hand and gathered all my courage. "I can." Raising my head, I straightened and pushed back my shoulders. "I will."

It was my "duty".

Holding my head up high, I stared into the Great Hall.

And then I saw them.

A trio stood at the back of the hall, their very presence commanding all of my attention.

Positioned as far away from the flickering candles as they could possibly get, their very presence seemed to suck up any remnants of light that dared make its way toward them. Each of their three faces was as hard as the stone beneath our feet as if they felt no emotion.

And perhaps, they did not.

Three sets of deadly black eyes stared straight ahead, their heavy gazes seeming to stare right into my soul.

Even with the expanse of the Great Hall separating us, the trio's collective beauty was so striking that it took my breath away. Their faces were so perfect, it almost hurt to look at them.

Almost.

Their beauty was unnatural and yet, it was entirely captivating.

I couldn't pull my eyes away, even if I tried. I didn't recognize two of the vampires, but the third...

I knew that face. Queen Marguerite's representative had given me a portrait of my future husband, and over the past two weeks, I had memorized every single line of his face.

My hand tightened around Papa's arm. "Is that... Why is he here?"

My father seemed just as surprised to see him. "Maybe he wanted to see you before the wedding?"

My mouth opened and closed, but nothing came out. In the end, I settled for continuing to stare at the trio.

They stood with little regard for the rest of the crowd, and their postures spoke of their desire to leave this place.

A male with skin as dark as the night sky stood on the right, and a pale female with long blonde, almost white hair, was on his left. She picked something from beneath her fingernails, a look of complete boredom on her face.

I barely paid them any attention.

My entire being was focused on the male in the middle. I thought that perhaps knowing what the Prince of Darkness looked like might have made doing my duty easier. Maybe by staring at his portrait long enough, I could have prepared myself for my fate.

An arranged marriage with a vampire prince.

I was wrong.

Nothing could have ever prepared me for this moment.

No portrait could ever do this male justice. No artist could accurately depict the aura of violence that surrounded this imposing male. Every single line of his face, every inch of his body, was the definition of perfection.

Two large black wings extended from his back, curved like a bat's and filling the dark space behind him. He was a head taller than the other two, his skin a shade paler than my perpetual tan, and his black hair hung ruggedly around his face. An obsidian crown was perched on his head, slightly askew.

He didn't need the marker of royalty. Strength and power radiated from him.

I sucked in a breath as his black, storm-filled eyes—a marker of his kind—met mine. For a moment, nothing else mattered.

Entire worlds were made and destroyed as we stared at each other. My heart ceased beating. My lungs forgot how to breathe. Moving was impossible.

The winged male I was going to marry raised a brow, tilting his head ever so slightly.

And then he...

Frowned.

Want to know what happens next? Grab your copy today.

Acknowledgments

No matter how many of these I write, they never seem to get any easier. Writing Of Ash and Ivy was very emotional for me. I've become very attached to these characters, and this is the middle of their story. I've passed the halfway point, and now, I can see the end.

First, I want to thank *you*. Thank you for reading my words. For hearing my story and for caring about the people living in my head. Thank you.

To the coven. You know who you are. Thank you for being such an amazing community.

To my writer's group, a million thank yous. You've listened to me as I bounced ideas off you and told you crazy ideas I had for this story when I first started writing it (I'm looking at you, Saena). You held my hand when I got frustrated with the characters (Xander, we all know I'm talking about you) and you wiped my tears when I cried. Thank you.

To the FaRo community. I am so blessed to be part of such an amazing global community of authors.

To my alpha, beta and ARC readers. Thank you so much for being present and reading my books in their raw forms. Thank you for being willing to deal with my anxiety and imposter syndrome. I am so appreciative for all of you.

Thank you to my husband, Aaron. Because even though he doesn't understand my love of books, he supports me every step of the way.

To Britanny and Jack. For letting me be your mom. I love you so much. One day, you'll be allowed to read these book.

And to you, my reader. Another thank you. You came with me on this journey, and I am so appreciative of you.

Thank you so much.

About the Author

Elayna R. Gallea lives in beautiful New Brunswick, Canada with her husband and two children. They live in the land of snow and forests in the Saint John River Valley.

When Elayna isn't living in her head, she can be found toiling around her house watching Food Network and planning her next meal.

Elayna enjoys copious amounts of chocolate, cheese, and wine.

Not in that order.

You can find her making a fool of herself on Tiktok and Instagram on a daily basis.

Also by Elayna R. Gallea

The Binding Chronicles (*Takes place in the Four Kingdoms at the same time as Of Earth and Flame*)

Tethered (February 13, 2023)

Romancing Aranthium (New Adult):

Opposite Ends of the Sea

The Pirate's Deal

Tarnished by Time

The Sequencing Chronicles (Young Adult) - a complete series

Sequenced

Rise of the Subversives

The Wielder of Prophecy

The Runaway Healer (a prequel novella)

Made in the USA
Middletown, DE
07 May 2024

54019828R00307